'A madcap romp through the 1980s with Ayrs... ... captures a world of indie rock and fucking wallopers with hilari... élan' Stuart Cosgrove

'An hilarious and caustic Boy's Own tale of achieving every wannabe pop star's dream … a No.1 Hit Single. The closest you'll ever get to being on *Top of the Pops*. A solid gold hit of a book!' Colin McCredie

'Full of comedy, pathos and great tunes' Hardeep Singh Kohli

'Warm, funny and evocative. If you grew up in the eighties, you're going to love this' Chris Brookmyre

'If you lived through the early eighties this book is essential. If you didn't it's simply a brilliant debut novel' John Niven

'Dark, hilarious, funny and heart-breaking all at the same time, a book that sums up the spirit of an era and a country in a way that will make you wince and laugh at the same time' Muriel Gray

'Like the vinyl that crackles off every page, *The Last Days of Disco* is as warm and authentic as Roddy Doyle at his very best' Nick Quantrill

'Took me back to an almost forgotten time when vengeance was still in vogue and young DJs remained wilfully "uncool". Just brilliant' Bobby Bluebell

'More than just a nostalgic recreation of the author's youth, it's a compassionate, affecting story of a family in crisis at a time of upheaval and transformation, when disco wasn't the only thing whose days were numbered' *Herald Scotland*

The Man Who Loved Islands

ABOUT THE AUTHOR

David F. Ross was born in Glasgow in 1964 and has lived in Kilmarnock for over thirty years. He is a graduate of the Mackintosh School of Architecture at Glasgow School of Art, an architect by day, and a hilarious social media commentator, author and enabler by night. His most prized possession is a signed *Joe Strummer* LP. Since the publication of his critically acclaimed, bestselling debut novel *The Last Days of Disco*, he's become something of a media celebrity in Scotland, with a signed copy of his book going for £500 at auction.

The Man Who Loved Islands

DAVID F. ROSS

ORENDA BOOKS

Orenda Books
16 Carson Road
West Dulwich
London SE21 8HU
www.orendabooks.co.uk

First published by Orenda Books 2017
Copyright © David F. Ross 2017

A catalogue record for this book is available from the British Library.

ISBN 978-1-910633-15-1
eISBN 978-1-910633-16-8

Typeset in Garamond by MacGuru Ltd
Printed and bound by CPI Group (UK) Ltd, Croydon CR0 4YY

SALES & DISTRIBUTION

In the UK and elsewhere in Europe:
Turnaround Publisher Services
Unit 3, Olympia Trading Estate
Coburg Road
Wood Green
London
N22 6TZ
www.turnaround-uk.com

In USA/Canada:
Trafalgar Square Publishing
Independent Publishers Group
814 North Franklin Street
Chicago, IL 60610
USA
www.ipgbook.com

In Australia and New Zealand:
Affirm Press
28 Thistlethwaite Street
South Melbourne VIC 3205
Australia
www.affirmpress.com.au

For rights information and details of other territories, please contact
info@orendabooks.co.uk

This one's for Karen ...
and the indomitable people of Ayrshire

'We're no longer as thick as thieves, no,
We're not as thick as we used to be.'

– The Jam: 'Thick as Thieves'

'Ye aw'right, though?'

'Aye. Ach fuck, who kens? You?'

'Ma mum and dad have split up. For good this time. He's away back up north. No' really surprised tae be honest. He was a total fish oot ae water away fae the city.'

'Sorry tae hear that, Joe.'

'Ach, fuck it. No' really that bothered. Him an' me … nae real connection. Fitba, that wis aboot it. No' like you an' auld Harry.'

It seemed like such a natural thing to say, but as soon as it was out there, Joey Miller regretted it. It still felt too soon. He was sitting on a damp wooden bench on the edge of the Kay Park lake with his closest friend, Bobby Cassidy; a friend whom he hadn't seen for almost four months.

'Ah didnae mean tae … ach, fuck sake, why am ah so fuckin' anxious here?' Joey admitted aloud.

Bobby smiled. 'It's fine. Ah ken whit ye meant, man.'

'So, ye gonnae tell me, or dae ah have tae keep guessin'?' said Joey, getting to the point of their meeting, from *his* perspective at least.

'Tell ye whit?'

'Where ye've fuckin' been since July?'

Joey was becoming exasperated. They had spent the initial ten minutes talking about last night's television; skirting around the main issues. Bobby had had a very tough time of it over the summer. His older brother Gary's Falklands War resurrection, and his father's sudden death all in the same week would have been hard for anyone to cope with, but rather than call on the support of his best friend,

Bobby Cassidy had effectively vanished, disappearing into the ether almost as soon as Harry Cassidy's body was in the ground. Hettie, Bobby's concerned younger sister, had heard nothing from him. His troubled brother had reluctantly returned to barracks in London, haunted by his own preoccupations. Even Ethel, his poor old mum, was now blissfully anaesthetised against her family's domestic carnage, countless tranquilisers keeping her in an all-day haze. Bobby's family – apparently once so close – had fragmented. Perversely, only Joey Miller seemed preoccupied with that.

'Ah had tae get away, man. Couldnae fuckin' cope wi' it aw. It wis just too much, mate,' said Bobby. 'Ah'm sorry. Ah couldnae really tell ye.'

'So where did ye go, then?' asked Joey.

'Benidorm,' replied Bobby.

'Whit, for four bloody months?'

'More or less.'

'Must be fuckin' great, eh?' said Joey sarcastically. 'Ye get a job wi' Judith Chalmers or somethin'?' The tone had changed.

'Don't start, Joe. Ah just dinnae need it, right?' Bobby eased himself onto the slatted back of the park bench. He zipped his black Harrington jacket up against the early-winter cold and folded his arms before haunching down on his knees.

'Thought we were meant tae be best mates, Bobby? Felt like a right fuckin' tit wi' everybody askin' me where ye were an' me huvin' tae say that ah didnae have a bastardin' scooby.' Joey looked away, readying himself for his principal objection. 'An' then Hammy … fuckin' *Hammy* … tells me yer away wi' Lizzie, an' he kens this because he got a fuckin' postcard fae ye in August.' Joey was angry but trying to keep it in check.

'So ye *knew* ah wis in Spain, then? So whit's wi' the Spanish Inquisition?' said Bobby.

'Where's *ma* fuckin' postcard, ya prick?' said Joey.

Bobby laughed, but Joey was being serious. Bobby reached into a side vent pocket. He brought out a folded card, which had a cartoon

of a blonde Diana Dors lookalike with enormous tits smiling seduc-
tively and lying on her back on a colourful beach towel, a broken
signpost pointing to her cleavage. The words on the sign read *Wish
you were here* … Joey snatched the card from Bobby and turned it
over. The only words written on it were his name and 'Onthank'
underneath it.

'Ah didnae post it. Couldnae remember yer exact address. Ah wis
never over at yours that often, you were always at mine.' Bobby's
tone was conciliatory.

Joey's wasn't: 'So whit wis ye dain' aw that time, sunbathin'? Sellin'
cheap sunglasses on the beach?'

'Lizzie got the chance ae a week away an' ah'd just had a fuckin'
massive barney wi' Gary. Ah thought *fuck it,* packed a bag, lifted
some money an' ma passport an' just went wi' her. Got a decent price
oan a last minute flight. We had nae intention ae stayin' longer than
a week, but one ae her pals wis workin' on the 18–30 stuff an' asked
her boss if we could stay a bit. We both got a job an' ah wis dain' a bit
ae the DJ'ing. It wis magic, man. Ye should come wi' us next year.'

'Whit aboot Hettie?' said Joey.

'Whit aboot her? She's got her ain life. We're no' weans anymore,
mate.'

'She's only fuckin' sixteen, Bobby … an' she's just lost her dad,
and her two brothers.'

'How has she lost us?' asked Bobby. 'We're still here, for fuck's sake.'

'Aye. Right.'

Joey's attitude was beginning to really irritate Bobby. 'Look Joe,
whit's the *Hampden* here? Aw this concern aboot Hettie, whit's it got
tae dae wi' you?'

Joey formed the words but then drew back from uttering them.
The truth would have put him on the back foot and he wasn't ready
for that. Instead he settled for a long and awkward pause. His best
friend had undergone a transformation during the last few months.
Where previously they had been inseparable, for Joey, it now felt like
little connected them.

'Did ye pick up the news that Weller had split the group?' said Joey at last, reaching for the old days.

'Not initially, but Hammy came oot in September, an' he…'

'Hammy?' exclaimed Joey, his annoyance ramping up a notch. He was now at Def Con Two. He felt like he had definitely been conned. Twice.

'So ye wurnae here for ma eighteenth, an' ye find oot aboot The Jam split fae Hammy fuckin' May?' A line had now been crossed.

'Well, nothin' lasts forever, does it?' That was harsher than Bobby intended.

'Aye, apparently so,' shouted Joey.

'Ah'd better go.' Bobby got up and stood in front of Joey. 'Ah'll maybe see ye at the weekend, then?' But Joey didn't answer him; wasn't even looking at him. So Bobby turned and headed in the direction of the town.

When Bobby was around fifty yards away, Joey stood up, intending to shout after his friend. But again the words didn't come. He wanted to say that he had missed Bobby badly and that he just wanted things to be back to some semblance of normality between them.

Instead, he simply whispered, '*Some* things last forever, pal.'

'Ah! yet doth beauty like a dial-hand,
Steal from his figure, and no pace perceived.'

(From 'Sonnet 104' by William Shakespeare)

Wide awake.

Wide awake in unfamiliar – but all too *familiar – circumstances. Wide awake when you know you shouldn't be; when every other person in a thousand-mile radius is asleep, readying themselves for the next cycle of work, or of play, or of whatever they will do that reminds them that they are alive. Or at least that's what my confused brain is telling me.*

'How can I be happily alone with my thoughts when all they do is torment me? When they haunt my sleeping moments until I wake, and then torture the waking ones until I can't escape them.'

The unbearable solitude of 3 am. Looking forlornly out of yet another anonymous hotel window. A now regular stop on the umpteenth circum-navigation of a ridiculously firm mattress. It's the same view as it was an hour ago; as it will be an hour from now. Blinking lights hint at life but there is none. Not yet anyway. Because every fucker in the world is asleep. Except me. Or so it seems.

I only checked in twelve hours ago and yet I know every square inch of this room, like I constructed it myself. Its maintenance-free parquet floor. Its lowest-common-denominator beige walls. Prints that are blood relatives of the ones in every other economy-priced hotel I've ever stayed in (business isn't quite as good as it used to be). Smoke detector. Sprinkler head. Siemens dials. Acknowledgments that this is a consistent set-up. An old silver Toshiba TV balancing unconvincingly on a Corian worktop in the corner. No upgrades to a flat monitor. Local channels in a language I don't understand. My distorted reflection in its slightly curved screen when the bedside lamp goes on again. Shades of veneers imitating real wood in finishes that don't quite match. Someone else's concept of traveller comfort.

Two white china cups. Both deployed into early service. A tiny kettle. It has worked hard; I'll give it that. Empty sachets of convenience tea or powdered coffee. Nothing in the fridge. Nothing to do. Back to the window. Pleading in vain for the sun to begin to rise. Just to make the loneliness go away. Back to the unrelenting berth. Lights out. Again.

Pains, both there and not there emerge. Some remnants from the sixteen hours it took to get here. Reminders that I'm too old to be doing this; that work-related travelling is a young man's conceit. Gentle, but jagged jabs in the blackness, which begin to score points for the illogical part of the brain. The part that subtly suggests I might never see my daughter again then leaves that thought to corrode. That points out how remote she is from me despite the world getting smaller. It skilfully plants seeds that instantly grow out of control like mutating Leylandi. The further away I am, the more disconnected from her daily routines I feel. Different issues. Different time zones. Half a world away. Out of sight, etc. The more reasonable part that allows me to function normally isn't fighting back. It seems to be the only part of me that is actually dormant. It is content to let irrationality dominate for the next few hours.

Lights on. Again. Hated the darkness when I was a child and now here I am, back there again. Yet another walk to a small, cracked basin in an adjoining space in this air-conditioned prison cell. A route that is becoming a circadian rhythm all of its own. Sharp, piercing light of a different kind. Shooting out from a horizontal tube above a small mirror. Reminding me that all I am is my father's son. The same corrugated contoured lines at the eyes. The same greying temples. The same elastic, leathery facial skin. The same paunch at which – every few months – I stare and resolve to remove. But I won't. It's a downward slide and I can't turn the clock back. Can't recover that feeling from when I looked a lot less like him. From the times when I felt I was made of different DNA. From when I wasn't going to make the same mistakes. From when I was going to be incomparable to him. Desperate to sleep and – at least for now – relegate regret to the sub-conscious.

The floor is solid not solely because it is easier to maintain, but because people like me would wear tracks in a carpet. Outside it's getting darker.

A fog is draping itself over the canyons of the city. The tops of the buildings are now invisible. But their inhabitants will soon witness the sun rise before me. And I'm jealous of them for that. Time, in this time zone moves painfully slowly. Dripping languidly, like Dali represented it. At least during the seemingly endless hours of the first few nights.

I put some music on. Nothing specific, just a shuffling Hobson's Choice through a never-ending mobile library. The Durutti's 'Otis', 'We're All Going To Die', 'Dress Sexy for My Funeral' … they don't intend to, but they just depress me more. Music, once so important, only underscores my mood and taunts me with its messages:

'Said somethin' I did not mean to say … all just came out the wrong way.'

He was right all those years ago; nothing lasts forever.

Tomorrow will be a bit easier. But perhaps only a bit…

PART ONE

BONFIRE OF THE PROFUNDITIES

Chapter One

October 2014. Shanghai, China

This was a watershed moment. *Finally.* He glances again at the words written on the folded page of the black A5 Moleskin journal. It might have been three days since the ink dried; perhaps even four. He can't remember actually composing the sentences, but he does feel a new clarity of thought that couldn't have been much in evidence when pen touched paper. At its best, Joseph Miller's sleep pattern is merely polyphasic, no better. He stares at the large clock in the corner of the room. It's a reproduction copy of an antique, its long hands apparently static, its elaborately enamelled second hand the only indication that it's still working. Time, for Joseph Miller, is slowing to the point where it feels like the wind-up key has gone missing. Days are like weeks. This isn't supposed to be the case. At his age, people lament the increasing pace of their lives, conscious of time appearing to accelerate as it runs relentlessly away from their younger selves. For him, it feels like it's gradually grinding to a halt. Nevertheless, rereading the words prompts a fleeting focus. He has decided on a task that initially seemed beyond him. A sense of responsibility has returned, though. He knows he has to make the best of this clarity before it evaporates in the polluted haze.

'*Mr Miller?* Mr Miller; is everything okay sir?'

Joseph Miller glances to his left, towards the origin of a sound that has softly punctured the silence.

'Mr Miller, your office in Scotland has been trying to reach you.'

It's a lovely sound, Joseph concedes; female, youthful, life-affirming, Californian: everything he isn't. He finds it strange that someone from the hotel is calling through a closed door. Housekeeping normally knock once and then just barge in. Why didn't reception call the room's phone to let him know about any messages? He glances at the telephone. Its red light is flashing. He also catches sight of envelopes that have been slid under a door he doesn't even recall locking. It seems likely that the voice out in the hall has been despatched to ensure that this particular guest hasn't fled; or died.

'Mr Miller?'

The sound entices him towards the door as if it comes from a siren. He knows the dangers that lie on the other side but he can't help himself.

The beguiling voice won't stop: 'Mr Miller, your colleagues wanted to wish you a happy birthday … and, on behalf of Double-tree Hotels, I'd like to as well.'

'Ah'm sorry. Just a minute, eh?' Joseph Miller clears up the various little brown bottles and their scattered pharmaceutical contents. He scans his reflection. *Mirror, mirror on the wall; who's that human car crash looking back at me. Not the fucking fairest in the land, that's for certain.*

He pulls on a white t-shirt. It has a dried coffee stain on it; he can't remember that happening. He yanks a pair of black Levi's on. His jaw is maybe a week of rough terrain. He might've looked acceptable if he was a mature, touring rock star. Despite his various hang-ups and anxieties, Joseph had always managed to look younger than his age. Until this last year, when the grey has descended down the sides of his head like a sudden avalanche. His skin, his teeth, and – bizarrely – his fingernails have all degenerated as if his body was a squalid apartment recently acquired by Peter Rachman. He turns on the cold tap, uses the water to pat down wild, freeform-jazz hair and sighs deeply.

'I'm sorry if I disturbed you Mr. Miller.' The entrancing voice belongs to a ludicrously healthy-looking young woman. Her naturally blonde hair hangs to just beyond the shoulders of her black business suit. Her teeth beam out, like xenon headlights, from a perfectly shaped mouth. Piercing blue eyes shine down at Joseph. She wears heels, making her taller than him. Her dazzlingly white shirt is open just enough to reveal about an inch of carefully constructed cleavage. She introduces herself as Megan Carter, Guest Relations Manager, but in a way that suggests everyone at the hotel is a manager of something. He notices that the description on her lapel badge puts the words in a different order. She seems nervous, as if this is her first day in the role. She is holding a large, wicker basket of fruit wrapped in cellophane. A purple bow with 'Congratulations' written in flowery silver script encircles it. In her other hand she holds a sheaf of notes and some envelopes. She hands both to him at the same time.

'I'm sorry; we didn't know it was your birthday, Mr Miller.'

'How would ye have known?' This sounds a bit harsher than he intended. 'Ah'm sorry, I'm just a bit … y'know … buggered.' He addresses her confusion. 'Tired. A bit of jet-lag still.'

She smiles. He doesn't reciprocate. It's been so long; he can't really remember how to without it appearing unnatural.

A few languid seconds pass in which neither of them speaks or moves. To the young Manager of Guest Relations, this seems like about an hour. Her experience of unusual or difficult guest situations is limited. She has only been a Manager of Guest Relations for a month – promoted internally to respond to an increasingly waspish clientele. The major World Expo of 2010 had opened Shanghai up to almost seventy-five million visitors during its six months, and The Doubletree Group had carefully plotted their customer demographics. Mainstream Western advertising campaigns followed and this particular hotel had boomed.

Megan Carter considers her training. Generally, residents only lightly brush against her honed, have-a-nice-day persona. She imagines they go about their business without much of a thought about her, save perhaps for a grudging acknowledgement that Americans really do perfect the art of service. A subtle and fleeting interaction: that is her purpose in life and – right now – that suits her just fine. Her polished and manicured veneer conceal a recent past that involves an abusive and criminal husband, his religious zealot of a mother and her own uninterested don't-come-running-to-me-when-it-all-turns-to-shit father.

She married the man almost six years ago. Madison Megan Carter and Vincent Antonio Sevicci: childhood sweethearts; Prom King and Queen of Albany High School. The façade of the American Dream was celebrated in front of family, friends and community in the beautiful little Epworth Chapel of the Holy Father. It was a crisp November day, which would go down in history as the same day her country elected its first black President. Shifting planes of history and optimistic dreams for many, but not all. Before the formal wedding photographs had been returned to them, her new husband had given her a heavily bruised eye socket and a broken clavicle. *She's always been a klutz* was the generally accepted analysis, following her complicit explanation that she'd fallen down the steep stairs leading to the basement in their new home. She had been blinkered. Love can do that to an idealistic young woman, she now reasons, to help her dismiss the distressing idea that her own hubris brought these troubles upon her head. She had known he was connected, but the Italians always looked after their women, or so she thought. For months after the wedding, Vinnie and his crew had met in their basement. She acknowledged the over-the-top respect they gave her when she took pizza and beer down to them. But also heard Vinnie's voice, followed by their loud forced laughter, as she climbed back up the stairs. She found it hard to ignore these hard edges like the other wives seemed to. They were paid for their silence in furs and jewels and dollars, but these things held little interest for her. She didn't want to be kept like a prized show dog. She wanted her own identity, to be able to follow her own dreams as well as the ones she had once believed they both shared.

She put up with the cocaine and booze-fuelled batterings, the unpredictable behaviour and the suspected – but unproven – sleeping around. Just over a year into this penury, when she announced that she was pregnant, her paranoid husband Vinnie kicked her repeatedly in the stomach, convinced the baby growing inside her wasn't his. He was a psychopath. It was barely conceivable that he'd been able to hide this throughout their high school courtship. But then hiding things was his speciality.

'Listen to me, honey. If you don't get gone, you'll *be* gone.' – The simple, but intuitive words from an experienced nurse, well versed in reading between the lines of those presenting with such distinctive body bruising. Vinnie had only left her bedside to go to the toilet but that one sentence was enough.

Losing the baby was the final straw. For it to make any kind of sense at all, it needed to be a full stop, too. Madison took a cache of his hidden money and, with the covert help of a close, trusted colleague from the bank where she had previously worked, buried it in a new personal account. Together they then manufactured a new identity, new papers and sufficient falsified references for her to get work and temporary overseas residency status, all without Vinnie even conceiving that it was being planned right under his Roman nose.

And then, one day, when Vinnie and his crew were concluding a deal in Miami, she just vanished.

The 'made' men Vinnie's crew answered to initially suspected a hit from a rival, but civilians – especially wives – had always been off limits. What betrayed her was the discovery that the money was missing – Vinnie had thought it was still buried under layers of ash in the solum of the basement. Even now she shudders when she recalls excavating those substantial sums without his knowledge, and shakes when she imagines him destroying the fabric of their house, wishing it was her face.

Maybe he's dead by now. The deep family values that underpin organised crime extend only so far. If some of that money was payments up the chain, honour wouldn't necessarily save him. It is a complex consideration for her: she doesn't ever want to see him again, but that doesn't mean she wants him dead.

Over four years – and a few detours – later and here she is in Shanghai, using her middle name as her first. The Pacific Ocean separates her from a past existence, and she will never go back.

Chapter Two

June 1986. Benidorm, Spain

'Ah'm fucking totally sick ae this Bobby.'

'Whit, aw the sparkling conversation an' jokey repartee? How could anybody be sick ae that?'

'If ah wanted constant bitin', cuttin'-edge sarcasm, ah'd fly back tae Ayrshire.'

'Well, maybe it's time up for it here then.' Bobby Cassidy said this under his breath but he was certain Lizzie King, his girlfriend of four years, had heard him. If she had, she wasn't acknowledging it, though. More times than not these days, it felt to Bobby like they were an old married couple. Being ignored by her wasn't so out of character in that context.

Bobby and Lizzie had been through a lot together since they had met back in Kilmarnock in 1982. Lizzie had been instrumental in setting Bobby's fledgling DJ career on its tottering way. Her eighteenth birthday party had been the first booking Bobby had taken in pursuing his dream of establishing a mobile DJ business with his then best friend, Joey Miller. She had been a shoulder – and an emotional release – for him during the surreal times of summer 1982, and for that he'd always be grateful. But their now overfamiliarity – a result of living and working long, tiring hours in claustrophobic proximity during the annual Benidorm summer seasons – was taking its toll on both of them.

They had headed to Spain four years earlier, both seeking escape, but for different reasons. Bobby's intention was simply to shrug off the pressures of life in the aftermath of his dad's untimely death and his brother's stressful return from the Falklands War. Lizzie had wanted to get away from an overcrowded council flat and the factory worker's destiny that seemed predetermined for her. She wanted to live her life away from daily family arguments about whether the rent would get paid before the bookies that month; about whether her unemployed father might eventually find something more productive to do with his life than impregnate Lizzie's step-mum. Christ Almighty, if reproduction was a specialist subject, Frank King would win *University Challenge* as a solo entrant. She lived with well-meaning people, but their life choices and the brutal steel of Thatcherism kept them struggling joylessly. Lizzie had only been eighteen then but she was already worn down by it all. She might not have had unrealistic dreams of being an air hostess, but Lizzie still wanted to experience a more colourful part of the world, even if it was one that seemed to have been transplanted from more familiar places in England; *Blackpool wi' sunshine an' a wider choice ae sexually transmitted diseases* being the way Benidorm had been described to her by a friend who'd gone out the year before them. That was enough though. It offered opportunities for personal development that none of those Tory, slave-labour redundancy displacement schemes could compete with.

Lizzie and Bobby had travelled out together for a few weeks in August 1982, and then returned for the whole season the following year. They worked long, tiring, but largely enjoyable hours: Lizzie as a junior rep for Twenty's and Bobby as an assistant bartender. Like everyone else, though, they also indulged like it was the last days of Caligula. Bobby's close friend, Hamish May, had come out sporadically – a week here, a long weekend there; but despite Bobby's attempts, Joey Miller – his best mate since schooldays – had always declined the offer. So he simply stopped asking. Lizzie liked Joey, but she could see that he had become a constant reminder of the things Bobby was fleeing: in particular his depressed and unhinged brother, Gary, who was unable to comprehend the madness of a war that he had survived; and Hettie, his younger sister – an insistent moral conscience at a time in his life when he wanted to act without such constraints.

Bobby Cassidy and Lizzie King ambled aimlessly along the Playa de Levante. Bobby surreptitiously checked his watch. He desperately wanted to head back to the bar. He had two thousand pesetas on Argentina to beat England in the World Cup quarter-final. Hamish – or Hammy as he preferred to be known – would be waiting for him, the San Miguels lined up. It felt to Bobby like he and Lizzie were already on their last waltz around the floor, but still he was reluctant to put the relationship out of its misery. If the end had to come, it would have to be Lizzie King that put the pillow over its face.

Even this late, the sun having long since departed, holidaymakers still lay on the gentle sandy slope of the beach. They were a mix of those trying to look like Madonna – both the young New York singer and the religious icon – and Andrew Ridgeley from Wham!. String vests predominated. Older men wore them because they always had; younger men because they were *de rigueur*. Some rebels favoured white espadrilles. Others bore the scalded, flaking signs of having lain far too long defying the big orange orb to try harder, as if daring it to fully char their pale, blueish British skin. Some, on the other hand, looked like they had just turned up, perhaps preparing to remain on the beach in the absence of any alternative roofed structure being available to them. More often than not sleeping under the Spanish stars was more pragmatism than romanticism.

Bobby and Lizzie strolled amongst those who may have been considering these options – as they had done on many occasions over the last three years – observing them in silence.

Finally Lizzie broke it. 'Don't be so bloody awkward, we need tae talk,' she said. 'Ah've barely seen ye for a fortnight. We've got stuff we need tae think aboot.'

'An' ye had tae pick tonight?' Bobby was finding the application and commitment needed to maintain their equilibrium inversely proportionate to the joy it now afforded him. They were both only twenty-two and their conversations already reminded him of unhappier times back at home in McPhail Drive, when Harry and Ethel, his mum and dad, argued over Gary. It wasn't supposed to be like this.

'Ah'm workin'', Lizzie. Just like you are! Ye knew this when we came out here. It's no' aw fuckin' sunshine in paradise, is it?' he scowled.

But, by and large, it actually had been. In their first full year as a working couple, they had been happily inseparable. Their lives were exciting. Admittedly, their wages were as basic as the lodgings they were forced to share with six other reps, but Lizzie was used to such domestic congestion. At least this new crowded house had sunshine, and for Lizzie it had Bobby. Things got a tiny bit more congested when Hammy May flew out late on in the season of 1982. Hammy was a clever young man. He had aced all of his Highers with considerable ease and his proud father had lined up a variety of options in the Diplomatic Corps, where he worked, on condition that Hammy's subsequent progress through university was smooth. A life of comparative privilege stretched out before him. All he had to do was work hard and follow this predetermined mouse trail.

In fact, Hammy had inherited Stanley May's pioneering spirit, but he had very different ideas about how he would apply it. Despite acceptances from numerous notable universities, Hamish May turned his nose up at all of them, preferring the chance to work five months of the year as a beach club dogsbody for an unscrupulous holiday company.

At each summer season's closing, they returned home to a bleak, lifeless Kilmarnock, which, when compared to the vibrant Costa Brava, looked like all colour had been drained from its structures and people. The three friends stayed in the Cassidy home, now free of any familial hassle. In a thoughtless move, which only widened the gulf between Bobby and his brother, the younger man betrayed their father's principles and used his part of the sum left to them to acquire the council house through Margaret Thatcher's right-to-buy initiative. He argued that it was an investment. Bobby's younger sister, Hettie had moved to the Dowanhill student dorms near Glasgow University in the summer of 1983, and his tortured brother

Gary had returned to his army barracks in London nearly a full year earlier.

Lizzie King's initial dissatisfaction with Hammy being the couple's third wheel quickly diminished. Her boyfriend was a young man who craved – perhaps even depended on – close and unquestioning friendship; and even his love relationships had to be resolutely optimistic and upbeat. There was no place for contemplative reflection of events past. Bobby was a laconic young guy but with a relentless eye for the present tense. Unshakeable positivity and a nonconfrontational attitude were the sole CV requirements for a position at Bobby Cassidy's side. Since Hammy and Lizzie both understood these crucial rules of engagement, they all quickly settled into their primary roles.

After only five weeks working in the hotel's outdoor beach bar, Bobby got his opportunity. Lizzie's friend, an occasional sexual partner of Sergio, the Entertainments Manager, put a word in for Bobby and he was given a week's unpaid trial as a DJ. Bobby had a degree of freedom to play his own music selections in a low-risk, unpressurised, day-time slot at the hotel. Even beyond his probation, the gig paid little, but it was a substantial step up from hearing *'Haw son, can ah have a Slow Comfortable Screw against a Wall, eh?'* five hundred times a day. Bobby loved the new job. It had been spine tingling for him to hear Afrika Bambaataa, Man Parrish or Indeep blasting out of the impressive speakers even if it was to a largely uninterested audience. It also gave him the space to practise blending and linking the records in ways that the old Heatwave Disco's birthday party or wedding function demographic hadn't permitted. He'd even tested out some unusual cuts, such as New Order's energetic New York-influenced 'Confusion' mixed into Prince's smooth pop classic 'Little Red Corvette'.

Soon after, Derek Dees, the semi-legendary DJ for Valentino's, the hotel's bar, vacated the booth, lured away by a bigger and better gig. So, after just a month as this old sorcerer's apprentice, Bobby nervously put his name forward as his replacement. His personal playlists would have to go but Bobby was more than happy to give up such experimental freedom and toe the party line when he eventually graduated to Valentino's main stage. The equipment decks and sound quality there were far more advanced, although his billing was unusual to say the least. DJ Bobby appeared in support of an astonishing magic show in which a dexterous Spanish woman, known professionally as Sticky Vicky, pulled unusual objects from her vagina. Lizzie didn't believe Bobby initially when he described the elegance with which ping-pong balls, eggs, sausages and even razor blades were excavated from deep inside this bizarre woman.

'Ye want tae see this,' he told a sceptical Lizzie and a stunned Hammy. 'She slides aw this stuff oot fae her fanny like she wis a fuckin' ballet dancer. It's like … art or somethin'.'

Hammy demanded to see it for himself. And their next night off, Lizzie and Hammy got complimentary tickets for one of Vicky Leyton's six-times-a-night, half-hour adult cabaret show. Bobby played extended remixes of Wham's 'Club Tropicana' on rotation until her performance began.

On their days off, Bobby and Lizzie participated in the occasional booze cruises, and often the midnight swims too. And until only very recently, Hammy had sex on various beaches with various female tourists. The frightening prospect of 'dying of ignorance' had become a real possibility, and thus curtailed his activities.

All three had only just left their teenage years behind them. They agreed that a prescriptive life of domestic drudgery and living on Thatcher's meagre and diminishing benefits back in grey, miserable Kilmarnock was for other mugs; the mugs who only got out here to sample this lifestyle once a year, for a week if they were lucky.

But, just as soon as it looked like it would propel them forward, their luck ran out. Lizzie got pregnant and had to return home to her family's congested flat. Having signed a contract for the rest of the '84 summer season up until November, Bobby – encouraged by Hammy – made the selfish decision to remain. Unsurprisingly, it was the beginning of the end for the young lovers. Lizzie suffered a miscarriage three weeks after returning to Scotland. Bobby and Hammy came home at the end of the season, but Lizzie continued staying with her family until they were due back out in spring 1985. Although the couple seemed to have put the heartbreak behind them, for Bobby at least, things were never the same. Too much had changed. Serious adult issues had intervened in Bobby Cassidy's Peter Pan lifestyle, and Lizzie King had been tainted by them too. He couldn't look at her in the same way. He couldn't ever admit to her that he was relieved. Better to just put distance between them and avoid any emotional confrontation.

Now – four years after immersing themselves in its uncomplicated warmth – the holiday capital of the Costa Blanca had suddenly lost all the appeal it had once held for them. Lizzie, the girlfriend that Bobby Cassidy once thought would be the love of his life, told him she was pregnant again. As she spoke the words, a loud roar went up from the beachfront bars. Diego Maradona had just punched the ball over Peter Shilton's head and into the England net. By the time he had waltzed and snaked through the entire English defence to score one of the greatest World Cup goals ever seen, Bobby and Lizzie's relationship was over. She had hurtfully jibed that this time the baby wasn't his, but Javier's; the head rep at the hotel complex where they all worked. Hammy later reckoned his friend had dodged a bullet, but it would take a while – and a decision to move to a different resort – for Bobby to see it that way.

Chapter Three

October 2014. Shanghai, China

Joseph Miller can't conceive that he has anything in common with this astonishingly beautiful and composed young woman. But there are many things: not solely time and circumstance. He too had once been able to conceal a darker side in the pursuit of businesslike normality. The development of new commercial relationships requires dogged positivity. No one at a conference junket or promotional lunch wants to hear about family pressures or depressed, dangerous thoughts. Such coruscating events are populated by the never-been-better brigade; recessions were things that happened to other companies, other people who didn't – or couldn't – work as hard. Others with less stamina. With smaller dicks. Men *and* women.

Joseph can't fake this master-of-the-universe bullshit anymore. For nearly a decade, he has been principally responsible for overseas business development at his firm of design consultants. He had foreseen that the ridiculous growth enjoyed by the construction industry in the first few years of the century was as false as the banking philosophies on which they were built. The boom years of credit-based prospecting couldn't possibly last, despite Tony Blair's deceptively unbridled and smiling optimism. Exporting expertise overseas to those countries whose public infrastructure was way behind the UK's was a clear strategy. His partners had backed his theory but on condition that he was the principal – or sole – focus of it. It had been a shot to nothing for them. Joseph and his small team had been successful; up to a point. This initially made him feel free. Free of the mundane matters of business management, but also free of the demeaning barbs and the financial handcuffs of Lucinda, his bitter ex-wife. Now though, he is finding it requires a level of energetic sociability that is as foreign to him as many of the customs he is expected to know and remember. While domestic work is on the increase once more, profits in overseas work are down. What's more, the high-risk international game that took Joseph from Libya to the Middle East to India and onto the promised land of China, has left a legacy in the form of an unsustainable level of financial exposure. In the early days the opportunities rolled in, their designs elevated the profile of the practice and some of them even resulted in projects that made decent profits. But then the Arab Spring changed much of the political and cultural landscape for many of the practice's foreign opportunities. Reckless American financiers and bankers did the rest for any necessary economic momentum. In the last year the firm has lost ground just as Joseph has lost interest. His impatient younger partners blamed the former firmly on the latter and effectively side-lined their firm's remaining active founder as a result.

'Sir, are you fine?' A new voice. Less serene, more insistent. An unusual turn of phrase.

'Em … aye. Yes, sorry.' Joseph is standing in the corridor. The hotel's Manager of Guest Relations has gone. An older Asian woman – presumably a fellow guest – is now leaning in to hear him answer. He has no idea how long he's been standing there. His room door is closed behind him and the colourful basket is parked carefully against the wall, the papers having been folded in half and tucked neatly inside the bow.

His journey down to reception to get a new room keycard is punctuated by a few strange looks and a small English child repeatedly asking his mother why the man in the lift has no shoes or socks on. No explanation is given by any of the adult occupants and the child remains ignored.

Later that evening, Joseph Miller walks aimlessly through the bustling lanes and squares of Xintiandi. He has polished shoes on and a freshly laundered, black Calvin Klein suit. A crisp white shirt, open at the neck, completes the metamorphosis. He blends in to the new cosmopolitan Shanghai seamlessly, like any other poised professional man of fifty years of age. It's a popular local demographic. When he puts his mind to it, the mask can still be very convincing. If only its power could be maintained. He strolls through the narrow passages with their carefully reconstructed facades, as he has done many times before. As an example of urban place-making, Joseph considers it to be amongst the best he's ever witnessed. It has all the proper emotional ingredients of yearning, romance, memory and connection that make all great public spaces magnetic. But it is all based on a lie; an elaborate stage set that has little real authenticity. What's more, to clear a path for it required the brutal displacement of almost four thousand Shanghainese families. This whole style / substance / collateral damage conundrum is one he understands only too well. He feels a curious belonging here. He is a stranger in a strange land, but one which has embraced so much in its relentless desire to be accepted on more recognisably Western terms, while stoically trying to hold onto aspects of a culture and tradition that are as old as any on earth.

He sits on the periphery of activity, observing people as they come and go. He watches a well-dressed couple approach, remarkable only in that the bulky man is wheelchair-bound and his tiny female companion struggles to push him across uneven cobblestones. She looks exhausted; he looks defeated, being unable to offer any assistance whatsoever. They are a difficult couple to age, but by Western standards they would never be referred to as elderly. The man appears almost totally dependent. The woman applies the brake at a table near Joseph's. She sits and the relief spreading across her face is immediately obvious. They don't speak or look at each other. Is he her cross to bear? Does their love for each other render such sacrifice beyond all question? Are there times when both crave the release that a suffocating pillow would bring?

The woman brings two drinks back to the table: one for her and the other, with a straw, for him. Before she has sipped from her own, she offers him the straw. His mouth barely opens to receive it. Liquid dribbles from the corner of his mouth and frustration flashes in his eyes. She lifts a napkin and dabs like a patient mother would a baby. Joseph is saddened by the scene; saddened more by the brutal truth of his own situation. At least the couple has company, compromised though it is. He opens his notebook and writes: *From the moment we are born, we are all essentially preparing to die. Some prepare better than others, that's all.*

Joseph Miller considers such things purely because he has never shared a love to light the fire of unquestioning devotion in his heart.

He nurses a coffee. He unfolds the papers printed and copied onto Shanghai Doubletree's headed notepaper. They comprise a month or so of increasingly concerned messages from home; from back in Glasgow. Amanda, his all-too-faithful secretary, has obviously been to the flat. He sometimes worries that she has too much access, but in truth there is nothing to hide. She knows it all. There's a note of gratitude from the Scottish Labour Party, thanking him for voting 'NO' to Scottish Independence, even though he didn't. He considers the Labour Party he had once been so loyal to much as he does the vinyl-era mobile DJs: on a downward arc headed towards virtual obsolescence. There is a scanned copy of a letter from the NHS. As fiftieth birthday greetings go it is brutally direct. It invites him to dig a wee wooden spatula into his poo and send it back to them. But at least they have bothered to write and mark the date, bless them. Unsurprisingly, there are no such acknowledgements from the tiny band of people he refers to as family. Those boats have long since been burned. The rest of the papers are exclusively from work. Records of numerous calls and printed emails from his younger business partners, apparently worried about his mental state since he went 'off the reservation' at the beginning of September. Amanda has clearly been tracking his movements through credit-card transactions. And there is one from his retired former colleague, Carlos Martorell, with whom he founded the practice almost twenty years previously.

This one intrigues him. The two men haven't properly communicated since the day of Andy Masson's funeral in 2004. Masson was the third 'M'. The practice had been christened M(cubed) to avoid any suggestion of hierarchy or the need to explain an alphabetical basis for the original Vaudevillian name, Martorell, Masson & Miller. In truth, Joseph Miller was the instigator of the practice, and formalised it along with his university friend from Barcelona. Joseph liked the idea of them feeling like a band; of them having values and principles that would govern their work. Andy Masson had come into the picture a few weeks later, when the Lennon & McCartney had realised that they needed a pragmatic George Harrison to keep their boundless design energy and innovation grounded in practicality. Joseph Miller held to the view that a Ringo wasn't necessary. It was all about the attitude and the creativity. The practice name hadn't yet been established and M(cubed) seemed clever and relevant. Andy had provided that sound judgement and business nous for twelve years, until cancer of the oesophagus took his life with brutal speed and at the tragically young age of forty-five. Andy was older than his two partners. He had married Carole when both were young and they had seemed blissfully happy. He was well liked by everyone at the firm and his measured, unruffled demeanour had defused many difficult meetings. In the latter years, his role seemed to be regularly reminding his colleagues why they had actually elected to be in business with each other in the first place.

Andy's death changed everything. He had – rightly in Joseph's opinion – been the driving force behind the development of a realistic succession plan: young, talented designers were openly encouraged to understand their potential place in the future of the practice. They were given their heads to a large extent, in terms of delivering projects, which freed up Carlos to focus on client relationships and Joseph to concentrate on the initial design concepts. It was a successful formula. M(cubed) won a number of regional design awards, it had a healthy financial position and when Andy was forced to withdraw from the practice in the summer of 2004, it employed fifty-eight people on a full-time basis.

The only time Andy had put a foot wrong in his time guiding the management of the practice was to promote Felix Masson to the position of partner. It was the decision that ultimately led to the end of Joseph and Carlos's friendship. In Joseph's opinion, Felix was a moronic product of a public-school system that continued to value connections, background and the status of an established family name over talent and an ability to empathise with people from all social levels. The time leading up to Andy's funeral had been understandably strained and difficult for everyone, but Felix's elevation to replace his dad as Finance Director had been rushed, and worse, agreed between Andy and Carlos without Joseph's full involvement in the discussions. Carlos had prompted the discussion for what he believed to be a good reason. The firm was going to lose a key figure and his shares would have cost the practice a considerable amount to buy back. Andy had therefore acceded to Carlos's plan to simply transfer the majority of them to Felix, at a price to be repaid to Carole over a five-year term. Joseph found out about this at Andy's expansive West Kilbride house only hours after they put him in the ground. Rather than accept that Andy had any part in such subterfuge, it suited Joseph to believe the manipulative Carlos had ulterior motives concerning Joseph's own 25% stake.

Henceforth, the two remaining founding partners of M(cubed) initially communicated by fax, more latterly by email and only occasionally by text. They had rooms at the opposite ends of the old converted brownstone building in central Glasgow that was the base of their operations. It passed into staff legend that the two partners didn't engage with each other, and although it seemed bizarre at first, the internal practice management systems simply adapted to accommodate them. This studio *apartheid* lasted until 2007, when Carlos Martorell negotiated a deal with Felix to leave the business, which involved widening the shareholding to a number of the younger members of staff. Joseph remained the principle shareholder but with an insufficient percentage to block the others under the newly amended shareholders' agreement. Having facilitated this, and with a sense of timing more aligned with luck than insight, Carlos left the practice with his shares inflated in value. The initial impact of the worldwide banking crisis hit barely six months after the ink was dry on his cheque. *That cunt would've come out with fish in his pockets if he fell into the Clyde* was Joseph's popular – and public – refrain in the early months of 2008 as the work began to dry up and the M(cubed) share price began to head in the direction of an extreme sports base jumper – and at a similar pace.

Joseph doodles on the inside cover of one of the Moleskin notebooks that have been his constant companion on this journey into the heart of his soul's darkness. It's a curved scribble, which he has absent-mindedly drawn many times in the last three months. On the limited occasions when he has been able to sleep, he has even dreamt about this scribble. The journals were intended to be part of a specific task set months ago. Following a debilitating illness, his young partners offered him an opportunity to take some time away from the business. In return, they asked Joseph to research and write a recent practice history, focusing on the many interesting projects in various countries that he had largely been responsible for taking the practice into. Joseph suspected the ulterior motives but nonetheless jumped at the opportunity.

He considers the brief he was given last summer. Carlos Martorell would've got wind of the exercise and his attempts to get in contact might be prompted by a fear that Joseph would disclose their peripheral role in the bribing of a local government official in Egypt in the early days of their foreign adventures. It's immaterial. The journals don't contain the story of professional success; of a relatively small, hard-working Scottish design practice triumphing overseas despite the emerging economic turmoil. Or of any secrets or skeletons that might incriminate those who are still alive. They contain a different set of words: a personal account of a past gone mad. Of a time when it all went off the rails. A confession of sorts. An atonement. A lament for a lost friendship. Joseph realised a long time ago that this was essential for his spirit to be able to rest. He doesn't expect it to be cathartic, but to honour the memory of who he once was, or might have become, it needs to be written down.

Chapter Four

April 1987. Ibiza, Spain

Bobby Cassidy had never been one for confronting personal and emotional challenges. His instinct had always been to run. So, aged twenty-three, and with Hamish May – his own personal *Passepartout* – in tow, he had run to the comparative peace, love and hippy tranquillity of Ibiza.

'The possibilities are endless,' said Bobby.

Hamish May had heard him say this around ten times that day and it was barely lunchtime. In the Bobby Cassidy wee black book of motivational clichés, it was up there with *You'll be rewarded in heaven*. Hammy had argued strongly for a flight transfer from the mainland. He'd once been cast adrift in a tiny rowing boat while unconscious, and that memory – combined with the shock of the recent *Herald of Free Enterprise* capsizing off Zeebrugge – had cemented a fear of travelling on water that even his inanely upbeat companion was struggling to counter. Hammy had spent the sailing with his eyes either locked on the horizon or directed firmly downwards, mid-vomit. It would be a good few hours before he was fully ready to embrace any possibilities, endless or otherwise.

The two young Ayrshire men gathered up their baggage and headed out of the port buildings into the blinding sunshine. Despite its fearsome reputation for overindulgence, the White Isle already seemed calmer than Benidorm, which, the previous summer, had become increasingly fractious, as Bobby's relationship with Lizzie King had finally dissolved.

'Hear that?' said Bobby as they clambered out of the sweltering taxi in Ibiza Town.

'Whit, the music?' said Hammy.

'Naw … well, aye, but the sound ae the crowds.' Bobby could see Hammy struggling to comprehend. 'Every cunt's laughin' an' happy … an' they're aw basically our age!'

Hammy smiled. He wasn't quite ready for anything more just yet; he hadn't picked up the vibe.

But Bobby was way ahead of him. 'Benidorm wis for auld folk wi' hankies on their heids. Fuckin' SAGA tours an' roast beef bingos. This is where the cool action is, man.'

They paid the driver, clawed their rucksacks out of his boot and headed off towards the bleached, bright centre of the town.

'Cool t-shirt, fella. You lads fancy a beer?' Bobby instinctively looked down as if trying to remember what shirt he had on. He was 'Choosing Life' in every sense of the words. He and Hammy were now outside a string of vibrant bars, having been carried along the waterfront streets on a euphoric wave of young, excited people of all colours and ethnicities. If Benidorm was an increasingly conservative colony of Brits abroad, Ibiza was an intoxicating melting pot – all vivacious flamboyance.

The bare-chested, blond-haired Australian six-footer handed them ice-cold Coronas – and flyers – on the proviso that they would return that evening. Bobby promised him they would.

'This place is gonnae be fuckin' great, man,' he said, clinking his bottle with Hammy's.

It was the middle of the afternoon and it felt as alive as Benidorm had at the height of a busy evening. Benidorm recuperated and recharged in daylight hours, like an elderly vampire. It was already clear that Ibiza just didn't stop. Decadence had long been the island's byword, its neo-culture founded on the liberal lifestyles of those who had opposed Franco's rule. The hippies colonised it in the 70s and much of their laid-back DNA remained. But just as Bobby, Lizzie and Hammy headed to the Costa Blanca in the early 80s, so the package holidays, the yachting set and the clubbers were spiritually drawn to Ibiza like it was an alternative, hedonistic Mecca.

Bobby and Hammy watched the people come and go in front of

them. The ultra-glamourous mixed with the beach-surf slackers and they all seemed to fit. Fishnets, spandex and leopard print, evocative of end-of-the-pier tackiness in Benidorm, looked positively prescient on the backs of some of the most beautiful women – and men – Bobby had ever seen.

'It's no' what ye wear ... it's the way ye wear it, pal,' said Bobby, apropos of nothing.

'F'you say so, mate,' said Hammy. He scratched his unkempt ginger beard and looked down at his own Dennis the Menace t-shirt and cut-away denim shorts. He looked like Shaggy from *Scooby Doo*. Hammy wasn't sure if Bobby was having a sartorial dig at him, but he let it go. The beer was only just settling his stomach and he didn't want to risk the bile rising again.

'Ah mean, look at this scene, man. It's fuckin' stupendous. Look at they two.' Bobby nodded at a gloriously made-up couple. They both had cheekbones like those carved into Mount Rushmore, and luxuriantly deep-brown skin. They were both as androgynous as Bowie and looked astonishingly self-assured. Bobby initially thought one of them was Grace Jones.

The next hour passed rapidly, hundreds more looking just as remarkable promenading in front of the bar.

'Holy fuck, it's like a fashion catwalk, this street!'

A skinhead rolled past them on roller-skates. Her wheeled, sequinned boots were thigh-high. A tattoo of Che Guevara was skilfully inked at the top of her leg, his famous beret partly concealed by the frayed edge of denim hot pants so tight they could've been spraypainted onto her. It was all topped off with a very bizarre-looking conical, pointy bra. She looked incredible but not in the slightest bit out of place.

Bobby was now wondering how he and Hammy had even been granted entry to this amazing Land of the Fucking Outrageously Beautiful. But whereas Bobby was energised, Hammy was now growing concerned that they would struggle to afford to remain here much longer than a day. They would have to find some work and a place to berth to avoid this becoming a short-stay holiday. Even in paradise, the working classes had to find a productive purpose in life, one that allowed them to sup from the same table as the higher-born. The youth hostels, bars and campsites were their starting point. And there were always opportunities for foreigners doing the type of menial jobs the locals didn't quite fancy. Emigration was built on such universal beliefs and dreams. Why should the Scottish diaspora be concentrated purely in the Americas and the Asia-Pacific? Bobby Cassidy and Hammy May felt like pioneers. They were starting again at the bottom of the ladder, but, like the Scottish engineers who invented the world, their aspirations were truly limitless.

'Some daft, wee Scouse prick's just bought me a drink tae celebrate the second summer ae love.' Bobby laughed as Hammy returned with three glasses. 'Don't even fuckin' ken when the first yin wis!' he said. 'Ah must've been in the bog havin' a big shite when it was here.' Bobby looked around the bay, expensive boats seeming to bob and weave along to the omnipresent soundtrack.

Everything in San Antonio had a syncopated rhythm. It had been nine months since they had first arrived in Ibiza and it remained an intoxicating, addictive environment. Bobby had worked solidly back in Kilmarnock at Mickey Martin's revamped Metropolis during the winter. It afforded him good festive-season wages for the return to the Balearics, and also a convenient excuse for avoiding any con-frontation with the ghosts of his recent – and more distant – past. Hammy had done his bit too, picking up some grave-digging work at the cemetery in Grassyards Road. Accordingly, they were flush, and while that wouldn't grant them complimentary Krug-laden access to Pacha's VIP zones, they could freely enjoy the spoils of the island when not working at the jobs they had returned to.

A waiter approached them. He placed two further beers in front of them.

'Fuck sake, Hammy, if yer Scouser's a bender, yer on yer own, pal,' said Bobby.

'From the lady, guys,' said the waiter. He nodded towards a distant table at the rear of the bar. 'Enjoy.' The dark-haired, bearded waiter swivelled his way swiftly through the thronging tables, like George Best avoiding defenders and law-suits, picking up as many empty glasses as his small circular tray could carry.

Bobby stared beyond him. 'Do you ken who that is?'

'Nae idea,' said Hammy. 'But she looks aw'right, man. If she wants a couple ae sex slaves for her dungeon ae depravity, then fuck it, ah'm game.'

'Aye … cannae see it, mind you,' said Bobby.

'S'pose,' said Hammy. 'She's probably got a knob that's bigger than yours!'

They both laughed.

'Haud up. She's fuckin' comin' over.' Hammy held his hand up to his mouth and breathed out, then sniffed deeply.

Bobby looked at him as if he had his jacket on back to front.

'Whit?' said Hammy, apparently satisfied with the smell. 'Ye just never fuckin' ken, man.'

'Hi, I'm Laurie. Laurie Revlon,' said Laurie Revlon. She held out a long, tanned arm. She had exquisite, perfectly maintained nails at the end of thin, talon-like fingers. A decorative cluster of gold rings interlocked on her forefingers like a glinting knuckleduster made by Tiffanys, Fifth Avenue.

'Hullo, yerself,' said Bobby.

'I was watching you on the decks the other night at Santorini's. You're good.' Laurie Revlon appeared genuine in her praise of Bobby's DJ skills.

He looked pleased with himself, even if he still wasn't sure where this was leading. She had that disconcerting manner of gazing into the middle distance while she was talking, as if there was always likely to be someone more interesting lurking just beyond a shoulder. But most of the London contingent here had that habit, so he couldn't call her out for that alone.

Bobby had stumbled into a regular DJ-ing gig at the small club three months before. During an extended remix of D-Mob's 'We Call It Aceeid', an overexuberant Pedro – the incumbent – had attempted to blow a flame by spitting a mouthful of alcohol at a lighter. He had burped before he was fully ready and accidentally sprayed the inflammable booze down his front, setting his abundant chest hair ablaze. The high-spirited crowd dancing on the open-air terrace had whooped and cheered until security arrived with an extinguisher and everyone understood it wasn't part of the act. Seizing his moment, Bobby Cassidy had offered to do the next three nights free, as a trial, and he had been there ever since.

Bobby and Hammy had bumped into Pedro a month after the fire. He took an admirably sanguine view of his self-inflicted predicament, bearing the young Ayrshiremen no grudges. He even showed them his scars. He hadn't recovered well. A track mark ran down through his remaining chest hair like a napalm strike in a Vietnamese jungle, and the flaking skin of his Latin torso now looked like a plasterer's radio.

But it was a break for Bobby, albeit at the painful expense of a fellow member of the international DJ fraternity. He and Hammy grabbed the chance with both hands. Bobby's ability to build an atmosphere was now regularly packing out one of Ibiza's smaller, 'third division' nightclubs, and interested people, like those working and scouting for Laurie Revlon, were raising an inquiring eyebrow. There were no histrionics in Bobby's sets – nothing that would cause him potential harm – just good, solid selections and mixes. He built on a different vibe to the one Pedro pushed, aiming at the chilled-out ambience that was gradually emerging. His slot began at 2 am and lasted for three hours, typically featuring cooler grooves from the likes of Soul II Soul, Inner City and even newer, trippier songs, like De La Soul's 'Me, Myself & I'. Bobby had even dispensed with DJ Pedro's trademark: the 'Erection Section' of plodding slow-songs. The amount of times he played 'Careless Whisper' for an audience who evidently couldn't have cared less, Bobby reckoned Pedro must've been on a cut of George Michael's royalties.

'It's Bobby, isn't it?' said Laurie Revlon.

Bobby nodded in acknowledgement

'I wondered if you might be interested in working for me.'

'Em … ah'm no' sure. Ah'm actually quite content here tae be honest,' said Bobby. 'Demis gie'd us a chance, ken? Seems only fair tae commit tae him for the rest ae the season.'

If this was barter, Hammy thought, Bobby was fucking bollocks at it.

Hammy coughed theatrically and then leaned nearer to his man. 'Fuck sake,' he whispered. 'He's Demis Dimitri … no' Brian fuckin' Clough, man! Ye don't owe the cunt yer livelihood because he plucked ye fae fuckin' Doncaster Reserves an' stuck ye in the Cup Final startin' line-up. Hear the lassie oot.'

Laurie had heard him, and smiled at her young, ginger-haired advocate.

'Just promise me you'll think about it, that's all I ask.' Laurie Revlon handed over a card. 'I'll come back and see you next week. If you're here, I'll assume you're interested. If not, there's no harm done. Deal?'

'Aye … seems fair enough. And thanks. Ah'm glad ye like the stuff that ah play.'

Laurie Revlon raised an eyebrow and sashayed away, all Joan Collins arse and Bardot pout. On her way out of the establishment, she air-kissed people at five separate tables; she was apparently well known to many on the island, if not the two she had just met.

Laurie Revlon had made a substantial personal fortune in the avowedly heterosexual world of English professional football. Beginning as a teenage secretary on work experience in the lower divisions, she had worked, slept and married her way up to a position as the most influential player's agent in the game. Her reputation as the most ruthless operator in football was cemented after an alleged bribing scandal involving medical consultants representing Inter Milan. In the early 70s – when she was still only in her mid-twenties – she negotiated the world's first million-pound transfer fee with the sale of Terry Dooley to the Italian club. Terry Dooley was universally lauded as the most promising young player of England's post-World Cup-winning era. Terracing rumours circulated that his controversial move to Italy was orchestrated by Laurie Revlon in order to remove him from the influence of a cabal of men who allegedly indulged in group sex with underage teenage girls. Many of these men – again allegedly – occupied senior positions within the English Football Association. Terry Dooley was an addict – of alcohol and cocaine, principally – but miraculously he passed a stringent medical in a Milan hospital. However, he would play only two games of the following Serie A season. Laurie Revlon was accused of collusion in a fraud investigation brought against both Terry Dooley's English club and Inter Milan by the governing body, UEFA. The case didn't proceed, due to a lack of direct evidence. The player had helped Leeds United to the league title the previous season. He had won thirty-two caps for his country and had even recently captained the national team. There were no obvious reasons to suspect that the transfer wasn't above board. Terry Dooley was found dead in a shallow Bergamo ditch on the last day of the 1976 Italian football season. While a postmortem recorded high levels of alcohol and heroin in his system, the coroner's verdict was 'accidental death'. Terry Dooley was twenty-four years old.

Laurie Revlon had her manicured fingers in every lucrative pie, it seemed. Yet she retained a relatively low profile. She continued in football for a few years after the Terry Dooley affair, but she already had eyes on bigger prizes. She set up a sports promotions business and put on a number of world championship boxing events across England. Then, in 1982, she moved the base of her operations to Spain. And in 1985 – having peripherally contributed to the success of the Live Aid concerts in London and Philadelphia – she moved to Europe's Pleasure Island, becoming the resident of a pristine-white, modernist villa overlooking San Antonio bay.

'Fuck me, whit a great arse, eh?' said Hammy. 'Ye'd need an experienced mountain rescue squad to haul ye oot ae a crack that deep. Ah'd certainly ram it!'

Bobby just smiled ruefully. It had seemed like a strange encounter. They had been around the nightlife of San Antonio for most of the past two seasons, Bobby working as a club DJ and Hammy as a handyman at the campsite where they stayed during the summer months. They were becoming better known to the locals, and they both got into the bigger 'first division' clubs, such as Amnesia and Ku, for free. But neither had ever heard Laurie Revlon's name mentioned. Bobby accepted that their lifestyle was myopic, but he still felt it was strange that they'd not come across the long, blonde, crimped hair, the power-dressing white business suit and the Marilyn Monroe posterior of this magnetic forty-five-year-old woman.

'Yous jus' need be careful, okay?'

The conversation with Demis Dimitri that evening was as strange as the meeting with Laurie Revlon. Bobby had anticipated a difficult discussion with his current employer, and initially it had indeed been strained. But when the Greek club boss inquired about where Bobby might be going, the answer led to a complete change of tone.

'She eat you up, spit you out, you no' careful,' said Demis.

'Fuckin' hope so, man!' laughed Hammy.

'You need to listen to Demis.' He looked around and behind himself, then leaned in. Bobby and Hammy reciprocated. 'Laurie Rev-*lon* ista total cunt!' he whispered.

As they walked back to the campsite, a full moon illuminating their way through the field, Bobby wore a pained expression.

Hammy couldn't understand it. 'Look, he's jist pissed off that yer leavin'. Dinnae take nae notice ae aw that fuckin' voodoo shite. Ye ken whit these Greek cunts are aw like. They smash their ain bastard crockery when they're fuckin' happy, fur Christ's sake!'

'Aye, mibbe.'

'Mibbe, nuthin'. This Revlon lassie's possibly gie'in ye a shot at somethin' decent … somethin' much bigger than Santorini's.' Hammy's upbeat-o-meter was redlining. 'Remember when ye first chucked it at the Metropolis? When ye telt Doc Martin it wisnae big enough for ye?'

'Aye, but that wis different.'

'Naw it wisnae. It's aw aboot ambition, man.' And then, the killer blow: 'C'mon … fuckin' get in there!' Hammy wrapped an arm around Bobby.

Bobby laughed. He had much to be grateful to Hamish May for. His relentless optimism in the face of all adversity had comforted Bobby in the early days of 1983, when his family pressures were at their greatest. He'd also steadied Bobby's emotional ship when his relationship with Lizzie King finally sank just off the east-Spanish coast. Hamish May was a rock of the ages, and whilst a significant part of Bobby still wished Joey Miller was here to share in it all, he couldn't have hoped for a better life companion than Hammy. Hammy was there for him all the time, through thick and thin, in good times and b—

'Hammy, where the fuck are ye goin'?' shouted Bobby, having just realised his friend had taken a different route.

A distant voice wafted back through the gloom. 'Doon tae the caravan park. On a promise ae a wee three-way. Met a couple ae Dublin women earlier. Ah'm ther' ultimate fantasy apparently.'

Bobby sighed.

'See ye in the mornin',' shouted Hammy. 'Away an' have a wee Sherman Tank tae yersel'. Think ae Missus Revlon scouring yer baws wi' a Brillo pad soaked in honey.' His laughter faded.

Bobby smiled. He recalled a time when he too was as bullishly buoyant about absolutely everything; a time before the Falklands War intervened.

Chapter Five

October 2014. Shanghai, China

''Scuse me?' Megan Carter, Manager of Guest Relations, turns around. It's a practised pirouette; as graceful as Fonteyn.

'Hello sir. How can I help you today?' she says.

Joseph reckons she must be in a perpetual state of mid-smile; like the personification of a Brian Wilson melody. It momentarily makes him forget his lines.

'Sir?'

'Aye … yeah. Look, ah just wanted to apologise for the other day. Y'know, wi' the flowers, an' that.'

Megan Carter's expression doesn't change. Joseph wonders if she has a twin. Or maybe she genuinely doesn't recognise him. He is more Charlie Watts than Keith Richards today, after all.

Then her glorious smile softens slightly. 'It's absolutely no problem, sir. To be honest, I wasn't having a wonderful day either, so I should apologise too.'

It isn't what he'd expected to hear and it takes him a bit by surprise.

She recognises his awkwardness, and she's suddenly serious. 'See, I shouldn't even have said *that*. I'm very sorry.'

'No, listen, there's absolutely no need. Ah was rude tae *you*, an' ah'm really sorry. Ah just felt ah should say.'

Megan's polished smile returns. Joseph smiles a little too. He hasn't done that in a while. He's lost count of the amount of times some fatuous cunt has informed him that frowning involved fewer muscles than smiling; but, given how unusual the upturned corners of his mouth now feel, maybe it's actually true. He turns slowly away. He wants to say more, but he has no connection with this girl beyond a few, inconsequential words.

'If you need anything else, just let me know, sir. My name is Megan.'

Joseph turns to face her. He is ten feet away now. *God, she is fucking beautiful.*

'Thanks. Ah will. Bye'

'Good evening, sir.'

Later, he sits on the bed. After reading an email from his duplicitous partners expressing shallow concern for his wellbeing, he paid for a substantial room upgrade. Gone is the inherent sense of fiscal responsibility he normally demonstrates. He unwraps one of two chocolates perched on pillows whiter than an Osmond brother's teeth. It's a farcical bed for a hotel room. Its width is its length and then half again. It is a bed fit for a Roman orgy, its size only seeking to remind this traveller of his solitude, not of the perceived royal grandeur of his upgrade.

He shuffles himself back up the bed and leans against the padded headboard. Six soft pillows create a nest for his body. It takes him a full fifteen minutes to flick through every channel on the wall-mounted TV. Chinese television is a confusing brew of talking heads, overdramatic melodramas and live-action table tennis, all presented with throbbing, surround-sound infographics. There are a few Western channels, principally 24-hour news, repeating the same stories every half hour but calling them 'breaking'. Joseph recalls the days when you had to make an appointment with the news. The impact of some of those news stories from his youth has remained with him. They were intertwined with the demeanour of the person delivering it at the time everyone heard it first. A succession of male anchors sensationally updating the numbers attributed to the Yorkshire Ripper as if he were a brutal bowler in a surreal game of cricket. An actor's voice replacing that of a blacked-out Gerry Adams every time an 'Irish atrocity' prompted his comment. The MOD spokesman, Ian McDonald, despatching devastating statistics from the Falklands, including one which wrongly included Gary Cassidy. How things had changed. Nowadays, news was everywhere. It found the recipient and latched on like bacteria, trivialising the impact of real tragedies by placing inconsequential celebrity scandals on an equal footing. To Joseph the news media of today thus seemed in a perpetual state of shock or outraged offence, but lacked the compassion or empathy that would make such emotions genuine.

The blinding graphic display is giving him a headache. He flicks the switch. Megan, the blonde-haired hotel emblem, slides languorously into his empty head, like honey dripping from a golden sceptre. His eyes close. He thinks about how her naked body might look if she was standing in front of him at the bottom of this rectangular island of a bed. He can't escape the thought of her sharing it with him: two castaways from the unforgiving ship of modern life. His hand is around his cock, although he hasn't even been aware of it developing into a hard-on sufficient to be useful to him. There is less feeling there nowadays – a byproduct of the inhibitors he takes to regulate his soaring blood pressure. In his subconscious, Megan is now stroking her own golden thighs and moaning as her delicate hand reaches between her legs. He is masturbating, trying to focus, but his cock is losing the brief hardness it had. He struggles to concentrate, guilty about using the girl like this, even though she is unaware of it. Eventually he ejaculates but not with any force or euphoria, more with a shameful, sputtering resignation.

Afterwards, his breathing is deep and forced, as if he is recovering from a long run or a steep climb. He gets up from the bed, rolling across the small wet patch he has just made, and walks, head down, to the bathroom. The light over the mirror comes on automatically and illuminates him as he wipes the sticky spunk from his belly button, and then the tears from his eyes.

The expansive reception area feels like the inside of a hollowed-out, multi-tiered wedding cake. An elaborate atrium stretches through its volume and becomes smaller with every three storeys until the top of it is barely visible. Joseph arches his neck back and stares up at it again. The building is a strange juxtaposition of the contemporary and the classical, or a pastiche of it, at least. Nothing in China seems authentic. It is a country lacking in identity, trying to become something it isn't. It makes Joseph briefly yearn for home and the more honest and thrawn environment of Jock Tamson's bairns. Even the buildings aren't allowed to get ideas above their station in Scotland. He looks at his watch. The date flickers. It is 13th October, four days since his birthday, and a full week since he arrived in Shanghai. He considers the time in Barcelona and then – holding the piece of paper from the flower basket far enough away to be able to see the numbers – he punches them into his phone. The long, single dialling tone for international calls sounds four times before it is answered.

'*Hola*.'

'Hello, Sophia? Sophia, it's Joseph … Joseph Miller. Is Carlos at home?' Joseph speaks slowly and clearly, sanding down the rough edges of his west-of-Scotland demotic. Sophia's English is good, but they haven't spoken at all for years and formal pronunciation seems appropriate.

'*Hola*, Joseph. How are you?' Despite obvious surprise, her tone is warm.

Joseph relaxes.

'Carlos is out at a doctor appointment, now, but I tell him you phone,' she says. 'He be very please to speak to you.'

'How's he been? I got a message from him. I'm over in China just now, writing. I wasn't sure if he'd have known I'd been away from Glasgow,' says Joseph, his speech picking up speed.

'Yes, he know. He not been so good lately. His skins are very sore. Difficult for him to paint now or do any things he loves.'

'I'm sorry to hear that, Sophia. Can you tell him I'll call again in a couple of days? I have to go to Huangshan for a day or two but I'll speak to him properly when I get back,' says Joseph.

'I will, Joseph. He need to talk to you. He has proposal for you,' says Sophia.

'Do you know what it's about?' Joseph asks her. This message from his old partner is becoming more intriguing. It is certainly unexpected.

'I should leave to Carlos to tell you,' Sophia says. He can't read anything into her delivery. It's neither positive nor negative.

'Okay, Soph. Thanks. Tell him I was askin' for him. Speak soon.'

'Bye, Joseph.'

'Bye.'

The discussion – such as it was – leaves Joseph Miller a little sidetracked. He'd no intention of contacting any of his current partners, but for Carlos Martorell to get in touch after all the acrimony, something significant must have happened. Whatever it is, it will have to wait. He has promised to visit Chan Li, his first client for a competition-winning cultural centre in the emerging third-tier city of Huangshan at the foot of the Yellow Mountains. Mr Li speaks no English, and Joseph has forgotten all of the basic Mandarin he picked up five years ago, but there is a bond of sorts between them, and Joseph is looking forward to seeing the older man again, as well as the building he designed for him.

He gathers up his papers, slides them into his small case and heads across the shiny marble floor towards a small army of smiling, uniformed hotel porters. The entrance is bustling. It is 5 pm and people of all nationalities are coming and going. Joseph ignores the *good evening, sirs* of everyone in a red tunic and walks out to hail a cab to the airport.

Outside, a commotion to his left catches his eye. Megan Carter, the special guest star of his recent impromptu fantasy wank, is at the centre of this too. She is being berated by a heavy-set English guy in baggy, flowery shorts as three others in similar garb laugh and egg him on. The Manager of Guest Relations is struggling to keep her composure over what appears to be a hire-car dispute. Joseph watches the Englishman go way over the top about the fact that the car isn't an automatic as he'd apparently requested. Joseph is about forty feet away, and he can't properly hear Megan's apologetic counters; only the cockney geezer's increasing personal abuse. Megan lifts her head and glances over, catching Joseph's eye, so she doesn't see the cockney's arm jolt out as if threatening to hit her. She flinches and her face transforms instantly. She wears a genuinely terrified expression. She moves back sharply and overbalances, falling over a small, perfectly trimmed plastic hedge. The back of her head hits the smooth concrete on the other side. The cockney's mates all laugh, and he turns to them and bows. Instinctively, Joseph drops his bag and runs over, but the cockney has spotted him.

'And who the fack are *you* then? *Her* fackin' dad?' he says, squaring up. 'Or maybe her fackin' grandad?'

The three mates laugh loudly again. It's clear they are all drunk.

'Hittin' a lassie, eh? That make ye a big man, does it?' says Joseph, shocking himself with his forwardness. From his perspective it looked like the man had actually connected.

'Ow, fackin' brilliant, boys. He's a poofy little Jock.'

'Give the cunt a right beltin', Jack … then let's go, yeah?' Cockney Jack leans in, weight on the front foot preparing to launch a south-paw fist at Joseph, but the red army reinforcements have numbered behind him, and the situation swiftly defuses.

Joseph's heart rate is accelerating, his temperamental blood pressure now five foot high and rising. The four Englishmen abroad head off in their non-automatic hired Hyundai with Jack mouthing, 'You're fucking dead, mate,' to Joseph through the windscreen as they reverse.

'Are you okay, hen? It's Megan, isn't it?' Joseph helps her to her feet.

She is shaking. And more than a little embarrassed. 'Em … sorry Mr … eh, Miller. Yes, of course. Yeah, sorry, yes … I'm perfectly fine. Thank you.'

Megan Carter clearly isn't perfectly fine. Her black jacket has a rip at the elbow and blood is evident through the blond strands of her hair. It seems to Joseph that there is more to this altercation than meets the eye. Two porters rush to pick up Joseph's bag, but none move toward their stricken colleague.

'You should get that seen tae,' says Joseph, indicating the emerging blood on the back of Megan's head.

'I will, thank you … Thank you, sir.' She looks him straight in the eye. He feels ashamed at his earlier private thoughts about her.

'It's Joseph. Please call me Joseph,' says Joseph.

'Okay.' She smiles. It's a fragile expression. 'Joseph. And I'm Megan.' She shakes his hand. Her touch is alabaster smooth, but still trembling. She turns to go back into the hotel but stops and looks back at him as she reaches the sliding doors. She waves to him before stepping inside.

Chapter Six

August 1990. San Antonio, Ibiza

'I really want us to take on Space,' said Laurie Revlon.

She had called a meeting of her protégés to outline her ambitious plans for the next decade. Bobby Cassidy was sat at the back. He looked bored. Two Italian DJs and three English ones, who had recently been added to the roster, sat in the front row. Bobby knew better. Laurie would occasionally lob in a live grenade and it was always those in the front row who had to quickly defuse it.

Bobby had been working for Laurie Revlon's organisation for almost four months. A year ago to the day, he'd signed a ridiculously long contract document without fully reading it.

'She's fuckin' payin' ye £750 a week, ya moron!' said Hammy. 'She could have first call on yer fuckin' vital organs for that. And *mine*! Other clubs are no' gonnae be comin' in for ye ... yer no' exactly the DJ-ing Mo Johnston, are ye? Get it bloody signed, mate.'

Bobby had smiled at the thought of his local deliberations causing as much widespread consternation as the Scotland striker's decision to turn his back on Celtic to join their fiercest city rivals, Rangers. Maybe one day they would, he mused. Hamish May – Bobby's de facto legal counsel – saw little benefit in deliberating over the small print. It was a four-fold increase on what Bobby was earning previously, and for two nights a week less. It had seemed mad to procrastinate. So Bobby didn't.

'We'll be expanding Revolution in the winter. I'm going to build a bigger area with open-air terraces around a new pool. I'm putting a wave machine in. We need to pull more people in. Amnesia is getting over five thousand punters a night now. The music scene is changing fast, and we need to be at the forefront.' Laurie Revlon spoke calmly but very assuredly.

There were some enthusiastic nods from the new boys.

'The days of chilling out and hippy-dippy beats while watching the sunset are gone, gentlemen. There's a hardcore rave transformation going on out there. It's going to be all about energy. High-energy music, high-energy drugs … and high-energy DJs.' She glanced at Bobby, who was demonstrating about as much energy as a two-watt light bulb. 'We're going to be open around the clock from next month.' Laurie Revlon continued. She now looked straight at the Italians. 'Sleeping is simply not an option.'

Bobby saw one of the lads from Rome silently mouth the words, 'Not an option,' as if hypnotised. *He'll go far*, thought Bobby.

'And we're going to be making our own mixes … putting them on our own CDs.'

If the earlier part of the meeting had been a bit 'meat and potatoes', this last bit was worthy of note. Bobby Cassidy was suddenly as attentive as the sparky Italians. Bobby had dreamed of making his own music mixes and recording them, as the emerging Ace Faces, Terry Farley and Danny Rampling were now rumoured to be doing.

Working under Laurie Revlon's banner at the new Revolution club had actually been good for Bobby. Laurie didn't get too involved. Her expansive team of associates and acolytes did all the interfacing with the DJs and, by and large, Bobby was free to play what he wanted. The club had had a slow start. It was a converted hangar in a remote part of San Rafael, on the outskirts of San Antonio. Several early technical glitches had saddled it with an unfortunate reputation that might have been more easily dealt with in a more central location. Faced with the journey out to an uncertain experience, the early-season clubbers had elected to stick with the tried and tested. But Laurie Revlon knew the right people. The Club closed for a week, dusted itself down and then reopened having had its turbulent electrics overhauled. And soon, with the help of an army of promotional fly-posters and PR workers, the sweaty clubbers and drunken tourists returned in substantial numbers. Bobby worked Tuesdays, Wednesdays, Thursdays and Sundays.

Hammy had also been promoted at the campsite and had a name badge that proclaimed him 'Assistant Campsite Manager'. His promotion was the result of his intervention in a fight between three English lads and a single German, who turned out to be the son of a friend of the owner. Hammy had suffered a black eye in his bid to calm the one-sided situation, and had received the equivalent of a £50-a-week pay rise for it.

Beyond Laurie Revlon's apparent ability to see into the future, it was clear that things were changing. The traditionally linear genres of music were already merging and crossing over into other territories. New Order – who had previously shared the same bedsit appeal as Echo and the Bunnymen and The Cure – had actually come to Ibiza to record an LP called *Technique*. Due to his fortuitously sharing a hotel lift with the band's lead singer, Bernard Sumner, Bobby was one of the first White Isle DJs to play a white-label promo of the LP's incredible opening single, 'Fine Time'.

In fact, the innovative Balearic DJs were at the forefront of an entire musical paradigm shift. Andy Weatherall and Terry Farley's influence on Primal Scream's new record 'Loaded' had indicated a dance-based direction for guitar bands, and in their hands cool samples were taken from a variety of unusual sources in ways that totally changed the sound of the source material. Weatherall even lifted Peter Fonda's audio dialogue from his film *The Wild Angels* to start the seven-minute 'Loaded' before reinforcing its groove with vocals from the Emotions and a drum loop from an Edie Brickell song. Heard lolloping out of the massive Revolution speaker stacks and into the warm Ibizan summer air, it sounded transcendental. It heralded a new philosophy in which the DJ was an imaginative innovator let loose in a classic record store with everything ever recorded at his disposal. Although self-produced, The Stone Roses 'Fools Gold' was another ten-minute journey into a sound that – especially when aided by other stimulants – could take Bobby Cassidy to another place entirely, a place where such music seemed like the only thing in life that actually mattered.

'Fools Gold' was heavily influenced by the Dust Brothers-produced Young MC track 'Know How', and also incorporated a guitar line from 'Theme From Shaft' by Isaac Hayes, and the break from 'Apache' by The Incredible Bongo Band. The song's basic repetitive lyrics made reference to the Humphrey Bogart film, *The Treasure of the Sierra Madre* and also, more subtly, Nancy Sinatra's 'These Boots Are Made For Walkin' and The Velvet Underground's Marquis De Sade-themed song 'Venus In Furs'. Only a few months earlier, Bobby had been part of a VIP group flown over to the band's momentous outdoor Spike Island gig: independent music labels in London were courting Laurie Revlon as a potential investor and there were a few spare seats on the Lear Jet. The experience had been incredible. Champagne bottles and solid-silver caviar dishes were everywhere. Perfectly formed mini-mountain ranges of Columbian marching powder adorned every flat surface on the plane. Blowjobs were being given as enthusiastically by beautiful company 'hostesses' as the boiled sweets to make your ears pop on landing were on more conventional flights. Turns out there were three possible interpretations of 'a Jack Daniels and Coke, please'. Laurie sat in the front row, calmly writing notes in a black, leather-bound diary with a diamond-encrusted pen like she was the madam of a flying brothel, marking up appointments on 'anything goes' night. When the small jet finally landed it looked like it had flown through a tornado upside down before Keith Moon had been drafted in to administer the final touches to its appearance of orgiastic excess. Bobby had thoughtfully kept the flight details from Hammy, who was already indignant about not being invited. Having missed the opportunity to have his balls sucked at 30,000 feet by a naked woman who looked like the twin sister of Cindy Crawford would have sent him over the edge. It was the Bacchanalian excesses of an industry built on extreme self-indulgence. Watching the Stone Roses at Spike Island from stage left, and with twenty-eight thousand fans separated from the stage by a strange, green-hued creek,

Bobby loved the ambition behind the gig. It felt like history in the making; like something you would tell disbelieving grandchildren about. To further compound its surreal quality, at the end he was almost certain he'd seen Joey Miller standing in the soaked crowd, being held back by a cordon of rough security men as the VIPs made their way to their limos. It looked really like him, but it couldn't have been. He'd have shouted or waved, surely.

Bobby began deconstructing these songs, the tasty melting pot of indie, dance, soul, rap and hip-hop that formed the ideas behind them. He kept notes and ideas in countless black books, and was spending more and more time in the club, watching those further up the DJ totem pole than him – which accounted for his current state of exhaustion in this meeting. Bobby had become a collector, a researcher and an alchemist all at once. The cultural clash of classic soul, indie attitudes and punk appropriation of cool movie motifs was the future of sound. He was suddenly appreciating what real DJ'ing was all about. It was about experimentation; about taking sonic risks and incorporating those risks into music that had evolved from its basic origins. About orchestrating the murmuration of thousands of clubbers all moving in a coordinated rhythm. Bobby Cassidy felt like he was an apprentice scientist, learning at the knobs and faders of the most important people in music … the DJs of the Balearics.

The two young men from Kilmarnock loved Ibiza during this frenetic period: the changing musical spectrum, the fashions moving back to a more glamorous era rather than the hippy slacker vibe, and the ecstatic drugs than made anything seem possible. They were both twenty-six years old and life was fucking magnificent.

Chapter Seven

October 2014. Huangshan, Anhui Province, China

The word 'democracy' can be difficult to define, and its meaning changes according to which part of the world you apply it to. Most in the West would consider it to refer to a form of government in which the people hold supreme power through representatives that they have elected. Hand in hand with this is a demonstrable sense of social equality. Even described in these terms, democracy can be a very abstract concept. For China, as it gradually emerges from being a closed and relatively unknown environment to one engaging far more directly with the rest of the world, the issue may be less about democracy and more about personal liberty.

It seems appropriate for Joseph to include a personal account of his time spent in China. It has been a considerable part of his own recent history and – he now accepts – a contributing factor in his descent into depression. He's had a few drinks, and the tiny bottles are piling up like skittles on his fold-down table. Music plays in his ear: 'Bigmouth Strikes Again'…

Prior to visiting China for the first time in 2009, my preconceptions about the country were fed by the media. I assumed it was a determinedly introspective, communistic place, where the individual rights and freedoms I take for granted are denied. In 2014, however, people in China have much more liberty than their parents had in the 80s – to love, work, shop, spend, enjoy, travel, speak, believe and, fundamentally, to live. With China recently overtaking Japan, becoming predominant in the new world order and the epicentre of world economic growth, the basic form of liberty that is required to survive the contemporary Chinese urban life does exist for all her citizens. However, it is becoming more evident that the extent of liberty is directly proportional to an individual's wealth and power. In that sense, Chinese society as it currently develops may be far more recognisable to Western civilisation than the USA and its allies might be prepared to admit.

'...and by rights you should be bludgeoned in your bed...'

If capitalism is an economic system based on private ownership of land, capital and the means of production, China is rapidly moving much closer to this model. But it is the issues surrounding ownership of land and personal advancement where the greatest anomalies remain. By the end of the Cultural Revolution in 1976, virtually all land was state owned. Private property rights had all but disappeared and land transactions were illegal. Since China is still fundamentally socialist in ideology, land remains mostly in government ownership. However, private developers can now purchase the rights to use the land. It's an interesting and subtle shift in approach; born from a policy rooted in socialism it has created a 'right of use' culture. Such rights are generally granted to those developers who have money – which suggests a more recognisable shift from communism to capitalism. Nonetheless, other factors, beyond differences in costs and land values, are now becoming more important and it is in this key aspect that times must change for China. By paying a huge price in social and environmental terms, China has achieved a strange mix of concern for the ignorance of its people and their human rights, and envy for the uncompromising momentum of its development.

Joseph ponders this complex contradiction. Lucinda Burroughs was very similar to China, he muses. Admired by everyone who knew her for her drive, ambition and no-nonsense attitude to ... What? Him? The people who worked for her? World fucking domination? She was feared – a fact in which she positively revelled. She was a total cunt. How had he not seen it, hiding beneath the veneer and the Max Factor mask?

'...I'd like to smash every tooth in your head'.

But this shift has also created an unsustainable acceleration in the real-estate market, leading to what many refer to as the 'ghost towns' of China. Built at breakneck speed in only five years, Kangbashi in Inner Mongolia is a state-of-the-art city full of architectural 'marvels' (not necessarily my term ...) and sculpture gardens. There's just one thing

missing: people. The city stands as a physical representation of an obses-
sion with GDP that makes no distinction between quantity and quality.
Similarly, the massive Three Gorges Dam project is considered in China
an historic engineering, economic and social success. The dam produces
electricity, increases the Yangtze River's shipping capacity and reduces
the regularity of substantial flooding downstream by the creation of flood
storage pockets. To achieve these things, more than 1.25 million people
were evicted. There were allegations that the funds for relocating numer-
ous farmers had 'gone missing', leaving them with no compensation.

Where these notes will fit in a memoir of accountability which
will attempt to explain everything to his daughter, he isn't yet sure.
He isn't entirely convinced she'll even read them; such is the canyon
that now exists between the two of them. But at least she'll have
them. She'll hopefully keep them, and perhaps one day she'll read
them. And then she'll understand. And that is all he craves.

'Bigmouth strikes again…'

For other countries trying (and failing) to keep pace with China's
relentless financial growth, the law, market regulation, the environment
and, most significantly, human capital are all highly topical and signifi-
cant issues. Many expect China to gradually adjust its economic structure
and reduce its environmental impact. There are also some small, but
nonetheless hopeful signs that in future, China's leaders might no longer
seek growth at any cost. In President Hu Jintao's summary, growth must
serve a 'harmonious society'. Harmony in this instance equates to a
narrowing of the poverty gap between countryside and city, and more
generally that the poorer inland regions catch up with the coastal ones.

It is these very complex contradictions inherent in China's rapid devel-
opment that make it such a fascinating place for architects to work. The
search for an architectural identity in an era of increasing globalisation is
relatively universal and not restricted to China. However, China faces a
very particular dilemma in regard to how its built environment develops.
Chinese culture is one of the oldest and richest in the world. Many ele-
ments of old China – Buddhism, Taoism and Confucianism – still play
an important role in society, representing for many what it means to be

Chinese, and demarcating Chinese culture from imports from other parts of the world. Unsurprisingly, these attitudes result in a focus on the past. On the other hand, the economic boom and the way the nation is reacting to global mechanisms have also created the desire for a new China, partly detached from the old, more restrictive traditions

'… and I have no right to take my place with the human race.'

He surprises himself with how easily the words flow. An extended delay during which he downed four gin and tonics on an empty stomach has loosened the pen somewhat. A tiny meal of rice and chicken might have soaked up some of that, had he not added another four during the flight. In some ways the sentences are of the nature expected when the task was initially set, but when analysed in the context of others he has already written about his times in Tripoli, Delhi and Cairo, they are merely allegories of his own complex contradictions and isolation. Joseph Miller has written most of these new words on the short flight between Shanghai's Pudong International Airport and its less refined regional neighbour, Tunxi Airport, at the foot of Mount Huangshan. The contrast between the two structures – one, a new, polished free-form temple to Western consumerism and efficient movement of people; the other a much older, tired, and constrained compromise of an operation – isn't lost on him as a metaphor for the relationships between himself and the two young women who are beginning to occupy his thoughts more and more.

He smiles ruefully. The printed paper sign reads 'MR JOSPEH MILLOR'. It is held by an atypical Odd-Job in a black suit. Most Chinese are slight but this lad is positively Sumo. Joseph knows there is no point in conversing even to ask his driver's name. Very few people speak English this far away from the first-tier cities. There is an acknowledging nod and the briefest of smiles as the car's door is opened for him, but that will be as far as the communication goes. It was one of the things he most liked about China when he first ventured further into the provinces, six years ago. Although Joseph feels relaxed enough now to do so, there's no pressure on him to talk the international language of commercial business: bullshit.

Mr Li's hotels are modest in scale but very comfortable. The interiors are adorned with expensive paintings, ceramics and furnishings. They are all built around a central, vaulted and mahogany-lined social space in which nightly staged performances take place. Private dining rooms with large, circular glass tables circle the void. Even when the shutters are open to allow views of – or simply the ability to listen to – the actors, ubiquitous wall-mounted television screens spew out their headache-inducing graphics. Chinese theatre is a magical mix of decoration and illusion, and although Huangshan has been preparing itself for a tourist influx since the maglev cut the journey time from Shanghai and Beijing by two thirds, these incredibly beautiful events are still being played out to largely empty halls across the region. None of this seems to have perturbed Chan Li, who, despite new legislation from Beijing strangling the hitherto massive profits of commercial developers all over China, has pressed on with proposals for substantial land-grabbing masterplans across the Anhui region. His new thing, apparently, is golf clubs.

'Mr Li want you to show him Scotland,' says the interpreter as they sit down for dinner.

'Tell Mr Li I'd be honoured to accompany him to St Andrews or Turnberry,' Joseph replies, knowing that ninety-nine percent of promises made to foreign clients are never called upon. He bows his head slightly and speaks directly to his host, who is seated to his immediate right. Joseph tries hard to recall the formal order of where people are seated relative to the most important person in the room. He assumes the man to Mr Li's left is his Managing Director. Two other, younger, men are obviously relations of Mr Li, given how closely they resemble him. The remaining five – including the only woman – are all company associates. The interpreter has no space at the table.

His host stands. Toast time. They are drinking tiny glasses of white spirit from the various glass jugs sitting around the table. Joseph is several rounds ahead of them. When first introduced to Chinese drinking culture, Joseph was mesmerised by it – all the rituals and customs and giving face. He now finds it tiresome. If toasted, you absolutely must remember to toast back, or cause offence. And a guest must tap the glass edge, stand and toast the whole gathering at least once during the meal … or cause offence. The Chinese aren't drinkers in the sense stereotypically associated with the Scottish, but, by Christ, do they enjoy trying to get their foreign guests drunk on this clear ouzo-like, aniseedy liquid. It isn't going to be difficult for them on this particular evening.

The perceived customs concerning the food are all thankfully false. It doesn't cause offence if a plate isn't cleared. It is simply bad form not to at least try the various things that pass for local delicacies. Healthy though the Chinese diet obviously is, a spin of the central glass disc on the table always presents a split turtle-shell soup or a fried scorpion. Joseph once watched aghast as a young woman seated next to him cracked an egg and swallowed a watery foetus. She briefly showed it to him before consumption. He was certain it had tiny feathers.

The social significance of eating is something Joseph once really admired about the culture. Regardless of what is happening elsewhere, everything stops abruptly for two hours at noon, and then again at 6 pm. This is when the real business is done. Now, however, he finds it boring and exhausting. Save for the odd nods, simple pleasantries and invitations to drink more, all conveyed via a third party, he is largely ignored. His thoughts keep drifting back to Megan Carter. He wonders what she is doing right at this moment, if she is over her earlier distress, if she is maybe even thinking about him. If she might be…

'Mr Li want you to go with sons now. They look after you, Mr Miller.' The interpreter bursts the bubble.

Joseph hasn't noticed that dinner has ended. Chan Li's sons are waiting for him. One has his coat. The other is holding his briefcase. A more suspicious reading of the situation might be that he is being disposed of; politely, and after being fed, of course. Like another suited Scotsman on Her Majesty's Service and from an earlier generation. But no, they are taking him out on the town, Huangshan-style.

Joseph Miller hates karaoke with a pained passion. But these people can't get enough of it. He simply wants to visit the completed building he designed. To see how it is weathering, how the local contractors and the design institutes have interpreted his team's drawings, whether they have cavalierly changed the specifications, the materials, its very appearance. Is it even recognisable as the same idea that once materialised in his head? But for that he will have to wait. He is being entertained whether he likes it or not.

The KYTV sign blasts neon into the atmosphere from the edge of the river. It is a ten-storey structure with an aesthetic supplanted from the monolithic Eastern Bloc era. The KYTV concept is simple: a multilevel legalised brothel where visiting punters can sing, have sex with young, apparently willing Chinese girls and drink until they can drink no more. *In communist China, everyone can find a worthwhile job; a way of contributing.*

Joseph is led, stumbling, to a private room lined, floor, wall and ceiling, with thick-pile beige carpet. Even the back of the door is carpeted. A massive beige U-shaped leather sofa circles a double-bed-sized, smoked-glass table with more whisky bottles on it than Joseph can count. In front of the table is the karaoke machine. In front of it, and just beyond the six-inch-high stage, is a mini cinema screen. Over to the left is a Corian inset washbasin, stacks of black towels and supplies of lubricant, condoms, wet wipes and an array of S, M, L and XL dildos.

A large whisky is poured by one of Chan Li's sons. Joseph is extremely uncomfortable. Earlier, outside the building's entrance, he protested, but in vain. If he wasn't forced into the establishment, it certainly felt like it to him. His head is swimming. The spirits are mixing; Scotch and Chinese and Gordon's. Taylor Swift is enticing him to the microphone. He can't get up from the sofa. The other Li son comes into the room leading a chain of five small Chinese girls. They look like schoolchildren being led across a road to a party by their teacher. They have numbers on their wrists and are dressed in long, beige dresses slashed to the upper thigh. Sharp v-shaped cuts go down past flat, immature breasts. Joseph Miller feels sick. The pixelated Taylor sings louder and more insistently. But he can't 'Shake It Off'. Chan Li Jr urges the girls to step forward one at a time. Joseph can barely focus. He is shaking and sweating. He is overheating. He looks up. Number one advances: it is Megan Carter. Number two steps forward: Hettie Cassidy. A muddy pain rises in his neck and slaps his lower jaw. The third KYTV Princess now … his daughter, Jennifer. She leans forward in a rehearsed pose of fake seduction, smiling but dead behind the eyes. Saying something he can't understand. His liver races upwards past his Adam's apple. He hears glass smashing, people moving quickly, his face deep in the shag pile like it was a rarely maintained Sunday league football pitch. His eyes close. He has scored high marks on the Glasgow Coma Scale multiple-choice quiz.

Chapter Eight

September 1992. San Antonio, Ibiza

'How do you feel about staying on, Bobby?'

'Whit d'ye mean … here? Wi' you?'

'Well, not staying *with* me, obviously, that would be ridiculous.' Laurie Revlon sniggered at the thought. 'But remaining here during the winter. To try out a few new recordings. I want the club to be up there with Cream and The Ministry … put out a Revolution Collection CD early next year, as part of the promotions.'

Bobby was exhilarated. He knew Laurie had been constructing a studio up in the hills away from the town, but he hadn't been invited up there yet. Laurie had only informed him that it was almost complete, and now, if he stayed, he was going to be one of the first to try it out. This must have been what Laurie Revlon had hinted at years ago when she first persuaded him to sign the complex contract with her. She had been as good as her word. His salary had increased substantially as the popularity of the club – and particularly his own slots – had grown. And now, Bobby Cassidy was about to get his chance. Now, all he had to do was break the news to Hamish May that he'd be returning to Ayrshire alone.

'Eh? Away an' get fucked!' Hammy wasn't happy. 'If you're stayin' here, then so am ah.'

'But the campsite's closin', man,' said Bobby.

'I'll fuckin' blockade it then … like that skinny wee *Tiananmen Square* cunt. Ah put up wi' aw the other pish, ah'm no' missin' oot on this!' Hammy was determined.

'But there's nae where for ye tae stay, man. The whole place is shuttin' doon.'

'So whit! Where are you gonnae be livin'?'

'Ah dunno yet. But ah think there's maybe a chance ae kippin' up at the studio. There's a back room an' that, an' Laurie seems quite happy for somebody tae be there aw the time, workin' an' lookin' after the place.'

'Well, ah'll stay there tae … unless yer tryin' tae tell me somethin' else.'

'Naw … naw, it isnae that. Ah just didnae want tae push ma luck, in case she fuckin' changes her mind, ken?'

'Well.'

'Well whit?'

'Push yer fuckin' luck, ya tube! There's nae way ah'm goin' back tae cuntin' Killie just as you finally dig yer way oot the trenches an' start reachin' for the stars.'

'Aye fine. Ah'll tell her yer ma new PA.'

'Whit's that stand for then?'

'Ma Personal fuckin' Arsehole. The yin that does aw the 'arsehole' jobs an' never fuckin' complains aboot it.' Bobby extended an arm.

Hammy considered it for a few seconds and then shook the hand at the end of it. Both men smiled.

'Deal,' said Hamish May. 'I'll be yer Arsehole.'

Predictably, Hammy was bored within a week of their new arrangement. He wandered about sullenly, hands stuck deep in the pockets of his camouflaged cargo trousers, farting in the sound-proofed rooms, where the smell couldn't get out. It was getting on everybody's tits. This was the first time Hammy had witnessed how an island totally dependent on tourists for its identity completely shut down during the times when they weren't there. It was as if a life-support system had been temporarily switched off and Ibiza had been cryogenically frozen. He found it depressing, but consoled himself with the thought that at least it wasn't literally frozen, as it most likely would be back in Ayrshire. During one recording session in mid-January, Hammy irritated the engineers working on Bobby's ideas so much that they walked out. He'd complained that complex international hostage negotiations had taken less time than one of them was taking in experimenting with a synthesiser sound.

'Fuck sake, Hammy … gie it a break, eh? These guys cost a bloody fortune.'

'It isnae your money, man. Whit are you greetin' aboot?'

'Ah've got tae get this track mixed and finished by the end ae the month, but that's no' gonnae happen if you keep pissin' every cunt off.'

'Ye've been at this one song for five weeks aw'ready. Jesus Christ, Bobby … nae disrespect, pal, but it's a fuckin' rave thing that just goes *Boom Boom Boom, Tiddly Bollocks, Boom* for half an hour! It's hardly fuckin' *Pet Sounds*, mate.'

Bobby had to laugh at Hammy's impression of the rhythm track. It was pretty accurate, but turn it up loud, neck a few Eccies, and it sounded like a bloody beat symphony. He knew. He'd tested it.

'So whit would you dae wi' it, then?' asked Bobby, principally to pass the time until the engineers returned.

'Ah'd stick a bangin' vocal on it, man,' said Hammy.

'On ye go then, Bono … grab the mic.' Bobby gestured through the glass panel towards the studio. He pressed a red button, and faded up the array of dials. *Boom Boom Boom … Tiddly Bollocks … Boom.* Bobby laughed again. How had he not noticed that before?

Bobby listened closely but he couldn't hear Hammy from his seat in the control room. Hammy appeared to be singing – or saying – something into the circular microphone, but because most of it was concealing his face, Bobby didn't know what it was. He faded the vocal track up. Hammy was whispering something. It sounded like 'feed me to the Lebanon'. But as the intensity of the music increased with the additional levels Bobby was adding, so Hammy's voice was increasing in volume. He was singing two lines. Bobby burst out laughing as he realised the first line – sung in a deep growl, like an irritated, constipated Scottish Barry White with a monster hangover – was 'dip me in chocolate'. Hammy repeated this in sync with the *booms*. And then, in a high-pitched girlish twang, and against the *tiddly bollocks* break he sang '…and feed me to the lesbians'. Bobby was in hysterics. Hammy couldn't see him and repeated the refrain over and over. Perversely, it sounded totally appropriate and uniquely great. The sentiment might've been a bit questionable, especially if Comrade Joey Miller had been here to hear it, but he wasn't. And this was Ibiza after all. Monster summer dance hits were made of hypnotic, repetitive, catchy loops. *Who really gives a fuck about the lyrics, anyway?* thought Bobby. *Only miserable peely-wally cunts who have never got over The Smiths split. Miserable cunts like Joey Miller.*

The White Isle was still vibrating to the irresistible Italo house cheesiness of 'Sueno Latino' as it lounged in a sunburned cocaine stupor on the Playa Bella. Laurie Revlon had been right all along. A new Eurocentric music was dominating and – as witnessed by the yearly Eurovision shambles – those cunts couldn't give a fuck about the words. That was where the real money was, not with these daft, smelly, studenty, wastes-of-space Nirvana fans in the UK, who hated themselves and wanted to die. Bobby Cassidy was convinced they could have a massive Balearic dance hit on their hands. Hamish May, a man who had started the day as someone's Arsehole, was ending it as an unlikely pop star-in-waiting.

The following decade passed by in a drug-fuelled, hedonistic, self-indulgent blur for both Bobby and Hammy, punctuated by two notable highs in its first quarter. 'Dipped in Chocolate' by MC Bobcat & The Rebel Hamster was one of the biggest hits of 1993. Although truly gargantuan in Europe, it was regularly cited as an example of that year's absolute nadir of British music. If Bobby was bothered by this, he didn't show it. By the end of the year, the pair of them had appeared on *Top of the Pops* seven times, including the Christmas Day Special, when Jimmy Savile leaped onto Hammy's back while he sang, as if he was a horse. He later offered to introduce Hammy to some real lesbians, but the Ayrshire man was fairly sure he was only joking. The only other locals who had achieved anything approaching Bobby and Hammy's level of pop fame were the archetypal one-hit wonders, The Miraculous Vespas, nearly a decade earlier. But in the wake of a major crime scandal involving gangland wars in Glasgow and leading to the unlikely abduction of a Boy George lookalike, the Ayrshire-based band and Max Mojo, their deranged young manager, had effectively vanished into thin air. That was a pity, as Bobby liked Max – or Dale Wishart as he was originally known to Bobby – and he considered their only recorded hit song to be a fantastic record. Nevertheless, if a James Hamilton Academy 'class of '82' school reunion was ever on the cards, Bobby and Hammy would absolutely walk it as 'those least likely to succeed … but who actually had'; if such a cumbersome accolade actually existed. Not that Bobby would have attended such a demeaning event but it pleased him greatly to suspect that he would have been celebrated *in asbsentia.*

In 1994, Bobby acquired Laurie Revlon's villa: one of the most notable on the White Isle. It had been her idea – a convenient Spanish tax dodge, Hammy was convinced – but Bobby thought this was immaterial. The 'sale' did come with yet another ludicrously lengthy contract, which seemed to Bobby to have more obscure foreign words in it than an original draft of *War and Peace.* On Laurie's advice – she was now Bobby's manager and looked after all of his financial and 'artistic' affairs – he signed it without seeking outside legal advice. When Hammy saw his room, and the extent of the 'salary' he was now drawing as a Personal Assistant to Bobby, his initial objections about Laurie Revlon being a modern-day Fagin evaporated. If it was merely a great wave, they should just surf the fuck out of it until it broke on the next shore. This was his new mantra.

A year later, though, MC Bobcat still hadn't followed up his hit single. Laurie Revlon was becoming more agitated. His Revolution DJ sets still drew in the punters, but in the opinion of Laurie and her advisors, he was flatlining. It was true: Bobby was struggling for inspiration. He and Hammy had become tabloid fodder, and even though they were now permanently resident 2,000 miles away, Britain's salacious press had grabbed both of them by the balls, although in different ways. Lizzie King – much to Bobby's resigned dismay – had somehow sold a barely feasible story to the *Daily Star*, falsely claiming that MC Bobcat was the real father of her eight-year-old son. To rub salt in the wounds, she'd named the kid Robert. The boy's sallow skin resembled neither his mother nor the wrongly accused 'father'. It seemed to matter little to the *Daily Star*, though, and the story ran over three days. A shouting match with his sister over the telephone ensued, the result of which was that an embarrassed and upset Hettie refused to speak to Bobby for over two years. But he couldn't stop himself feeling sorry for Lizzie. She was a fundamentally decent person who had probably grabbed the opportunity to provide for her and her kid. He would probably have done the same in similar circumstances. At least that was how Bobby Cassidy tried to move on from the incident. No point in bearing grudges. Life was too short, and despite what Liam Gallagher would have everyone believe, it didn't last forever.

Hammy felt differently about his inglorious moment in the Fleet Street spotlight. So-called 'friends from school' – none of whom Hammy could even recall – told tales of his voracious appetite. *He'd eat anything!* said one; *I once saw him eat two tins of dog food for a bet,* said another. A third joked that as far back as primary school, the finger of suspicion had fallen on Hamish May when the class pet had gone missing. *The Sun* reprised its most famous headline: 'The Rebel Hamster Ate Our Hamster!' it screamed. This was Hammy's Warholian fifteen minutes of sun-drenched fame. And rather than shrink from the coverage, Hammy revelled in it, and for a month in mid-1995 t-shirts with the newspaper's headline were as ubiquitous as the 'Frankie Says Relax' ones from the previous decade.

Success had brought undeniable comfort to Bobby, but at the cost of personal motivation. Whereas previously he'd work – and watch others work – endlessly, perfecting his DJ'ing as if it was a complex and detailed craft that had to be mastered and tamed, he now treated it like those poor, ordinary saps back in Kilmarnock heading out to Johnnie Walker's Bottling Plant at 6 am for an eight-hour shift pasting labels on bottles. How quickly it had become a chore. The disdain for 'Dipped in Chocolate' had gotten to him. His skin wasn't as impervious as The Rebel Hamster's, it transpired. Bobby had discovered that fame was a double-edged sword. *Hideous tricks to be played on the brain*, right enough. Maybe Morrissey had been right all along. He yearned to do something worthwhile; to create something with music that others would admire; that others would be proud of. Others like Hettie, Gary ... and even Joey Miller.

And then, just when Bobby was starting to feel the lash of Laurie Revlon's tongue and the constant reminders of *contractual obligations in perpetuity*, a miracle happened. Literally.

Max Mojo rang Bobby's drawbridge-mounted doorbell. The story of The Miraculous Vespas had passed into cult legend, principally because Max, the band's enigmatic, delusional manager, had disappeared without trace along with Clifford X. Raymonde, the veteran producer of their only major single 'It's A Miracle (Thank You)'. The four-piece themselves had broken up, and had maintained a more dignified silence about their last days as a band, which only added to its mystique. However, industry rumours persisted about a legendary LP, the only tapes of which had been lost in an arson attack that had destroyed Raymonde's Ayrshire recording studio.

'Get that will ye?' shouted Bobby Cassidy despite being closer to the CCTV monitor and release switch than Hamish May. 'Who is it anyway?'

'Gie's a fuckin' minute, ya lazy bastart,' shouted Hammy. 'Ye've got yer ain fuckin' legs, man ... even though ye rarely bloody use them these days.'

'Aye, okay. Just tell us who's there!'

'It's some old cunt. Cannae work him oot. This screen's aw grainy, Bob.'

'Get oot an' clean it then, fuck sake!'

'Jesus,' said Hammy.

'Whit is it?' said Bobby.

'This aul' duffer's got a face like a ninety-year-old Jamaican scrotum that's been turned inside oot!'

Bobby snorted at Hammy's description, then got up to look for himself. Although presented in monochrome, the old man's leathery skin was clear to see on the distorted image leaning in to the camera and looking back at them.

'Bit auld tae be a windae cleaner, an' too scabby tae be a Mormon, ah'd have thought,' laughed Bobby.

'Aye, an' either too deaf or fuckin' stupid tae realise ye've got tae press the button tae speak back tae us. Look … fuckin' walloper.'

They watched in hysterics as the old man acted out a full expressive story of explanation in total silence.

'Open the fuckin' door an' let us in, Cassidy, ya gadgie that ye are!'

Bobby jumped back. The voice was familiar but it wasn't coming from the old man, it came from Max Mojo, who was hiding behind him.

Max Mojo and Cliff 'X-Ray' Raymonde had dropped on Casa Cassidy out of nowhere. In their possession were the 'lost' tapes of an album that many wanted to hear but most believed to be nonexistent. It took a while for X-Ray to get the LP tapes sorted but, with the money fronted by Laurie Revlon, and the recordings held at Revolution Studios, it was clear to everyone who heard the initial playbacks that this was a phenomenal record. And to herald its return, Max Mojo wanted his old mucker, Bobby Cassidy to remix 'It's A Miracle' and reposition the band as part of the cool Balearic indie-beat scene.

With Laurie Revlon's contractual blessing, Bobby Cassidy worked wonders on the original single. He increased its speed and mixed it in a higher key. Unusual samples from Simple Minds' 'Promised You a Miracle' were added and random dialogue from the Martin Scorcese film *Taxi Driver* was scattered liberally around the backbeats. It was pressed, bootleg style, as a twelve-inch single in a simple, blue transparent plastic sleeve with a yellow title sticker. Max – high at the time, naturally – had initially insisted on a Peter Saville-designed

'4D sleeve … so folk can fuckin' feel the music through different time zones'. But that was officially ruled out as being 'cost-prohibitive', and unofficially ruled out due to no one having the slightest fucking clue what he was talking about. There was no B-side and, in order to appease the band's temperamental singer/songwriter, Grant Delgado, the words 'Anti-Complacency League, Baby! (Slight return)' were scratched into the run-off grooves. The record was an incredible critical and radio success. It revived Bobby, both professionally and personally. He was certain Joey Miller would've loved it.

Chapter Nine

October 2014. Shanghai, China

Joseph scans the room, unsure of where he is. It's a large, uncluttered room, but some form of balanced Feng Shui order seems to have been applied. *Unlikely to be heaven, then,* he figures. *More likely the other place.* 'IKEA, maybe?' he whispers to himself.

'Ah, Mista Miller. I hope you are fine now.' The voice comes from behind him. He hasn't even appreciated there *is* a 'behind him'. He lifts himself up slowly on his elbows and edges gingerly against the collection of soft pillows before sinking into them.

'Where am I?' he croaks. A familiar face wanders into view. It is the interpreter.

'You are in Mr Li's clinic, sir. You fell last night.'

'Fuck sake, last night.' Recollections instantly accelerate into his head like Formula 1 cars racing for the first bend. Some of them collide. His addled brain bears the brunt. Joseph looks around quickly. He isn't in a recovery room. There don't appear to have been any unauthorised procedures carried out. He is in silk pyjamas that don't belong to him but other than that he seems fine.

'What happened tae me?' he asks hopefully.

'Doctor think you have suffer anxiety attack, Mr Miller,' says the interpreter. Joseph feels embarrassed. 'He say "too much alcohol, not enough sleep". Ah ...' the interpreter searches for a word. He looks across the ceiling as if he might find it written there. It comes to him. 'Dehydrate.'

Joseph sighs, not quite knowing what to do next. A full reconstruction of the circumstances of the previous evening is slowly forming. He won't see Mr Li or his sons again, not even to apologise or express gratitude to them. He is now being dealt with solely by the lower orders. He hasn't caused them dishonour, but he has prompted a loss of face – mainly his – with the owner of the KYTV establishment.

'Doctor come back to check. Remove drip. Then you go?' It is said very politely but to Joseph, it translates as: *Make sure the cunt isn't going to die on the premises then get him to fuck out of here!* Joseph looks at his hand. There is no sign of any saline drip within the room, but the small plastic connector that facilitated its route into the vein is still taped and embedded there. He hasn't noticed it. He gets out of the bed. He is unsteady. The interpreter holds out a hand but appears relieved when Joseph declines it. He steps gingerly over to where he assumes the shower is. He is like Bambi on the ice. He reaches the door and holds its handle tightly.

'Where are my clothes?' he asks. The interpreter simply nods in the direction of the en-suite. Constantly smiling, but – Joseph surmises – internally raging at being stuck with this embarrassing fuck-up.

They drive the short distance to the airport in total silence. The short flight back to Shanghai is turbulent, and Joseph – normally a very good flyer – feels ill and disorientated when they land. He heads straight for a toilet near the baggage collection carousel and vomits violently. He arrives back at the hotel. He pays the taxi driver. He is still dehydrated and exhausted. He sits on a sheltered concrete plinth and opens a bottle of water. He reaches into a jacket pocket and takes out his phone. He punches the numbers.

'Carlos? Is that you? It's Joseph.'

'Megan, I'm sorry to have to tell you this but we've received a serious complaint from a guest.'

Megan has foreseen this. Cockney Jack would have expected her to seek her own redress and, in anticipation, he has acted quickly with a counter. That doesn't mean it will be any easier for her to accept, or to address with her employers. The Doubletree Group has a fixed and very formal process for dealing with customer grievances.

Megan Carter sits in the air-conditioned office as Alison Wang, the new Head of Human Resources, adjusts her glasses and her posture and delivers her considered adjudication. Cockney Jack and his cohorts have all written letters on Doubletree headed paper claiming Megan ignored their polite requests regarding the type of hire car they ordered. Furthermore, she became extremely abusive, and used foul and threatening language. Having tripped and fallen backwards over a small hedge, she then accused one of the guests of pushing her when he was in fact trying to help her to her feet. In all the years of their firm's patronage of Doubletree Hotels, claim the tersely worded statements – it is the most unacceptable service and treatment by a member of staff that any of the Cockney Jack lads has ever witnessed. The letters stress that action should be taken or their organisation will take its substantial custom elsewhere. CCTV footage indeed illustrates her fall, although the guests threatening gestures have been ruled out as a cause. One of her Chinese hotel colleagues who witnessed the contretemps has substantiated the complaints of the hotel's guests. Megan is devastated that a fellow worker thinks so little of her, but the complicity has been bought. She is given a two-week suspension to appease the complainants, but on full pay. The English party of four have a substantial corporate bill reduced by fifty percent. Their company's patronage is very important to Doubletree.

'Megan?' the voice surprises her. It is familiar, but also caring in its tone. She looks up. It comes from Joseph Miller. 'Is everythin' alright? You've been cryin'.'

'Ah … I'm sorry. Yes, I'm fine. Just had a bit of bad news,' she says.

'Aye, me too.' He smiles, hoping it will help the moment. It doesn't. She affects composure like a professional actress hearing the word *Action!* But Joseph is equally practised in rehearsed deception.

'Let me get that for ye,' says Joseph. He can see she is upset and struggling to manoeuvre through the heavy, glass side door that Joseph himself has just come through. He walks back out into the hotel's covered forecourt. Crowds of tourists and business people jostle for space near where the taxis are stopping. For a country so otherwise regimented, queuing is a totally alien concept. It will be some time before the excitable throng clears. He offers to walk with Megan, carrying her bags.

Despite herself, reluctantly, hesitatingly, she accepts.

They walk slowly. The humidity is stifling. The unseasonal heat has remained constant through September. Thunderstorms have been predicted, but they have stalled off the coast of the East China Sea, as if they are contemplating their next move; deciding in which direction to drift next.

'Cappuccino?' he says.

'Yes, that's me. Thanks,' she says. She has ordered. She has spotted a seat by the window. He has told her to sit down. He pays. He wipes his mouth on a napkin and picks up a metal box of mints. Despite the water, the flat, iron taste of sickness remains in his throat.

'So what happens now?'

'Em, I'll have to take the two weeks away and then go and see the Regional Manager when he returns.'

'From holiday?'

'No,' she smiles. 'They never seem to take holidays. He's over in the Philippines training people apparently.'

'Ah, right. Ah see,' he says. He lifts his cup but then spills some of the coffee on his trousers. 'Fuck!' he mumbles. 'Do ye no' have yer own holidays?' he asks. 'Somewhere tae go just tae get away, like?'

As they strolled to the coffee shop Joseph offered to speak to the hotel's management and ensure such blatantly false complaints were countered. Megan didn't want that though. It perplexes Joseph that she seems content to let these lies blemish her work record. He can't quite understand it.

'No,' she says. 'I mean, I have breaks, but I don't really have any … I'm happy just staying at home,' she says.

'An' where is home, then?' he says, smiling.

She visibly stiffens.

He briefly wonders if he has said something different from what he thinks he said; something more threatening. 'Ah'm sorry. Ah didnae mean tae…'

'No. No, sorry … it's me. I don't have many friends here. This isn't … it's not home. You become accustomed to your own company, you know?'

'Aye,' says Joseph, 'ah know that only too well.'

'Are you working in Shanghai?' she asks him.

'No, well no' really,' he says. There is a difficult pause. Their conversation is like two people separately navigating a maze, not entirely sure where it is going, occasionally bumping into each other by accident, constantly trying to recall the route they took before hitting a dead end, and starting again.

'Dae you live on yer own then?' He says this, and again immediately regrets it. It sounds like a chat-up line from the early 80s.

She doesn't react. These exchanges are like a game of battleships.

'What do you do? Back home, I mean?' Her questions are a defence against having to respond to his. She is fascinating. It is clear to him that she is hiding something of herself. She sits back in the chair and her arms only unfold to reach her cup.

'Ah'm a designer. An architect, although ah'm no' sure for how much longer,' he says. 'Have ye always worked in hospitality?'

'No.' A pause, then. 'Not always. What do you mean by not for much longer?' She is a challenge.

'Ach, ah think my partners are forcing me out,' he says.

'Oh, that's terrible,' she says, but in a non-committal way, as if it simply seems like the right thing to say. She is being led by his downbeat delivery.

'Aye, fuck it. It's a young man's game an' ah'm no' that anymore,' he says. 'Too tired. Too many aches an' pains, ye know? Mental and physical. It's hard tae keep up wi' the pace of things nowadays.'

She relaxes, but only a bit.

He continues. 'It's a lonely life, wi' all the travelling an' that. Ah mean, look at me for Christ sake! Ah'm really only thirty.'

He smiles. She does too. Her face lights up when she does.

'Don't be so hard on yourself, you look very good…' Her voice tails off, not because she doesn't believe it; she just can't comprehend she has actually said it.

He looks perplexed; a man out of practice at receiving any form of favourable compliment.

She blushes. '…I just meant, you know … for your age … for a man who's just turned fifty…'

She laughs. He does too. He finds her ham-fisted attempts at flirtatious small talk endearing. He laughs only because his are no better.

'Aye … it's fine. Ah know what ye mean. The George Clooney effect, eh? Middle-aged guy in a black suit wi' a white shirt, greying hair? He's done wonders for our demographic, so he has.'

She smiles again. Her face radiates warmth.

He orders another two coffees. She relaxes into one of the coffee shop's brown leather sofas, kicking off her heeled shoes and pulling her legs up to her side. Her shoulders drop, a weight lifted from them. Solitude has made him a miserable bastard, but her response to it seems almost enigmatic, like she craves it. He tries a different approach.

'What'll ye do if the hearing disnae go well?'

She looks like she's sifting through his words and the tone of their delivery for hidden traps or unexploded ordnance.

'I'll maybe move on. I've been here quite a while now, anyway. It's a nice city but there are others.'

'How long?'

'What do you mean?'

'How long have ye been here?' He is aware of her searching his face for any clues regarding his veracity. She is determinedly hiding something significant about her past. It is none of his business, but he still wants to know what it might be. His own past is so brutally and irrevocably fucked that probing someone else's dysfunction is a convenient way of avoiding his own, albeit temporarily.

'What are ye runnin' away fae, Megan?' He surprises himself with the directness of the question.

She puts her legs down, and straight into her shoes, the last thirty minutes have been a soft-touch polygraph test that she has just failed on the final question. Flustered, she rustles her things together: a phone, a small mirror, a pair of glasses, a lipstick, an open pack of handkerchiefs all collected and thrown carelessly into her bag. He catches her by the wrist. She instinctively stiffens but still holds his gaze, shocked not that he's touched her but by something else. There is something about him; something different from others who've tried to get close these past five years.

'You're hurting me,' she says softly.

He releases his grip.

'Ah'm sorry. Ah didnae mean tae grab…' He sits back. 'Look, ah recognise this. Ah don't know whit it is, but yer boltin' fae somethin', or someone.' He is aware that a Chinese couple at an adjacent table are looking at them, having stopped their own conversation when he grabbed her wrist. They will be analysing the human dynamic: Desperate father and disrespectful daughter? Inappropriate employer and angry employee? An affair between an older man and a younger woman that has just reached a conclusion? They won't interfere, but externalised public displays of emotion are notable, even in the cosmopolitan cities.

She glances at the Chinese couple with a look that indicates embarrassment but that they need not be concerned. The Chinese couple look away. If they have concluded anything from the potential options, their faces don't betray it.

He continues. 'A few years back, a really close pal died an' ah've been drifting ever since. The remorse was terrible, an' even though ah couldn't have prevented it, ah felt … ah *still* feel … responsible. Ah should've done more. Ah should've seen the signs. Ah should've listened when he wis tryin' tae find a way tae communicate.' He leans back in his seat. 'Ah'm here in China supposed tae be tryin' to write this stupid fucking book – a practice monograph – but mostly all ah've written about so far is sort of about him, an' all the stuff leadin' up to the end, in order to try an' explain it all tae somebody else.' He sips from the small glass of water that has come free with a preposterously expensive coffee. 'Earlier on, just before ah bumped intae you comin' out, ah wis on the phone tae my former partner. He's retired an' he lives in Barcelona. He told me that the firm – the one that we founded together over twenty years ago – had been sold tae an American company an' that my current partners – devious bastards to a fucking man, by the way – have bought me out without my consent.'

She thinks she sees the brief flicker of a rueful smile on his face but perhaps not.

'Ah haven't seen or spoken to my only daughter in years, since her manipulative cunt ae a mother has completely turned her against me.' It is beginning to sound like the worst blues song ever, but he hasn't finished. 'Ah presume every muscle twinge tae be the start ae a heart attack, every slight stomach cramp tae be cancer, every head-ache, a brain tumour. Ah suffer fae regular anxiety attacks an' ah take more pills than The Grateful Dead.' He smiles as his eyes moisten. 'And ah've lost all contact wi' the only people ah've ever really cared for. The ones that ah could maybe have confided in about it aw.' He sighs. 'Everybody's runnin' from somethin' Megan.' He dabs at his eyes.

She leans forward slowly and nods. 'I stole $450,000 from my husband six years ago. He had physically and mentally abused me every day that we were married until he beat me and I lost our baby. He was part of an organised crime family and some of that money was theirs. That's what I'm running from.'

Checkmate.

Chapter Ten

August 2006. Ibiza, Spain

'C'mon, man … ah need tae go. This Geppetto cunt'll be waitin' for us.'

'Take the fuckin' car then.'

'Naw, ah want tae walk. We don't dae enough walkin' these days. We're turnin' intae fat slobs. You're gettin' a belly like the yin wee Jimmy Stevenson used to have.'

'Whit ye sayin'? Ah'm now your bastardin' full-time chauffeur?'

'Ah'm no' askin' ye tae drive me down the day, ah'm ah? So stop greetin' an' hurry the fuck up!' Bobby was becoming agitated. The interview had been set for 2 pm and it was now nearly half past one. He had been persuaded that it would be a worthwhile idea. His profile had diminished in inverse proportion to his waistline over the previous five years. His remix work on The Miraculous Vespas singles of 1995 and 1996 had reclaimed some of the critical ground he'd lost after 'Dipped in Chocolate'. But he hadn't followed it up. Hammy put it down to core, inherent laziness, but in truth, Bobby had been affected by a sudden and sharp loss of confidence. It coincided with Laurie Revlon's illness. This had happened a full ten years ago, whilst she was on a personal quest in Africa to adopt a child. Her acquaintances, Elton and Madonna, had talked about it often. Laurie wanted to be the first. She had selected a six-year-old boy from the floating-village slums of Makoko in Nigeria. The adoption process had been completed and the boy had been renamed Laurence. But, on their final day in Africa before returning to the Balearics, Laurie had suffered a stroke. It was not severe enough to halt her motherhood ambitions, but she was fifty-three at the time. Some additional payments were needed to officials in Lagos to ensure no reconsiderations were contemplated by other interested Nigerian authorities. Laurie wasn't totally debilitated, but it did knock her world-domination plans off track for a year or so.

At the same Bobby Cassidy had been slipping down the rankings within Laurie's team, not helped by his emergent sloth. Now, though, an opportunity to raise his profile with an Italian dance magazine had presented itself. They were doing a major retrospective on the Ibizan superclubs of the late 80s and had sent one Guiseppe Gennaro to speak to anyone who was part of that scene and was still alive.

The walk down the narrow, hairpin tracks from the villa to the tiny local bar where he had agreed to give the interview took a full thirty minutes. Bobby was sweating profusely. The heat had been far more intense than he'd anticipated and his shirt looked like it had been used to mop up beer spills at the saloon adjacent to the OK Corral. Unfortunately, Guiseppe had brought a photographer with him, so Bobby instructed Hammy to run back up the steep hill to the house to get him a new shirt, and the car for the journey home. Hammy was understandably angry about this, and more so since he'd predicted it happening before they left.

'Fuck off, an' stop moanin', ya lazy bastard,' Bobby shouted at him before Hammy reluctantly turned back. Hammy was possibly out of earshot when Bobby yelled, 'This kinda shite is what ah fuckin' pay ye for, remember!' In the guilt-ridden days and weeks and months that followed, Bobby prayed that Hammy hadn't heard him.

'MC Bobcat, thank you for this interview. How are you now?' The shift in tone from the young Italian from casual to professional at the flicked switch of his tiny, metallic tape machine took Bobby by surprise. As did the use of the recording name. He hadn't heard anyone use it for a while. It grated like nails on a blackboard.

Bobby paused before answering. A young waitress brought over their order: bruschetta and still water for Guiseppe; a burger the size of a car's hub cap and a flagon of beer for Bobby. The waitress fluttered around the handsome young journalist but barely looked at the forty-two-year-old DJ.

'Ah'm fine, pal,' said Bobby. 'Whit aboot you?' Guiseppe sipped his water and ignored the reciprocity.

'You first came to Ibiza in…' He checked his notes. '…1987, right? What was the club scene like back then? Were you aware of the, em … explosion that was about to happen?' Guiseppe's English was excellent. His pause wasn't about searching for an evasive word, it was about selecting the right one. This wasn't going to be as straightforward as Bobby had anticipated when Laurie Revlon's PR department had informed him about the opportunity.

'It was excitin', tae start wi',' said Bobby.

Guiseppe was writing copious notes in addition to the recording process, presumably to ensure that the interviewee's rapidly delivered dialect could be deciphered properly back in Milan.

'Aye, the Brits aw headed tae The Star Club. Most ae them were in San Antonio so we pitched up there tae,' said Bobby between beer burps. 'It was like a place lookin' for an identity. An' then the following' year Oakenfold an' Farley an' Holloway an' aw them dropped Es at the Amnesia, an' well … ye ken the rest, eh?' Bobby launched himself at the burger two-handed.

Guiseppe's mouth gaped a little before he collected himself. 'Who were your DJ heroes, back then?' Guiseppe's questions appeared to be pre-determined, if a little randomly sequenced.

'One ae your lot … Toni Oneto. He did really cool stuff at Nightlife up the West End.'

Guiseppe was fairly certain that Toni Oneto wasn't Italian, but made a mental note to check.

'…And Derek Dees. He wis a fuckin' legend, man.' Bobby registered the puzzled look on Guiseppe's face. But he hoped the magazine would give his Benidorm-based mentor a namecheck. The auld cunt was probably stacking shelves at a Carrefour nowadays but maybe he'd somehow see the eventual article and get a few free dinners off the back of Bobby's benevolence towards him.

'What else has changed, for good and bad?' Guiseppe asked.

'Fuck me … well, ah had a bit more hair,' Bobby laughed.

Guiseppe didn't, he simply scribbled notes. It was disconcerting that he wouldn't even look up after delivering a question.

'Well, ah suppose … Privilege was called Ku. Stupid fuckin' name by the way. Whit else … George Michael wis still straight an' ye could trust the cunt tae run ye hame in his motor. The England fitba team were still pish … aw, aye, an' fuckin' DJs didnae earn the same amount for playin' other cunts' records as David Beckham does for wearin' a fuckin' sarong!' Bobby's voice was growing in volume at the same pace as his general irritation. Someone had put mayonnaise on the burger when he had expressly asked them not to. His blood pressure was rising. It was hotter than hell itself and Hammy was still nowhere to be seen with his change of clothing. He scraped the top of the remainder of the meat and then clamped his jaws around as much of it as possible.

'What's exciting you now about the Balearic scene, MC Bobcat?'

Since this wasn't a live radio interview, the second use of the stage name just seemed unnecessary. Bobby felt something more than a journalistic jibe sticking in his throat.

'Fuck all,' he said, coughing. He gulped more beer. It didn't help. 'There's a wee bar up west … used tae be Plastic Fantastic … *cough* … it's just called Plastik now … *cough* … It wis a great … *cough* … record shop an' now it does DJ competitons … *cough cough*.'

Unknown to him, Bobby's face was reddening. Guiseppe's head remained down, looking at the words he was writing.

'…*Cough* … It's great. It's changin' the face ae San Antonio, man … *cough cough*. Ah'd love them tae ask me tae work there…'

Guiseppe looked up sharply. Bobby's voice had changed from deep growling to squeaky struggle. He now sounded like the Wicked Witch of the West as she evaporated. Bobby's face was beetroot red. He was struggling to breathe.

Guiseppe jumped up and pulled Bobby off the stool. He grabbed him from the back and manoeuvred him as Heimlich had dictated. After three jerks, a piece of gherkin projected across the bar and hit the menu blackboard behind the wooden servery. Guiseppe let

Bobby go and he fell breathless to the floor. The observers in the bar applauded and – spotting her chance – the young waitress ran forward and hugged the Italian hero, accidently stepping on Bobby's hand as she did so.

'So, MC Bobcat, one final question. How did it feel to find out that your record 'Dipped in Chocolate' was voted the worst dance song ever, by *Mixmag*?'

It had been nearly an hour since a pickled cucumber had almost killed Bobby Cassidy. This interview wasn't doing much for his health either, but he now felt obligated to Guiseppe Gennaro to complete it. The interview certainly wasn't what the Italian had anticipated either. He hadn't admitted as much to Bobby, but his brief was simply to grab a few background quotes in order to add depth to a wider piece. From Bobby, however, he'd gotten so much more: an intimate portrait of an angry, disgruntled has-been from the Balearic Beat days, whose bitter recalcitrance would now be the central theme of an expanded study.

It was almost 4 pm. Guiseppe Gennaro left in a taxi as soon as that final, brutal question was addressed. Bobby knew the record was widely derided but the Italian's reveal had been like a hook from Mike Tyson to the solar plexus. His response had attacked and blamed all manner of people, from 'that snidey wee cunt, David Guetta' to 'Thatcher's fuckin' bum boy, John Major'. His acridity was redolent of a professional footballer who'd retired penniless the season before the Bosman ruling came in to force, or before the Sky money dropped and grossly inflated the salaries of even mediocre players. Bobby Cassidy was depressed. He knew it but couldn't admit it to anyone else, least of all Hamish May. The last ten years since the highs of The Miraculous Vespas triumph had been a relentless downhill slide. Everyone else was still riding that crest to a differing degree: Max Mojo had a villa in the South of France. He was often on the phone to Bobby talking about getting into film, purely in order to be able to walk to the Cannes Festival just down the road from his house. Old Cliff Raymonde – whose mahogany-tinted skin Bobby's own now most closely resembled – had taken over Laurie Revlon's studio, converting it so that it had proper accommodation and making it among the best in Europe. Laurie Revlon's own business had also grown and adapted. Revolution still thrived, but Bobby Cassidy hadn't worked there since, coincidentally, the night of the 9/11 attacks in New York, five years earlier. He'd made a thoughtless joke after playing an old, jazzy Style Council track entitled 'Dropping Bombs on the White House'. Hardly anyone was in the club that night. Most were at home, glued to televisions, still unable to fully comprehend what they were watching. Angered words got back to Laurie Revlon. Laurie had a close friend who worked for Silverstein Properties on the eighty-eighth floor of the north tower. It would be three full days before Laurie knew she had made it, shocked and traumatised, but safely out of the building before it collapsed. By which time Bobby Cassidy had been suspended. Laurie liked Bobby, but he would never work at Revolution again.

Bobby's temper was rising as he looked back on a decade of increasing obscurity. He strode back up the steep hill, preparing himself for an outpouring of rage at his disrespectful subordinate. Hammy had evidently simply left him at the bar. And the photographs for what should have been an important, profile-raising interview would now surely show him to be out of shape, filthy and the red-faced victim of an assassination attempt by a rogue pickle. A sweat-sheened fury was consuming him.

It took him fifty minutes to reach the approach to the house. He felt like he was physically melting. He must've lost at least a stone on this climb.

Fifty yards from the gatehouse, on the tightest of Can Germa's mountain bends, a car was on its side. Water and oil was flowing from its exposed underbelly, steam rising in the melting heat from its bonnet. A young male driver was being breathalysed by an even younger Ibizan police officer. A female passenger sat shaking on a piece of stone by the side of the road. A thick puddle of fresh, red blood and the marks of rubber evidenced what had happened.

Bobby's heart stopped in its tracks. It seemed inconceivable that Hammy had been involved, and yet he hadn't returned to the bar for Bobby. *He'd be in the house*, Bobby told himself, as he ran past the crash scene. *But what if he wasn't?* His heart was racing. *What the fuck would he do without Hammy?*

Chapter Eleven

October 2014. Shanghai, China

He sits in her living room. It is compact but its elevated position offers an exceptional view of the Bund, especially now, late at night, when the dazzling neon and the effervescent sodium mix and dance across the Huangpu's rippling blackness. The flat is a model of frugal minimalism. There are no material trappings. Nothing on the walls. No Western consumerism that many of those born here so crave and fear in equal measure. There is no television in the principal room. He knows the programmes are mediocre for the most part, and downright irritating for the remainder. So, maybe that view is enough? It isn't a home. It is an enclosed, heated space from which someone can disappear within fifteen minutes, leaving little trace that they have even been there.

Megan pours him a glass of red wine, one sizable enough for him to deduce that she is happy with him staying for a while. He still isn't sure why he is here, beyond the instinctive feeling that he wants to be. After the nadir of the Huangshan visit, being here, in the flat of a beautiful, young, English-speaking woman is incredibly comforting. Joseph suspects that she too craves some form of emotional solace. She has no close friends to speak of. He isn't blind to the suggestion that his earlier intervention on her behalf was, for her, motivated more by paternal protection than by sex, as he had briefly imagined.

She returns from her bedroom. She is wearing a loose white t-shirt, bleached jeans and white Converse shoes. Her blonde hair is tied up. She looks totally different; beautifully natural. In her work clothes, she could really be anyone. Attractive certainly, but more reflective of the organisation she works for – polished and professionally classy but not remarkable. He realises now that she is only truly relaxed within these walls. And she has let him inside. He appreciates how much that must have taken for her.

She sits on the sofa next to him, watching the ships and cars slowly start to outnumber the people on the Bund as late evening becomes early morning. They talk for hours, her telling him that he should get back in touch with his best friend, him affirming her determination never to return home. She is a nomad and the anonymity solitude affords her comforts and sustains her. Isolation from the people and places that made him feel most alive is slowly but surely killing him. Difficult though it would undoubtedly be, she is convinced Joseph needs to see Bobby Cassidy; to atone and account for sins past; to try and recapture something of the relationship they once had. Perhaps some form of happiness or contentment might come from that. It is surely worth a try, she feels. He isn't convinced but he has to conclude recounting some of their teenage experiences has been refreshingly enjoyable. It has been a very long time since he has laughed as much. It has been a similar amount of time for her, too.

He looks down at her. She has fallen asleep, her head on his lap. Telling him more about Vinnie, the crushing shock and subsequent terror of his immediate switch into Mr Hyde, and about the circuitous route to reach possibly the one country he won't think of looking for her has exhausted her.

She sleeps.

He can't. But he is happy, comparatively speaking. His hand rests on her shoulder. As clichéd as it sounds, he assumes she simply needs a father figure; someone to reassure her that she did the right thing all those years ago and that she should never go back. In the future, another Cockney Jack cunt will destabilise her and another Joseph Miller will hopefully be there to protect her from her doubts. He wishes he was younger, that he could be the one who was always there for her.

She sleeps.

He can't. So he sits awake, dreaming: that Gary Cassidy never went to the Falklands. That he and Bobby never fell out. That Hettie Cassidy never met that cunt Pete D'Oliveira. That he never met or married Lucinda, the architect of all his pain. But then he'd never have had Jennifer in his life, however short-lived, and although that road is currently blocked, Megan has reassured him there remains some hope of connection via the words he is writing for her.

Joseph Miller lifts Megan Carter's head and gently lays it down. It is almost sunrise. She stirs. He fears she might be disorientated and will panic at the sight of a strange man in her apartment. But she doesn't. She smiles warmly at him.

'Some breakfast? I don't have much in, but I could fix an omelette.'

'That would be good, aye,' he says. He watches her rise, shake her hair and walk to the kitchen worktop at the rear of the open living space.

'Put some music on if you want,' she says.

He picks up her iPod. It is connected to a tiny speaker. Portability is the prime characteristic of Megan's lifestyle. He flicks through a few playlists. There aren't many. He presses shuffle on the Motown Gold collection.

'(Love Is Like a) Heatwave' by Martha & The Vandellas. ... *Fuck sake*, thinks Joseph Miller. The signs are everywhere.

Chapter Twelve

October 2014. Ibiza, Spain

Bobby Cassidy stares out over the Mediterranean through freshly cleaned, frameless glass. It provides a clarity of view – if not thought – that has been missing for the past four months. The few remaining rivulets of moisture succumb to gravity and fall slowly. Everything seems to move at such a pace at this time of the year. With the previous weekend's closing parties signalling the end of the season, the vibe has shifted. It has packed up its stimulants and its effervescence and has headed for the hills to hibernate and recharge.

Ibiza has been the perfect form of isolation for Bobby: secluded and protected from much of the negativity that has ruthlessly enveloped other parts of the world's economy and security. Only facile positivity has prospered here. But that is different now. Bobby still misses the buzz of the early 90s, but he isn't sure why. It was a time of excess; of numerous, faceless, nameless young women. A vacuum of emotions that ended up spilling out on roulette wheels and shamefully destructive, early-morning card games. He sometimes feels he misses it simply because it feels like he should. He misses Gary only because something inside him tells him he should. But in more lucid moments, he recognises these feelings as guilt, not nostalgia.

It is maintenance time at the villa, when the reckless disregard shown for it at other times of the year is normally rectified. Bobby used to love this time almost as much as the anticipation in late May of it returning refreshed; but not anymore. His body aches. More pertinently, his fingers ache. He stretches them and tries to place them flat to the glass, but – like other parts of his body – the disobedient bastards won't play ball. Fleshy saddle-bags of relaxed muscle drape under the back of each arm. Everything is descending as gravity swoops like Ali in Zaire. Bobby Cassidy had it whupped in the early rounds, but now he's fucked from all the effort. He has nothing left to give. He watches the dark clouds amassing on the western horizon. As climatic metaphors go, it is still too early to say whether they are a portent of unsettling and restless times to come, or a reflection of the unsatisfying and unhappy year just past. They seem to be static – undecided, threatening – a gathering vapour shelf like the Assyrian army, which once prepared for invasion from a similar position.

'Storm's comin'. Ah'm headin' intae town for some stuff before it hits. Ye want anythin'?' Hamish May's voice drifts down through the sparse, open-plan volumes. It echoes and bounces and pirouettes on the cool terrazzo before finally reaching Bobby Cassidy.

'Naw,' says Bobby without turning his head. It is unlikely that Hamish has heard his reply, so mournfully was it delivered. A squeak of distant wheels and then the door shuts. Bobby is alone; only him and his fevered thoughts.

The house became his in 1994, back in the days when it seemed impossible to conceive of life being any better. For the past twenty years he has lived here with Hammy – the ever-faithful Hammy – whose very existence Bobby Cassidy has materially altered for the better; and then for the worse. He acquired the house when the money started rolling in. He was the toast of the Balearic Beat scene at the time. *Worlds and oysters*, he thinks. The cool, minimalist, modernist structure rising through the verdant pines and olive groves of Can Germa was the perfect motif for his success. It is notched into the sloping hills of the White Isle, with panoramic views over San Antonio bay. After negotiating a snaking road, which narrows significantly as you approach foreboding gates, the house is entered at the top of the slope and at its highest point. Visitors to it traverse a rooftop bridge across the dramatic rocky terrain below. Those with vertigo struggle with the open, metal-mesh floor. The house is separated from the rest of the land like a modern-day castle; if constructed in the early part of the island's inhabitation, archers and serfs with vats of boiling oil would've manned its parapets. Bobby and Hammy drove golf balls off the roof in the early days, trying to hit hole-in-ones into the various swimming pools that punctuated the hillside below them.

Those lucky enough to make it inside cascade down four levels until they reach the voluminous main living space with its prominent terrace, looking to all purposes like a ship's bow. Or at least they used to. The party set don't come up here anymore. There are other, better experiences, ones not promoted by a lonely, depressed fifty-year-old club DJ chained to a previous era and unwilling or unable to leave it. The fear has set in and it is preparing for the long haul. Where once an invite up to the hills was an indication of cultural acceptance by the 'in' crowd, it now represents a journey back in time; like a reluctant stop on a tour of Ibiza's many sites of historic interest. Cultural enlightenment is not the type of sightseeing Ibiza is known for. Hedonism doesn't live in the past. It doesn't actually care much for the future either. It is myopically focused on the here and now.

Bobby's 'here and now' has become a prison sentence of the mind; an 'open' sentence, admittedly, and one being served out in a beautiful paradise, but he still feels just as confined as those incarcerated in the moderate freedom Devil's Island once afforded. The drawbridge once signified a lifestyle of enviable exclusivity; now it simply reinforces its occupier's isolation.

The house was once described as an 'architectural icon'; a refined steel and glass composition lauded by European design journals, influenced by such luminaries as Le Corbusier and the early houses of the American modernist architect Richard Meier. With Bobby's music industry connections, it was, perhaps more prosaically, used as a location for music videos. This initially increased its value. On one of these shoots, Simon Le Bon casually offered Bobby £3 million for it. The worldwide financial crisis of 2008 hit the tourist-reliant islands hard, and Hammy urged Bobby to reach out to the singer to determine if he was still interested. But Bobby mined hidden depths of natural optimism and convinced Hammy it was right to hold back; that all of life's various crises invariably pass. Six long years have passed since then, and – like the house they occupied – any remaining remnants of that optimism have crumbled due to lack of regular care and attention. Now it represents a millstone around Bobby's neck. Even the critics have reassessed their opinion of both the house and its once-revered Spanish designer. Letters discovered after his death have exposed him as a Francophile fascist and his most famous structure – the current Casa Cassidy – is now universally denigrated as a 'big, white, sterile fridge dropped brutally and insensitively to intimidate an unsuspecting sylvan context'. Its perceived sterility is apparently contagious. Bobby turned fifty in January and a hastily arranged out-of-season party attracted only five guests, all of whom were male and two of whom were even older than Bobby. Each guest had a choice of two bedrooms, and two exercised that choice before 11 pm. Some white powder was distributed but only in the form of an *Askit* to fend off a guest's developing headache. In the crushing aftermath, Bobby has considered the potential of returning to Scotland, although he's been resident on this sun-drenched Mediterranean rock for the same amount of time as the bigger, wetter one where he grew up. Home, to Bobby, is now a vague, out-of-reach concept where the past means something tangible and where real friendships and family connections sustain him, not torment him. Hammy's is a friendship that endures, but Bobby accepts that Hammy, too, is trapped, and by more obvious and practical circumstances than his own. He regards the storm clouds that are most definitely heading towards him, and he yearns for that past and for all of the people he ruthlessly and recklessly dismissed.

The rain pounds against the glass. For men who grew up in the west of Scotland, attuned, year-round, to leaning in, head down, collar turned up against the elements, it is still a remarkable sight. Rain such as this, carried on volatile weather systems working their way up and over from the African edge of the Mediterranean, doesn't visit these islands often, but when it does it brings life to a complete standstill. Perversely, it only makes Bobby Cassidy miss that evasive notion of home even more.

It has only been five days since Bobby's last night at Las Dalias, but already the daily winter pattern has been established. The Scotsmen get up around midday. Hammy makes lunch and then heads out into town. He comes back around four in the afternoon and they watch television for around four hours until it is time to eat, and then generally to think about going back to bed. Bobby has just turned on the large, flat-screen in the main room. He flicks through around thirty music channels, all playing variations of essentially the same song. Everything here sounds like 'Summer', which was presumably Calvin Harris's original intention. Bobby Cassidy was once where the superstar DJ from Dumfries is now, albeit without the worldwide coverage and the absurd *Galáctico*-style remuneration. He is now totally sick of anything 128 bpm. It has been everywhere, every day; the island's national anthem for the year. A decade ago, a younger Harris – then going by the name of Adam Wiles – asked Bobby for an autograph. He happily obliged. The present-day Harris, briefly visiting, blanked Bobby when he sought a few brief words with him. Both men are from western Scotland, but Bobby considers that one has apparently forgotten the common courtesy inherent in sharing a background. As far as Bobby Cassidy is now concerned, Calvin Harris can go and fuck himself up the arse with the nosecone from one of his fleet of private Lear jets.

They have taken to watching a British Gold channel. It shows repeated black-and-white classics, which remind Bobby of summer holidays from their school days.

'Hammy, hurry the fuck up … this is comin' on,' he shouts.

'Aye, gie's peace, for fuck's sake, ya miserable prick. Stick it on *pause*.' Hammy rolls into the room.

'An' for the love of God, will ye get they fuckin' wheels oiled?'

'Ach, ye know whit … ah knew ah'd forgotten something. Ah

went aw the way into *Toni* tae get oil,' says Hammy, melodramatically, 'an' guess whit?'

Bobby sighs.

'Go on,' Hammy continues, 'guess whit?'

'Bugger off,' says Bobby turning the volume up.

'Despite being stuck in this bastard wheelchair mornin', noon and night, wi' its nonstop incessant fuckin' squeakin', gettin' the oil tae lubricate the cunt slipped my mind … cos ah wis out gettin' shit for you!'

'Ah'm sorry, right?' says Bobby, exasperated but meaning it. 'It needs a new wheel. Ah told ye this aboot a week ago. Ah ordered a new yin, remember? It should be here on Friday.'

'Look, ah said ah'm fuckin' sorry. Ah've nae mind ae ye tellin' me, man.'

'Aye. Right. Typical.'

A few days into the close season and they are already getting on each other's nerves. Bobby is struggling and Hammy knows it. But his escape – his day-release programme from the sanction of living with Bobby's misery – is to spend time with a woman from the medical centre where he receives fortnightly physiotherapy. She is a voluptuous fifty-five-year-old Spanish *señora*. Her name is Esta Soler. She is an amputee, and she is married to the local police chief. Once a patient herself, she now volunteers at the centre. Hammy considers these to be details that only he needs to know. Wider knowledge only increases the risk of them getting caught, and in his situation, both fight and flight options are totally out of the question. A defiantly self-centred Bobby is too preoccupied with his own decline to question such small details, which would have otherwise cornered Hammy. Fortunately, Bobby dismisses Hammy's apparent forgetfulness on his daily trips to the small supermarket in San Antonio as just that. Esta introduced Hammy to Viagra more than three years ago, and since then Hamish May has undertaken a voyage of intense sexual discovery that the court of Louis XIV would have roundly applauded for its diversity and dexterity.

Hammy manoeuvres the armless chair into a position where he can see the television more clearly. The late, low-lying afternoon sun has returned, drying out the effects of the storm but reflecting on the flat screen from around fifty percent of the room's potential viewing points. The electronic, scrolling blackout blinds that would otherwise have dealt with this problem have been faulty since 2012. Bobby presses the remote and the distinctive haunting rumbling notes of the theme tune reverberate around the bare, white room. The rolling waves, the stark titles and the words of Robert Hoffman not quite matching up with his lip movements. It is time for *The Adventures of Robinson Crusoe*. For the third day running, Bobby is in tears by the end of the twenty-five-minute episode. His own Man Friday is rapidly running out of patience.

Chapter Thirteen

October 2014. Shanghai, China

Megan looks at the five questions written in black ink on the heavy paper ripped neatly from his notebook. It is a strange feeling for her – simultaneously fun and nerve-racking. He laughs as she tells him it feels like they are cramming for a Green Card application as a newly married couple. She isn't objecting but it shocks her to acknowledge how open she is prepared to be with a man she only met two weeks ago, and, what's more, in the routine context of work rather than as a personal choice.

'Ooh … you'll just laugh,' she says.

'Ah won't, honest,' he replies.

'Hmm.' She isn't convinced. 'Okay, but I'm warning you.' She wags a playful finger at him. 'It's *Pretty Woman*,' she says.

He laughs. 'I'm sorry,' he says.

'I told you.' She lightly slaps his knee. It is the penultimate of her five questions. Another straightforward one for her following safe ones about her favourite food, place and music. They have promised to be totally honest with each other, but she is a little embarrassed at what she assumed he would think a clichéd answer.

'Have tae confess, ah like it too,' he says.

'You do not,' she counters.

'Ah do!' he says. 'Los Angeles, sunshine, big shoulder pads, posh folk playin' polo, Richard Gere givin' zero fucks about everythin' except a big Rodeo Drive hoor … what's no' tae like?'

'True. All human life is in there,' she says, laughing. 'Okay, my turn. Since we're on the subject, what's your favourite movie?' It was a coincidence that it was also one of her questions, albeit she has changed the order of them.

He has fielded slightly more searching ones about a fond childhood memory and what he is most afraid of. He ponders if it constitutes a stereotypical gender split: her questions about emotions and feelings; his, the assimilation of status via lists of cultural touchstones.

'Hmm. That's a tough one. Ah've got lots,' he says. 'Too much time spent watchin' DVDs on ma own. Hundreds tae pick fae … hmm. There's probably two main ones.'

'But you're only allowed one, Joseph. You have to pick,' she says.

'Aw okay. *The Pope of Greenwich Village*,' he says.

'I don't know that one. Who's in it?'

'Mickey Rourke,' he says.

'The bad guy from the *Iron Man* 2?'

'Eh … dunno. He might've been in that. Ah haven't seen it,' he admits. 'This is a bit ae a cult film fae the early 80s. About two cousins: one's a real kinda go-getter, ye know? The other yin's a fuckin' balloon, but they really care about each other. Because they're family, like.'

She nods.

'The Eric Roberts character … the balloon … gets them intae a load ae trouble with local neighbourhood gangsters an' Mickey Rourke has tae get them out ae it. It's brilliant. Really cool wee movie,' says Joseph. 'It reminds me ae the way Bobby Cassidy an' me used tae be. Everythin' was a great laugh, even though some of it wis really dangerous.'

'Do you miss him?'

It's the simplest of questions but, still, it jolts him. Perhaps because no one in recent years has either cared enough, or knew enough about him to ask. She is the first person he has talked to about Bobby and Gary and Hettie in more than five years.

'Aye. Ah do. Ah really do,' he says, as if recalling a fallen comrade on a particularly poignant anniversary.

'You really should get in touch with him,' she says. It seems like the most obvious thing in the world, and she can already see that it's what he needs, but that he can't take the first step for fear of yet more rejection. 'You can go back into that world, I can't. I'd love more than anything to be able to see my friends again … even my dad,' she says. Her eyes well up. 'My mum dying really killed a bit of him too. He couldn't live with the rage inside of him, that whole feeling of unfairness, of them having their years ahead stolen from him.'

Joseph puts an arm around her shoulder and pulls her closer. It amazes him how quickly this has gone from feeling awkward to feeling very natural.

It amazes her too.

'I'm sorry,' he says. 'This was just a daft wee game. Ah didnae mean tae upset you.'

'It's okay. It's actually good to remember, don't you think?' she says. 'I was very bitter towards him for years. I couldn't comprehend why he wouldn't defend me … why he couldn't see the pain I was going through, but it was because he was so consumed by his own.' She wipes her eyes and forces a smile.

She is truly alluring when she smiles. He has taken countless pills and capsules for depression and anxiety, but in this moment it feels like he could replace them all with that sparkling smile.

'Okay, next question,' she demands, tapping a pen on the table in deflection.

'What's the secret to real happiness?' he says. He'd deliberately left his *Joker* for last.

'Unconditional love,' she responds – immediately, without blinking, staring him straight in the eyes. It is a statement of absolute conviction, but she delivers it like it is a personal challenge. She is a set of jump-leads for his serotonin. She smiles again. When she does, he finds it incomprehensible that someone would ever deliberately cause her pain.

Megan takes Joseph's hand. He wasn't always burdened with vertigo; it has been something he's become aware of following his treatment.

His anxiety manifests itself everywhere and in almost every given situation. It has essentially left him convinced that danger lies around every corner, despite how irrational that might sound to an intelligent man. It is what ultimately led to the enforced period away from work and the realisation – from his partners at least – that Joseph could no longer cut it. It is less than a year since he took time off indefinitely. He has been petrified that his own shadow might take up arms against him, yet here he is, walking across the thick glass floor, one hundred storeys above ground, in the observation deck of the Shanghai World Financial Centre Tower. Joseph's head is in the clouds. And all because she is holding his hand.

Joseph admires this building very much. With the modern predilection for adorning unusual buildings with nicknames, it is now known as the Bottle Opener. There are so many actual bottle openers in the gift shop, Megan naively assumed they were the stimulus for the design concept. Unlike many skyscrapers, though, the design isn't ostentatious. It is relatively sleek and simple; elegant – at least in comparison to its nearest neighbour, the Jin Mao Tower with its serrated edges and aggressive corners. Joseph smiles to himself as he considers the juxtaposition between Megan and Lucinda Burroughs.

Megan remarks that she's been in the city for a while but has never even thought to observe it – or map its incomprehensible growth – from the top of its more notable buildings. That just seemed to her like something tourists did. Other people; normal people. She asked him to go up in the express lift with her. Megan laughed when Joseph said he couldn't venture to the top. She said she'd take care of him.

His knees are shaking. She can feel the tremors in his hand. She clasps it tighter. They stare out across the distinctive bend of the Huangpu, left and right towards the four bridges that connect the new, wealth-orientated districts of Pudong New Area, where they have spent the day strolling, with the poorer west-bank areas where many of the displaced have been rehoused. It is one of the most populated areas of Shanghai. Paradoxically, that is due to the amount of immigrants like Megan Carter who have come here to contribute to this driven and powerful financial hub.

'So … any regrets?' Her question takes him by surprise.

'What, about comin' up here? Naw, it's fine. Ma legs are a bit…'

'No, I meant that's my final question.' She didn't asked it earlier. Following her response to his, he leaned in to kiss her. She turned her head and he kissed her ear. It was awkward and he felt like an idiot. But, like many things in his life, it was just bad timing. As he withdrew, she touched his face tenderly and held it there, kissing him gently and briefly on the mouth. Neither of them was sure what to do next. There was a prolonged pause. Perhaps it wasn't the Year of the Horse anymore. Maybe it was the Year of the Absolute Prick. They were both clumsy, ungainly. They stood up from the bench in unison. The takeaway sushi she had bought them remained half eaten. It wasn't really his thing. He'd once eaten raw fish fingers but only because his dad had been too drunk to cook them properly. He had smirked at the thought of his traditionalist, narrow-minded father seeing him now.

He breaths deeply and leans forward, his forehead on the glass, looking straight down, 500 metres to the ground. He gasps and she grips his hand.

'Ah've got regrets about everythin' … absolutely everythin',' he says. 'People ah've let down, people ah should've paid more attention tae. Ah listened tae people ah should've ignored, an' ignored the very people ah should've listened tae. It's just a big fuckin' mess.'

'But it's not too late. You can still fix it,' she says.

And he almost believes her.

'You said it yourself … your partners are actually doing you a favour. They've set you free, Joseph. You're just scared about what that freedom means. I totally get that. I left Vinnie and all his mob bullshit, and I swapped it for this … to be free from all of that. You can use that freedom too … find a bit of happiness, and a bit of *purpose.*'

Ah, *purpose* … that relative term connected to *function.* Function means a lot to designers. If something has no function, it's essentially fucking useless. Pure ornamentation. Form even follows function! But what's his? What's his purpose now that the constants of employment and relationship are no longer there? He wants to believe her. He wants to stay with her. He wants to be younger, so that the possibility of staying with her wouldn't be so fucking risible.

'But this isnae freedom, Megan. Yer livin' on a witness protection programme, but wi' nae protection. How can that be livin'?'

'It's living, because all I was doing before was barely surviving. We were in that closed community where everyone who knew us would've known what he was doing to me, but nobody would ever, ever say anything about it. I knew he wouldn't go to the cops … about me *or* the money. That was my chance and I took it. I've no regrets, Joseph.'

He turns away from the view and looks at her. It is the most resolute she's been in the four days they have spent together.

'But ye said yer no' stayin' on here. So that's you on the run again. Fuck sake, Megan, ye cannae keep doin' that for the next fifty years.'

'I'm fine. That thing with those British guys could've happened to anyone. It's just made me think that it's time to transfer. Doubletree are really good that way. They actually like having people like me … happy to move, no responsibilities. It's pretty straightforward to get a transfer in those circumstances.'

'Well ah certainly couldnae do it,' he says. 'Although ah'm no' sure what ah am gonnae do.'

'You need to go and see Bobby,' she says. 'You need to find a bit of closure.'

He laughs and she looks puzzled.

'Sorry,' he says, 'it's such an Americanism, that word, eh?'

'Are you mocking me?'

'Naw, ah'm not. Ah'm just deflectin' … it's what we do, we Scots. We're miserable, dour bastards.'

'No you're not.'

'How would you know? How many Scots have you met?' he says.

'*Ach* … loads,' she says, laughing.

'Right, you are just takin' the fuckin' piss now, is that it?' He laughs too.

'Mel Gibson, Scotty from *Star Trek*, Mrs Doubtfire … the big fat baddie in the *Austin Powers* movies. I grew up with lots of Scotties.' She puts her arms around him and cuddles him.

He catches sight of their reflection in a shiny metal panel. He feels detached from the reality of the situation. It feels like he is watching another couple; like he is acting on impulses he is struggling to comprehend. Joseph is simultaneously anxious about what might happen when he lets her go and experiences the feeling that his entire life has been a preparation for what he will say next.

'Why don't ye come back wi' me … back tae Scotland?'

Chapter Fourteen

October 2014. Ibiza, Spain

Sebastian Tellier's melancholic 'La Ritournelle' fills the house. It is such an expansive, layered song. It is the rich, musical equivalent of whisky fermenting. An aural comfort blanket. Bobby Cassidy has the Sonos powering on repeat, and the song is on its umpteenth circuit. Windows are wide open and a cool breeze wafts its way around the interior, investigating all of its open space and available corners. A 'David Essex in *Stardust*' metamorphosis seems to be under way. It isn't a good sign. Hamish May can still navigate the mood swings of his friend by the musical accompaniment. Based on the last few days, Bobby is only one nostalgic trip away from a Leonard Cohen career retrospective.

'Jesus, it's fuckin' freezin' in here!' says Hammy as the door to his room closes sharply behind him. 'At least it'll shift the bloody smell, mind you.' Hammy considers whether Bobby did actually go to bed last night, or if he simply stayed in the same spot where his friend left him, watching Laurel & Hardy DVDs with the sound turned down.

'Ye no' gonnae get changed oot they clothes, mate?' asks Hammy hopefully.

'Nae fuckin' point,' Bobby replies.

A half-eaten bowl of Cheerios sits disregarded on the glass table. It fights for space amongst the scattered detritus of empty beer bottles and potato crisp packets from last night, which Hammy now assumes Bobby has left for him to clear away. He is eating at least. That's something.

'Get yer scabby, crusty scants aff, ya blacko,' Hammy laughs. 'Then once we've chased the bastards 'roon the hoose and caught them wi' the big tongs, we'll wrestle them intae the washing machine an' fumigate the cunts.'

'They're fine. Ah'm no' takin' them off.'

'C'mon tae fuck, Bob eh? Ah no' ah'm here tae help ye, but for fuck's sake help yersel', ya useless auld cunt!'

'Gie's peace,' says Bobby.

'Look at ye,' Hammy says. 'Ye look like Catweazle at a Hugh Hefner lookalike contest.'

Bobby knows he looks bloated. He is at least two stones over what would be classed as a normal weight for him. The various full-length mirrors in this austere art gallery don't lie. His thinning hair is grey and hasn't been cut for months. His stubble is rougher than the surface of the moon, and he's been wearing the same boxer shorts and silk-sheened dressing gown for six days now. They used to be white, like virtually everything else Bobby wears.

'Haw, Howard Hughes … whit the fuck's goin' on here? Is there somethin' ye're no' tellin' me, man?'

Bobby's expression becomes more vacant.

'Fuck sake, please tell me yer no' back at the gamblin'.'

Bobby takes a few deep breaths then slowly shakes his head.

'Are ye sick?' asks Hammy, fairly certain that he would've noticed something more serious than a general malaise.

But what Bobby is about to say has taken time to build up to, and he still isn't sure what it might mean for them. He sighs.

Hammy is now worried.

'Laurence is cancelling us for 2015. That fuckin' barney wi' thon Rough Guide cunt a month back wis the last straw. Ah'm fucked.' Bobby sits down. The weight of those few words seems too much for him to carry standing up.

'So,' says a relieved Hammy. 'Big fuckin' deal. We'll get another gig, an' a bit closer tae San Ant than oot at that fuckin' hippy market tae.'

'That's no' gonnae happen, Hammy. It's finished. *Ah'm* finished. Ah don't get the vibe aboot here anymore,' says Bobby. 'Ah'm yester-day's man.'

Hammy looks at his watch. This had better not take long. Esta will be waiting and she has a 'beeg, beeg sooprise' for him. He rolls his noisy chair over towards where Bobby is reclining like a fallen Caesar on the white chaise longue. It was only a few sentences, but Bobby hasn't said this many words in days. Hammy appreciates that his role here is simply to listen and then talk his charge down from the edge. Again.

'Ah think ah want tae go home, Hammy. Ah mean it this time. It's by for us here, mate.'

He's never said this before. Hammy is suddenly perplexed by Bobby's use of the word 'us'. As far as Hammy is concerned, this is their home.

'Ever since the start ae the year, ah've felt like total shite. Like ah've nae idea what ah'm even dain' here.'

Hammy knows that much but has just put it down to Bobby turning fifty and the acceleration of the arthritis that now so forcibly pains his joints.

'Ah've been thinking aboot Hettie, an' Gary … an' even fuckin' Joey. Ah want tae see them aw again.'

Hammy briefly thinks Bobby's marbles have gone, along with the dexterity of his digits.

But Bobby corrects himself. 'Well, no' Gary obviously, but ye know whit ah mean, aye?'

'Look, Bob … ah get it. Yer fifty, yer feelin' fucked, an' frankly, yer needin' a good fuckin' shaggin' … although we'd need tae hunt for the skankiest, dirtiest hoor on the strip wi' you in that condition.' It isn't the most erudite psychoanalysis, but Hammy suspects it's pretty accurate. 'There's nothin' back in Scotland for us now. Fuck sake, we didn't even get tae vote for it tae become independent! Look how fuckin' angry that made ye.' Hammy sighs. This isn't going as he hoped. He wants to get away, to dissolve into the ample cleavage of the rampant Esta Soler and to feel whole again as he does every day he's with her. 'Ah'm no' even sure ae the point ae goin' home … wherever the fuck that actually is noo. Ah mean, Hettie'll no' even see ye, man … ye know that. An' dae ye even know where Joey Miller is?' Hammy watches Bobby meekly shake his head. 'An' whit the fuck ah'm ah gonnae dae back in Scotland, eh? Look at me! That snidey bastart Cameron's hardly featherin' nests for disabled cunts like me is he?'

How his friend has changed, and not only over this last year. He tries to shake the thought, but the truth is Bobby Cassidy has been on the slide since the day a young drunk driver out for a tour of the island mowed Hammy down, taking the use of his legs away from him.

That was almost ten years ago. Paradoxically, the accident and its aftermath have freed Hammy, but simultaneously imprisoned Bobby Cassidy. Hammy knows Bobby feels responsible and that self-reproach and regret have been mounting ever since. But now they have seemingly combined forces and are beginning to consume him.

'Ah need tae go, pal. Ah've got physio … an' the joints are aw a bit sore, y'know?' says Hammy, wincing theatrically but to no response. 'We'll sit doon later oan an' figure it aw oot, right? Ah'll go an' see Laurie Revlon tae. Work oot a deal. Ye're still a big draw, Bob. You're MC fuckin' Bobcat for fuck's sake! You helped build this bastardin' island.'

'Aye … once upon a time, maybe,' says Bobby mournfully. 'But that wis then.'

Hammy leaves without anything else being said but content that Bobby will just sit aimlessly watching *Belle & Sebastian* repeats in monochrome as opposed to hurling himself from the villa's elevated roof.

Esta Soler is a *Sangre Naranja*: a small group of local, wealthy, middle-aged women who meet regularly to play poker, smoke cigars and discuss the details of their specific ongoing extramarital sexual encounters. It is a closed community with as many secretive codes and rules as the other order with whom it shares a colour. The similarities stop there, though. The Blood Oranges are solely about female gratification. Hammy has often wondered how such a small island community of notoriously loose-lipped Catholic females can keep schtum about such things. Is it only their priests who are taken into any form of confessional confidence? He's even wondered if the perversity of their husbands stretches to participation, as willing and encouraging voyeurs. But the risk of exposure simply seems to be part of the game for these feisty women. In its present manifestation, the *Sangre Naranja* comprise fifteen members. Esta Soler is the group's current organiser and leader. She is in the middle of a three-year term. It is her responsibility to set challenges for the women and their carefully selected covert partners as if they were all merely part of a suburban Woman's Institute group trying out cake recipes. However, the tasks all involve increasingly daring sexual exploits upon which they then have to report like participants in a contemporary Masters & Johnson academic research study programme.

An austere Alicante hospital rehabilitation centre was the scene for the first meeting between Hamish May and Esta Soler. It was November 2008, two years after the car accident. An unconscious Hamish May had initially been taken to a small hospital in Ibiza Town. He was in the flat back of a car being driven by Bobby Cassidy's closest neighbour, a German surgeon who had bought his house as a holiday home only three weeks prior to the accident. In his first week in the house, only a loud 'FORE!' had prevented Hammy hitting him with an almost perfect five-iron shot from the roof. On the direct advice of the Ibiza Town surgeon, Hammy was immediately flown to the specialist hospital in Alicante.

Hammy subsequently spent a significant period of time in the same hospital, undergoing twenty-three separate operations, as Spanish orthopaedic surgeons attempted to repair the damage of extensive compound fractures to both tibias and the fibula of his right leg. To exacerbate this, he contracted MRSA while in the hospital, causing further tissue and muscle damage. Was it not for this, a long recovery might have resulted in him being able to walk again unaided. Hammy's mum and dad, and several of his large extended family flew out to see him several times while he was in hospital. Fragmented relationships were repaired, despite Hammy having made it clear to all of them he had no intention of returning to Scotland. With Bobby Cassidy paying all of the horse-choking medical bills, Hammy's allegiance remained firmly in Ibiza.

'*Eso me ha dolido incluso incluso a mi*,' said Esta, opening that first conversation while sitting in the chair opposite Hammy. She had been staring at the elaborate tapestry of scars on his exposed lower legs. They looked like they were the template for an abstract game of Snakes & Ladders.

'Eh ... ah'm sorry, ah don't speak any Spanish,' Hammy replied, smiling, before adding '...An' ah dinnae dae the English much better.'

Esta smiled back at him. 'Ah ... jour leg, painful no?'

'Aye. Fuck me ... the worst ah've ever felt, an' ah once got seriously electrocuted tae.'

Esta looked bemused, as if waiting for Spanish subtitles to appear across Hammy's chest.

'Sorry,' he said, recognising that he'd spoken far too quickly. 'It. Was. The. Worst. Pain. Ever.'

Esta's brow furrowed a little. Hammy felt that he had perhaps patronised her, but she was merely expressing empathy.

'How about you?' said Hammy, pointing at the space where her lower left limb should've been.

'A ... eh, infection. Bad,' she said slowly. 'Had to lose leg.'

Hammy sighed, Esta shrugged. Two resolute survivors, it seemed. He, there for his first – and last as it transpired – physiotherapy session; her, there for a fitting for a new prosthetic. Despite the chasm across which their ability to communicate had to leap, they talked further over lunch, watching the historic events taking place across the Atlantic, where Barack Obama had earlier been announced as his country's forty-fourth President. They were staggered to find out that they would both be returning to the same island later that evening. On Esta's suggestion, Hammy began attending a clinic-based thera-peutic class in Ibiza Town that Esta helped run. After a year of close attention, Esta Soler took it upon herself to widen the clinic pro-gramme to include sexual therapy. Hammy accepted a deep-rooted personal desire for strong female domination. He'd already recog-nised it within himself before leaving Kilmarnock more than thirty years before. He had never thought of himself as a 'mummy's boy', but with a father rarely at home, perhaps he had been. It wasn't something he could readily discuss with Bobby for fear of ridicule, but when Esta initiated him into the ways of the *Sangre Naranja*, she found an only-too-willing student.

'Where have jou been?' She is a little irritated.

'Ach, it was Bobby. He's going a bit…' Hammy circles a pointed finger at his head, wide eyes going in different directions.

'Loco?' says Esta.

'Aye,' Hammy laughs, 'fuckin' loco. That's the very word.'

'We need to do quick,' says Esta.

Hammy knows not to correct her. He gets the message. He's driven out to the agreed location. It is forty minutes to the north from Can Germa on the PM-812. He's followed her written instruc-tions and has arrived at a remote farm steading closer to Sant Joan de Labritja. Hammy has seen most of the island, but he hasn't been near here before. Those in the Order from the south of the island use locations in the north for their activities, and vice versa, although lately, Hammy and Esta have been meeting to make plans at a small bar close to Bobby's villa. Esta Soler has been kept waiting for over an hour. Hammy, even more than usual, is happy to do as instructed.

'Een the back room,' she says, gesturing towards a closed door in the rear of a tin shed which has, until fairly recently, been the home for a substantial amount of livestock.

Hammy briefly wonders where they are now, and the same about their owner. He wheels his chair through the dung. It will need a sharp hosing afterwards. He suspects he probably will too. Nervous anticipation grows in the pit of his stomach. Esta has accepted that he never wants to do anything that will cause him pain; it isn't that kind of domination he craves. But, as he approaches the closed door, he knows some form of mechanical contraption will be involved. On a previous outing, involving the suction pipe from an industrial hoover, Hammy insisted on a safe word. He chose 'Heatwave'. As he sits contemplating what is on the other side of this potential room 101, he hopes Esta has remembered it. His cock is now javelin hard, not from the thought of being strapped onto some form of combine harvester, but from the Viagra he has taken at the time instructed by Esta's note. It is that, more than the fear of a lashing from her that has made him leave the villa abruptly. Hammy couldn't risk Bobby, apparently in the early phases of a potential breakdown, spotting him with a hard-on growing in his shorts. That would've been way too difficult to explain. So Hammy bolted, his penis thrusting its way up like an inflatable helium rocket at a kids' fair.

The back room is hot, the sun baking its crinkled metal roof all day. It is a nondescript space, apart from the apparatus at the centre of it. Hammy can't conceive what it would normally be used for. Storing hay perhaps, but that might've been about it.

'De bed is for me. De harness ees for jou,' says Esta with authority.

Hammy looks up at the roof. Two parallel ropes hang from it, supporting a seat that looks like a toddler's swing. The 'bed', on the other hand, looks like a bizarre gurney on which a condemned person might be lethally injected. Hammy is relieved that it isn't for him. Esta carefully helps Hammy out of his clothes and into the swing. He is naked. The ropes have a little stretch in them and he bounces up and down a bit while she undresses herself. She then parts the legs of this modern-day stretching rack and her plan becomes instantly clear to Hammy. Supported by the sling, Hammy will enter her from behind while she uses the electronically controlled base to manoeuvre her vagina to a level so that Hammy can easily swing into her. Hammy finds it endearing that she has given considerable thought to him shagging her from behind while 'standing' up. His skinny, redundant legs contain little working muscle now with which he could support himself. But his upper torso is arguably larger and stronger than it has ever been. He is all out of proportion, much like the body of a cartoon superhero drawn by a child.

Esta removes her prosthetic limb and clambers on the open-legged table. A flick of the remote spreads her – and the bed's – legs. Another button pressed and her magnificent arse rises, propelled by a break in the middle sections of the bed that Hammy hasn't even noticed.

'Okay, Hamma … jou get in now,' she pants.

Hammy grabs his throbbing cock with one hand and swings the harness closer with the other. His feet touch the concrete floor but they are of little use beyond counterbalance. He edges closer and slides into her easily. His hands grab her arse cheeks, both for balance and for propulsion.

'Mmm … Ahh,' Esta moans. 'Harda Hamma … Fasta!'

He's imagined having sex standing up for years now, but has never thought he'd ever do it again. *Fuckin' Viagra, man. Greatest invention ae the century*, Hammy thinks as his rhythm improves.

Esta is now pushing herself backwards in syncopation. *This fuckin' woman.* They were surely meant to be together.

Despite struggling to get up a consistent pendulum or purchase, Hammy's confidence is growing. He decides to pull out of her, swing right back and then re-enter her on the downward curve as if he was one of the Flying Wallendas. She moans loudly as he pulls out and pushes back from her sweating, arched arse. He sniggers as images of Billy Connolly's most famous joke materialise. But he has pushed too hard and the swing has gone back too far. The bed also rolls forward slightly on tiny wheels that Hammy hasn't even noticed. His weak and ineffectual feet, now off the ground, he overbalances and tips sharply forward, like the star of an X-rated Punch & Judy show being operated by drunken puppeteers. The back of Hammy's head is now where his cock has just recently been, his wasted legs flail around as the blood rushes downwards towards his head.

'*Dios mio… ¿qué ha pasado?, ¿estás bien?*' Esta lifts herself forward and Hammy consequently rotates. He is upside down.

'Heatwave, heatwave. HEATWAVE!' he yells.

Esta hops around. Hammy is still hard. Supporting herself on one of Hammy's ropes with one hand, she wanks him off with the other, before righting him and releasing him from the swing.

'What a fucking woman,' says Hammy, exhausted; blood rushing back from his head like the salts in an inverted eggtimer, streams of sweat flowing in the same direction. They both dissolve into hysterical laughter. He never wants to leave this place; nor to leave her and the life-affirming excitement of the illicit relationship they have.

Chapter Fifteen

October 2014

Bobby Cassidy watches himself on the flat screen. Tears are racing each other down the pockmarked slopes of his face. Some slow and stop on the crest of his cheeks, as if part of a relay team waiting for a colleague in the same lane before setting off again towards the chin. A couple of fat ones drop into his glass and ripple his latest whisky. He has lost count of how many have preceded it. The film playing on his DVD player brings back substantial memories of an earlier – and much happier – time. The DVD case is in his hand. It is the remarkable story of *The Rise & Fall of The Miraculous Vespas*; a story with a postscript in which Bobby Cassidy played a key part. Bobby reluctantly took part in the documentary film as a favour for Max Mojo, who was keen to relaunch the band with a thirty-year anniversary package. Now, he is watching a snippet of an interview he gave months ago but can barely remember taking part in. The LP went on to achieve legendary status, cited by the likes of Noel Gallagher and Alex Turner as a major influence on the work of their own bands. Both of these titans of modern music bookend the piece delivered by Bobby Cassidy – formerly MC Bobcat – the Ibiza-based DJ whose remixed single lit the fuse of the reclusive band's rocketing reputation.

Bobby raises his glass: '*Here's tae us, wha's like us, damn few … an' they're aw deid.* Or they fuckin' might as well be!'

Joseph Miller packs the bigger of his two silver, hard-shell cases. He searches for his passport, finding it under the bed. He scans it quickly, checking the date on his visa, as if hoping to find that he's miscalculated. Maybe there was one more day available. The cost of a cancelled flight would have been worth it. Carlos Martorell was right, hard though it is to admit it: the settlement offered by Felix Masson on behalf of his own new partners is very fair, more than reasonable in fact. Like Megan, he now has more than enough money to live the comfortable lifestyle he once imagined for himself, he just can't remember what that was. Her lifestyle is spartan, and her acquired money is merely an emergency escape fund. His could fund a freedom that he doesn't know how to take advantage of and has no one to share with: a painful emotional paradox.

'Fuck sake, Bob.' Hammy tries to rouse his friend. There is no imminent danger of him choking on any vomit. His head is draped over the edge of the white sofa at an angle similar to that recently experienced by Hammy.

'C'mon, pal, eh? Look at the fuckin' state yer in, man.' Hammy lifts Bobby's head. His straggled, sweating hair sticks out at right angles from the back of his head. 'Jesus Christ, have ye fuckin' tanned aw that Johnnie Walker in the time ah've been away?'

'Um … dunno. Time is it?' Bobby slurs and dribbles.

Hammy wipes his face.

'Whit day is it?'

Hammy laughs. 'It's fuckin' Wednesday, ya tube!'

Bobby shakes his head. He puts his head in his hands. 'Where have you been, anyway?' Bobby asks this in a manner that suggests he has no interest in the answer.

'Jist oot. Divin' aboot an' that.' Hammy knows he can get away with such evasion. It has been obvious for months that Bobby Cassidy is wallowing in a well of self-pity so deep that it is totally immaterial to him what is going on up at the surface. Hammy has been relieved about this. But now it saddens him to see his friend in such pain. He phoned Laurence Revlon at Revolution that morning. Laurence is an arrogant prick in Hammy's opinion, with none of his mother's class or consideration. She can be as hard as nails but there is always fairness from her too. Hammy can't stand Laurence's cut glass Eton accent. He constantly fights the temptation to remind the twenty-five-year-old that, with his 'shanty-town, rice an' fuckin' beans' background, he should be less of a cunt to others, 'just in case his Ma decides to send him back'. Hammy bit his tongue when Laurence told him Bobby was finished. He remained silent as Laurence described how Bobby had been drunk on his last shift, and had taken offence at a young man photographing him behind the Las Dalias decks. The young man was a Rough Guide writer, covering – with Laurence's permission – the less well-known clubs in the Revolution portfolio; the ones way off the beaten track. Laurence could detect the resignation in Hammy's breathing as he explained the nub of the issue: Bobby left the DJ area and pursued the young man through the club, diving on top of him and yelling 'He's got a rucksack, he's a fuckin' Al-Qaeda terrorist … everybody get down!' Hammy knew it was over. There would be no appeal to the Higher Court of Laurie.

He looks at Bobby. He is unsure of what to do, but he knows he has to do something if he is to salvage a future here in his Esta-shaped Paradise.

'Listen,' says Bobby.

'Whit?' says Hammy. Maybe a depth has finally been reached; a profound realisation is imminent.

'Some wee polis guy wis here lookin' for you … Soler, he says. Juan Soler.'

Hammy chokes. 'When?'

'Fuck should ah know? Ah dinnae even ken whit day it is, man,' says Bobby. He buries his face in his hands and his head shakes slightly at the hangover raging inside his skull. 'Whit ye been up tae anyway?'

'Nothin'.' Hammy is suddenly hyperventilating. 'See whit ye were sayin' aboot headin' back? Tae Ayrshire an' that? Mibbe it's no' the daftest idea.'

She has her hands deep inside her pockets. It isn't cold by Joseph's hometown standards, but she does seem to be shivering slightly.

'Right, that's my flight gettin' called,' he says.

'Joseph, I've really enjoyed these few days together with you. It's reminded me a bit about … I dunno, just being content.'

'Come over, then. Fuckin' hell, we've got tons ae Premier Inns in Scotland,' he says. 'Ye might have tae sleep wi' Lenny Henry, or listen tae the bastard's jokes tae get a job wi' them though.'

Megan laughs. She has no idea who Lenny Henry is.

'Look, just think aboot it. Ye know how tae get in touch wi' me. Nae pressure, okay?'

'Okay,' she says.

'We'll go up round the Highlands … tae aw the islands. Everybody's fuckin' anonymous up there, that's the whole flamin' attraction ae the place. Miles an' miles ae sheep, an' daft big cows an' jaggy heather an' fuck all else!'

'It sounds fabulous,' she says. 'Maybe someday.'

She says this in the tone of a parent promising something outrageous to a nagging child, just for a bit of peace. It makes him feel even more insecure and childish. She moves around and leaves little trace. In a few weeks, she'll have a new mobile phone, a new number and to all intents and purposes, a different identity. He won't know where she is. They won't meet again, because she doesn't ever look back. 'Don't Look Back': one of his favourite songs. The irony twists and torments him. She leans in and kisses him. It is a goodbye kiss from a Goodbye Girl. His heart hasn't ached like this since the day of Gary Cassidy's funeral. Or immediately following the aftermath, when it felt absolutely certain that he'd never see Bobby Cassidy again. But he is now heading to the Balearics. Only two hours after

Megan convinced him to get in touch with Bobby, Joseph's now-former PA forwarded an email to the hotel that the Glasgow studio had received. It was from Hamish May. It was marked urgent. It described Joseph's best friend, Bobby Cassidy, in a very bad way, and desperate to see him one last time, having been given the last rites.

PART TWO

THE MAN WHO LOVED ISLANDS

'Loneliness has followed me my whole life. Everywhere. In bars, in cars, sidewalks, stores, everywhere. There's no escape. I'm God's lonely man.'

(Travis Bickle, *Taxi Driver*)

Chapter Sixteen

November 2014. Ibiza, Spain

Joseph Miller is nervous. But this is different from his natural state of heightened anxiety. He doesn't feel in any danger, just a generalised uncertainty. What will he say or do faced with his stricken former friend, whom he last spoke to six years ago, in a profanity-strewn, abusive and angry parting shot. If Bobby only has days – possibly even only hours – left, how to reconcile all that has gone before?

Joseph is also exhausted. He can't get Megan out of his mind. He has texted her daily in the week since he left China, but the responses are already drying up. There's nothing quite as pitiful as middle-aged male desperation in the pursuit of youth, be it buying a scarlet-red Porsche, growing a ponytail or phone-stalking a female more than a generation younger. Joseph Miller is no Rod Stewart or Ronnie Wood; he has little to offer and he knows it has to stop.

His already fragmented sleeping pattern has been rearended by the message from Hamish May about Bobby's condition. The details were scant. Hamish left a phone number but he hasn't been responding to any calls, and Joseph can't contact Hettie. He assumes she must be out here at her brother's bedside, having buried her own Bobby-shaped hatchets in advance of having to bury him. Seeing Hettie will be difficult for Joseph. He made a total fool of himself – again – on that cataclysmic day in Bethnal Green back in 2008. Even the passage of time won't erase that humiliation.

Joseph looks for his bag. The flight from Glasgow has been delayed. The plane's baggage is now mixing with other incoming flights from Frankfurt and Copenhagen. He didn't want to bring a large bag. He didn't think he'd be staying long. If there is to be a funeral, he expects it to be back in Kilmarnock, but even if it isn't, he'll return for it to avoid hanging around in the atmosphere of death with a morose Hamish May. He's made the decision to wear a black suit to travel, partly out of respect for Hettie, but also just in case it's needed more quickly than anticipated. T-shirts and jeans and toiletries are all in the bag he was forced to check in.

Flights are clearing quickly. Copenhagen disappears from the board, replaced by Madrid. Then Frankfurt, substituted by Berlin. Paris makes an appearance. Glasgow has long since gone. There are a few people he recognises from his plane, all coming to terms with the fact that their baggage hasn't made the same flight as they did.

He wanders out into the arrivals hall. He will have to return tomorrow for his luggage as he can't give lost property a forwarding address. Joseph has left voicemail messages for Hamish to plead for an address and an update on Bobby's condition. In a text reply, Hamish has merely confirmed that he'll pick Joseph up.

The cool blast that comes through the open doors makes him gasp. By Scotland's standards it is still warm, but the Ibizan summer has long gone. Hammy is wearing a chunky knit sweater and a New York Yankees baseball cap. Despite looking like an elderly Scottish folk singer at a Hogmanay Ceilidh, Joseph doesn't see him. He scans the heads, looking for a ginger-haired six-footer. He hasn't seen Hammy in nearly twenty years and even though he realises Hammy's appearance will have changed, he doesn't think his own has so much that he wouldn't be immediately recognised. Of course, given the chaotic nature of the few messages since the initial email, it is entirely likely that Hammy is late, or has gotten the fucking date wrong.

'Haw mister, can ah watch yer motor for a fiver?'

Joseph turns round sharply. It's Hammy. But his head isn't at the level Joseph expected.

'Aye, we dinnae really like "disabled", but it's a fuckin' step forwards fae "handicapped", ken?'

'Aye … ah can appreciate that.'

This is a surreal experience for Joseph. Hammy, wheelchair-bound and driving a converted BMW; repeatedly calling him Joey, despite

Joseph's insistence that he doesn't. And, moreover, Hammy's apparent determination not to clarify how Bobby is or explain what's even happened to him. Hammy has also slalomed past questions about how he lost the use of his legs with all the dexterity of Franz Klammer, preferring to focus on the positives of the situation.

'Ah mean, we've even got our ain fuckin' Olympics noo! It's no' the stigma it used tae be,' says Hammy.

'Naw. Ah suppose it isnae.' Joseph figures Hammy is still in some form of shock.

'Christ, wi' that fuckin' geezer fae the X-Men wheelin' aboot on they groovy chairs, weans'll actually be *aspiring* to be fuckin' disabled soon. It's gonnae be a fuckin' life goal, ken?' Hammy is being ridiculous now.

'Don't talk pish, Hammy. Kids would gie up their legs just for a chair just because ae an actor, or some guy that wins a gold medal for wheeling a bogey up The Mall? Away an' shite!'

'Sometimes legs are no' everythin'. Look at you … fuckin' grimacin' just walkin' tae the motor earlier. Yer joints are aw fucked, eh? Ah can oil mine, but you're stuck wi' yours creakin' an' achin'. Ah bet ye ah could beat ye doon this hill in a race!'

'Aye,' says Joseph, 'but ah'd be able tae fuckin' stop at the bottom ae it, ya daft bastard.'

Hammy laughs, and eventually, grudgingly, so does Joseph.

'It's fuckin' good tae see ye, Joey … after aw these years, man, it really is.'

'Look ah telt ye, it's Jos—. Ach, fuck it, whatever.' Joseph/*Joey* stares out over the lush plantation to the sea beyond as they climb away from the urban fringe. He is surprised by an island he expected to be brash and vulgar. It is undeniably beautiful. Not as beautiful as Megan Carter, but then, even nature has its limits.

'Hammy, for fuck sake, where are we goin'?'

'Just up tae the house. It's up in the hills. Ye'll like it … It's aw *architecty* an' stuff.'

Joseph imagines his old friend, Bobby Cassidy, lying prone in a bedroom lined wall-to-wall with frightening medical apparatus, countless drips plugged into his arteries, keeping him alive purely to allow this one final emotional reconciliation to take place. Joseph shudders at this, though. It would have perhaps been easier to see him in a hospice or in an intensive-care unit or somewhere that would have helped them both accept the inevitable.

Hammy points the house out through a gap in the trees as they climb slowly up through the tight bends and undulations in the narrow road. Joseph is staggered. He knew the building by its reputation. It astonishes Joseph Miller that a 'career' playing the records of other people could be so lucrative, especially as Bobby Cassidy was far from the top of that particular tree. He considers his own path: office junior; the college stage; seven long years at university, and even then he still required some of Lucinda Burrough's family money to sustain his part of the practice when the difficult economic times came. Now that he was finally free of her – and the practice – he was financially secure, but this appeared to pale in comparison to his former Heatwave Disco DJ'ing partner. *But then, appearances can be very deceptive,* he thinks.

'Dive oot, an' nip ower the bridge, Joey,' says Hammy. 'Ah left the door open for ye. Ah need tae take the motor doon tae the garages 'roon the side. Ye'll find him inside. Ah'll see ye shortly.'

Joseph hesitates. How will he react? Will Bobby even know him through the depth of his medicated haze? This all makes no sense, to be here now, and in this context of finality. The whole experience has a surreal air, like being forced to watch a thirty-year-old home movie while tripping on LSD.

Joseph edges the door open. 'Hullo,' he says but in a tone so low, someone standing less than five feet away would've struggled to hear him. 'Fuckin' fuck, Hammy,' he whispers to himself.

The house is impressive. It needs a good clean, admittedly, but in terms of its fluid spatial quality, it is breathtaking. Joseph Miller isn't from that postmodern school that now denigrate the structure simply because its creator was a right-wing fascist cunt. That would have been like denying Oscar Pistorius was once a decent 400-metre runner.

'Bobby? Where are ye, man?' Joseph descends two flights of the open stairs, having quickly peeked into the principal rooms on each floor. The house is designed to be sparse, focusing more on the quality of the spaces and the way the brilliant Mediterranean light infuses them. *Only prostitutes and architects look at ceilings:* a maxim Joseph's always remembered. He sniggers then feels that to be inappropriate. He catches sight of movement through the three-storey glazed front-age. Even this late in the year, the glare from the low sun is blinding. It reflects off a tiny splash pool recessed into the external wooden deck. Joseph's sunglasses are still in his delayed baggage. He lifts a hand to shield his eyes. A heavy man lies face down on a garish pink inflatable lilo. It bobs gently on the clear water. He heads towards it. This might be Bobby's carer. Shouldn't he be at Bobby's bedside – and dressed more appropriately. Maybe this indicates an improvement. *Or maybe the selfish bastard is already fucking dead.* Joseph's heart is racing. He slides the glass door back, impressed at how quietly it operates.

''Scuse me, sir?' Joseph leans over the pool's edge.

The man jumps, startled. In turning around sharply, the inflatable overturns and submerges. The man surfaces, choking back swallowed water.

'Joey?'

Joseph is speechless. 'Bobby?' he says at last. 'Bobby fuckin' *Cassidy?*'

'Aye ... aye, it's me, man! Whit the fuck ae you doin' here? Wait a minute ... is somebody deid? Is it Hettie?'

Before Bobby can reach for a poolside towel, Joseph has launched himself, still fully suited, into the water.

'Ya fuckin' cunt, ye ... last fuckin' rites, my arse,' he shouts as they splash around furiously. Joseph has his hands gripped around Bobby's throat. 'Yer no' even a fuckin' Catholic,' he screams.

'Aargh ... get fuckin' ... aargh ... *cough* ... Get affa me, ya mental case!'

A freezing cold blast of water shocks the two of them. Hammy sits at the side of the tiny pool. He has turned the hose on them.

'Right, now that ye'se have got the opening remarks oot the way, can we stop fuckin' about an' get doon tae business?' With the author-ity – if not the diplomacy – of a United Nations envoy, Hamish May has kickstarted the middle-age peace process. Stan May would finally have been very proud of his son.

Chapter Seventeen

November 2014. Ibiza, Spain

'Right. Start talkin',' demands Bobby. 'Whit the fuck were ye thinkin', bringin' that bampot here?'

'Ah spoke tae Laurence,' says Hammy. 'He telt me the full story.' Bobby's head dips. 'Yer a mess, man. Yer headin' for a flamin' break-down. Aw this "constant regrets" stuff. Man, it's really gettin' ye doon … it's fuckin' gettin' me doon. Ye need to pull out ae the tailspin or we're both fucked. Gettin' Joey here wis the only thing ah could think ae.'

'An' whit's he gonnae dae, Hammy?' Bobby sits at the kitchen table. He is holding a bag of frozen peas against the emerging lump under his left eye. Joseph's uncoordinated swinger had caught him as they scrambled gingerly out of the pool.

Hammy is at one end of the solid wooden table. A place has been set and is waiting for Joseph. Hammy is making a point. Joseph is off having a shower and, despite Bobby's protests, selecting something from his reluctant host's closet to wear until his own clothes arrive on the island. Joseph drew the line at borrowing underwear. He would put his own in Bobby's fridge overnight, knowing they would then feel fresher for the morning's recycling.

'Ah'm totally fuckin' depressed, man. Ah cannae shake it. Him showin' up unannounced wi' his *ah'm-a-big-shot-designer* tin flute on just makes it aw worse. Here tae fuckin' gloat about how great eve-rythin's turned out for him, nae doubt.'

'Is he fuck, man. He's here 'cos ah telt him you were dyin',' says Hammy. 'The cunt fuckin' cares about ye.'

'Well, ma life's total shite an' ah don't ken whit tae dae about it.'

'Aye, thanks for that,' says Hammy sarcastically. Bobby's deepening solipsism is rendering him almost unreachable. 'How aboot startin' wi' patchin' things up wi' him then? Ye ken the date, an' there's nae better time than an anniversary for forgivin' an' forgettin'.'

It later surprises Hammy to find out that Joseph has actually forgotten the exact date, whereas Bobby has been thinking about it constantly for almost two weeks. He was sure it would have been the other way around.

Hammy bursts out laughing. 'Jesus, Joey … ye no' think tae put the light on when ye were in there lookin' for stuff?'

Joey slopes towards them, still angry. 'Fuck up,' he says.

'A vest an' a pair ae raggy three-quarter length troosers? It's an island but yer no' a fuckin' castaway, pal.' Hammy is roaring with laughter.

Bobby remains silent.

'Hey, they're his bloody clothes, no' mine. Have a word wi' him!' says Joseph. 'An' by the by, have you got anythin' that isnae white? Or at least used tae be when ye first got it?'

'Ah'll "him" ye … fuckin' blowin' yer mouth aff, when yer in "his" hoose,' says Bobby. 'Uninvited.'

'It's hardly fuckin' uninvited when this lying prick invites me, is it? "Come quick, Joey … Bobby needs ye, Joey … He's no' got long tae go, Joey." Ah should fuckin' sue the pair ae ye!'

'Ach, fuckin' gie's peace, man,' says Hammy. 'Yer hardly bein' held against yer will. Yer gettin' a bloody holiday. An' ye look like ye could dae wi' one, ya miserable bastard. And anyway, ah wisnae lyin'. Fuckin' look at him!'

Bobby gets up from the table and saunters away from them.

'Ah'll have tae stay here, 'cos ah didnae book a hotel, an' ah'm nae stuff either, but ah'll get a taxi first thing an' ah'll be ootae here before you two doss cunts are even up,' says Joseph. It's going to be a long night.

An hour passes. Barely a word is spoken. Whisky is consumed, plenty of it; and, much to Joseph's disgust, three Pot Noodles are served. It seems hardly surprising that Bobby is considerably heavier than the last time Joseph saw him. That last time was six years ago to the day: a pivotal moment for a number of people.

Barack Hussein Obama said 'Yes, we can' to the American people. Megan Carter said 'Yes, I do' to Vincent Sevicci. Hamish May said 'Aye, ah will' to Esta Soler. And Joseph Miller said 'Naw, ye fuckin' willnae' to Bobby Cassidy before both of them tumbled, punching and kicking, into the open grave that they had just helped lower the coffin containing the body of Gary Cassidy into.

It's approaching 11 pm. From the moment he decided to intervene, Hammy knew things would be strained, but he naively hoped for a thawing of the ice, a ceasing of hostilities. Hammy wasn't in London for Gary's funeral. He was in Alicante, getting acquainted with his new female friend. He now understood that Bobby's curtailed account of what happened may have been diluted. Maybe the wounds ran way too deep for any form of reconciliation.

'Anywhere about here ye can get a drink this late?' Joseph asks.

Hammy sighs. Bobby ignores both of them, puts a pair of Beats Bluetooth headphones on and continues watching the Barcelona match recorded earlier.

'Look at this fuckin' wean, eh?' says Hammy, nodding at Bobby. 'Stay here, Joey. Fuck sake, we've got plenty ae booze. It's actually the only thing we've got plenty of. An' that daft cunt fuckin' needs ye, man. He's just too bloody stubborn tae admit it.'

'Naw, Hammy. Ah need tae get out ae here. Get some air an' that. Is there somewhere?'

'Aye, there's a wee place doon the hill ... stays open right through if there's folk in there tae drink aw night,' says Hammy. 'Auld couple run it wi' their son, Albert. Ah think they actually just dae it for the company tae be honest. It's about half an hour's walk though, mate. An' they roads,' he says, pointing to his legs. 'Watch yersel ... fuckin' dangerous, man.'

Out of Joseph's earshot, Hammy pleads with Bobby to go after him, but Joseph sets off alone. He has kept the daft white trousers on, but has diminished their laughable impact by pulling on one of Hammy's long, dark-blue sweatshirts. He has lifted a pair of black opened-toed sandals. Judging from their barely worn condition, they are probably a pair belonging to someone else; someone who left them there. Joseph is staggered at how mild the late-night temperature is. It must be twenty degrees. It is midnight, and it is November.

A full moon and a clear sky provide him the necessary illumination and he finds his way to the small roadside bar easily. A tiny fluorescent strip lights the name 'Salazars' from above. The bar is essentially a covered area to the left-hand side of a small house. The debris and amateurish scaffolding suggest the house is undergoing a transformation, but at a pace that indicates the American TV detective, Petrocelli, is the contractor. As Hammy assured him, it is still open. A family group indulge in a fairly robust conversation in Spanish while sitting on the small, cantilevered timber terrace. The two women in the group are wrapped in shawls. One of the six men is bare-chested. He is the one who spots Joseph first. He stands up to greet him warmly.

'Drink, sir?' he says. His English is remarkably good. There is only the slightest hint of continental influence in it.

'Eh, aye. Cheers. Jack Daniels an' Coke, please.'

'Of course, sir.'

'An' have one yerself, yeah?'

'Ah, thank you, sir. Very kind. I'm Albert,' Albert extends a hand across the bar.

'My name's…' Joseph hesitates. 'Joey. Joseph Miller.' He smiles.

'Pleased to meet you, and thank you for coming to my bar,' says Albert. 'You're from Scotland?'

'Yeah. Just got here today.' Joseph automatically softens his accent and speaks more slowly.

'You know Hammy? The Rebel Hamster?'

Joseph laughs. 'Yes. He's a mate. We go way back. Went to school together. Ah'm sorta staying with them.'

'He's a very good man,' says Albert. 'Looks after his Bobby very well. He always drops in here with his friend when I'm away … to make sure they're okay.' Albert nods over to the table where his parents are sitting.

'Aye, ah can't deny he's alright, is Hammy,' says Joseph. 'His friend … you mean, Bobby?'

'No. Sorry, his *woman* friend. Bobby never comes down here anymore. Not for years. In fact, probably not since Hammy's accident.'

It is a major surprise to Joseph that Hammy might have a female friend here. An assumption he made earlier in the day was that Bobby and Hammy might now be a couple; admittedly one with a relationship as dysfunctional as Steptoe & Son, but still, more than just housemates. It matters little. But this news explains even less. If Hammy has an alternative, and he is evidently still able to access that alternative, why does he choose to remain up there in the miserable, chilled air of Castle Hotpoint?

Joseph hands Albert a five-euro note. The barman holds his hands up, smiling warmly and says, 'later.'

Joseph walks over to a table in the opposite corner of the covered bar area, noticing the old jukebox partially concealed behind a curtain. He finds a soft armchair seat and turns it round to face the sea. Albert and his group continue with their discussion as if he isn't even there. Joseph lays out the pad and pen he has taken from Bobby's kitchen. He'll transcribe what he writes to his laptop later.

The story is nearly complete:

It wasn't always bad; these things never are. It's just that disappointment and regret are blinding. They grow out of control, like a forest fire, to obscure and destroy any good there once was. I used to be amazed at how quickly a bottomless hatred can develop in a relationship. People will do and say things to each other that would be inconceivable to them only a few short years earlier, when they shared a life ... when they created *a life. And it's all down to that sense of intense disappointment; of having lost something that can never be recovered. Time, mainly, but also to have invested emotionally, for no return. For no apparent benefit. To be back at square one.*

Those great times we had, laughing until our sides were sore ... tears running down our cheeks. Thinking that life would last forever. That we'd grow old together, still liking the same things, still teasing each other about the same differences. Recalling fondly the stupid names we had for each other. Planning to revisit places that held personal and memorable significance.

We had all this, your mother and I, even though it was only for a very brief time And then it evaporated. I called it a misunderstanding, but she knew the truth. I just loved someone else.

Chapter Eighteen

August 1984. Kilmarnock, Scotland

'How ye holdin' up, Hettie?'

'Ach, aye. Ah'm fine … y'know, considering.'

Hettie Cassidy had seen Joey Miller walking through the cemetery gates from a distance. Her family's plot was high up on the steep contours of the Strawberrybank hills. From that vantage point she watched Joey, dressed in black and carrying flowers, for a full five minutes before he reached her. He wore a long trench coat despite the late-summer sunshine. He was walking slowly: it was a warm day and he couldn't quite remember exactly where Harry Cassidy had been buried two years earlier.

'Ah'm really sorry about yer mam, Hettie,' said Joey.

'Aye. Well … maybe for the best. She was a poor soul at the end,' said Hettie.

It was clear she had been crying recently, but she was more together than Joey had anticipated. He didn't expect her to be here, but he was glad she was. Joey didn't want to probe too deeply but he didn't have to.

'There wis so many things at the end,' said Hettie. 'One thing after another. But it wis the pneumonia that did it. She just didnae have the strength to fight it.'

Joey sighed.

'Christ, Joey, ah'm no' sure ah can really comprehend these last couple of years. Both parents gone before they were fifty.' She began to cry. 'It's just so bloody unfair.'

Joey kneeled down next to her, put his arm around her and drew her closer. 'C'mon, pal. It'll take time, but ye need tae try and stay positive, eh?' These seemed like useless platitudes, but they seemed to help.

'Thanks Joey,' she said. She wiped her eyes on his jacket. Her tears left a wet stain on his shoulder. 'Ach, look at the state ae me. Ah've blubbed all over ye. Whit ah'm a like?'

Joey smiled at her. Hettie smiled back. He helped her up. They arranged Joey's flowers, along with the ones Hettie had brought earlier.

'Nice colours,' he said.

'Aye,' said Hettie. 'She loved chrysanthemums. Thank you.'

'The least ah could do, Hets,' said Joey. 'Ah'm sorry ah wisnae here for the service an' that.'

'It was lovely. Gary wis a bit ... arsey, but just because Don McAllister sorted aw the arrangements. Then him an' bloody Bobby fell out about it all. To be honest, ah was really grateful tae him for everythin'. An' him and Auntie Mary had been lookin' after her since ... well, Dad ... y'know, so ah don't really know where Gary got off, havin' a go at him for it.'

'Ach, he's got his own shite tae deal wi' though. Cannae be easy, ken?'

'Have you seen him, then?' asked Hettie, sounding surprised.

'Aye ... ah have, recently tae,' said Joey hesitantly. He had been in England when Hettie's mum, Ethel, had passed away two months before, and had missed the funeral. But he was aware that her death had pulled out a pin in a grenade that none of her three children had been able to defuse.

They had all been so close growing up: Bobby and Hettie, both so laid back and free-spirited; Gary, their protector and shield when things got increasingly strained between their parents. To Hettie he had seemed so different to her and Bobby: so robust and capable. But in the emotional aftermath of the Falklands War, in which he had served, been lost, presumed dead, and then resurfaced, with all the attendant media pressure, he had changed immeasurably. He'd returned to barracks in London, and Hettie hadn't seen or heard from him for over a year. Then, out of the blue, he came back home, with his girlfriend Deb and their tiny baby son, James, named for

Harry, but taking his middle name. Harold seemed way too formal, and its shortened version sounded too much like an old man's name to Deb. Gary hadn't even phoned to let Hettie know James had been delivered safely; she had been incredibly upset by that. But Gary, uncharacteristically, shrugged it off like it was no big deal.

When Hettie finally welcomed them all to Kilmarnock in late 1983, Gary seemed smaller to her, as if he had physically shrunk. He was stooped. He had put on weight and that whippet-leanness was gone. He chain-smoked, too, and was clearly drinking too much. There was no joking around; no playfully teasing Hettie as he had always done. He was edgy and anxious, constantly looking at his watch as if there was somewhere else he should be. Deb was also a bit distant, but her anxiety seemed connected to his; like she was anticipating an outburst and trying desperately to deflect the potential of one. They didn't come across as the loving, dedicated couple Hettie expected newborn parents to be. Gary didn't communicate much during the five days they were up. When he did, there was a bitterness to his words. Cynicism and sarcasm infused the few sentences he offered. Hettie pitied him his suffering and understood the intense pressure he was under, but he wouldn't respond when she asked him what the army were doing to assist him. She wanted to try to help her brother, but he wouldn't let her in. Gary Cassidy was a locked, dilapidated shell of a structure with a demolition notice pasted on the outside. Someone she once knew and dearly loved was squatting inside, but he was too terrified to come out into the light. She still loved him; just didn't really know him as the same person anymore. Any intervention would have to wait. Gary, Deb and little James departed on the National Express and Hettie didn't see any of them again until two days before Ethel's funeral on 20th June 1984.

'Jeezo, what happened to you, then?' said Hettie. She hadn't initially noticed the marks on Joey's face when he had approached; he had walked up from the west. But now they had turned, and she had her back to the sun. The scars on his face were healing, but lit from the other side, she could see how many of them there were. It looked like he might have been whipped.

'Ach, ah wis down at Orgreave, a couple ae months back. That's how ah missed the funeral, like. Went wi' the Labour Party guys ah'd been hangin' about wi'. Got involved, got locked up, got a batterin' off the polis, got let go.'

'Bobby thought ye might've been there,' said Hettie.

'Aye? Did he?' said Joey. He wasn't expecting Bobby to have even mentioned his name at the funeral.

Hettie didn't elaborate. *Bet that stupid cunt, Joey Miller's doon at that miners' riot, chuckin' bricks at polis horses, the fuckin' bampot:* Hettie didn't feel Joey needed to know the full context of Bobby's words, or that they had been the catalyst for his argument with Gary afterwards. *At least that* 'fuckin' bampot' ... *yer best pal, remember ... believes in somethin' bad enough tae fuckin' fight for it.* A fight had followed but in a contest between an aggressive angry soldier and a truculent, part-time slacker DJ, there was only ever going to be one winner.

'It wis absolutely terrible, Hets. Just bloody legitimised state violence. We were aw there tae picket peacefully, an' then ye just got the sense that the polis saw it as a battle right fae the off. They were meant tae be maintainin' order but they were just bloody out ae control ... hundreds ae the bastards, chargin' aboot on enormous big horses, batterin' anybody that stood in the way.'

'Ah saw it all on telly, Joey. It wis terrible,' said Hettie.

'Aye, but the flamin' BBC edited it back tae front. They news reports showed the pickets throwin' stuff, an' then the horses chargin'. That's no' how it was. Ah wis right there.' Joey's voice was becoming strained, as if he was on a witness stand, trying to get his point across under cross-examination.

'Ah wis ower in Maltby just days earlier tae, when that young guy Joe Green got killed by the lorry. There wis a sense that it wis aw kickin' off after that,' said Joey.

Hettie was no supporter of the Thatcher administration but

neither was she an activist. The miners' strike had seemed shocking but it also seemed remote from her. She sensed Joey Miller was desperate to share these events with someone, anyone. She felt instantly sorry for him. Not only had she 'lost' Bobby; he had, too. He seemed a bit disoriented, which was presumably how he had ended up in England, trying to replace one small gang unit with another, much bigger one. Belonging was always something Joey Miller craved. Hettie knew it from the way he had spent more time at the Cassidy family house than at his own. There were even times, when Bobby and Lizzie King had started going out, that Hettie had found Joey in Bobby's bedroom on his own, practising with the mobile DJ decks.

'Ah tell ye, Hettie, this country's fucked. The way the polis, the government an' even the media are aw colludin', it's the biggest frame-up in history.'

'Ye cannae win in those circumstances, it's true,' she said.

'But that shouldnae stop ye tryin', should it?' he said.

They walked on into the town, saying little.

'How's Uni?' he asked her after a while.

'It's good, aye. First year was a bit tough. Ah actually preferred the photography tae the fine art. The lecturer was better an' ah got on much more wi' him. But, aye, it's good. Good tae get away fae Killie. Too many deadbeats an' arseholes left about here,' she laughed.

He wasn't sure if she meant him.

'Whit aboot you. Whit ye up tae when yer no' punchin' polis horses?'

It was intended as a joke, just to lift the mood. But he thought she was making fun of him.

There was a long pause. He didn't answer her question. Instead he said, 'Ah saw Gary an' Deborah an' the wean a wee while ago.'

This caught Hettie off guard. She now knew she'd hurt him. This was his subtle revenge. 'Ah got lifted after Orgreave, but after gettin' a bleachin' they let us go. Ah wis stunned by all of it, we aw were. Ah didnae want tae go home, so ah went tae London. Went tae the barracks an' hooked up wi' Gary. Figured *he* might've understood.' This was a counter-dig, aimed to hurt. He saw it did, and he immediately wished he hadn't said it. 'Gary was askin' for ye, Hettie,' he lied. 'Told me tae come an' see tae ye, ken. Make sure ye were aw'right.' One lie leading to another. 'Said tae tell ye he wis fine, that he wis gettin' help fae the army.' A litany, now. He was trying to recover lost ground; to curry some favour. 'He gave me this for ye.' He passed her the Polaroid he had taken from his wallet. It was a photograph of Gary, Deb and wee James that he had taken for them but then asked if he could keep.

Hettie wept again when she looked at the picture, but not at the cuteness of her new nephew; not at the shared joy of a young family captured at the start of their new life together. Hettie Cassidy wept when she saw the haunted, strained, look on her brother's unsmiling face. *The Man Who Wasn't There*. A young man who had experienced brutal, traumatic events that had led to him retreating from contact with his remaining family, and – as it transpired – from his own comrades.

Joey Miller put another consoling arm around his former best friend's younger sister. She would maybe phone London later, and his fencing match with the truth would be revealed. But having intended to hurt, he then only wanted to heal. He would have to take his chances.

Chapter Nineteen

July 1985. Glasgow, Scotland

Hettie had packed a larger bag than would have normally been required for an overnight stay. She put it down to nervousness. Spontaneity was the usual characteristic almost everyone she knew associated with her. She smiled at the thought of them watching her now. This bag had been packed, unpacked and repacked countless times in the days before they were due to leave. But now she finally felt ready. She still had to wait for Joey, though. But once he got up, they'd be off, back to London. She sat the bag down close to the front door and laid her duffle coat over it. Then she went into the kitchen and put the kettle on.

She was close to Joey, but they weren't a couple, although many of the people they hung around with assumed they were. She did care deeply for him, but she didn't want a relationship. She'd known him since she was only ten years old. He'd always just been there; her big brother's best friend – normally a no-go area for teenagers anway, at least in terms of acting on any stronger feelings, and in truth, she had never specifically had them for Joey. But he'd been a support for her in the difficult months after her mum had died, when her brothers weren't. She also revelled in his passions: for politics, for music. He took her to gigs; and out of herself. She recalled his enthusiasm about science-fiction, and allowed herself to smile at his theorised, nerdy certainty about the future: cars that drove themselves and telephones the size of a matchbox, which you could carry around and use anywhere. Since Bobby was no longer around, Joey had picked up the mantle of idealistic dreamer and Hettie absolutely loved that about him, even if there might have been a degree of opportunism about it. Nonetheless, he made her believe anything was possible at a time when, aged only eighteen, she had struggled to see any future happiness in her life.

'Are you ready? We'll need tae go or we'll miss the train.' Hettie rapped heavily on Joey's bedroom door, for the fourth time that morning. There was no irritation in her voice but she had already decided that this was his last chance. If there was no indication that he was up by her next circuit of the flat, she'd be barging in and dragging him out of his bed. It was 4 am, admittedly, and also a Saturday, but since this whole trip had been Joey's idea in the first place – and he'd insisted they get there in time to see The Style Council – there was going to be no soft-soaped sympathy for him not being a 'morning person.'

'Right, ah'm comin' in … ah don't care if yer starkers!'

'Ah'm up, ah'm up,' he replied. 'Christ's sake, ah hear ye.' The door opened slowly. Joey Miller edged through it. He had his jeans on, and presumably pants underneath them. 'Five minutes tae I get a quick wash, eh?'

'Joey, the train is at ten tae five! Ah'll need tae phone a taxi now.' Her earlier mocking tone had shifted to one with a more vexed edge.

The bathroom door shut. She headed towards the shared phone out in the communal hall of their Dowanhill student dorm.

Joey Miller had been renting with Hettie Cassidy and two other young women – Alexa and Persephone – for six months now. The arrangement seemed to suit all of them. Tony Macari, the previous incumbent of the room at the end of the hall, had been mentally unhinged. He had been stealing things from all three girls for a few weeks before they confronted him. When they did, he had grabbed Alexa and held a kitchen knife to her throat, before edging both of them towards the front door. Her neck still bore faint marks from the cut, although she still didn't think he had intended to harm her. Alexa tended to see the good in everyone, and not the salient fact that Tony was a drug dealer who preyed on the Glasgow University fraternities for his livelihood. His bedroom door had remained constantly locked, he didn't engage much with his flatmates and there was an undeniably dark side to him. But still, when the police investigation began, the depth of his criminality had shocked the girls. When he had been in their company, he was usually very pleasant; and he was very good-looking too. They couldn't blame themselves, though; his police interview described a very plausible, if totally fabricated life: *A practised liar and career criminal.* After his exit, though, the girls needed the additional income, and from someone who could respond positively to the following challenge: *Flat-mates must be of good character. They must not be two-faced or addicted to alcohol. They must not use shameful ways to make money.* Hettie was a bit unsure of this, but since Alexa had suffered the most, she was given the casting vote. Hettie showed the draft text of their advert to Joey to ask his opinion. He was certain it had been lifted from the Bible, but regardless, had put himself forward as an appropriate candidate. Almost a year earlier, Hettie had persuaded him to swap a college course that he hated for studying architecture at Glasgow University. Joey had reluctantly applied and – with his Ordinary National Certificate providing sustenance to his art-centric Higher qualifications – had been accepted. When the flat-sharing opportunity came up, a move to the city seemed the logical one. Although he certainly wouldn't have qualified to be a church deacon, Hettie could attest to his character, and that was enough for Alexa and Persephone. He was in, sharing a flat with Hettie Cassidy, and now, preparing to head to London with tickets for both of them to go to Live Aid at Wembley Stadium.

The train from Glasgow Central was packed, predictably. Hettie was so glad this trip had been preplanned. Her old, spontaneous self might've just turned up and hoped for the best, but Joey had stressed the importance of reserving seats. That was one of the main ways in which he had irrevocably changed her. It had taken a while, certainly, but she now looked forwards. She anticipated, whereas before, in the ashes of that tormented summer of '82, she had just reacted, gone with the flow. Previous boyfriends – admittedly, there hadn't been many – were regularly late when meeting Hettie. They had all been young students, free of the bonds of home for the first time; flexing their wings in the big city. Strutting peacocks, more obsessed by their looks than most women. He might not have been an official boyfriend, but Joey was different to them in so many ways. Alexa had decided he was unconventionally handsome, and apparently unaware of it. He was also clean-shaven at a time when the emerging Glaswegian student counterculture was threatening to put local barbers out of business.

'I need a coffee. Want one?' said Joey.

Hettie shook her head.

He got up to look for the buffet car, which the conductor had told them was in the next carriage. He wasn't sure *which* next carriage; left or right of their seats. She watched him squeeze between a group of youngsters all carrying balloons and Union Jack flags and then disappear behind four tall skinheads all wearing ripped t-shirts with the words 'Fuck You' scrawled across them. Paradoxically, they smiled broadly and politely stepped out of Joey's way when he asked them to excuse him. Everyone else, including the conductor, had been eyeing them suspiciously since they had boarded the train at Birmingham New Street, as if they were aliens, intent on mass abduction. Hettie felt sure the skinheads wouldn't be heading to Wembley. The billed acts were a bit corporate, and music-business safe. Although her own tastes were less narrowly defined than his, Hettie agreed with Joey that including The Smiths and Echo and The Bunnymen might've made the British side of the event a bit more representative of contemporary UK music. They probably would've rather stuck pins in their eyes than play Geldof's matey-driven games. But at least U2 were in and she loved them. Bowie too, and if putting up with the record-business old guard of Phil Collins and Queen was the penance to be served for that, she was sure it would still have been worth it. A brief flurry of local rumours had hinted that The Miraculous Vespas – the Kilmarnock band who had hit the number one spot with their debut single the previous autumn – would be appearing. Joey knew their manager and had hoped that backstage passes might be possible. Subsequent counter-rumours had quashed these hopes. The band had been pawns in a bizarre, large-scale gangland vendetta and for anyone on a witness protection programme, appearing in front of an estimated global audience of 1.9 billion wouldn't have been the smartest move.

'It's 12 noon in London, 7 am in Philadelphia, and around the world it's time for Live Aid.'

Joey and Hettie were walking casually onto the Wembley pitch when these words by the Radio One DJ, Richard Skinner, opened the show. They both turned to each other and laughed, suddenly swallowed by the atmosphere and excited by the whole sense of history happening around them. Joey had been cynical about the motives for most of the acts appearing. It was fairly obvious that all would benefit from a significant boost in both sales and profile. But it would have been churlish to deny that Bob Geldof had indeed put together something that was uniquely special. He already felt certain that they would both recall this moment exactly in the same way as their parents recalled the assassination of JFK or Neil Armstrong's first step on the moon. It felt momentous, and they were carried away in the mass euphoria that greeted Status Quo, the first performers, who took to the stage after the Coldstream Guards' Royal Salute.

'This is fuckin' brilliant, isn't it?' said Joey.

'It is, Joey, aye,' said Hettie.

'Ah wish Bobby was here tae see it,' he said; automatically, and as if the last three years hadn't happened.

'Me too, Joey.' She could see he was excited. She was too. Perversely, she'd rather have shared this moment with Gary than Bobby.

'Ah'm gonnae regret bringin' this coat,' said Hettie. It was hot and she'd been forced to tie it around her waist. He had been carrying the rucksack since they had left the flat. She had two full changes of clothing in it, and toiletries. He had a spare pair of pants and socks. It would've been a bit much to ask him to take her coat too, so she wore it over bleached denim dungarees, until the heat became too much. As usual, Joey was dressed in black. Drainpipe jeans, a ripped Clash t-shirt and a black Levi's jacket. They both wore Doc Martens boots. They looked like a cool, young indie couple. Appearances can be deceptive.

They worked their way closer to the front but they were still only at the halfway line when Paul Weller appeared on the stage: red jacket, white jeans … blonde streaks. The moment above all others that Joey Miller had travelled 450 miles to see.

'Aw, ah love this song,' said Hettie. She put her arm around Joey and danced with him. She smiled warmly, the sun shone brightly. It was a moment, for him more than for her. Music's unerring capacity for capturing emotions otherwise buried. Tears formed. She swayed. She rotated and bumped into him, facing him.

'Ah love you, Hettie,' he said and kissed her hard on the mouth. It was unexpected and she pulled back, pushing him away with more force than she meant. She knew he had feelings for her but, in truth, she'd tried to avoid confronting them; to compartmentalise that part of her life that saw him purely as a friend, and still as her brother's friend at that. Weller continued to sing 'You're The Best Thing', but, immediately and rudely sobered, it didn't feel like that anymore to Joey. He immediately tried to put it down to the moment, tiredness and too much canned lager consumed on an early-morning train. Hettie shrugged it off, but it felt suddenly awkward, like a door having slammed shut behind them, one which led to the calmer, safe place they had come from; one which they now couldn't find. They had only been at Wembley Stadium for an hour, there were still over nine of the merciless fuckers left to go. She had just turned nineteen, he was nearly twenty-one. They had both witnessed death and marital break-up close hand, but still neither was quite mature enough for this moment. How to withdraw gracefully, so that feelings wouldn't be hurt and their close friendship wouldn't be tarnished. It was regrettable for her, but crushing for him, like being back at primary school, forced to select a girl from across a gym hall, for 'social dancing' one at a time, while classmates sniggered; a brutal and hideous experiment in child cruelty by way of state-promoted embarrassment. The pretty girls went early, sought out by those already demonstrating alpha-male tendencies; but for the shy suitors like Joseph, the more desirable ones with the better personalities carried equal risks of humiliation, just like now. He wanted the Wembley turf to swallow him whole as it had done to countless Scottish goalkeepers over the years.

They didn't speak for about an hour, instead watching the bands, trying to absorb the consequences of his rashness. They both now knew that a relationship meant different things to both of them. A string of fairly unremarkable performances didn't do much to help lift Joey's mood. And then finally, a solo and inspiring Elvis Costello reminded everybody, rather prosaically, that all they needed was Love. Joey Miller already knew this, but it momentarily stopped him feeling sorry for himself.

'Ah'm just goin' to find a loo,' said Hettie. 'Will ye wait here, for me?'

'Aye, no problem,' he said, a bit too matter-of-factly.

'Will ah get ye a beer, or a hot dog or somethin'? Ah'm quite hungry now.' Normal conversation as a sticking plaster.

'Aye. Okay. Just a beer though. Ah'm no' hungry,' he said. Petted lips had no place here, he knew that. There were bigger things; bigger issues. 'D'ye need any money?'

'No, it's cool. Ah've got this.'

They caught each other's gaze. Hers was apologetic. She was telling him she was sorry, but without uttering the words. He understood. Life is punctuated by such moments. This one would take a while to absorb, for both Hettie Cassidy and Joey Miller.

She was gone for so long he thought she might even have left the stadium. He stayed in the same spot. She could just be lost. They had planned for such an eventuality and said they'd meet up at the main gate at 6 pm if it happened. But she returned just as the live hook-up with JFK Stadium in Philadelphia kicked in. Four other people were with her; four men Joey didn't know, but that Hettie clearly did. She was more drunk than when she'd left him and happier. Perhaps as a consequence.

'This is ma pal, Joey … ma flatmate.' she slurred.

'Pal Joey,' laughed one of her new comrades. 'Is that not a movie?' They all laughed, apart from *Pal* Joey.

'Ye'se aw'right?' he said, sizing them up.

'Never better,' said another. 'What a superb atmosphere, eh?'

'Aye, ah suppose,' said Joey.

'I'm Pete,' said the oldest of the men. 'Pete D'Olivera.' Joey raised a hand. 'And this is Grant, he's Oscar and that little runt there is Rupert.'

'Hey: "little runt"?'

'Sorry Rupe,' said Pete, theatrically. 'I meant little cunt. My mistake.'

Hettie's new pals laughed like braying donkeys. Hettie smiled broadly and then shrugged in Joey's direction. Joey was still struggling to work out the dynamic. She hadn't just met them, that seemed certain, but they were all older than her, and Pete – their apparent leader – looked over forty. He had the air and aesthetic of someone who hadn't been able to leave the flower power era of Haight-Ashbury. He had that seasoned puffer's ability to smoke a cigarette from one corner of his mouth, whilst exhaling from the other. A constant fug engulfed his head.

'I'm Heather's photography tutor, by the way. She's got a fantastic eye,' he said, more salaciously than Joey felt was appropriate.

Oscar whispered something to Grant. To Joey, it sounded like 'And you've got a fantastic eye for her arse'.

Things were deteriorating fast for Joey. Jumping in and defending Hettie's honour from these privately educated fuckwits would backfire if Hettie didn't actually want her honour defended. But she seemed oblivious to the tensions that were now climbing all over Joey. She whooped and hollered with no inhibition. U2 had come on.

They were well into a song that lasted almost fifteen minutes before Joey realised that Hettie and the four interlopers had moved away from him and out of his sight. He was alone, and since she was now pretty smashed, he figured the chance of reconnecting with her later would be remote. The initial reaction from those around Joey Miller was that U2 had blown their big chance. He was beginning to know how they felt. Most of the acts were getting a slot comprised of four songs, but 'Bad' *was* essentially the Dublin band's set. In the midst of it, Bono pulled a young woman from the front of the crowd and danced with her on the Wembley stage. From his cramped viewpoint, Joey initially thought the girl was Hettie. It wasn't. She was elsewhere, out of reach; with four older guys. The day was fucked. Joey Miller left Wembley Stadium before Queen appeared on stage, before David Bowie sang 'Heroes', and long before Paul McCartney's microphone packed in. It was one of the most memorable nights in British music. At its UK conclusion, Hettie Cassidy was staggering back into the centre of London, heading to Pete D'Olivera's hotel room. Joey Miller was already asleep on a sofa in the emotional war zone of Gary Cassidy's flat in Bethnal Green. And the Youth Hostel room they had booked and paid for remained unused.

Chapter Twenty

May 1987. London, England

Joey Miller had retained his Labour Party membership. His dad used to talk about the apathy and cynicism that regularly descended, washing away youthful political activism. It usually occurred after a couple of bad election results – depending on your perspective, of course. But it always happened, 'as sure as night follows day', according to Joey's dad. Joey was determined to be different. He didn't see his father much these days, but with both of them living in Glasgow, their fragile relationship had definitely improved. Joey's father grudgingly respected that his son was now at university, studying for a profession, no less. But it didn't stop him being even more convinced that Joey's politics would slide gradually to the right, the older he got, and the more money his chosen profession afforded him. Joey was intent on that not happening to him, and at the successful conclusion of his third year, instead of going off immediately to start a year out in practice, Joey signed up to work on the merchandise stalls for the second Red Wedge tour.

The Red Wedge agenda was specific: the ousting of Margaret Thatcher at the forthcoming election on the 11th June. The collective, formed of left-leaning musicians, had been established in the dying embers of 1985. Fronted by Billy Bragg, Paul Weller and Jimmy Somerville – the Glaswegian singer with the Communards – they coordinated a series of gigs and media engagements throughout 1986 in support of the Labour Party's election campaign. Joey Miller had been to a few of the gigs, particularly the ones featuring cameo appearances by The Smiths and Elvis Costello. Although she had moved out of their flat at the start of the year, Hettie Cassidy went with him to one held at the Edinburgh Playhouse. The Blow

Monkeys, Lloyd Cole and Jerry Dammers were amongst the contributors, and although the songs often sounded unrehearsed, the joy of the people on stage, collaborating in each other's sets, gave the gigs a spontaneous vibrancy they otherwise wouldn't have had.

Joey and Hettie's friendship had been strained in the aftermath of the Live Aid concert. Hettie – who had been privately hankering after the attentions of her former photography tutor – had subsequently moved in with him. He no longer tutored her, Hettie having now shifted the focus of her course onto fine art. Her work was developing impressively. It was highly personal and largely figurative: expansive canvases filled with exaggerated, impressionistic images of the body. Like Lucian Freud – her biggest influence, and Jenny Saville – one of her classmates, Hettie's paintings were direct, authentic and confrontational. Many were self-portraits and Joey felt uneasy looking at the nudes, especially as they seemed to reflect how she saw herself.

Joey had remained in the flat. Persephone Wilcox had filled the financial gap left by Hettie's moving out by encouraging her friend from riding school, Lucinda Burroughs, to move in. Lucinda was a pretty girl but extremely distant. She looked down her nose at everyone, especially Joey. They didn't communicate much, and he was convinced she was trying to have him evicted in order to move her sister in. Lucinda was adopted, Persephone had informed him, but by one of the wealthiest men in the west of Scotland. She reeked of ruthless entitlement and upper-class, Thatcherite attitudes. She was dismissive of the working class as lazy, workshy Neanderthals, and Joey Miller came to regard her as an inverse image of him in virtually every regard imaginable. Hettie didn't like her, naturally, but since Joey positively hated Pete D'Olivera, he would regularly find himself defending Lucinda Burroughs purely for the contrary position it afforded him.

Joey was participating in the background support for the Red Wedge 1987 Comedy Tour, along with Gary Cassidy. When Joey dropped into Gary and Deb's tiny eighth-floor flat in Bethnal Green on the evening of Live Aid, 1985, a tumultuous argument had just taken place. Furniture was on its side, a mirror above the mantelpiece was smashed and domestic debris lay everywhere. It was as if Bill Bixby had just been kicked out and anger had transformed him into The Hulk. The following morning, a returning Deb had confided in Joey that Gary's violent mood swings were becoming a massive problem for the young family. While she stopped short of suggesting that there had been any actual personal violence, her growing fears it was somewhere down the slippery slope Gary was on were apparent.

Joey had stayed for a week. And he had returned faithfully at term breaks. He had initially visited Bethnal Green following Gary's discharge, because he felt he simply had nowhere else to go. But subsequently, Deb welcomed him with open arms; and Joey Miller had a strangely calming effect on Gary Cassidy. Now, they were both off around the country, working and campaigning against Thatcher, selling t-shirts at comedy gigs involving the likes of Ben Elton, Harry Enfield, Lenny Henry and Craig Charles.

'Who the fuck's this?' said Gary, dismissively.

'It's Porky the Poet,' said Joey.

Gary stared at the Hammersmith Odeon stage. It contained a single microphone stand and a heavy-set young man, illuminated by a single spot light. He was delivering a poem entitled 'Beano'. Joey Miller thought it was great.

'This is fuckin' pish, Joe.' Despite his traumatic experiences defending a Margaret Thatcher-led incursion on the other other side of the world, Gary Cassidy thought the protestations of a bunch of smelly comics and ranting 'studenty' poets was embarrassing. Porky – or Phill Jupitus as he was known post- and pre-gig – was a support act on this particular evening. The hall was still pretty empty, and Gary and Joey were manning the merchandise stall at the rear, near the main doors. Gary found it hard to be upbeat about much, but, perversely, Joey's mood always soared when they were together. They were Yin and Yang: if Gary was like a younger, Scottish Alf Garnett, Joey was like Else, Alf's long-suffering wife. Joey Miller craved companionship and was always prepared to adapt his outlook on life to accommodate a partner, even if their demeanour was often challenging.

'Thank fuck for that,' said Gary.

'What?' asked Joey. He had just returned from the bar with a couple of beers, so he had his back to the stage.

'Some cunt's just lobbed somethin'. It's hit Porker oan the heid. Doon he went like he'd been tackled by Gordon McQueen.'

The downing of the unfortunate left-wing, bedsit raconteur did little to lift the prevailing downbeat mood for Gary. Joey was concerned about him; his tension was visibly mounting, even though Joey considered the comedy gigs to be a far less anxiety-inducing environment for Gary than the incendiary volumes and headache-inducing light shows of the Red Wedge music events.

'Christ, that's no' good, man,' said Joey. He'd been jostled at the bar by a group of muscle-bound skins, all wearing Fred Perry shirts. It was becoming increasingly difficult to differentiate the old ska kids, who still followed Madness or Jerry Dammers' latest incarnation of The Specials, from those at the other end of the spectrum, who often appropriated similar clothing. It was beginning to look like the bouncers on the doors of that night's gig had been having the same problem.

John Tyndall had formed the New National Front in 1980, and then changed its name to the British National Party in 1982. They, alongside the Conservative Monday Club, had campaigned against the increasing integration of the UK into the European Union. However, Tyndall's reputation – his brutal, street-fighting background and his open admiration for Adolf Hitler and the Nazis – was preventing the party from gaining any respectability. So they developed a policy of eschewing the traditional far-right methods of extraparliamentary movements, and were concentrating instead on the ballot box, increasing tensions in England in the run-up to the 1987 election.

'*Fack* are you lookin' at, you *cunt*!' An aggressive skinhead the size of a Shortlees single-end spat venom at Gary and Joey as he was being ushered away from the stage. These were tonight's bottlers, an aggro-group intent on disrupting the Red Wedge gig with a display of aggression and intimidation. It had clearly worked. The shouting skin approached the stall. Joey Miller stepped back instinctively. Gary stared back impassively.

'Fancy a fuckin' go then, do ya son?' The skin's head was forward, a British bulldog dressed in DM's, shin-high jeans, Fred Perry and red braces. He stank of the pubs, the prisons and the politics, just the way Weller had famously described them.

'Ah'll batter your fuckin' cunt in, you don't stop lookin' at me!' The skin advanced as if to topple the stall over.

An ineffectual security detail was struggling to cope with the skin's fellow fascists. Joey started to shrink lower. It was one thing standing up for a political cause, it was an entirely different proposition to get your head kicked in for it, he reasoned. He would have been no use in Detroit in '67, or in Prague in '68, and perhaps for the best, he had been no use in Orgreave in '84 either. He had long since acknowledged that he was a passionate but pacifist supporter of liberal-socialist causes. Actually *fighting* for your rights was for other, stronger people.

Suddenly Gary was on the other side of the table. Joey wasn't sure how that had happened, so swiftly had the former soldier moved. In one brutal movement, the skin was down. Gary had shot an arm out straight and connected with his opponent's throat. Then Gary Cassidy went to work, pummelling and battering the stricken skinhead in a rapid flurry of blows that left everyone watching with open mouths. In less than a minute, Gary Cassidy had rendered the skinhead unconscious but was still over him, punching his pudgy, rugby-scrummed face to a bloody pulp. The white Fred Perry shirt was now the same colour as the red braces. Young girls screamed and young men turned away; even the remaining skinheads were rendered motionless by the severity of this wiry, ginger-haired merchandise-stall man's attack.

Eventually Gary Cassidy stopped. He looked at his bloodied right fist as if it wasn't attached to him, and then put it in his pocket, like a child trying to conceal the evidence of a theft. Standing over his victim, he glanced down and yelled, as if shocked by what he'd done.

Joey reached over, trying to calm Gary down. But as he pulled Gary's arm back, the former Scots Guardsman swivelled on one foot, and in the same motion swung a right fist and connected with Joey Miller's lower abdomen.

Joey didn't feel the pain he thought such a gut punch would bring, though. He felt something cold and sharp. Gary's shocked and tearful expression now mirrored his friend's. He dropped the small knife and slumped to his knees, seconds before Joey Miller did the same thing.

Chapter Twenty-One

February 1988. London, England

'Gary Cassidy, you have been found guilty of the charges against you. In reaching an appropriate punishment for your violent actions on the night of 11th May 1987, I have acknowledged the testimony and positive character references offered by former Strathclyde Police Superintendent, Sir Donald McAllister, and also that of one of the men you assaulted, Mr Joseph Miller. I have taken into account your service for your country in the Falklands conflict and the significant commendations you received for valour. However, the severity of the assault and the consequence of your actions for Mr Andrews leave me with no alternative but to impose a custodial sentence.

Gary Cassidy, I am sentencing you to ten years' imprisonment for the armed assault of Kevin John Andrews and Joseph Miller. You will serve a minimum of four years before there is the possibility of parole. Take him down.'

Chapter Twenty-Two

July 1991. HM Prison Wormwood Scrubs. London, England

Hi pal. Hope things are good with you and Lucy. I know she hates it if you call her that but Lucinda just seems way too formal, do you not think? I'm only kidding (but don't tell her I said it anyway. She seems pretty scary!)

Don't worry about last month, you can't get down every time. It's too far and you've got your finals coming up. Plus, you've got a wedding to plan.

Thanks for coming down a couple of months ago. I really appreciate it, and all the stuff that you left me. I'd just been getting into the Stone Roses, and even The Smiths … 'I wear black on the outside but black is how I feel on the inside' … Fuck sake, that's me to an absolute tee. But the guy who I'm in with got caught with some weed. Bloody screws turned the cell over and broke the wee cassette player.

Things are good now though in here. I don't get much hassle now that the Nazis have been moved. And there's some high-ranking government investigation going on into the warders and their brutality, so they're on the best fucking behaviour at the minute. It's actually quite funny to watch. And Deb brings wee James around every now and then. She said she saw you coming in last time and decided against it herself because you had travelled so far. We're over obviously but she's still letting me see my boy, which is great.

Hettie wrote a few weeks back but she said in the letter not to tell you. What is it with you two? She said she didn't blame you for telling her not to come to the trial. She knows it was me who made you do that. Go and see her, for Christ's sake. I think she really wants you to. You're both as stubborn as each other at times.

I didn't tell you this before but Bobby visited too. It was about a year back and totally out of the blue as well. He was over here for some festival gig on an island. I don't think he said who was playing. As you can guess, it was tough and awkward for both of us. Didn't know whether to hug him or just shake hands, and we ended up doing neither. He was asking about you. He said he thought he had seen you at the island thing. Anyway, the reason I'm telling you this now is that I went to my therapy session after it, and I talked more than I had done ever before. It really helped, and the doc suggested I write my feelings down. Haven't done any of that since the Falklands, and those daft letters that probably only made things worse with my dad and me.

But I did write, and I've ended up studying for an English Higher, which I'm hoping to sit in here next year. Here I am, turned thirty and back at bloody school! Fuck knows what I'd actually do with it if I passed, but it's therapeutic. It's helping me to come to terms with all the shit things I've done.

So Joey, I have a favour to ask. I've got a creative writing piece drafted for the exams. Can you read it over and tell me what you think? It's a few words over the 500-word target, so if you can suggest any ways to cut it down, I'd be really grateful. It's a bit of a rip-off to be honest. *Tom Sawyer* and *The Adventures of Robinson Crusoe* are the only books I've read right to the end in here. My story is called *The Man Who Loved Islands*. I hope you think it's okay.

See you next time, pal.

Gary.

The Man Who Loved Islands by Gary Cassidy

I bought an island, or to be more truthful, I won an island. I won it in a card game from the man who owned it, but I had to pay a lot of money to get into the game, so in effect, I bought an island. I had never sought solitude before. I always considered isolation to be depressing. How can I be happily alone with my thoughts when all they do is torment me? When they haunt my sleeping moments until I wake, and then torture the waking ones until I can't escape them. But such thoughts are always about the perception: the fear of what others will think if I express my true side, the one that is scared of other people, of myself, of what I might do to them. They would never understand that everything is just a cry for help from an inarticulate man.

But as I came to regard my prize, I started to feel differently about those things. My world occupied by people had been relentlessly painful. I had to hide my shattered emotions from everyone, for fear of upsetting them, or in case they misinterpret them as threats. My island was odd looking, just like its owner. It was anchored in between other landforms but spoke to neither. It sat proudly, ignoring everything else, revelling in its awkwardness; proud of its brutal sparseness. I admired it the minute I saw it. It wasn't a remote island, and certainly not a desert island, no … far from either. It was easily accessible but no one bothered because there was nothing of interest there to entice other people. Nobody wanted anything from it. It had nothing to offer. It had no oil reserves; it had no natural beauty other than the abrasive ruggedness that only I could see in it. It benefitted from no sunny climate and it could not be exploited for commercial gain. No tourists were ever interested.

So I made plans. I hired a boat. I needed no human companions; my dog would be enough. I began to acquire provisions and to prepare for moving to my island. I watched it every day from the shore. Naturally, it never changed, but it changed me. For once I was positive; excited even. Soon I would be there. Alone, except for the gannets and the gulls. In splendid isolation surrounded by water and completely free to do as I pleased with no debilitating fears about how others regarded me.

But when I got there, circumstances had changed. Not my circumstances; they remained constant. It was the island's appeal that had changed. The devious card sharp had done a separate deal with another man. We met and the initial impressions were worrying. He had the same papers as I did. We had the same dilemma: to share or to give up our half. My half faced the west of Scotland. His half faced the north of Ireland. I love my island but he said he did too. I'm not sure if I can share it with anyone. Although we have agreed to keep strictly to our half, I worry about his ability to keep to our new deal. I fear he will try to invade. I want to have my island to myself. I fear I will have to kill him, before he kills me.

(559 words)

Bobby and Joseph both found out the news that Gary had died in the same way: via a mobile-phone message. Bobby listened to Hettie's emotional statement of the basic facts three days after their brother's death. She had called him seven times over those three days. He'd missed them all.

Deborah was still listed as Gary's emergency contact. Since their acrimonious and turbulent split, however, Deborah hadn't kept in contact with Gary's family. Calling Hettie now seemed too much for her, so it was a nervous young policewoman who informed Hettie of her brother's death over the telephone.

Joseph's number had been given to Deborah by Amanda, his secretary, who felt certain he'd want to know the news. Deborah had some things: personal items, such as the two well-thumbed books that Gary had taken from the prison. She figured that Joseph might want them.

There had been many times in the past when Joseph had anticipated hearing just this news. But not in recent years, though, with Gary's treatment seeming to be going so well. *Press 2 to listen to this message again.* He did, as if doubting its veracity. *Press 3 to delete.* An ignominious full stop.

Chapter Twenty-Three

November 2014. Ibiza, Spain

Joseph Miller has read the words on this piece of paper hundreds of times before, most notably at Gary's funeral on 4th November 2008. He has carried it with him ever since, like it is a definition of his life's purpose.

These words, written on a piece of discoloured notepaper bearing an HM Prisons stamp, were the catalyst for Joseph's disagreement with Bobby at Gary's graveside. A distraught, drunken and possibly even stoned Bobby lunged for the paper in Joseph's hand as he read out the words. Tempers had been simmering between the two for days. Bobby felt the reading inappropriate given that Gary's sudden death meant he'd left no instructions for how he wanted to be remembered. Joseph had angrily argued that, since Bobby barely seemed to remember that he even had a brother, he had little right to dictate the order of service. One as obdurate as the other, both tumbled into the deep hole in the ground as the small group of assembled mourners – and a local chaplain – looked on, first in disbelieving shock, and then in apoplectic rage. Two forty-four-year-old men emerged from the grave, swinging and slapping like a couple of toddlers high on an overdose of blue Smarties. They were yanked out of the hole by an irate Benny Lewis, who's life Gary had saved when they had served in the Falklands.

'Show some fookin' respect, you bastards!' he shouted.

Pete D'Olivera led Hettie away from the sodden graveside. She was sobbing uncontrollably. Young James, Gary's fifteen-year-old son, put one arm around his mum, and held up the large, black golf umbrella with the other. The burial in a far corner of a Bethnal Green Cemetery had begun in drizzle and ended in a sudden torrential blizzard.

Joseph Miller and Bobby Cassidy stared at each other.

'You're a fookin' disgrace, the pair of ya!' said a disgusted Benny Lewis. 'I hope this day haunts ya both forever, you pair of selfish cunts. He was the best man I knew.' And with that he turned and headed after the others.

Only Joseph and Bobby remained, their suits covered in mud and wet grass-stains. They had fought on the lid of the coffin of their friend and brother. Being haunted by that forever was only beginning to hit home for both of them. They said nothing more to each other. What was there to say? It was well and truly over between them. They headed in separate directions: Joseph to try and vainly apologise to Hettie and Deb; and Bobby to find a Casualty department to ascertain whether he had – as he now suspected – broken his wrist as he landed on Gary's wooden place of rest.

Joseph Miller sits at a table in a bar on a small Balearic island six years to the day since that cataclysmic fight with his former best friend. Tears well in his eyes as he reads the words again. As well as a forensic insight into Gary Cassidy's state of mind while in prison for putting one man in a coma and stabbing another, the story has become something of a metaphor for Joseph's own life. He too initially craved the isolation of his own company when his marriage to Lucinda Burroughs fell apart. There was no solace to be found in domestic work and he now realises the increasingly fractured relationships with his business partners were precipitated by his own unreasonable behaviour. Running away to develop opportunities overseas was Joseph's version of buying an island. But, just like Gary's, it was built on a false premise. The grass is always greener on the other side of the world. Except that, eventually, it isn't. Unless it's the rolling hills of Hollywood astroturf, it still needs to be maintained and properly looked after. People need foundation and the sustanance of a loving relationship. Megan Carter was right about the definition of true happiness. Hettie had it with Pete D'Olivera and, although perhaps unlikely at the time, Joseph now has to concede that he was wrong about Pete back in the mid-80s. Hettie was never going to be his.

Following Gary's trial and Joseph's enforced rehabilitation at the flat in Glasgow, he grew closer to Lucinda. It seemed like an unlikely relationship, given her earlier antipathy, but they started to get on better. Lucinda found socialising as awkward and alienating as Joseph, and they spent many weekends at home together. Neither of them had a close circle of friends. It was a strange courtship but almost by accident rather than desire – perhaps out of a growing feeling that this was as good as it was going to get for both of them – they became engaged. Like those shy, embarrassed kids at the school dances, everyone else had been picked; only the two of them remained.

They were polar opposites, and while there is a certain clichéd attraction in that realisation, it ended up not being enough. Those things that divided the two of them grew in number and intensity, creating a chasm. Increasingly, the only thing that connected them was her father's money, invested in Joseph to provide him with the necessary capital to fund his share in the formation of a new design practice. It became a stick for her to beat him with, especially in times of recession, when the amount doubled and the possibility of repaying it seemed remote. Her father was a decent man, but Lucinda carried with her an intense bitterness that Joseph could never fully work out. Life had been good to her, latterly at least, and whilst they weren't her birth parents, her mum and dad had lavished more love and attention on Lucinda and her sister than might have otherwise been the case. Perhaps that was the core problem.

When Jennifer was conceived in 1995, it was a surprise. William – Lucinda's father – had died a month earlier, and it changed her briefly: she was suddenly vulnerable and accessible. For a short period, Lucinda and Joseph communicated in ways that they hadn't before. They went on holiday, for the first time since their short honeymoon.

But after their daughter was born, things went back to the way they had been. The stables where Lucinda had gone riding since she was a child had been acquired as a wedding gift to Lucinda from her sister. Since the wedding, it had taken up the majority of her time. That was *her* island. As soon as she was able, Lucinda went back to work and hired a full-time nanny, against her husband's wishes.

Joseph Miller folds the papers that are scattered across the bar table. He's been absorbed in his writing and hasn't noticed that the sun has come up, or that Albert's group is now down to two people: Albert and an older man, who must surely be his father. Albert has put a shirt on and has covered his sleeping father with a shawl. It is cold outside the bar. Albert's breath is visible in the crisp, November-morning air. Joseph has been in the bar for six and a half hours.

'Would you like coffee, sir?' asks Albert. He has risen, having seen Joseph preparing to do the same.

'Aye … please. Sorry for keeping ye up, mate.'

'It's no trouble, I don't sleep.' Albert smiles. He goes through a small door behind the bar. Joseph turns his chair one last time to look out at the sea. A coffee, and then up to see Bobby. To do what Megan suggested he do. *People need people,* she said; her being the apparent exception to this rule. He is aware of movement behind him. He doesn't turn round, assuming it's Albert returning with his coffee. But the movement is followed by a sound; a strangely familiar one:

'There's an old piano and they play it hot behind the green door…'

'Remember this yin?' Bobby Cassidy stands at the jukebox.

Joseph sighs. 'Aye,' he says before slowly turning around. His shoulders relax. 'Ah fuckin' hated that song, man.'

'Got us through that first night, mind you, didn't it?'

Joseph laughs. 'Aye, it did that, ah suppose. Good auld Shaky, eh?'

Bobby sits down at the table. He too turns his chair to face out over the mist forming on the sheen of beautiful azure water. 'Can ah tell ye somethin'?' says Bobby.

Joseph prepares himself for criticism.

'That's the actual record, Joey.'

Joseph is speechless. 'Hammy bought Albert's aul' man the jukebox years ago, an' then we gie'd him a stack ae the auld records fae Heatwave Disco. Hammy comes doon here every noo an' again just tae listen tae them. It makes him feel happy.'

Joseph smiles at the thought.

They have both missed this so much; the close companionship of a friend who has seen you at your worst as well as your best. It is difficult for Bobby to explain why, increasingly, Hammy just isn't enough. It's perhaps to do with Hammy's fiercely independent streak, whereas the younger Bobby and Joey seemed to be somewhat diminished when not in each other's company. A Wise without the Morecambe, or a Dec without the Ant. A Hardy without the Laurel.

'Whit makes you feel happy, Bobby?'

'Fuck all, these days, man.' Bobby sighs deeply. 'Ah've made such a cunt ae everythin'.'

They watch the moon's reflection rippling.

Neither speaks for a spell.

'Remember some ae the daft things folk used tae say tae ye?' Joseph reaches back.

'Aye. Ah remember some absolute poultice demandin' that ah play a David Bowie song, when ah wis actually fuckin' playin' one right at the same time! Ah says, "That is Bowie" … He looks at me as if ah'm mental, an' then says, "Aye, but no' that yin!" So then the pished bastard leans in, aw Winalot dug-breath, an' starts hummin' the very same Bowie song that's just been on! Fuckin' arsehole.'

Joseph laughs. 'Ah don't remember that, but see the night ae the Henderson Church riot? That night where you'd picked up a mysterious last-minute injury…'

'Hmm, ah vaguely recall somethin' like that.'

'Aye, ah'll bet ye dae. Anyway, before it aw kicks off, this fuckin' gypsy sidles up tae us, an' whispers in, "Play an ABBA yin, an' play it fuckin' soon … 'cos we're gonnae be leavin!" Ah mean, Abba! For fuck's sake … an' fae a guy that helped wreck the place, five minutes later.'

Albert brings a pot of coffee, and two cups.

'On the house,' he says.

'He's a nice geezer, eh?' says Joseph.

'Aye, he is,' says Bobby. 'Hammy would rather spend time doon here wi' him than wi' me, nowadays.'

'Ye sure it's wi' him? Whit about this woman he's seein'?' said Joseph.

Bobby looks confused.

'Whit woman?'

'He's got a burd on the go, according tae Albert anyway.'

Shakin' Stevens finishes and Aneka's 'Japanese Boy' fills the room.

'Fuck me, man. Remember that night … the daft bastard electrocuting himself?'

'Aye, couldnae stop laughin' at the time. Huvnae thought about they days for years.'

'Ah've been spendin' a lot ae time lately … thinkin' aboot them. You an' me. Gary,' says Joseph.

And suddenly they're at it: the nub of it all.

'Look Joey, ah wis a fuckin' arsehole back then when … y'know … Gary went.' This is difficult for Bobby but there is a sense of it being cathartic. 'Ah shouldnae have tried tae stop ye honourin' him an' ah've felt fuckin' suicidal … just aboot … every day since.' Tears are forming in Bobby's eyes now.

Stripped of context, Albert briefly thinks he's put salt in their coffees rather than sugar.

'Ah wis out ae control at the funeral. Like a true selfish bastart, ah'm firstly thinkin' it should've been held back in Kilmarnock rather than London. Ah had nae thought for young James an' whit he had just lost. Then ah'm angry for such a wee turnout for a man that wis a national hero, an' then got his whole life fucked up as a result ae it. An' none ae they government or services cunts gie'd a flyin' fuck aboot him. Aw these poor bastarts, returnin' fae the Falklands, or Iraq, or some other fuckin' war-torn shitehole that we send them tae … they come back fucked up in the heid because ae whit they've been through, an' rather than treat them, our system puts them in fuckin' prison when they dae somethin' stupid 'cos they cannae cope wi' aw that trauma.' Bobby says all of this calmly and with no obvious rancour; just a sense of depressed acceptance.

Joseph's eyes moisten but he stares ahead intently.

'An' then the worse bit ae all of it … ah felt fuckin' ashamed ae myself. After ma da died,' Bobby choked. 'After he went, ah fuckin' blamed Gary for causin' it. Just yet more *Gary* stress an' bullshit for him tae deal wi', only this time the auld fella couldnae. After ma da's funeral, ah knew right away that Gary wisnae ma real brother. Rather than fuckin' help support the poor bastart, ah just vanished.'

'Fuck sake, Bobby, ye were just a wean yearsel, more or less. Gie yerself a break man,' says Joseph. He finally knows it's time to move on.

'Ah'm findin' it hard tae cope, man,' says Bobby. 'Every year, it gets worse. Ah'd gie anythin' tae have Gary back, tae turn the clock back … wi' Hettie as well. Ah totally fucked that up tae.'

'Naw ye haven't,' says Joseph. He is blowing his cheeks out and wiping his face with a napkin that he has absent-mindedly doodled on. It has the same sketch that he's been drawing and dreaming about for months. 'She's still there. Back in Glasgow. Go an' see her.'

'Dunno,' says Bobby. 'Ah tried that before … swallowed it aw up, phoned an' made plans an' everythin', an' ah could tell she was sceptical. Convinced it's aw just bluster, an' that it'll fall through,' says Bobby.

'So … whit happened? When was this?'

'Fuckin' April 2010,' says Bobby. He looks at Joseph as if this should be enough.

'And?'

'And some fuckin' volcano erupts in bloody Iceland and shuts doon Europe's entire airspace.' Bobby holds his hands out pleadingly. 'Whit can ye dae, eh? Had the fuckin' tickets booked an' everythin'. Ye couldnae fuckin' make it up, man!'

Joseph laughs. It breaks the tension and Bobby does too.

'So, that's nae big deal, is it? The flights were aw back oan a month later,' says Joseph.

'Ah phoned, Hettie. An' ah wis pished at the time. Another big mistake. Hammy telt me tae leave it, but naw, naw … ah wouldnae listen. Ah knew better. She wis convinced ah wis pleased about the whole Act ae God shite. Telt me tae just forget it. Ah ended up thinkin' it *wis* an Act ae God, but the act wis him punishin' me for bein' a total fuckin' prick ma entire life. Ah started thinkin' it would take nothin' short ae Cilla fuckin' Black divin' in the front door an' shoutin' "Surprise Surprise". So, ah just gave up … more or less.'

It is hard for Joey to know what to say. Bobby Cassidy slumps in the seat. The confession has taken so much out of him. Terry Hall is singing 'Too Much Too Young': the story of their lives, it seems.

'Ah think we should go home,' says Joseph.

'Aye. Ah think yer right. It's time,' says Bobby.

PART THREE

LAUREL & HARDY RIDE AGAIN

'Didn't you once tell me that you had an uncle?'
'Sure, I've got an uncle. Why?'
'Now we're getting somewhere. Is he living?'
'No. He fell through a trap door and broke his neck.'
'Was he building a house?'
'No, they were hanging him.'

(From *The Laurel-Hardy Murder Case*)

Chapter Twenty-Four

November 2014. Ibiza, Spain

'Christ, tell ye one thing for nothin',' says Bobby, 'the quality ae the grub has dramatically increased this last week.'

He is wolfing down a healthy pasta dish that Joseph has made for them all. More out of necessity than desire, Joseph has taken over the culinary duties. Hammy's mind has been elsewhere, and his interest in cooking food has apparently accompanied it. He seems distant and worried. Bobby puts it down to the anxiety of returning to Scotland. But in fact, for Hamish May, it can't now come quickly enough.

It has been a week since the breakthrough summit meeting at Albert's. It has astonished all of them how quickly they have shifted into a different groove, as if the perceived grievances of the past thirty years were deep-layered soot and mould stains on a rendered wall that just needed a concentrated power-washing to return it to its original condition. They watch and laugh at old black-and-white comedy movies well into the early morning, quoting remembered lines before the actors do. There have still been occasional raised voices between the three childhood friends, but as the days pass these become less frequent. Much of this is down to Hammy breaking out his hitherto secret stash of cannabis. A different perspective on everything – from their original fall-outs to the current perilous state of Kilmarnock Football Club, on to Thatcher's legacy and including Simon Cowell – has accrued from such imbibing. They have smoked Hammy's beefy, hand-rolled joints deep into the night while reclining on Bobby's deck loungers. All three of them justify this drug-taking by claiming that its therapeutic qualities are the principal reason for their indulging in it; and, for their different reasons, this is actually true. All three have suffered physical or mental pain that getting high combats. Equally, their historically fractured relationships looked totally different when viewed through the prism of the mild, relaxed euphoria that the prime-quality dope provides.

The personal transformation in Bobby Cassidy during these last few days has been nothing short of miraculous. Having gone through the denial and anger stages during the mid-80s, he extemporised the bargaining stage through his increasingly desperate gambling. Depression – the longest and most recent of his personal grief stages – has now finally morphed into a form of acceptance. The most obvious sign of this can be seen in his appearance. He now sports a decent haircut for a man of his age. The straggling rat's tails have gone, replaced by a number-two buzzcut to balance out the thinning top, and the white clobber has been superseded by tones and colours more appropriate for a European man of his vintage. Astonishingly, he has risen early for three days in a row, and has shocked his long-term companion by going out running. He now looks years younger, pounds lighter and immeasurably happier. The now-clear fact that Bobby's deepening depression was merely a pining for Joey Miller – as if the two men were Siamese twins separated at the onset of adulthood – initially irritated Hammy, but the real source of his agitation lies elsewhere. Hammy aside, there are now far more occurrences of nostalgic laughter and juvenile piss-taking as Bobby and Joseph become reacquainted. The house seems less cold and austere as a result, just as they are making plans to leave it.

'So, whit dae ye think ae the idea?' Bobby says.

'Aye, ah like it. Ah think he'd definitely have appreciated it,' Joseph replies. 'Even though ah'm still no' quite sure what "it" is yet.'

'Ach, we'll get tae that later. Important thing is that we're gonnae honour his life in some way. That'll get Hettie back oan board, eh?'

'Aye,' says Joseph. 'That should be yer main aim, in my opinion.'

'Well, aye, but let's keep focused on Gary. We need tae think more about whit he would've wanted.' Bobby stands up and cranes his neck to the side. 'Haw, Ironside … whit d'ye think?'

THE MAN WHO LOVED ISLANDS

After a pause, a dejected-looking Hammy wheels himself in. 'Aboot whit?' he says.

'Aboot a fuckin' memorial tae Gary, ya tube! Have ye no' been listenin' aw week?' says Bobby.

'Build the cunt a statue … or name a fuckin' boat after him or somethin'. Fuck should ah ken? He wis *your* brother!'

Bobby and Joseph look at each other. Something serious is eating away at Hammy. He hasn't seemed himself all day, but this latest outburst is another level of uncharacteristic.

'Whit's up wi' ye, Hammy? Has Chorlton phoned demandin' his Wheelies back?' says Bobby.

Joseph laughs. Hammy's face remains stony. Joseph looks at Bobby for an explanation.

Bobby shrugs. 'Hammy?'

Hammy turns his chair and wheels it a few feet away from them. It's almost as if he can't face them. 'Ah'm in a spot ae bother,' he says eventually.

'Has the island run oot ae WD40?' says Bobby.

Without turning around, Hammy says, 'Aye, it's aw fuckin' jokes wi' you now, eh, ya selfish cunt. Yer pal's back an' yer like a fuckin' wife in the 1940s whose man's just returned out ae the bastardin' blue fae the war! For near ten years, ah've had tae put up wi' the *other* Bobby … the Gamblers Anonymous posterboy, the yin that's just one *Our Tune* story away fae a wrist-slashin'.'

Bobby sighs deeply. He is embarrassed and ashamed.

'An' now … when ah actually need you, where the fuck are ye? Headlinin' at the local comedy club. Fuckin' typical.'

'Aw, look Hammy … ah'm sorry, mate. Ah just thought ye were pissed off aboot us headin' home, man,' says Bobby.

'Pissed off? *Pfft.*'

'What's goin' on, Hammy?' asks Joseph.

Hammy breathes in deeply.

'Is it about this woman yer seein'?' says Joseph.

Hammy stares away. There is no clue from the back of his head as to how he took that question. Then suddenly, his chin drops down onto his chest.

'Whit's the script, man?' presses Bobby.

Hammy sighs. 'Fuck!' he mutters. 'Aye. It's true,' he adds, confusing the two as regards what he is actually verifying. 'Ah've been seein' this woman for aboot six years, on and off.'

'Fuckin' dark horse, Hammy,' says Bobby. 'Kept that yin quiet. Aw they times ye buggered off, ah just assumed ye were at a bingo club or ye were doin' the early-bird dinners.'

'Aye. Well. There's … em, a reason … em, ah huvnae telt anybody,' he stutters. There's a pause, punctuated only by Hammy's shallow breathing.

'Well?' says Bobby, trying to conceal his impatience, and the increasing thought that Hammy might've murdered her.

'She's a Blood Orange,' says Hammy.

'A *what*?' asks Joseph.

Hammy remains focused on the view outside. They can't see his face. His confession, painfully slow that it is, seems to require this condition.

'She … *cough* … she's part of a secret, em … middle-age sex club,' says Hammy.

'What, like a swinger?' asks Joseph.

'Fuck sake, pal. Ye've landed on yer … em … wheels there, Hammy,' says Bobby.

'Ah'm fuckin' warnin' you, Bob!' growls Hammy.

'Whit?' Bobby pleads. 'Yer gettin' yer fuckin' Nat King Cole regular, like, wi' a Spanish swinger. Stop greetin' 'cos we're goin' home. Christ, bring her wi' ye. Ah'll pay for it.'

'She's married…' says Hammy.

'Oh,' says Bobby. 'That changes the game a bit.'

'…tae the local polis chief in San Antonio.' Hammy's head sinks a bit lower.

'Oh fuck!' says Bobby. 'Ya stupid cunt. Ye'll need tae go … em … on the run, then.'

Hammy turns sharply, picks up a coconut from the fruit basket next to him and throws it at Bobby. It hits him square on the forehead.

'AAARGH! Jesus fuck … that wis sore!'

'Hammy, how do ye know?' says Joseph, intervening as Bobby hunts for a mirror.

'She told me this mornin',' says Hammy. It's clear now he has been crying.

'Ya fuckin' daft bastard. That's gonnae leave a big mark!' shouts Bobby.

'So how did he find out? Did she tell him?' asks Joseph.

'Naw,' says Hammy. 'One ae the other women in the group had *her* man round earlier in the week. He's intae aw this *autoasphyxiation* bollocks. She's prancin' aboot in the scud in front ae him while he's got one ae her stockings on his heid, and another yin tied round his neck an' ontae a door knob.'

'Fuck sake, Hammy. Did they get caught?' asks Joseph.

'No' exactly. She'd put one ae they wee clementine oranges in his mouth as an extra touch, ken?'

'Aye,' says Bobby. 'Ah think so,' he adds, struggling to hold in a laugh.

'But the cunt tipples ower tae the one side. He's making aw these weird groaning noises, an' she's wearing a mask an' she cannae see him, so she just fuckin' keeps on gyratin', thinkin' that he's just aboot to shoot his load.' Hammy puts his hands up to his head. 'But the poor bastard wisnae cumin' … he'd swallowed the wee fuckin' orange an' he wis chokin'. By the time she's finished the Dance ae the Seven Veils, the guy's fuckin' deid!'

'Fuck me,' says Joseph. He shoots a dagger at Bobby, who is silently wetting himself.

'Ah'm fucked,' says Hammy. 'The woman panics, calls the polis an' it's Esta's man, Juan, that turns up. The aul' bitch fuckin' dobs everybody in … names, addresses, favourite fuckin' positions … the whole lot. Esta's warned me that Juan Soler's a total cunt. Mental mad wi' the jealousy.'

'…an' she couldnae have told you that before ye started bangin' her?' says Bobby.

'That's when she *did* tell me!' says Hammy. 'Made it more excitin', like.'

'Aye, an' look at how excited ye are now, ya balloon,' says Bobby.

'So what's happenin' now? Is he headin' up here for ye?' asks Joseph.

'He had tae go tae the mainland an' file the reports an' take the body back an' that. He's gonnae be back in two days an' then he's comin' for me,' wails Hammy. 'Whit the fuck ah'm ah gonnae dae, Joey?' he says, appealing to whom he considers the most balanced person in the room.

'What's he comin' for, Hammy? He cannae arrest ye for havin' affair wi' his missus! It's no' against the law, is it?' says Joseph.

'He disnae gie a fuck aboot the law, man. He's comin' wi' bruisers. Ah'm gonnae get taken oot on a fishin' boat an'…' Hammy tails off as if he can't contemplate what Juan Soler's men will actually do to him.

'…ye'll be made tae walk the plank?' whispers Bobby.

'Shut the fuck up,' says Joseph. He notices his right hand is trembling. 'Yer no' helpin' here.' Joseph scratches his chin to hide the hand tremor. 'Ah've got an idea, but we need tae act quickly. Ye got a printer here?' he asks.

Hammy nods.

'Right, well … we're in business then.'

Two days later the plan has been thoroughly rehearsed. Two flights back to Glasgow have been booked. Bobby is remaining on Ibiza for a month or so and then returning to Scotland early in the New Year. He needs to sort out storage and then the repatriation of their belongings, and also to square the circle with the terminally ill Laurie Revlon and her demanding son and business heir, Laurence. Joseph and Hammy have packed and are waiting at the house until the last possible minute before heading to the airport. If Juan Soler is in fact on the hunt for Hammy and potentially heading this way, Joseph's plan will only work if they are cornered at the house. Hammy is still holding out hope that Juan Soler's flight back from Alicante that morning has been delayed or that he's missed it. A flashing light on his phone quickly dispels that notion:

Hamma, yo need go now. Juan he back. He's on you!!!! You care take. I luv yo!!!! I hope see you agin. Esta XXXXXXXX

Hammy holds the mobile telephone screen up to show Joseph.

'Joey, ah'm fuckin' shitin' myself,' Hammy admits.

'Aye. Me too,' says Joseph. 'But let's just play it cool, right. We'll be fine.' Joseph pats Hammy's arm. 'Okay, go and get the cuffs,' says Joseph.

Hammy rolls off to his bedroom. He returns some minutes later with a pair of handcuffs wrapped in fluffy pink fur.

'Ye might've fuckin' mentioned *that*!' Joseph takes the cuffs and throws them to Bobby. 'Scrape that feathery shite off them. Christ, they would get us a doin' on their own.'

When Bobby returns, they fit the handcuffs on Hammy. Their travel bags are already in the car outside.

The buzzer sounds.

It's Juan Soler and his men.

'Fuck sake, look at these two cunts here wi' Boss Hogg,' says Bobby.

Hammy and Joseph advance to look at the screen. The buzzer rings again. Juan Soler is getting impatient.

'Fuck!' Hammy exclaims. The smaller, fatter police chief is bookended by two giant Peter Howson subjects, who seem to have peeled themselves away from one of his canvases and are now intent on battering the fuck out of someone before their painted flesh dries. 'They're no' fuckin' polis … they're intae human waste disposal!' Hammy shivers.

Joseph's heart is thumping. He feels that it must be visible, like he is a love-struck Bugs Bunny. He breathes deeply and slowly, in and out, to control the rising anxiety. The buzzer rings again, this time for longer.

'Eh, hullo. Can ah help ye?' says Bobby.

'Open please. Policia.'

'Em, what's it aboot?' says Bobby nervously.

'Open please. We need speak to Señor Ham May,' replies Juan Soler. He isn't dressed as one might expect of a local police chief. He acknowledges this and shows his badge to the security camera above his head.

Bobby ponders whether the thugs will look normal-sized when he lets them in, or be even more distorted than the fish-eye lens of his security camera is currently making them. It's a frightening thought, either way.

'Look, are you part ae this ongoing operation tae?' says Bobby. He has now shifted into the script that Joseph outlined. Juan Soler looks genuinely puzzled. He turns and mouths something to his expressionless associates. Bobby can't decipher it.

'Open please … or we will be force to break your door,' says a now clearly aggravated Juan Soler.

After a few seconds, Bobby presses the button, and the wooden door slides back into its concealed housing in the wall. Bobby watches the two burly henchmen's impressed expressions.

It takes them a minute or two to work their way from the top of the house down to the living level, by which time Joseph is wheeling Hammy outside in the handcuffs and pushing him to the large black car, with the blacked-out windows that they have borrowed for this purpose from Laurie Revlon.

'Hold sir,' shouts Juan Soler. 'That man is wanted by local Policia,' he proclaims.

Joseph and Hammy stop at the gravel base at the bottom of the steep slope down to the car-port.

'Stay there you,' Joseph says loudly to Hammy.

'An' where the fuck dae ye think ah'm likely tae go?' he replies theatrically.

Hammy is dressed in a beige suit with a clean white shirt. Joseph has his black Calvin Klein suit on with white shirt and black tie. His shoes are gleaming. His hair is Jehovah's-Witness-perfect. A manufactured bulge in the upper jacket, fashioned out of a pair of Hammy's old braces, make him look like he's carrying. Joseph spots both of Juan Soler's associates scanning the bulge as if they have x-ray vision.

'And who are jou?' says Juan Soler.

'What business of it is yours?' replies Joseph, trying to sound as intimidating as possible, but getting the order of the words wrong. English not being their first language, he gets away with it.

'This man is wanted…' says Juan Soler unconvincingly. He is still trying to size up the situation.

'Yes, I know … and we are extraditing him back to the United Kingdom right now, so please don't curtail this serious investigation.'

Juan Soler is temporarily flummoxed. He has imagined driving up here, picking up the cripple and dropping the bastard – still chained to his metal chair – off a boat out in the Med. This unexpected shift is making him lose face.

Joseph recognises that this is his chance. He steps closer and reaches into his jacket. The thugs visibly tense. He pulls out a card. It has his face and name on it, together with the stamp 'MI5' in the top corner.

'Special Agent Joseph Miller,' he says. 'Hamish May has been on the UK Government's Most Wanted list for more than four years. He is a principal suspect in the ongoing Operation Yewtree, which has identified him as the leader of a group of men who are actively trafficking young girls from Europe … from the Spanish mainland … over to the UK. We finally tracked him to here, and he has now been apprehended.' Joseph quickly flashes another letter as they all gravitate out to where Hammy sits. 'This letter exchange between our governments has agreed the terms of his extradition.' Joseph's fluttering stomach is in knots, but Bobby Cassidy – an ineffective observer to all of this – has to tip the hat to his convincing performance.

Juan Soler has no answer.

'So,' Joseph continues. 'Whatever he is wanted in connection for on the island, it will have to wait. You will have to contact your own security officials and take your case from there.' Obviously, that isn't going to happen.

Bobby steps towards Hammy and slaps him hard across the face. 'Ya dirty kiddy-fiddlin' bastart, ye!' he shouts. 'Livin' under my roof an' runnin' a child sex exploitation business fae yer bedroom? Ye deserve aw that's comin' tae ye, ya filthy perverted cunt!' Bobby slaps Hammy again, harder.

This is taking the method acting too far. Hammy determines to get even with Bobby for this.

'Bastardo!' shouts Juan Soler, and he swings a dull punch into Hammy's jaw. A big, circular sovereign ring acts as a de facto single knuckle-duster. Hammy slumps, howling in pain.

'Okay, that's enough,' says 'Agent' Miller. 'I hate this scum for what's he's done, but I don't want him gettin' off on a police brutality technicality.'

Hammy is then briskly bundled into the back of the car, Juan Soler eyeballing him constantly. Joseph gets in the driver's side and the window slides down.

'Thank you for your assistance and cooperation in helping capture this man, Mr Cassidy,' says Joseph. 'I'll make sure your country knows how much personal danger you put yourself in.' And with that, the car screeches away, throwing gravel chips backwards as it accelerates up the steep driveway.

'Fuck sake!' Hammy complains. 'Ye coulda stopped the cunt fae rattlin' my jaw, Joey.' He draws a breath sharply in through his teeth as if just reading an estimate for cosmetic dentistry. 'An' whit the fuck was aw that kiddly-fiddlin shite, eh? That wisnae in the script! Thought ah had sold secrets tae the Russians … like that Wikileaks tosser! Ah ken it wis just an act, but lumpin' me in wi' the Jimmy Savile brigade … fuck sake, man!'

'Better that than sleepin' wi' the fishes, pal,' says Joseph, looking in the rearview mirror.

'An' as for that prick, Bobby,'

'Well, we're ootae trouble now, eh?'

'Ach, aye. Ah suppose,' says Hammy, finally managing a relieved sigh.

Suddenly, Joseph slams the brakes on. Hammy is thrown forward, the seatbelt snapping tightly and painfully across his chest. Joseph opens the driver's door and staggers to the side, visibly shaking. He vomits loudly into the undergrowth.

'Holy fuck, Joey, that wis sore,' says Hammy. 'An' can ye take these fuckin' cuffs off noo?'

Joseph frees him, before starting the car again. 'Ya ungrateful bastard, ye!' he says.

'Ah appreciate it, man,' says Hammy. 'Ah dae, ah really dae. Where did ye get the MI5 badge by the way? That even had me convinced.'

'Ah worked out in Libya. We went out there as part ae a Tony Blair delegation aimed at bringin' Gaddafi back intae the international fold, so we could buy the oil off him rather than the Russians. The sanctions got lifted, an' the trade was goin' tae be UK teams providin' designs for schools an' hospitals and aw kinds ae community shit. In order tae get full security clearance, aw the advisors got badges and citations. Ah just never handed mine back.'

They are at the airport in less than twenty minutes. Joseph parks the car where Bobby can pick it up and return it later. Hammy gets into his chair. A reddish purple welt has formed on his jaw line.

'Hamma … Hamma!' It is Esta. She runs to him, leans down and hugs him.

'Are jou okay?' she asks him.

'Aye … fuck it, 'Nam was much worse.' He laughs.

She doesn't get it. 'I have dis for jou,' she says, handing him a long package. 'I never forget jou.' She kisses him tenderly.

Joseph is touched. Their relationship was more than he'd assumed it to be. He feels for Hammy.

At check-in, Hammy plays it straight. He admits having been given something to carry on and that it is a gift and he isn't sure what it is. It gets unwrapped and cleared by security. A sobbing Hamish May boards the plane clutching one of Esta's prosthetic legs. When he lands, he will text her that he will never sleep without it.

Chapter Twenty-Five

December 2014. Glasgow, Scotland

He has been back in Scotland for almost a month and Hamish May is still struggling to come to terms with the many changes in his immediate environment. He is living with Joseph Miller in his fourth-floor, brownstone tenement flat. The lack of a lift in the old Victorian structure has confined his movements and has persuaded him that – although they are getting on reasonably well – this isn't a long- or even medium-term solution. He can't keep relying on Joseph to help him down four flights. That realisation is percolating. It needs attention and reasonably urgently. Hammy rolls his wheelchair the short but congested distance through deep slush from taxi stance to ticket office. The snow didn't last long. Odds on a white Christmas had been slashed to evens by some bookmakers, but an upsurge in temperatures has saved them. All that remains is this dismal, wet, grey mush – which is still dangerous for people out walking and vehicles traversing the ungritted roads.

Hammy is en route to Buchanan Bus Station and the bus back down to Kilmarnock. Hammy wishes he hadn't left it so late. He regrets not taking the train. He is travelling on the last day of the year, and, as a result of not having phoned ahead, he has to get the more local service and not the express one. This means a journey of an hour and half, through countless stops on an extended circuit of the suburbs of Glasgow, as opposed to a forty-five-minute one straight down the M77. He will be staying with his old mum for a few days. She is a sprightly seventy-six-year-old; much of Hammy's determinedly independent spirit comes from her. Having looked after himself – and to a large extent Bobby Cassidy too – for some years, requiring any form of assistance from Joseph to get down the stairs and get out and about seems like the start of a slippery slope. Hammy needs some alternative options. Joseph has suggested he buy a mobility scooter but Hammy argues that people who use such things are as likely to be obese and lazy as disabled, and he wants no such judgement cast on his own condition. Joseph can't immediately see the logic in his argument. It appears to be based solely on the fat Americans Hammy has seen motoring around in a television programme about Disneyland.

He arrives in Kilmarnock. A kindly driver assists him to get his chair down a mobile metal ramp. He pulls on his gloves. He navigates a route from the local bus station through a sad and largely redundant Burns Mall, stopping at an RS McColl's to pick up some flowers for his mum. Kilmarnock hasn't changed much since he was last here. A Greggs has replaced an Olivers, and vaping shops and mobile phone stores have replaced virtually everything else. He laments the accessibility of these public spaces. They seem much worse in a Scottish town centre, with all its new DDA regulations, than on a tourist-orientated, steeply contoured Spanish island. But he also acknowledges that he is actively finding fault.

Heading back up to the taxi rank at the base of the multi-storey car park on the Foregate, his wheelchair is stopped in its tracks. Literally.

'Hammy?' A blonde woman has stepped right in front of him.

Out of context, he takes a minute, but then says, 'Lizzie? Fuck sake, is that you?' He knows it is. Unlike him, she has barely changed since the last time he saw her. But since Hammy pinned his colours to the mast regarding Lizzie's newspaper betrayal twenty years earlier, he was simply hoping she hadn't seen him.

'How are ye?' she asks, immediately realising the general stupidity of the question. 'Sorry,' she says, 'ah didnae mean … Look, ye got a minute for a coffee?'

'Ah'm headed tae see ma mam, Lizzie … ah'm a bit pushed for time, ken?'

'It's important. Please,' she pleads, still blocking his route. 'Just five minutes, eh?'

'Aw, it's good tae see ye, son. Ye look rerr,' says Maggie May.

Hammy hands a bag to his mum. It contains three packs of biscuits. Maggie May beams like a five-year-old being given a present from a department-store Santa. When BN biscuits were mysteriously banned in the UK, Hammy regularly sent packs of them home to his mum, who had developed a mild addiction to them. Legend has it that they were banned because of small quantities of cocaine being added to the chocolate filling. The biscuits' sinister, smiling, winking faces merely reinforced this theory. Regardless, Hammy and his mum have both been hooked for life.

A taxi has dropped him at the large semi-detached former council house in Kilmarnock where Hamish grew up. It is, of course, far less congested than it used to be then. Maggie lives here alone, apart from two ginger cats. Maggie's husband, Stan, died from a heart attack in 2009. Hammy wasn't well enough to travel home for the funeral but they were at least reconciled following his accident. Hammy's brothers and sisters are scattered to the four winds. Two are in different parts of Australia, one is in New Zealand, another works in the town planning service in Orkney, and Glendale, his younger brother, is currently in jail in the American Deep South. The remaining two – his twin sisters, Dolly and Aretha – still live in Ayrshire, and will be visiting tomorrow. The fabric of the house has echoes of all of them, but Maggie doesn't let their various absences drag her down. She is stoic and resolute. She's glad her boy is back, but equally, now that he's a fifty-year-old paraplegic, she doesn't want to become his full-time carer. In such a large and pioneering family, independence has always been important. Hammy knows it and he has been grateful for that legacy over the last twenty years. Such characteristics have helped him survive. There has never been time for self-indulgence or self-pity in the May household.

Hammy's mum has made a bed for him in the living room. All the other bedrooms are upstairs. He's happy with this and he knows it's only for a few days, but she returns to the pressing subject as they eat and watch the *Strictly Come Dancing* New Year's Eve Special.

'Jeezo, ah thought Bruce Forsyth wis deid!'

'Naw, that's just the guy that writes his jokes,' his mum says.

'Man, ah thought the Spanish telly was rubbish,' says Hammy. 'Ah've never ever heard ae these so-called celebrities.'

'Most of them are soap stars or reality telly folk,' says Maggie. 'Ah hope the boxer wins … he's lush!'

'Lush? Where the hell ae ye gettin' aw this?' Hammy says, laughing.

'What … are we no' allowed tae have a wee bit ae slap an' tickle at oor age?'

'Jesus Christ, mam,' Hammy chokes. 'An' what's wi the "we"?'

'The Bowlin' Club lassies,' she says, pausing before adding, '… an' the lads.'

'Lads? Whit's goin' on wi ye, mam?' The Blood Orange ethos is not limited to the Mediterranean, it seems.

'Ah've got a fella,' says Maggie, proudly.

'Eh?' Hammy can't quite believe what he's hearing. 'Yer whit … seventy-five?'

'So whit,' she replies, not adding the additional year that he has omitted. 'Dinnae be a prude. Seventy-five's the new fifty!'

'Is it fuck! Fifty's always been the auld fifty.'

'Hey, watch yer language,' says Maggie, scolding her son. 'Would ye want me stuck in here aw day, bored wi' life, just waitin' tae die and relyin' on Phillip Schofield for the only stimulation ah get until that happens?'

Hammy dismisses the unwelcome image of Phillip Schofield stimulating his old mum, but it is quickly replaced by one in which the daytime TV presenter sticks his hand up Gordon the Gopher's arse. Hammy isn't sure which is the more disturbing.

'That's whit you're needing, son,' says Maggie.

But Hammy's head's gone. 'Whit? Phillip Schofield's hand up ma arse every mornin'?'

Maggie looks puzzled. 'Ye talkin' aboot? Naw … a companion. Someday that can love ye an' look after ye.'

Hammy thinks back to what he had with Esta, and with Bobby, in Ibiza. Sunshine, sex and Sangria: it's the ultimate in clichéd 'Brit abroad' holiday aspiration but Hammy had it year round. What the fuck was he doing back here in the sleet and the cold and the inaccessible kerbs?

'So where are ye livin'?' says Maggie.

'Ah'm bunkin' wi' Joey Miller up at his flat but that'll no' dae. Too much hassle. We're gonnae sort somethin' when Bobby comes back, dunno what though.'

'Well, ye can stay here for a wee while, but this isnae ideal … ye ken that, eh?'

Hammy doesn't want to stay with his mum, but is curious about the way she has said it; there was a *definitely not* emphasis, as opposed to a *definitely maybe* option.

'Why no'?' he asks, testing his theory.

'Well, there's nae room for a start.' She sees his *Aye, right!* expression. There's more space than she knows what to do with, and were there the impetus, a 'Thora Hird' stairlift could be fitted to make access to a bedroom possible. But there is something else; something she's reluctant to tell him. He stares her out. Eventually she crumbles.

'Ach, it's Bert. He's movin' in in a few days,' says Maggie. She looks down.

'Bert!' shouts Hammy. 'Who the fuck's Bert?'

'Hamish May! Language!' She stands up. He can't. 'It's Bert from the club. Bert Bole.'

'Bert Bole? Jesus Christ, mam … he must be about a hundred years old. That daft auld git was the cruise singer on the Titanic!'

Maggie May removes their plates and takes them through to the kitchen. She is trying not to smile. That last remark was quite funny.

When she returns, Hammy has calmed down a little. He has given thought to this unlikely coupling and figured that maybe there isn't a world of difference between his mum and him: both trying to find a bit of happiness and excitement where they can before it's too late. And neither his mum nor Bert Bole is married to anyone else. Hammy's in no position to cast the first stone.

'So how did that come aboot, then? he asks.

'He wis doin' the club bingo night an' he did ma song. It melted ma heart,' she says.

Hammy's dad was a decent crooner and his party-piece was, unsurprisingly, 'Maggie May'. Hammy reflects on the sweetness of his mum's story. Although his parents spent a lot of time apart due to Stan May's job, they were totally devoted to each other. Hammy knows his dad would approve, as long as Maggie is happy. He picks up his mum's hand and kisses it.

'Ach as long as he makes ye happy, eh mam?' She rubs his cheek.

'But if he ever, *ever* cheats on ye, or steals yer false teeth,' he says, 'then ah'll hunt him doon an' put three holes in his colostomy bag!'

Hammy's mum laughs. She is glad he's back.

Joseph Miller rings the doorbell. A dog barks. It sounds like a small dog in close proximity, as opposed to a big one that might be at the other end of this vast, detached, stone-faced Pollokshaws villa.

Hettie has done well for herself. Her art remains very much in vogue and the bigger pieces sell for tens of thousands of pounds. The house reminds Joseph of the one he used to live in, with Lucinda and Jennifer. It is ostentatious and muscular; a house not to be trifled with or contested in divorce proceedings. Lucinda Burroughs had their house put in her name as a condition of her father's financial support for the architectural firm. Limit the liability, they argued, and Joseph acceded. She knew what she was doing.

The door opens and Hettie walks out and throws her arms around him without speaking, crushing the flowers he has brought her between them. Even though she knew he was coming, her hands and arms and hair and clothes are heavily flecked with paint. He assumes his clothes will be too, but when he checks he is pleasantly surprised. It's Hogmanay and yet she's still working.

'Jeez, Joey,' she says, standing back to look at him. 'How are ye?'

'Ah'm fine, Hettie. You look well.' 'Aye, ah'm a bit tired, but, yeah, things are good,' she says.

Joseph wasn't sure how this would go. It has been more than six years since he has last seen her, and four years since they have spoken on the telephone.

'Come away in,' she says, sounding older than she is. He moves into a huge reception hall, bigger than the one he used to call his. It is a bohemian space with a couple of big canvasses hanging either side of an old, knotted-wood stair. Three chairs of different design typologies sit close together, like shy, awkward wallflower party-guests who haven't been introduced to the others yet. There's a high-backed Charles Rennie Mackintosh formal piece, a Jacobsen swivelling 'egg' chair, and an austere metal-and-leather Berlin seat. It's hard to determine the prevalent influence and he finds himself wondering, like Loyd Grossman, 'who actually lives in a house like this?'

'Ah just need to finish somethin' up,' says Hettie. 'Make yerself at home though, eh? The main room's through there. Ah'll just be five minutes.'

Joseph watches her go and then deliberately wanders into a room adjacent to the one she suggested. It is lined wall to ceiling with books: expensive ones, not airport paperbacks. Joseph's never been much of a reader. He has acquired a lot of books too, but he rarely reads any of them. He is so uncomfortably aware of this contradiction, he even knows that the Japanese have a name for such a person: a *Tsundoku*. He wonders if this extensive library of books is just for show, too. He suddenly feels superior. Like Nick Carraway slinking away from Jay Gatsby's party, Joseph Miller thinks that he has stumbled on a façade; uncovered a falsehood. But the pages of the random selection he makes are cut and well-thumbed. These books are cherished and loved.

The remainder of the house is as much of a stylistic melting pot, full of collected bits of furniture and fittings, and *objets d'art* – as he imagines Pete would refer to them. Like many houses of the Victorian vintage, it feels dark and foreboding. These interiors are dominated by dark-wood panelling. It gives the house a definite feeling of permanence and strength, but its lack of a lightness to its main spaces is a touch depressing, Joseph thinks.

'So?' she says. She has seen him scanning the details of how she lives like a property agent about to value it for a third party.

'Sorry,' he says. 'Force ae habit. The house is really interestin', Hettie. It's bloody massive tae.'

'Aye, most ae the stuff is Pete's. Ah'm not a collector, he is. He hoards stuff that he places a value on … which is basically everythin'. Come on through tae the studio. Ah just need tae finish up a bit an' then ah'll get dinner.'

They wander through a sequence of rooms before emerging into one flooded with north light – so much in contrast with the remainder of the house that Joseph takes a few seconds to adjust to it.

'Pete likes the house tae be quite dark. Aw they years stuck in darkrooms, y'know.'

'How is he?' Joseph asks. He assumes he'll see him later at dinner, although Hettie hasn't made that clear.

'Ach, no' great,' she says, then pauses. At first he thinks she won't elaborate. 'But he's lasted longer than he thought he would.' She smiles, but it is painfully forced.

A central part of Joseph's previous humiliation at Gary's funeral in 2008 was his forthright insistence that Pete D'Olivera had never been right for Hettie; he behaved like a spurned boyfriend, jealous his former girlfriend's attentions were going to another man. Only Joseph hadn't ever been Hettie's boyfriend, and the scene he made, at the age of forty-four, was rendered all the more shameful as a consequence. 'Look at him!' Joseph shouted. 'He's a miserable auld prick.' Pete had been diagnosed with emphysema three weeks earlier; his 'misery' at that news compounded by the need to give up smoking or face a prognosis of two years, max. Paradoxically, it was Joseph's misery that prompted the outburst. A long, drawn-out and bitter divorce from Lucinda Burroughs had been made final just about the time Pete was receiving his own bad news. Late 2008 had a lot to answer for, Joseph often acknowledges.

Pete is now in his mid-seventies. He claims to not know his exact year of birth, having been born in a commune in India sometime around the outbreak of the Second World War. Pete's mother was an opium addict and her fall from grace was swift. The identity of Pete's father was also a mystery but, for the early part of his life, he had grown up in a protective, if dysfunctional and unconventional, extended 'family' grouping. Pete and his mother and three sisters reluctantly moved to London in late 1947, when Partition made the Punjab a dangerous place for people without financial connections. Only a donation from an elderly British gentleman, who Pete's mother regularly serviced, made their passage from India possible.

Both Pete and Hettie have accepted his fate and, by and large, they have been content here in Pollokshaws in the six years since his diagnosis. Now though, as Hettie is explaining, Pete is on the last lap, essentially confined to a converted ground-floor family room, full of life-prolonging apparatus, which looks out onto an expansive garden.

'My God, this is fantastic,' says Joseph Miller of the dinner he is eating.

'Thanks,' says Hettie. 'En Croute Catering – they never let me down,' she admits. 'Ah've nae time for cookin', an' nae real interest in it. It's hard when yer just makin' things for yerself, ye know, and at all kinds ae daft hours?'

'Aye,' says Joseph. He knows that only too well.

Earlier, Hettie showed him a preview of work for a new exhibition. It was very clear from the subject matter that Pete D'Olivera wouldn't be joining them to eat. Countless black-and-white photographs – self-portraits – were pinned to every surface. From left to right, they mapped a steady chronology of the ravages of terminal illness on the outward surface of the body. Hettie's paintings were all of Pete, too: gaunt and decaying, but trying to capture something dignified out of the toll it took on the inside; on his mind. Despite the brutal realism of these painfully honest figurative works, Joseph saw some kind of frail and fragile beauty in them. They were vast canvases. The workshop extension at the rear of the house was designed and constructed specifically for them. Hettie remarked that she thought Pete was defying death simply to allow her to complete this portfolio of work, but it was essentially his work too. She had three other paintings to finish and then it would be complete. It was a document of Pete's decline over the last three years and the portfolio was entitled *All This Useless Beauty*. Joseph wasn't really sure what to think. The finished paintings unnerved him. They made him pity Pete and then conversely, the experience made him feel that it was actually an invasion of Joseph's own privacy to be invited to view them at all. Hettie explained that all of these reactions – and the complex shades in between – were the principal objectives for an artist in this – and by extension, all – figurative art.

'Look, ah know ah said this before but now ah'm here in person, ah'm really, really sorry for everythin' ah said about Pete,' says Joseph now, as they eat. 'Ah know how painful that must've been.'

'Lets no' dwell on the past, eh?' says Hettie.

'Ah know, but ah kinda need tae get past this,' says Joseph.

'Look, we've aw moved on. More important stuff tae be gettin' on wi',' she says, casting her eyes to her left.

He recognises that he came here craving her unconditional forgiveness and feeling that it was perhaps the missing link in his own personal rehabilitation. But she's always loved him, anyway, just like she has always loved her brothers. Her lack of contact wasn't to do with vengeance or disinterest; it was simply a consequence of her attention being necessarily focused on someone else's needs. He feels childish and selfish for not appreciating that until now.

'So you and Bobby are back on the prowl, then?' she says, laughing.

'Aye, seems so.'

'God help us!'

'This thing for Gary's goin' tae be great, whenever we work out what it actually is.'

'Well, if ah can help, tell him ah will,' she says, leaving the possibility open that Joseph Miller might still need to mediate somewhat.

'He'll be back in January, once he's dealt with the house an' stuff. Ah'm sure he'll be here tae see ye the minute he lands,' says Joseph.

'Aye,' she says. 'Ah'll maybe no' hold my breath though, eh?'

Bobby sits on the edge of a bed that feels bigger than his splash pool back at the villa. He feels awkward being here on Hogmanay but has already acknowledged that the dawning of a new year has different connotations for someone as ill as Laurie Revlon. She is currently asleep, propped up on a few, sizable white pillows. Everything in the room is white. Every surface, every fixture and fitting. He imagines Laurie waking and momentarily thinking that this is in fact heaven. *Perhaps that's the point,* he considers.

Laurence has shown him up to Laurie's bedroom under some duress. Laurence has never fully understood the favour in which his mother holds this dishevelled, redundant Scotsman, but he doesn't know that Bobby Cassidy inadvertently provided Laurie Revlon with an escape route at a time when she needed one more than the incarcerated hero of The Shawshank Redemption.

In the early 90s, Laurie Revlon's business was in trouble. An oil-price recession at the beginning of the decade had accounted for much of the decline in the distributed financial profits in her organisation. A new investigation into Terry Dooley's unexplained demise was brewing, and developing a music business based in the Balearics was very much her last throw of the dice. Her capital was all but used up and her banking credentials – like many others who'd overextended in pursuing Thatcher's capitalist dream – were worth little. But then along came 'Dipped in Chocolate', an unexpectedly massive worldwide smash-hit single. Consequently, the restrictive contract she'd drawn up with Bobby Cassidy had paid off and then some. The civil suit brought by Terry Dooley's family surfaced after a *Panorama* investigation. So Laurie settled privately with the family and agreed an ongoing royalty percentage from the record, in perpetuity. Rather than paying for the issue to go away, it looked like a benevolent act of support for the dependents of a former client. But beyond the convenient timing of the record's success, Laurie was fond of Bobby – and of Hamish May, as it happened – and had resolved to look after him and his newly appointed personal assistant. Bobby's DJ'ing sell-by date had long since expired, and even though she accepted that Laurence wanted him out of the A-list clubs in San Antonio, Bobby would always have a place at the table, even if it was out in the comparative clubbing wasteland of Las Dalias.

Laurie had been made aware of Bobby's decision to return home to Scotland and had asked to see him one last time. A visit was the least Bobby could do.

'Well, don't be a stranger then.'

Bobby has been staring out the window at a large yacht cruising slowly past the rocks just beyond the flat, green land that marks the Revlon private estate. He turns. Laurie has her cheek inclined and he bends across the bed to kiss it. Even now, with death hovering impatiently in the atmosphere, she looks serene; a woman for whom age and beauty have no ongoing dispute. Her hair has been brushed and some light make-up provides the only colour.

'Hi Laurie,' his voice trembles. He isn't good with this sort of situation. 'How are ye, then?' he asks, thoughtlessly.

She laughs, and the exertion of this makes her cough. 'I'm good, Bobby. Peaceful. It's been a good life. I have loads to be grateful for.' She motions to him and he helps her sit up a bit higher in the bed. 'More importantly, how are you?'

'Things are really good, Laurie. Ah'm lookin' forward tae gettin' back now, y'know? Seein' ma sister an' dain' somethin' special for Gary, ma brother.'

'That's good, son,' she says. 'I'm really pleased.' She hasn't seen him in person for over a year but Laurie Revlon is well aware of the personal demons that have been strangling the very life out of him.

'Look, Laurie, ah just wanted the opportunity tae say thanks … in person, like … an' for everythin', y'know?' The 'everything' includes clearing his debts, giving him a place to stay for nearly twenty years, giving Hammy a paid job and sponsoring their original permanent-residency applications. Although Hammy has always implied that Laurie took far more than she would have otherwise been entitled to from 'Dipped in Chocolate' and the Miraculous Vespas remixes, Bobby knows that this has been balanced out by her covert financial support during the many wilderness years since. Unlike John Lennon's, Bobby Cassidy's 'Lost Weekend' has lasted for a generation.

'No need,' says Laurie. 'We've been good for each other. I wasn't going to forget that in a hurry.' Laurie reaches to her side and softly presses a button on a remote control. Bobby looks around, expecting curtains to close, or a massive, flat-screen television to drop down from a narrow slot in the ceiling. But nothing happens until footsteps are heard on the terrazzo outside.

'I'll meet you outside, Bobby. There's something I want to talk to you about.' Bobby is ushered outside and two other, black-clad, helpers begin the task of preparing Laurie Revlon for what could easily be her last stroll before the disease that's consuming her finally eats its relentless way through her internal organs.

'It's really, really beautiful here, isn't it?' whispers Laurie.

Bobby doesn't answer. It is rhetorical; as if Laurie Revlon is justifying the choices she has made with her life before it comes to an end.

'I've always been fond of you, Bobby. I know Laurence hasn't treated you as well as I would have, and I'm sorry about that.'

'It's fine,' says Bobby. 'Ah haven't exactly made it easy for him, y'know?'

'Still,' says Laurie, before wheezing. 'He didn't understand the background.'

'*Que sera*, Laurie,' says Bobby. 'Ah've no' done badly out ae knowing ye.'

They sit quietly for ten minutes or so.

'Just promise me you won't fall back into the old ways … the gambling and the drugs,' she says at last.

'Don't worry. Ah know how lucky ah wis tae get out. It took a while but ah'm fucked if ah go back down that road, ah know that.'

'Good,' she says, patting his arm.

The crisp air is biting into Bobby's hands as he sits on the stone bench at the edge of the garden. Laurie is wrapped up tightly, like a tiny baby, and her wheelchair is transporting her and the oxygen tanks that are assisting her breathing. She won't be able to be outside for long, she has warned him, as the lucid breaks away from the morphine are getting shorter with every passing day.

'So Bobby, what are your plans?'

'Eh, no' totally sure. But when ah go back there's some paperwork tae sort out. Tax and registration an' stuff like that. Folks are bloody mental about tax avoiders in Scotland just now. Aw those Glasgow Rangers bastards, they've fuckin' spoiled it for the rest ae us genuine tax exiles.' He's joking, and she smiles even though she's been away from football too long and the downfall of the Glasgow giants means little.

'Do you have money saved?'

She knows of the debris of his gambling problems, and he understands this is what she is really asking about.

'Ah'm straight for five years, Laurie,' he says 'an' for one reason or another, me and Hammy have been livin' like bloody monks up there. Frugal disnae even cover it.'

'So?'

'So, aye … we're aw'right. This memorial thing for my brother might take a bit ae financial plannin', but we should have enough.'

Laurie reaches inside her shawl, and a frail, white, gloved hand emerges with an envelope. She passes it to him.

'Whit's this?' he says 'A bill?' He's only half joking.

'Open it,' she whispers.

He does. He reads down the length of the papers. 'Laurie … ah, don't … what does this actually mean?' he stammers. He thinks he knows but it seems too unbelievable to be true.

'I'm leaving you the villa, Bobby,' she says. 'You've been someone I've always been close to. You always made me laugh, even when you didn't mean to. This is a small token of my appreciation for the good times we shared.'

Bobby is in tears. 'Jesus fuck, Laurie … it's a five-million-pound house! It's hardly a small token.'

'There's no pockets in shrouds, Bobby,' she says.

'Christ … ah don't know whit tae say,' says Bobby.

'Don't say anything. Just remember me fondly,' she says. Bobby leans over and hugs her, kissing her cheek at the same time. How could he ever forget her?

Chapter Twenty-Six

January 2015. Troon, Scotland

'How are ye?' Bobby Cassidy stands as he says this. He feels nervous, tension rising from the middle of his back. It reaches his shoulders and grips them tightly, like a grapple hold from Giant Haystacks. Hammy has informed him that Lizzie knows he's back and is desperate to see him. He put off calling her for the first couple of weeks but then thought it would be interesting to catch up. Now, though, with her in front of him again, a mild panic has set in.

'Ah'm actually good, Bobby,' says Lizzie King, in a way that suggests she has imagined he expected her not to be.

'Ah, that's good,' says Bobby.

'An' what can I get you both?' asks the attentive young waitress.

Bobby does a double-take. It astonishes him how much this young woman looks like Lizzie when she was a similar age, more than thirty years ago. He thinks Lizzie has noticed this too. They order breakfast. After the waitress wipes their table and leaves, they say nothing for a few minutes. It's a breathtakingly beautiful morning: freezing cold, as befits the season, but the low angle of the sun is giving a strange, liquid, painterly quality to the evaporating mist that rests over the boats moored in Troon harbour. The view is magnetic, and Bobby and Lizzie seem unable to converse properly with such a serene backdrop.

'Bloody lovely, down here, eh?' he says.

'Aye, it is,' says Lizzie. 'It might only be ten miles up the road, but the air seems cleaner here than in Kilmarnock.'

'It would make ye think about buyin' a boat,' he says.

'Aye ... an' sailin' it away intae the sunset, never lookin' back,' she says, laughing.

'Ye haven't changed, Lizzie,' says Bobby. He means it, and thinks

now that, actually, Lizzie looks not much older than the young waitress, who has just returned with their cutlery.

'Aye, a bit wiser maybe,' Lizzie says. 'An' the roots take longer an'
longer tae hide.'

Bobby laughs. 'Aye, mine tae,' he says, running a painful hand
through his thinning strands.

'It's good tae see ye, Bobby, especially after aw that crap wi' the
papers. Ah wasn't convinced ah'd ever get the chance. Ah'm really,
really sorry about that.'

'Ah know ye are,' says Bobby. 'That's no' why ah got in touch.'
He instinctively pats her forearm. It doesn't feel awkward. 'Look, it
wis donkey's years ago. It's a bloody tidal wave that's gone under too
many bridges, Lizzie. Ah treated ye badly when ye … when *we* lost
the baby. Too self-centred an' insensitive. Ah wish ah could get aw
that time back an' dae loads ae things differently. That's really why
ah'm back. Ah want tae save my life while ah still care about it. It's
just … we left it aw on such bad terms an' ah'm sure a lot ae that
was ma fault.'

'Thanks,' says Lizzie to the waitress, who has just brought their
breakfast.

'So are ye back for good?' Lizzie asks. Bobby's mind immediately
jumps to a punchline about Gary Barlow and unpaid taxes, but it's
perhaps not the time.

'Aye,' he says instead. 'We're puttin' on a big memorial thing for
Gary.'

Lizzie looks up. 'Christ, ah'm sorry, Bobby, ah didnae ken he had
died.' She leans over and touches his hands. They have become tactile
much earlier than both would have imagined. 'When was it?'

'Eh, November … 2008.' He sees her reaction. 'Aye, ah know.
It's taken a while tae get tae it. Ah wis in a bit are a bad way, like.
For years. Depressed, an' that. Addiction issues. Everybody looks
at ye like yer jacket's on back tae front when ye hint at goin' doo-
lally while yer livin' somewhere like Ibiza. But ah was. Reminded
ae illness an' fadin' health everywhere.' He holds his arthritic hands

out and stares wistfully at them. 'Ibiza's a tough place tae get auld in, y'know?'

She nods, but she doesn't know.

'Ye become sort ae invisible tae the young,' he says. 'It's like they dinnae want tae confront the reality that you are what they are gonnae become.'

'Can't blame them for that, Bobby. Remember whit we were like,' she says. 'So what changed?'

'Joey showed up.'

Lizzie smiles knowingly at this.

'What?' says Bobby.

'The real love ae yer life, eh?' She laughs and he does too. 'When we were together in Spain, near the end, ah kent ah couldnae compete. An' it wisnae wi' Hammy; it wis wi' the ghost ae Joey Miller.' She says this without rancour; almost pleased for him that, by his own admission, his life seems back on some form of track.

'So what about you, then? Ye must still be beatin' them off wi' a big stick.' He'd watched her arrive, fashionably late, and walk across the Scott's Restaurant car park, her arse still as impressive as it was the first time he saw it walk away from him at the Sandrianne, on her eighteenth birthday. She was always a lovely-looking woman. Although he knew it made him seem shallow, this fact had helped him assuage any vengeful feelings he had when she 'betrayed' him back in the mid-90s. Strange, how attractiveness can help sway someone's thinking.

'Nope,' she says. 'Ah'm an independent woman, always have been.'

Her conviction, however, masks a sadness – one that many single people of her age work hard to conceal. Bobby Cassidy himself practises that very same public bravado. Hammy dutifully passed on the information that Lizzie is generally fine and now living in Troon, from where she runs her own cleaning business. She was quick to point this out to Hammy, for fear that he might hint to Bobby that this meeting was about money. She's made that mistake before. It won't happen again.

'What about … em … Javier?' Bobby genuinely struggles to recall the name which was central to their break-up.

'Christ Almighty,' says Lizzie. 'The minute he kent about Robert he was off. Bullets have left guns slower.'

Bobby apologises.

'No' your fault,' she says. '*Que sera.*'

'So how is he? – Robert, ah mean.' Bobby quickly does the maths. 'He must be, what, nearly thirty, eh?'

Lizzie turns her head away.

'He's dead, Bobby.'

This strikes Bobby Cassidy like a baseball bat to the legs. He temporarily thinks he has misheard her. He coughs. He hasn't misheard. She is wiping away a tear.

'Jesus, Bobby … sorry. Ah wis determined ah wisnae gonnae cry when ah seen ye. Noo look what ye've made me dae. Is my mascara runnin'?' She affects a playfully scolding tone.

But he remains too shocked to respond. This isn't the conciliatory chat over morning coffee he had envisaged. Only half an hour in and both have shared news of tragic personal loss.

'When he was wee, he started gettin' sick regularly,' she says, more serious now. 'Loads ae coughin', an' pickin' up daft illnesses that he couldnae shake off. So ah took him tae see aw these different doctors, an' then specialists. They eventually determined that he had a rare form ae leukaemia. He was only about eight at the time.' Lizzie stops. Her young doppelgänger is clearing the table. She leaves for the kitchen with their plates. 'My dad an' Anne did what they could, but *he* wisnae well either. Ah was workin' double shifts just tae keep afloat, an' then the service got privatised an' all ae a sudden … nae job. The treatment wisnae really workin' an' this doctor suggests we should maybe go private … he recommends a specialist clinic in Switzerland. Ah'm firstly thinkin' that this daft bastard in the white coat obviously thinks ah've got the same background as his.' Lizzie pauses, takes a drink of water and a few deep breaths. 'But deep down, ah knew he wis right. It was the only chance we had. Ah'll no' hear a bad word against the NHS, they were great, but the waitin' times for treatment back then, y'know? Then you had the big hit record. Aw these newspaper guys are swarmin' around Killie, lookin' for dirt on the two ae ye'se.' She turns to look at him. Her face is strained.

He now knows that this moment is why she called him, to hope-fully meet with him; to explain. It will be a necessary catharsis for her.

'This grubby tosser fae London offers me a few grand tae say you were Robert's dad. He said it didnae even matter if it was true … if you ignored it an' said nothin' the story would be verified. If ye denied it, folk would probably believe it aw the more.'

Bobby feels instantly sorry for her and terrible that she had been painted into such a difficult emotional corner.

'Ah was desperate, Bobby. Ye'd do anythin' for yer wean if they're sick. Nowadays, ah'd start a social-media campaign, run a marathon, but back then gettin' cash off the papers seemed like ma only option. My only hope was that ye'd understand, if ah ever got the chance to tell ye in person. Ah'm really sorry Bobby, ye didnae deserve any ae the pain that ah put ye through.'

In truth, there was little pain. Short of the double-barrelled ire he caught from Hettic at the time, his self-imposed exile from the UK meant that any local opprobrium passed him by. The additional fact that he was out of his head for most of the 90s only made this whole situation feel like it had happened to someone else. It was reminiscent of watching an old television show or a film – one whose plot he couldn't quite remember, but if he watched it now, he'd recall. It was his turn to take her hand.

'Fuck Lizzie, ah'm so sorry. Losing the wean at that age … Jesus Christ! Ah wish ye had just asked me for the money, though. Better it goin' tae some positive use than gettin' tipped away in fuckin' slot machines or roulette wheels.'

'But he didnae die, then,' says Lizzie. 'He recovered.'

Bobby's eyebrows rise.

'Took about two bloody years, but gradually the cancer was in remission. He went on tae university. Studied tae be a lawyer in Edinburgh.' Lizzie smiled briefly, her pride instantly obvious. 'An' then he's out celebratin' finishin' his finals. May 2011. There's a local Hibs an' Hearts fitba match. Two groups ae drunk fans spillin' into the same wee pub in the Grassmarket. A big fight breaks out, an' in the midst ae it, Robert gets stabbed. He died in the Royal later that night. After everythin' he'd been through, everythin' he'd beaten … he's gone because ae some daft wee yobs an' their tribal rubbish – 'cos he intervened in somebody else's argument. He was tryin' to stop these three big lads batterin' a wee yin. Why could he no' just have left them tae it, eh?'

Bobby stares at her. He knows she has gone over this in her mind thousands of times, trying to find a new way to explain it. But she can't. That most painful and crushing of rhetorical questions: why?

He doesn't know what to say. Scott's upper floor conservatory overlooking Troon marina is empty. They are alone. It's a quiet time for the restaurant, deep in the winter season. Bobby moves his seat around to be next to Lizzie. He puts his arm around her and pulls her close. He kisses her forehead. There are no words.

'This is me,' she says.

'Nice,' says Bobby. He looks up at the three-storey block.

'I'm at the top,' she says. 'The view's good.'

Bobby turns away from the block and examines the panorama from ground level. They have been walking slowly along the promenade so he hasn't paid it much notice, but yes, from twelve metres up, a view out towards Arran and Ailsa Craig must been lovely.

'Want a cup of tea?' says Lizzie.

Bobby checks his watch. 'Aye, time for a quickie,' he says, and she laughs at his unintentional double entendre.

He has a bus to catch and another meeting to go to, but Lizzie makes him feel far more relaxed and comfortable than he would ever have thought possible. They have a nice time together. Once past the mutual mourning and painful memories, as they remember happier ones, they laugh and giggle like the teenagers they once were. A couple of daft kids; wide-eyed and legless as they discovered a world way beyond their parochial upbringing. Too much too young though. Just *way* too much.

Her flat is, unsurprisingly, adorned with photographs of her son. Bobby can track a life from these images: school, hospital, clinics, holidays, football teams, part-time jobs, university.

'Good-lookin' boy,' he says.

'Aye, his dad might've been a total fuckin' arsehole but his cheek-bones were definitely in the right place.'

She heads through to the small kitchen. Bobby wanders over to the window in the front room. He stares at the Ailsa Craig, perfectly framed by the Heads of Ayr to the left and Arran to the right. The water is flat calm. It's unseasonably peaceful. She comes back and hands him a cup.

'Cheers,' he says. 'Gary loved lookin' at that big lump ae rock. He'd have thought this flat was great.'

'How did he die?' she asks.

'He was run over by a bus,' says Bobby, matter-of-factly. 'A total accident. Naebody's fault. Ah didnae see it like that at the time, mind you. Ah was desperate to find somebody tae blame. But there was nothin'. He staggered out ae a wee shop, blinded by lights and noise, across the pavement an' intae the path ae a double-decker. Shopkeeper said he just freaked out when the fire alarm went off.'

'God, that's awful,' says Lizzie.

'He wis gettin' treatment for his depression and trauma at the time. Makin' good progress as well.'

'Aw that's just terrible, Bobby.'

'Aye. Ye'll know the worst thing about no' gettin' tae say cheerio, eh?'

She nods sadly at this.

'Ah hadn't spoken tae him in years. Stupid family shite, an' my complete an' utter selfishness,' he says. But there's an upbeat tone to this, like he's come to terms with it. 'So we're gonnae dae this right … me an' Joey. If anythin', he took Gary dyin' even harder than me at the time. Ah'd nae idea that they were even mates at the time, that's how fucked up ah wis.' Bobby doesn't want to talk about Gary's violent episodes, about his prison time and the incident that got him incarcerated there. There are some things his memorial planning doesn't need to acknowledge.

'So what's yer plans then?' Lizzie asks.

'Don't really know,' he replies. He stares into the distance, across the Firth of Clyde.

'Ye should do somethin' really memorable; somethin' big that would have made him proud,' she says.

'Aye,' he says, but he still stares, transfixed.

The doorbell rings, breaking the spell.

'Look, ah should go,' he says. 'It wis good tae see ye again, Lizzie. Can ah see ye again, sometime?'

'Let's see, eh,' she says. 'Couldnae take too many emotional breakfasts like that yin every week!' She smiles.

'Aye, a bit intense, eh? We should just take it slow … be a bit like the Nescafe Gold Blend couple.' He heads to the door, shimmying past a plumber who has arrived to fix Lizzie's temperamental boiler.

Bobby says goodbye and kisses her on either cheek; he's a continental, she remembers. He emerges from the shared-entry front door. Ailsa Craig is right in front of him. It seems closer than it did from the third floor. An optical illusion, no doubt, but it reinforces a new idea that flashed into his head just as Lizzie spoke to him. He fishes his mobile out of his inside jacket pocket. He punches a speed-dial number.

'Joey? Aye, it's me. We need tae meet. Ah've got it … the big idea, ah mean!'

Bobby makes another call; a very overdue one. It's to his sister Hettie. It isn't a long conversation. Despite the more intense emotional history with Lizzie, Bobby found it easier to converse openly with her than with the youngest member of his immediate family. He puts this down to the inescapable notion that he wronged Hettie. His guilt over this has had him believe that she has never forgiven him. But now he needs her to. And, over the course of the ten-minute phone call – the first time they have spoken in years – she does just that. It is the catalyst they need to move on and start repairing their fractured relationship.

Like many things in his life, he can't fathom why he didn't reach this cathartic point sooner.

Chapter Twenty-Seven

February 2015. Crosshouse, Scotland

Max Mojo wanders around the church hall of the Manse in Crosshouse, where he grew up and where The Miraculous Vespas were born. When he looks up at the ceiling, as he does often, he puts his monocle in.

'Dae you actually need that daft fuckin' piece ae glass, or is it a Chris Eubank thing?' says Bobby Cassidy.

Max ignores him.

'Whit the hell are ye lookin' at, Max? Ah cannae see anythin' up there.'

'The future, Bobcat ... ah'm lookin' at the future.' Max has a look. It's one that many past associates took cover from. It usually meant trouble of some description. 'Ah'm gonnae turn this place intae a museum, man.'

'A museum? Are they no' aw aboot the past?'

But Max isn't listening. 'A museum celebratin' the greatest an' most influential rock an' roll band there's ever been.'

'Whit ... the Goombay Dance Band?' jokes Bobby.

Again, this floats way past Max Mojo. He's in the zone and outwith the reach of west of Scotland bampottery. 'When's that cunt Joey turnin' up?' he barks,

'He's just comin',' says Bobby. 'Ah've also got a meetin' wi' him about this gig we're thinkin' about, so he better be here soon.'

'Gig? Whit gig? Who's playin'?' Max is suddenly interested.

'Ach just a wee thing tae honour ma brother, Gary. We're gettin' the Heatwave Disco Show back th'gither,' says Bobby proudly. 'Maybe in a wee school hall on Arran or our auld school in Killie, just for a laugh, ken?'

'Fifty-one-year-old DJs in a tiny school dinner hall that's aulder than them?' says Max dismissively. 'An' on a bloody island, tae! Aye, fuckin' sign me up for that yin! Hope *Emmerdale*'s no' on at the same bastard time.'

'Fuck off, ya sarcastic prick,' says Bobby.

'Where's yer ambition? Dae a "gig", aye … but for fuck's sake dae it right. Yer brother'll be up there in heaven tellin' aw his deid mates "Look at whit ma wee bro's gonnae dae for me",' says Max theatrically. 'He's gie'n it "Wembley Stadium this, an' the Hollywood Bowl that", an' then you go an' book the hall at the Arran YMCA? Ye'll make the poor cunt a fuckin' laughin' stock up there! He'll never be able tae walk doon the Paradise Promenade wi' Hendrix an' Cobain again.'

Bobby laughs. There is something in Max's bizarre analogy. The original idea that emerged as he left Lizzie King's Troon home was to do something on an island. He and Joey Miller spent hours talking about the words Gary had written and why they had meant so much to him. But Bobby had tempered that initial dream, fearing that Joey – Mr Pragmatism – would ridicule him for it, or worse, accuse him of not taking the whole thing seriously. So he took the easy route; the low-budget, low-risk venture. Max Mojo was madder than a box of frogs on LSD, but at least he pursued his ventures with commitment and conviction. Perhaps there was something to be learned from that.

'Aye, finally,' says Max, looking up. 'It's ma high-priced design consultant.'

'High-priced, eh?' says Joseph Miller. He has worn a suit to reinforce his professionalism. 'That mean ah'm gettin' paid then?'

'In kind, brother Joey, in kind,' says Max, extending a raised hand, high five-style, which Joseph takes awkwardly.

Joseph spots the two Laphroaig bottles: one empty, one heading that way. 'Ye can keep yer blowjobs, Max. Ah'm by wi' aw that now.'

'How ye been, Joey? Whisky?'

'Aye, fair tae pish, generally speaking. You?'

'No bad, buddy. The fuckin' film's dain' well an' there's clamour for the band tae, like. Me … ah'm restin' up ower in the South ae France. Life's fuckin' magic.'

Bobby Cassidy observes this exchange from the edge of the low, wooden stage at one end of the hall, but his mind is elsewhere, preoccupied by other concerns.

Joseph Miller wasn't ever close to Max Mojo, or his earlier incarnation, Dale Wishart. But Joseph did once work for Max's father, Washer Wishart. While Bobby Cassidy and Hamish May spent the mid-80s working in clubs overseas, the young Joey Miller was designing one for Max's father, in the very building they are all now standing in. As the extensive fallout from Operation Double Nougat diminished, the infamous Glasgow ice-cream gang wars – which almost swallowed this small Ayrshire community, and certainly derailed The Miraculous Vespas' career – forced change. Washer planned to convert the church hall into a nightclub. Legitimate business was the aim, and it was also a principal part of the post-trial conditions of the family's involvement in the Malachy McLarty sting. Washer's lieutenant, Gerry Ghee, knew that a local kid, Joey Miller, was studying architecture. The student was approached with an offer-he-couldn't-refuse-style deal and appointed to design a new club. For three years, his outrageously expensive creation was lauded. It was named The Biscuit Tin after the record label Max had started from his bedroom. It had a sparse, industrial-style aesthetic, and, as the second summer of love fizzled out in a late-80s dilated, smiley-faced haze, the club became a focus for thrill-seeking kids from all over the west of Scotland. However, as its reputation grew, based on innovative music and edgy, provocative DJs, so too did its attraction to both the local police and assorted drug squads. In 1990, raid after raid eventually forced its closure. Nevertheless, The Biscuit Tin retains a legendary status that persists to the present day. Max Mojo, who held onto the building after his father died in 2007 and his mum moved to be with him in the South of France, is back and looking to invest in a new business.

'So, what's the script then?' asks Joseph.

'Ah'm lookin' at a museum … but one wi' a stage an' a bit tae get some fuckin' food, an' maybe a couple ae guest bedrooms an' a massive fuckin' jukebox an' memorabilia … oh, an' a big cunt ae a film screen showin' cult movies tae.'

Max Mojo is pointing at various parts of the hall as he rhymes off the component parts of the brief. It's clear to Bobby and Joseph that he already sees it all in his head. Even in the wake of suspect financial viability, such a vision is addictive and inspiring. And Joseph thinks he may well have something. Bobby, though is lost in his own daydreams. His eyes are growing wider. Joseph Miller is, therefore, a practical anchor between two drifting dreamers. It is a position he knows well.

'So, whit dae ye'se fuckin' think boys?' says Max.

'Ah think we're gonnae dae the Heatwave Disco gig on the Ailsa Craig,' proclaims Bobby Cassidy.

Joseph and Max turn sharply to look at him.

'Ye whit?' says Joseph.

'Now yer fuckin' talkin', ya cunt,' says Max, simultaneously.

'Aye … the gig for Gary, we'll dae it on the island. A Heatwave Disco rave on a remote desert island. It'll be fuckin' magic!' says Bobby.

'How much ae that stuff have you had, mate?' asks Joseph.

'S'a fuckin' brilliant idea … like somethin' Bill Drummond wid dae,' says Max.

'Who?' says Bobby.

'The dude fae the KLF. Used tae manage the Bunnymen tae, an' sent them oan that mental tour ae the Western Isles, 'member?' says Max.

'Aye,' says Joseph. 'Lost a fuckin' fortune. In fact, he burned a fuckin' fortune at the Brits, did he not?'

'Mental,' says Max, full of obvious admiration. 'But in a good way, like.'

'Ah dunno, Bobby,' says Joseph, pouring another whisky.

'Come on, man,' says Bobby. 'Let's fuckin' go for it.'

'How dae ye know this is whit he would've wanted?' says Joseph.

Max gets up and walks through into the main house, leaving the two other men on the stage. Darkness is descending outside, but not in Bobby Cassidy's heart.

'The words … his story, it's aw there, man. It wis you that showed me them!'

'But they last sentences … the ones about killin' somebody. That doesn't indicate happiness.'

'*The Man Who Loved Islands* … it's right there in the title. *He's* the *man*. It's him! We've got tae dae it there!' says Bobby.

There's a pause as both think about the premise: Bobby Cassidy, on the possibilities, Joseph Miller on the complex logistics.

'No' sure, man' says Joseph.

'Only one way tae find oot!' says Max. He has returned with a box under his arm. 'Ouija board … let's ask the cunt!'

Despite Joseph's scepticism, they set up the board; three men in their fifties in various stages of spirited drunkenness.

'You believe in ghosts, then?' Joseph asks Bobby as they watch an energetic Max create the right conditions for some of them to visit.

'Naw. The closest I've come to seeing a ghost is watching Hammy trying to put on a white duvet cover.'

Joseph says, 'Maybe we should just go an' ask Fat Franny Duncan. That auld cunt knows more about dead folk than a bag ae maggots.'

'Fuckin' hell, is he still livin'?'

'Dunno. Let's ask Mystic Max here tae check.'

Max has lit candles and brought down his old record player and a few boxes of records – one of the principle attractions in the planned, new Miraculous Vespas / Biscuit Tin Records Museum.

'It's like a fuckin' Madonna video in here,' laughs Joseph.

'…But without the virgins or the Jesus yin!' observes Bobby.

'Ah'm like the Jesus yin,' says Max. 'An' naebody fucks wi' the Jesus. In fact, when aw this is by, ah'm gonnae be bigger than that cunt!'

'Aye, aw right Lennon, haud yer pish in, eh?' says Joseph. Max puts the needle to the record.

'Whit's this?' asks Bobby, of the elegiac, ethereal music coming out of the record player's speaker.

'Cocteau Twins,' says Joseph before Max can.

'Every cunt kens that Liz Fraser's voice is the first thing ye hear when ye get tae heaven. Ah'm just tryin' tae make yer brother feel at hame.'

Max seems convinced of this course of action. Bobby and Joseph are simply indulging the former Miraculous Vespas svengali. He's clearly bonkers, but entertainingly so.

Elizabeth Fraser's celestial vocals fill the church hall. Max has put on the *Treasure* LP. It might be the whisky, but Bobby is starting to feel a spiritual vibe.

'Right, get 'roon the table,' Max commands. He has set up a small tressle table right in the middle of the hall.

A beautiful acoustic guitar line gives way to Liz singing impenetrable and indecipherable lyrics in praise of Ivo Watts-Russell, the 4AD record label boss. One of these days, Grant Delgado will sing similarly in praise of Max, he's sure. The whisky bottles now number three. The board is wooden and rectangular in shape. It has black letters of the alphabet in a soft curve, and the words 'Yes', 'No', 'Good' and 'Bye' around them. Max uses a guitar plectrum as the planchette. *Nice touch*, thinks Bobby. Max reaches into his pocket and brings out a bottle. It looks like it's for perfume. Bobby and Joseph glance quickly at each other before Max suddenly sprays both of them in the face.

'Fuck sake, Max!' shouts Joseph.

'Aye, whit's the Hampden?' Bobby yells.

'Holy water!' says Max. 'Calm doon, for fuck's sake. Ye'se never done this before? Ye cannae summons the spirits without protection!'

'Think you've summoned too many spirits aw'ready, ya daft bastard!' says Joseph looking at yet another empty glass at Max's wrist.

Max has turned the music down but its otherwordly ambience is still detectable.

Max begins: 'If there's any evil or harmful spirits here wi' us, get oot now an' never return,' says Max, as serious as either Bobby or Joseph has ever heard him before.

Joseph sniggers.

Max digs his nails into Joseph's palm. 'You are no' welcome … ye've never been welcome … an' will never *be* welcome here!'

Joseph thinks Max is speaking to him until he realises he isn't.

'Now … if there's any good spirits in here, especially yins called Gary … if ye want tae talk tae us, we're here, an' we're aw ears!'

'What if we get Gary Glitter?' whispers Bobby. 'Ah dinnae want tae talk tae that dirty bastard. Should ye no' have been more specific?'

'Shut the fuck up, there's somebody about!' whispers Max.

'Gary Glitter isnae fuckin' deid anyway,' says Joseph.

'Ach, ye know what ah mean,' says Bobby.

'Gie it a fuckin' rest, eh? The spirits are assemblin',' whispers Max.

Suddenly the planchette moves. All three have their hands on it. Joseph is convinced Max is moving it. Bobby isn't so sure.

'Is there anybody there?' asks Max. The plectrum seems to be vibrating. The door to Max's spirit world seems to be opening. The plectrum with fingers from the three men touching it moves to 'Yes'. Joseph remains sceptical. Bobby is mesmerised.

'Do ye ken anybody here?' asks Max.

The plectrum moves closer to 'No' before swiftly and smoothly gliding back to 'Yes'.

'Are you happy, spirit?' asks Max.

The plectrum moves to 'No', and stays there.

Max looks worried.

'Maybe we've got the cunt up out ae his bed,' says Joseph. 'Maybe he was oan the night shift!'

The plectrum moves sharply to 'Good Bye'.

'Fuck sake, man. Ye've upset that yin. Ye need tae fuckin' take this seriously or else there's nae point.'

Joseph reluctantly accepts this rebuke from Max Mojo. It is approaching midnight and they'll now need to stay the night in the Manse. It would be counterproductive to provoke a fight. More whisky is poured. Varying the theme, but only slightly, This Mortal Coil's LP is now playing. They begin again.

After the preliminaries, a new spirit is asked: 'Are you Gary ... of the Ayrshire Cassidys?' Max has asked this in a way that makes the Ayrshire Cassidys sound like a family dynasty from *Game of Thrones* rather than McPhail Drive. But Joseph manages to stifle the laughter.

'Yes' indicates the plectrum.

Joseph can detect Bobby's deeper breathing.

'Do you know anybody here?' asks Max. Slowly, but again surprisingly smoothly, the plectrum spells out the words 'B-O-B-B-Y' and 'J-O-E-Y'.

'Do ye have a message for us, Gary?' asks Bobby, his voice trembling slightly. Max looks at him sharply as if he has spoken out of turn.

Bobby looks back and shrugs his shoulders.

The plectrum says 'Yes'.

'We want tae dae a memorial in yer honour, Gary ... somethin' ye would be proud ae, an' ah've had this idea tae hold it oan the Ails—'

'Haw,' Max interrupts. 'Too much, man! Short questions or the spirits cannae answer them,' he scolds.

'How no'?' asks Joseph.

'Fuck should ah ken!' says Max. 'Ah just ken. Somethin' tae dae wi' the narrowness ae the communication lines,' says Max.

'Nae superfast broadband in heaven then?' Joseph jokes. Max glowers at him.

'Spirit, are ye still there?' asks Max.

'Yes', indicates the plectrum.

'School Hall or Island?' asks Max, cutting to the chase.

Joseph wonders if the spirit has been fully aware of the context of the question, but says nothing.

The plectrum spells out 'I-S-L-A-N-D'. They all glance at each other as if a breakthrough has just been made.

'Do you want a memorial on the Ailsa Craig?' asks Max with the formality of a High Court Judge.

A wind whistles through the cracks. The candles blow out. And an almighty thudding bang is heard outside the church hall.

'Jesus Christ, man!' says Joseph. 'Nearly had a fuckin' heart attack there.'

They remove their fingers from the plectrum with it yet to respond and get up to investigate the source of the noise. Max opens the church doors. Across the road and beyond the church's high boundary wall, a white van has crashed headlong into a concrete lamp standard. From their elevated position, they observe that the driver seems dazed but unhurt. The front of the van is crumpled and steam is rising relentlessly in the cold winter air.

'Look,' says Max pointing at the van. 'There's yer answer.'

The van carries an advertisement for a local optician. The words 'Eye – Right' are as conclusive an affirmation to a sozzled Bobby Cassidy as the will written bequeathing him a multi-million-pound villa in Ibiza, the sale of which would now fund this magnificent folly.

'Meant tae say tae ye'se … fancy comin' tae London wi' us next week? Ah've got tickets tae the BAFTAs.'

The casualness with which Max Mojo makes the offer is typical of him. They are clearing up after the impromptu séance and he just came out with it.

'*The Rise and Fall* film's up for Best Documentary an' ah've got the guest tickets, but the band dinnae want them!'

Bobby and Joseph stare at each other in astonishment. A national televised awards event in which he might well win a significant award and Max Mojo has just asked two interlopers to accompany him with less than a week to go.

'Too fuckin' right,' says Bobby Cassidy.

Chapter Twenty-Eight

February 2015. London, England

'This is brilliant, eh?' says Bobby.

'Aye, it is mate.' Joseph agrees, and he means it.

They are sharing in the Dorchester Hotel, but the room they are in is truly enormous. And there's another one only marginally smaller through the door. When Max gave them the details it sounded like they would be sharing a double bed in a shoebox-sized room in somewhere remote, like Barking, being forced to traverse into the centre by cramped tube while dressed in dinner suits. Their accommodation was advertised as a 'double' room but it is in fact a suite, and a sizeable one at that. They haven't seen Max since the night of the séance. He is in the same hotel but he is on a separate floor, booked by the film company who made the documentary. They are conducting press and media interviews in the expectation that their film documenting the travails of a legendary but dysfunctional Scottish indie band and their driven but delusional manager will actually win the Best Documentary Award.

As they flew down the night before, scribbled notes and a strange drawing materialised amidst the British Airways snacks and copious gin and tonics. These described an idea that a week ago seemed derisible. Now though, with funds from the sale of the Ibizan villa back to Laurie Revlon's son Laurence propping it up, it appears not only possible but likely.

There is much to consider, the list not limited to: How do you get various pieces of disco equipment over to a remote island with little in the way of a jetty and with no services or general infrastructure? Having tackled that, how do you then get the people who buy tickets for the event there and back? If there's nowhere for them to stay overnight, will the whole thing need to be conducted during daylight hours?

There are so many imponderables and there does seem to be a certain slapstick lunacy to it all. But nonetheless, the venture has galvanised the pair and nothing is now going to stop them attempting to deliver a Heatwave Disco reunion on Ailsa Craig for a bunch of their old friends and colleagues, in honour of Gary Cassidy: The Man Who Loved Islands.

They approach the room. Both are wearing black dinner suits, with cummerbunds and black bow ties. They scrub up well, and whilst Daniel Craig need not worry about his franchise gig being threatened, Joseph still feels they look a bit too conventional, especially when he tries to imagine how Max will be dressed. They have passed three levels of security, from the initial 'girl with clipboard' at the lift lobby, right up to 'Head of PR' for the film company: a stern no-nonsense woman named Marge. She makes them show their passes to three different people before she allows them to progress further down the hall. They reach the open door. Max Mojo is lounging on a large purple sofa. He is dressed in a wildly colourful smoking jacket. He has a fur-lined fez on his head and black leather trousers around his legs. Numerous lights are focused on him. Black Raybans make the task of focusing easier for him. A chair faces him and, as they peer in to the room, acknowledging Max's wave, they see a serious-looking man with an unusual hairline sit down in the chair.

'Is it aw'right if ma associates sit in, man?' asks Max of the man.

'Yes, no problem,' replies the man, but in a way that implies that he feels it's an imposition.

Max waves Bobby and Joseph in and ushers them towards a side room out of the line of the camera. As they watch transfixed, Bobby and Joseph understand that this is a piece for a BBC Arts programme. The journalist, a remarkable-looking man with longish hair flowing down from a balding pate introduces himself as Will Gompertz. At the beginning of the recording he asks Max Mojo a whole series of searching questions about The Miraculous Vespas. Max responds calmly to all of them, apart from a spiky one, to which he responds by pondering on the irony of a bald man splitting hairs. Will Gompertz takes this in good part, and by and large; Max is on his best behaviour.

Bobby knows most of this incredible story, having taken part in – and watched – the completed film. But much of their extraordinary rise and fall is news to Joseph Miller. He was aware of the band's tumultuous rise and the incredible success of their one recorded hit single, 'It's a Miracle', but he has no real idea about the criminal back story, and he hasn't appreciated the depth of the legacy of the band's only recorded LP. He therefore finds the interview fascinating, particularly as it opens up a side of Max Mojo he hasn't previously realised existed. Max sounds reflective, reasoned and rational. He laments the break-up of relations within the band and regrets the various subsequent legal actions taken in terms of royalties.

'So, Max Mojo, given the likelihood of a success at the BAFTAs tonight, and the likely clamour for the band to reform, what does the future hold for The Miraculous Vespas?'

Max scratches his chin and leans forward to look straight down the camera lens, just over Will Gompertz's left shoulder.

'The band are reforming,' he announces, to the surprise of everyone in the room. 'We're doin' a special one-off gig later in the year,' he says.

'Glastonbury? T in the Park?' asks a surprised Gompertz. He thinks he's hit on a major arts exclusive.

'Naw,' says Max. He looks up at Bobby.

Joseph knows what's coming but Bobby hasn't got there quickly enough.

'It's called The Big Bang an' it's bein' held on the Ailsa Craig.'

Bobby laughs, thinking it's a joke.

'Fuck sake, Max!' says Joseph.

'Can we edit that?' Gompertz asks a colleague, before wrapping up the interview.

'These are the promoters,' announces Max, proudly.

Will Gompertz simply nods, and then a lightbulb goes on over his shiny dome.

'Max, gentlemen, can we secure the first interview with the band?' he asks.

'We'll see, pal,' says Max. 'Loads ae competiton for that exclusive. Big money deals, ken?'

'We'll definitely be in touch, Max,' says Will Gompertz, packing up his gear. 'And good luck for tonight, guys. I hear it's a bit of a certainty.'

He stands, shakes hands with everyone in the room and then leaves. His sound and cameraman remain, dismantling their own equipment. Max ushers Bobby and Joseph through to an adjacent bedroom; a room the size of the penalty box on a football pitch.

'What the fuck wis that?' asks Joseph angrily.

'Whit?' pleads Max.

'What actually just happened there?' asks a stunned Bobby Cassidy.

'This devious cunt has just nicked oor idea!' says Joseph.

'Whit? Have ah fuck!' says Max. 'It's the same fuckin' idea, man.' He sees the glazed look that remains on Bobby's face. 'Look, nae disrespect, but who the fuck's gonnae pay tae be imprisoned on a tiny island aw day just tae see you two geriatric clowns playin' Shakatak records?'

Bobby and Joseph don't speak but both know Max has zeroed in on a major flaw in the plan.

'Ye need fuckin' headliners, Bobby,' says Max. 'Ye need profile. It's a fuckin' event, but yer approachin' it like it's just a dream tae score affa some cunt's bucket list.'

'Aw that might be so, Max,' says Joseph, 'but it wasn't your fuckin' prerogative tae reveal it tae the media before ye'd even spoken tae us!'

'Look, opportunity knocked, Joey. That's how it fuckin' works some times. A door opened an' ah dived through it. Ah figured you two would be fine wi' it. A much bigger problem's gonnae be the band. They cunts aren't even speakin' tae one another.'

'Whit?' screams Joseph. 'Ye huvnae discussed it wi' the band?'

'No' exactly,' says Max.

'What dae ye mean "exactly"?' asks Bobby.

'Well, ah meant "at all",' Max admits.

'Holy fuck,' says Bobby. He sits down and puts his head in his hands.

'Look, we're gonnae win this stupid fuckin' award th'night. Then the offers tae reform'll be floodin' in.'

'Disnae mean that they'll aw say aye though, does it? No' every cunt's driven by money,' says an exasperated Joseph.

'That's pish!' says Max.

'The Smiths? Oasis? The fuckin' Jam?' says Joseph. 'If they don't fuckin' speak tae each other, how are ye gonnae get them tae agree?'

'You leave that tae me,' says Max. 'You two need tae get on wi' organisin'. Get a date set. Get promotion material sorted. Get a Facebook account goin'. Sort oot support acts an' the stage an' everythin'. An' most important, get permission affa the cunts that own the fuckin' place.'

This last point jolts Bobby. He has simply assumed that an uninhabited island is freely available to anyone who wants to visit and occupy it.

Joseph feels foolish for not having considered this, even though it is only a matter of days since the idea has even materialised.

Max grabs Bobby and waltzes him around. '…So, take a chance on a couple ae *crooks*, hung up on *some dancin'*,' he croons.

Bobby and Joseph refuse the lines of cocaine Max has just cut for them. They feel high enough as it is. Max hoovers up all three. The septum separating his enlarged nostrils is as inconsequential as a tennis net, Joseph notices.

The rest of the evening passes by in a total blur for Bobby and Joseph. *The Rise and Fall of the Miraculous Vespas* film does indeed win the Best Documentary Award and both of them stagger blindly onto the stage, propelled by a febrile Max, and with four other film company executives. They shake hands with Stephen Fry, and kiss Olivia Coleman, who is presenting the award. Max naturally takes the prized mask statue, thanking everyone he's ever met, but especially his close friend, Bobby Cassidy – MC Bobcat – whose 1995 remix of the band's single lit the fuse of this renaissance. He finishes by dedicating the award to Clifford 'X-Ray' Raymonde, who passed away in 2008, and saying straight to camera: 'Grant ... ah love ya, man. See ye soon, buddy!'

In a loft apartment in downtown Portland, USA, a fifty-year-old man sits calmly at a typewriter in his study. It is mid-afternoon, and he has just returned from an Alcoholics Anonymous meeting. He is typing some notes for a new novel. It is about addiction but it isn't autobiographical. Later, he will be heading out for dinner with his son, Wolf, his daughter-in-law, Carrie and their six-year-old son, Aaron. The man's partner, Maggie, is on an assignment in South America and can't help the family celebrate. The man's acclaimed novel *The First Picture* has been acquired by the American actor Steve Buscemi, and, that very day, a film treatment has been fast-tracked by his production company. The man's name is Grant Dale, and he has no idea of the shitstorm of press interest that is about to descend.

Chapter Twenty-Nine

February 2015. Portland, Oregon, USA

He lives a disciplined life now, by necessity. Predictability has replaced spontaneity. His younger self would baulk at the boredom of his existence. But then his younger self would've driven him headlong into a concrete wall, like a crash-test dummy. Circumstances force change. Nowadays, his repetitive daily routine causes no abrasion. He gets up early. He makes breakfast: scrambled eggs on brown toast with coffee. He reads the newspapers; an activity in decline, he accepts, but he'll persevere with it. He writes for three hours. He goes to a gym and boxes – the heavy bag a metaphor for his demons, real and imagined. He goes to the cinema, alternating this with addiction meetings, as required. He returns and rereads and corrects his earlier writing. He cooks, often for just himself, or when she's home, for Maggie too. He watches television for an hour or so: sports, or heavyweight, literary dramas, such as *The Sopranos* or *Breaking Bad* or *Fargo*. He goes for a late walk around the neighbourhood. He goes to bed. It's a routine that is consistent regardless of weekday or weekend. Only events like a dinner out with his close family to celebrate a birthday – although never his own – interrupt this monastic schedule

His neighbours don't know about his history. He isn't especially close to any of them in any case, and those that care simply know him as Grant Dale. For all official purposes, including his publishing deal, he uses his original surname. Some have remarked on his astonishing likeness to Steve Jobs: the gauntness, the round-rimmed glasses, the thinning, greying hair and light stubble, and the predominance of black in his attire. But this isn't deliberate. Before it was mentioned to him, it hadn't dawned on him that he shared the ordinariness of his appearance with one of the most extraordinary people in history. All Grant wanted was simply to vanish.

Grant Dale was, once upon a time, Grant *Delgado* – the controversial singer and songwriter of The Miraculous Vespas, one of the most influential and mysterious rock and roll bands of the twentieth century. The bizarre and barely believable story of the band's rise and subsequent fall has been documented in a new film, scripted by their visionary but deceptive manager, Max Mojo. It is a truly astonishing tale of success and excess on the band's own independent terms in the early 80s, before their peripheral part in a major Scottish police crackdown on organised crime destroyed their future. Max Mojo has somehow turned this into legend, and when tapes of the band's only recorded LP surfaced in the mid-90s, far from being cast as irrelevant, one-hit wonders, The Miraculous Vespas were being hailed as the missing link between New Wave and Britpop. And for Grant Delgado and his fellow band members – Maggie Abernethy and the Sylvester brothers – that's where the problems really started.

The phone rings. It is such a rare occurrence that Grant has to think about where it is located. He tracks it down.

'Hullo?' he says tentatively.

'Hello, is that Grant Dale?' It's an unfamiliar voice with a pronounced New York accent.

'Eh … aye. It is. Who's this?'

'Sorry, for callin' you directly, Mr Dale. I hope you're having a great day,' says the voice. It pauses.

Grant is blindsided. Is he supposed to answer? It seemed rhetorical. They must be selling some shit that nobody wants. It'll be gauged as a successful call if the New York voice can keep him on the line for more than five seconds, he assumes. 'Eh, aye … it's alright,' he says. 'Look, ah'm actually workin'…'

'Yes, sorry Mr Dale. I'll get to the point. My name is Alexis. Alexis Amberson. I'm the head of Mr Buscemi's production company. We recently acquired the rights to your book *The First Picture*.' Again a pause, to let him absorb this.

'Ah, okay. Right,' he says.

'I contacted your agent, and explained our perspective, but perhaps she hasn't been in touch yet,' says Alexis.

'No, she hasn't,' says Grant. No surprise there though. Relations with his agent are fractious at best. Despite *The First Picture* being shortlisted for the Man Booker Prize in 2012, Grant refused to attend the prize-giving in London. He also avoided any of the promotional duties the exasperated agent suggested. Although the book was a modest commercial success for a small publishing house, selling around 12,000 copies in the European market alone, it achieved this on the strength of the writing, not as a result of the sparkling personality of its author.

'Well, we floated an interesting idea past Ms Burke. She seemed positive but pointed out that any decisions, especially about investment, would be yours alone.'

'Investment? What d'ye mean?' says Grant.

'We have a proposal about how to get the film fast-tracked and without it being diluted by the bigger studios to broaden its appeal,' says Alexis. 'Steve is keen to meet you to discuss the option of you becoming Executive Producer.'

'What does that involve, like?'

'Well, you'd have a far greater level of input into everything – the look, the casting, the story, the music etc – in return for—'

'How much?' he says abruptly.

'Steve would like to meet you for lunch to talk through the options. Can you come to New York?' asks Alexis. 'We'll obviously cover any costs.'

Grant feels his internal anxiety-meter rising.

Long ago, Grant Delgado developed a reputation for being difficult – and deservedly so. It was the result of the band's final, incendiary appearance on *Top of the Pops* during the Christmas Day Special of 1995. The Miraculous Vespas had been persuaded to appear together for the first time in almost ten years to promote a remixed, rereleased version of their debut single 'It's a Miracle'. Rather than miming, as instructed, Grant took off his shirt and taped up first his own mouth and then that of his fellow bandmates. The *Top of the Pops* executives were furious. Various legal actions were raised. The act killed any possibility of the band reforming, but simultaneously guaranteed their legendary status in rock and roll history. From that point on he was regarded as a modern-day Syd Barrett; something of an innovative genius, but not one you'd want to spend a long-haul flight sitting next to. For ten years, his descent into a form of personal, provincial madness robbed him of his creativity, his sanity and his relationships with everyone he cared for. But the roots of his unreasonable and volatile behaviour were sown in the late 80s.

Maggie's motivation to return for the Top of the Pops gig was purely in order to support Grant, who had only agreed to it for the money. But he had selfishly tried to cut the Sylvester brothers' percentages down further from the paltry £1,000 they were both offered by Max Mojo. The already fractious inter-band relationships descended into pure acrimony, and in the various settlements that followed the dissolution of Biscuit Tin Records in 1997, Maggie had had enough. She departed for a new life in America, taking their young son with her.

Grant Delgado disappeared from view for more than a decade. The early part of those years was characterised by increasing lone-liness, depression, anxiety, drug dependence, claustrophobia, and, latterly, agoraphobia. But there were also intermittent periods of cre-ativity. They manifested themselves in Swiftian stories that combined the absurd and the transcendent. These gradually worked themselves into a novel – an allegory for the self faced with an impending and increasingly bleak denouement.

The First Picture initially reads as a twenty-four-hour, dreamlike meandering odyssey through key places in an unidentified Scottish city in the mid-90s. A recovering addict searches for something very personal and important to him, which he has lost, or has had taken from him (although there are hints, the reader never exactly finds out what it is). His uncoordinated search forces him to confront various challenges and temptations, the decisions he has made, his broken relationships, the places he somehow can't leave, but also the joy and hope in things he's previously taken too much for granted. Overall, the journey seems to represent the catharsis the protagonist needs. The book's time sequence is uncertain and the story could take place over a year, rather than a day. There are four phases – morning, afternoon, evening and night – each with different weather, reflecting the narrator's changing emotions.

The First Picture takes place in 1997, a time when Britain is undergoing a substantial cultural and political transformation, and on the surface, the mood is optimistic. The narrator is the middle of three sons. He is thirty-two years old as he begins his story. His older brother is a social worker, and while capable of helping the narrator, he has given up on him. Their youngest brother has been killed in 1991, aged only twenty-three, when a stag-night prank suggested by the main character went tragically wrong.

To the irritation of his publishers, Grant pored endlessly over the blurb for his novel, insisting it communicated what *The First Picture* is about: transformation, and seeing things – relationships, the city, his life – with a new clarity, but not always with the positivity the storyteller has assumed that would bring. The storyteller ultimately comes to the conclusion that, although he knows it will soon kill him, he prefers the anaesthetised life of an addict, in which he doesn't have to deal with or confront the pain he has caused others.

The First Picture by Grant Dale was published by a small independent publishing house in spring 2011. The critics responded favourably, one describing it as 'a mesmerising portrait of modern Western civilisation, with claustrophobic cinematography by Cormac McCarthy and a scatological screenplay by Irvine Welsh'. And for its author, it allowed him to emerge on the other side of his personal wilderness. Grant Delgado found he had rediscovered Grant Dale: an optimistic kid brought up in a socially deprived Scottish council estate during the Thatcher Years. He felt the trajectory he'd reclaimed was an authentic one; one that allowed him to be expressive on his own terms, that didn't ask him to justify himself to anyone, least of all tiresome leeches like Max Mojo. The 'rock star' years were alien to him now. They offered little that was positive, save for the relationship with Maggie and the life they both created.

Grant had moved to Portland, Oregon eighteen months before his book appeared in print. Maggie had never stopped loving him; she just couldn't live *with* Grant Delgado. And Grant *Dale* couldn't remain in Glasgow. Creativity needs room to breathe, and the hangers-on, dealers, and nosy music journalists interested in an exclusive, suffocated him, denying him the ability to function. Bewilderingly, he had rediscovered it, himself and the love he felt for Maggie and Wolf, in the city that was now widely recognised as having the most vibrant music scene in the United States.

Grant ends the call with Alexis, having agreed to meet Steve Buscemi. Little does he know that Steve wants to recast the book in New York. The American will argue that all cities undergo the same type of complex transformation as that of Glasgow, against which the protagonist's dilemma is painted. The UK in 1997 saw the beginning of the Blair era; New York City had a returning, preening Rudy Guliani, who presided over the lowest crime rates in over twenty years just as many lamented the loss of the city's soul to cosseted exclusivity and urban gentrification.

'Hi, how's things?' says Maggie. She is on a location shoot in Argentina and the line isn't great. The distance between them is reinforced by the audio quality.

'Aye, fine ... ah think,' he replies.

'What d'ye mean?' she asks.

'Ach, this film deal thing ... the guy wants tae meet me in New York next week.'

'That's great, Grant, isn't it?' Maggie detects his hesitancy. The reason for her calling him might only exacerbate this, she fears.

'Aye, ah suppose so. It's just that he's lookin' for us tae invest. It's still low budget but in order tae maintain control and get a slot at Sundance, it needs to be financed quickly.'

'Oh,' she says. Grant has been struggling with writer's block lately, and due to his tempestuous relationship with his publisher, an advance for a new book has not been forthcoming. Maggie's salary offers them a degree of financial comfort but investing in a film production is another matter altogether. 'How much?' she asks.

'Not sure yet, but ah'm guessin' half a million.'

'Jesus! Pounds or dollars?'

'Might as well be gold fuckin' nuggets,' he says, laughing.

'Well, let's no' rule it out right away.'

Grant is surprised by Maggie's response. Raising this amount of money will be nearly impossible. Maggie has a good job with regular commissions, but Grant's earnings from his writing are limited. The acquisition of the film rights to the novel is a timely boost, but he won't promote his work in person and his rate of creative output is laborious. It's far from the security of a regular and consistent monthly income that a bank might loan against in the new, post-Lehman Brothers era.

Maggie knows she has to broach her next subject carefully, like a helicopter attempting to land on an oil rig in a force-ten gale. One wrong move and everyone on board is fucked. Nonetheless, she thinks Grant's unexpected dilemma has given her an opportunity.

'Grant, ah've had a few calls earlier today, about the Vespas.'

'Aye, what about them,' says Grant. His tone has changed.

'Well … Max…' she pauses. 'Max has told a journalist that we're gettin' back together. Doin' a tour an' that,' she says.

The reception is getting worse. Maggie is outside and it's clear to Grant that the wind is rising.

'An' … so what?' says Grant. 'Let him talk aw the shite he wants. Disnae make any difference, does it?'

'But, what if the money's good? Maybe we should think about it,' she says.

'Sounds like you aw'ready have,' says Grant. It sounds just as bitter as he intended.

'It's a one-off, Grant. One gig, an' a big payment for everybody. We aw need it, for various reasons.'

'Hey, haud on! You've spoken tae him, then?'

This was the difficult bit for Maggie. Time to just tough it out. 'Aye. He phoned earlier. He didnae want tae call you 'cos he was sure ye widnae have spoken tae him.'

'Well, he'd have been fuckin' right then!'

'Look Grant, this a small gig on a remote wee island. But Max has got sponsorship an' a load ae interest buildin'. Look at it as the key tae gettin' the movie goin'.'

Grant isn't really sure what to think. She mentioned a tour to begin with, but now it's apparently only one gig. He starts to sense that Maggie has known about this for longer than a few hours. His mind races as he contemplates the likelihood that she has spoken with Max Mojo more than once recently, and to the Sylvester Brothers too. But the whole fucking deal depends on him, and whether he is capable of overcoming a number of things: his distrust and hatred of his former friend Max Mojo; his embarrassment over the way he treated Eddie and Simon Sylvester; and, perhaps worst of all, the chronic stage fright he has concealed from everyone for over twenty years.

He hangs up the phone.

PART FOUR

THE BIG BANG (IN THEORY)

Chapter Thirty

March 2015. Crosshouse, Scotland

It is three weeks since Max Mojo has announced to an unsuspecting world that The Miraculous Vespas are reforming. The news has been met with amazement, excitement, apathy and disdain, generally in that order. Max knows they have to act quickly. The downside of twenty-four-hour news media is that everybody's attention span is shortened. He needs a campaign: a series of stunts that keep the YouTube subscribers interested and active.

Grant Delgado, the band's frontman and the key to the whole venture still hasn't responded to Max Mojo's numerous emails and calls. So Max is now focusing solely on Maggie Abernethy as his conduit to Grant.

For his part, Grant has stopped answering his home phone landline. And, in a fit of anger at the upsurge in 'Have you been mis-sold PPI insurance?' calls – which he has put down to his number being widely shared back in Scotland – he has thrown his mobile phone into the Willamette. Any negotiations with him are now being conducted via Maggie Abernethy.

Maggie wants the band to do the gig, and at least one Sylvester Brother is definitely interested. So everthing now rests on Grant Delgado.

The unopened letter Max has in his hand may provide the answer.

Max has called a meeting – the venture's first formal one – at the new base of Heatwave Promotions Ltd: the church hall adjacent to the former Crosshouse Church Manse. The attendees include the three Directors (and equal shareholders) of the company, Max Mojo, Bobby Cassidy and Joseph Miller. Share certificates and Shareholders' Agreements are yet to be issued – this has been left with Max, who has set the company up with his regular accountants. Each man has contributed £100,000 of their own money to provide the necessary working capital for the ambitious project, which has become known as The Big Bang, due to the noise made when the sign-bearing white van crashed outside. The Big Bang, as noted on the company papers and witnessed by Max and a slightly detached and uninterested Hamish May, will be a one-off music festival held on the tiny Ailsa Craig on the edge of the Irish Sea, just off the west coast of Ayrshire. The date for the event has been set for Saturday, 29th August 2015, giving approximately six months to organise everything. This doesn't seem like sufficient time to Joseph Miller, but both he and Bobby are being carried along on Max Mojo's building wave of inspirational optimism. Also in attendance at the meeting are Hammy, who has been given the job of Project Administrator, and Hairy Doug, fresh out of retirement and back to control sound and light equipment, on the promise of recovering the money still owed to him when he was a small shareholder in Biscuit Tin Records.

The main business of the day is the allocation of specific tasks and an assessment of progress on the ones that were informally discussed when the new business venture was set up. But first comes the opening of the letter from America, which has just been received. The Teenage Fanclub compilation CD, which has been playing in the background, is muted; fittingly, the track was 'The Concept'.

Max scans the letter, his brows going up and then down like a pair of dancing caterpillars as he digests the contents.

'Well?' says Joseph.

'Hmm,'

'Fuck does '*hmm*' mean?' says Bobby. 'Are they in or out?'

'They're in,' says Max.

'Really?' says Joseph. He previously suggested a Plan B, since all of the available evidence pointed to Grant Delgado telling Max Mojo – through a paid intermediary – to go and fuck himself.

'Aye ... but at a fuckin' price,' says Max.

'Of?'

'They'll dae it for a million,' says Max. 'Sterling, no' bucks.'

Bobby isn't sure which is worse. The UK's recent political uncertainty seems to have totally shat on the pound to the extent that it often feels like the economy is heading back to one solely based on barter.

'A million fuckin' quid!' Joseph is trying hard to stifle an ironic laugh. 'He's havin' a bastard laugh. Christ almighty, they've done one album and one single, and if it hudnae been for that film, nae cunt would even give a shite about them. It's the Ailsa Craig, for fuck's sake … no' Oasis at Knebworth.'

'Well, that's that idea shafted, then,' says Bobby. 'Who wis next on the list ae bands?'

'There's nae next,' says Max. 'It's The Vespas or nothin'.'

Joseph senses something doesn't quite fit. Max seems too calm. 'Are you behind this, ya devious bastard?' he asks.

'Meanin'?' says Max, defensively.

'Have you done a deal wi' the band on the basis ae yer split loyalty as a partner here, an' their manager?' asks Bobby.

'Any idea how fuckin' mental that is, ya cunt? They're suin' me for usin' material in the film that Grant hudnae agreed tae.'

This is new information to Bobby and Joseph.

'Eh? So how the hell are ye gonnae get them tae play while a fuckin' law suit's ongoing?' Joseph is perplexed. Max's buoyant optimism suddenly seems holed below the waterline.

'By payin' the cunts a million, evidently,' says Max, as if explaining simple arithmetic to a toddler. 'The rest ae it is just business, man. Fuck sake, cunts sue each other aw the time in this business. Most ae it's just tae maintain profile. They always settle oot ae court. calm doon, the two ae ye'se … ah ken whit ah'm dain' here.'

Max Mojo is mad, Joseph is convinced of it now, but since everyone in the wider Mad Max world seems to be equally so, perhaps his conviction is enough for now.

'So, we raise the million an' agree, right? Ah wis anticipatin' this, so we need tae make it seem like a fuckin' bargain. A campaign strategy that makes this the music event ae the bastart century. If ye miss oot', ye'd regret it for the rest ae yer life. Like the Sex Pistols at the Manchester Free Trade Hall in '76 … or Oasis at King Tut's in Glesga in '93 … or, even better, The Stone Roses at Spike Island in 1990.'

'Ah was at Spike Island,' Joseph announces. 'It wis fuckin' pish!'

Bobby is staring at him with a bemused look on his face.

'Jesus, ah fuckin' though *that* wis you!' he says. 'Ah saw ye, but ah didnae…' he tails off.

'Aye, ah fuckin' know ye did. We were aw soakin' an' then had tae get held back in a massive crush just tae let a bunch ae arsehole VIPs out.'

'Aye,' Bobby smiles and looks into the long distance. 'What a great night that wis!'

'Look, the point is, it's an event,' says Max while Joseph glowers. 'There wis only aboot thirty fuckin' folk at the Pistols gig, an' wi aw his mental dancin' they probably counted Ian Curtis twice!' Max took a deep breath. 'But if ye believe the fuckin' internet, there wis about fuckin' forty thousand there. Folk are lyin' cunts when it comes tae this kind ae shite. Ah ken whit ah'm talkin' aboot.'

'So, if we can only get about five hundred at it, how much are we gonnae have tae charge for a ticket?' Joseph asks. He can see Hammy trying to work something out on his notebook, in the hope of making a contribution.

'Let's come back tae that. There's other stuff we need tae talk aboot first,' says Max.

Hammy continues scribbling.

'So if we've got the band … at a price, whit aboot the venue?'

This is Joseph's allotted responsibility. While ruminating over their future plans back in Ibiza, a hallucinating Hammy proclaimed that the 'eyelid' sketch Joseph had been scribbling resembled a stage, similar to the outdoor one at the Hollywood Bowl. It had lodged in Joseph's subconscious until just a few weeks ago, when the prospect of actually needing a stage recalled it from the vaults. Joseph has proposed turning the sketch into a lightweight-timber, floating stage, securely moored to prevent the bands getting seasick. It is an interesting if unlikely idea and it will mean that the audience can be retained on the beach, so to speak, and as a result, no additional accommodation will be needed. Of all the tasks, Joseph's seems to be the most straightforward. And as it is a temporary construction, it falls outside of conventional Building Regulations. In fact, the local council has been totally unsure of how to even categorise the project. Joseph is pressing on with design drawings and detailed discussions with potential builders, while the council searches for some guidance on how to evaluate the structure's general suitability. Development on the island itself is very strictly controlled, due to sensitivities related to the neighbouring seabird colonies. However, Joseph's structure floats, it isn't really a building; in fact it might be more appropriately subject to maritime design regulations. But no one seems quite sure. Max Mojo has covertly contacted local councillor, Cramond Crockett to check.

Bobby's principal responsibility is securing permission to actually occupy the island for the designated weekend. Ailsa Craig is owned by the Scottish peer, Archibald Angus Charles Kennedy, the eighth Marquess of Ailsa. Following an initial approach, which the Marquess's representatives rubbished as a drunken prank, they subsequently referred a persistent Bobby Cassidy to estates and property agents in Glasgow who are acting for the Marquess. Just like Max Mojo, Bobby Cassidy has exclusive news just received in the last day or so.

'The dude that owns the island isnae gonnae grant permission for us tae use it. He's said that there's too many environmental restrictions oan it for him tae agree.'

Once again, there's a detectable 'well, that's us fucked, then' atmosphere in the room.

'Whit the fuck does that mean?' asks Max. This issue looks less easily fixable; Max's default setting of throwing money at a problem until it goes away looks unlikely to work.

However, Bobby goes on to explain that Ailsa Craig is home to one of the largest gannet colonies in the world, with about thirty-six thousand breeding pairs. The Royal Society for the Protection of Birds looks after the colony, which he says it describes as a 'bustling seabird city, with gannets, puffins, black guillemots, razorbills and peregrines some of the special residents'.

'Who the fuck ae you, all ae sudden … Johnny Morris?' Max attempts levity.

Bobby shushes him. 'There's strict controls oan any development oan the island, so's tae protect the birds' breedin' ground,' he reaffirms.

'But we're no' buildin' oan the island, though,' says Max hopefully.

'Exactly, but it disnae matter 'cos the geezer isnae gonnae grant permission. He thinks it would damage his reputation.' Bobby pauses, then smiles. It's not only Max Mojo who has some slick tricks. 'So … ah bought the fuckin' island off him!'

No-one speaks; Bobby is sure they don't even breathe. Only Hammy looks relaxed.

'An' ye can thank that dopey cunt for this turn ae events.' Bobby nods at Hammy.

They all turn and look at Hammy with a mix of admiration and confusion.

Hammy winks. 'He comes back fae a meetin', aw "Boo-Hoo, the gemme's up", like somebody's eaten his last Munchie, ken?'

They all smile knowingly apart from Bobby.

'So ah digs through the internet, an' fuck me, is the island no' up for sale. It wis put up first in 2011 for £2.5m, but nae cunt's bitin' at that price. So they drapped it back to £1.5m. Wi' the recession still bitin', the pound carryin' aboot as much value as a *Jim'll Fix It* badge … there's nae chance ae sellin' it. So Bobby—'

Bobby dives in. 'Ah went back tae them. Ah offered a million,' he says proudly. 'An' ah got the confirmation last night that they've accepted.'

No one knows what to say; least of all Hairy Doug, who is contemplating what impact all of this boundless spending might have on his eventual cut. The meeting has been in progress for less than half an hour and already two million pounds in unforeseen costs have been added to the debit column.

'So … we own a fuckin' island?' asks an excited Max.

'Naw,' says Bobby. 'Ah own a fuckin' island. Ah'll use some ae the dosh fae the sale ae the villa in Ibiza.'

On reflection, they all realise that this makes sense. Bobby has the money; he sold the Ibiza house for four million euros, largely on the deathbed advice of Laurie Revlon, who'd privately told him to hold out for that amount.

'Whit've ye actually bought then?' asks Joseph.

As if reading straight from the sales schedule, Bobby describes an uninhabited, dome-shaped land mass lying ten miles off the Scottish coast, colloquially known as 'Paddy's milestone', due to the island being situated mid-way between Glasgow and Belfast, as the crow flies. He knowledgeably informs everyone that geologists believe the island is a plug left behind from an extinct volcano. He confirms that it constitutes 220 acres and comprises a ruined castle, a derelict row of small cottages, a lighthouse and a working granite quarry. He clarifies the extent of the gannet community and how it thrives, now that the migrating rats that found their way there from numerous passing vessels have been eradicated. In a special 'Did You Know?' section, Bobby explains how the Ailsa Craig is renowned as the source of the majority of the curling stones currently in use across the world. The granite hewn from the quarry is very dense and non-porous, which prevents moisture from penetrating and pitting the carved stones as they lie on the ice. There is an audible 'Oooh' at this revelation. If the Ailsa Craig is ever a specialist subject on *Mastermind*, Bobby Cassidy will clean up.

'Well, that's a fuckin' bonus, then, eh?' says Max.

Bobby and Joseph exchange looks. The Big Bang was originally intended to be a memorial for Bobby's brother, but they are both beginning to feel that Max has conveniently forgotten this fact. He has taken over so much, the project is starting to feel like his vision alone.

However, Bobby is quick to mention that he intends to rename the island the Ailsa Cassidy. With his ownership seeming like the only option if they are to make this event as memorable as Max is painting it, Bobby's actions might just help retain the original spirit of their plan, in the face of all Max's bluster and any other purposes he has in mind. There's no getting away from the fact, though, that the whole thing is a ludicrously expensive way for Bobby to compartmentalise his guilt.

'We're no' out ae the woods yet,' Bobby says. 'The environmentalists aren't chuffed at the prospect ae a music festival. We'll need tae keep an eye on that yin.'

'Ach, we can just bung them a year's free supply ae Trill.' It's not clear if Max is serious.

'Right, next: you're up, Hairy.'

Thirty years ago in this very hall, Hairy Doug almost separated Max's head from his shoulders for his apparent disrespect when referring to Doug, and his former wife, Fanny in this way. Now though, the septuagenarian can't be arsed appealing.

'The sound system will be an issue, no doubt,' says Hairy Doug, his bizarre concoction of regional dialects having not withered with age. 'But I think we can do it.'

'That's aw ah need tae ken, big yin. Just keep us posted on the costs ae aw the infrastructure,' says Max. 'Finally, there's ma bit ... the campaign!' He picks up some papers and leans forward on the table, adjusting his monocle to see the words more clearly. 'Loads ae money bein' spent, but nae real idea ae how tae recover it,' he announces. 'An' ah get that's gie'in some ae ye'se sleepless nights, but ah dinnae want ye'se tae worry about that.'

There is a detectable sigh of relief from all of them. Their *de facto* leader has a plan. He understands that, in order for the event to wash its face, its credits and debits need to match. He has obviously considered the economics of ticket sales and transport expenditure and…

'It's gonnae be a free event!' he announces proudly.

'Ye whit?' shouts Bobby, incredulous at this notion.

'We're gonnae gie the tickets away,' says Max.

'Ah was right aw along,' says Joseph, folding his arms. 'This daft cunt's no' the full shillin'.'

'Look, shut the fuck up, an' hear me oot, will ye?' It appears they have no option. 'We create an event campaign oan FaceBook, Twitter and aw forms ae social media. Controversy sells. Carefully made adverts done like abstract social statements ... a bit like Banksy's. Every cunt starts talkin' about them. The buzz builds up. We make it as exclusive as we can. Most folk want nuthin' more than tae feel like they're in a club that only they can get intae: "Yer name's no' doon, yer no' gettin' in!" Ye get it?'

'No' really,' Hammy admits.

'Once we've created the expectation, we put the briefs oot intae circulation the week before the gig. The kids have tae fuckin' hunt for them, like Willy Wonka's golden tickets. Only we put them oot via a social venture. We put oors in sealed copies ae *The Big Issue*!'

Joseph was starting to piece this together. Maybe Max wasn't quite as mental as he'd thought.

'But how dae we recover the costs?' asks Bobby.

'Sponsorship, mate ... sponsorship. Think ae the companies that want tae be associated wi' a noble social cause. They watch their brands an' how they're being perceived. Look at how quickly every one ae them drapped that cheatin' bastard Lance Armstrong like a fuckin' stone ... or aw these worldwide brands rethinking their financial support for FIFA. Aw these organsiations dinnae mind avoiding their corporate taxes or gettin' their ain shite made by slumdogs in fuckin' Calcutta, but ask them tae maintain a position wi' some other cunt that's dain' the same? Naw ... aw we're doin' is playin' on their rank hypocrisy. We're supporting the homeless an' chargin' fuck all tae dae it, an' it's aw because your Gary – a war hero, dinnae forget – cared passionately aboot the mental-health epidemic an' how it affects folk wi' nae place tae live,' says Max, 'an' wi' that...' he tails off, knowing that Joseph has it now.

'…ye can license the music through iTunes, sell film rights tae the highest bidder, get free promotions fae the likes ae McDonalds for the catering … an' get the record companies tae pay through the nose for their artists tae actually appear.'

'Exactamundo,' says Max Mojo. 'So let's stop fuckin' aboot. There's work tae be done!' Only Hairy Doug looks bemused now, but he knows his place: source the light and sound gear and then get it over on a boat and rigged up to generators and onto the floating stage. Simple.

'Bobcat,' says Max. 'You an' me are off tae London th'morra. Breakfast TV booked an' a day ae startin' tae make announcements. Noo that ye've went an' bought the fuckin' rock, ah've got another idea. Hammy, dae a letter back tae Maggie Abernethy accepting aw the terms. That'll put the shiters right up Grant Delgado!'

Max Mojo is a blur of intense activity. Like a fifty-one-year-old Tasmanian Devil. Irrefutable evidence that the right drugs do in fact work.

The following morning on the way to the airport, Max Mojo makes a string of phone calls. None seem to last more than a few minutes but all fit a predetermined pattern. Bobby Cassidy can't help but be impressed at his new business partner's drive and grip of the situation, even though he only hears Max's side of each conversation:

Phone call #1:
    'Hullo. Izzat you? Aye. Aye. Aye, definitely. Naw, fuck that. Nae explosives. Right. See ye!'

Phone call #2:
    'Hi. Aye … it's me. We're oan. Maggie's twisted the cunt's arm so ye'll get yer bung. Have ye spoken tae yer brother yet? Whit d'ye mean "he's found God"? Well tell him tae take the cunt in an' get

the reward an' then get his fuckin' arse in gear! Aye. Ah'll phone
ye wi' the rehearsal details. Cheers.'

Phone call #3:

'Hullo … Hullo! Aye, aye, ah'll hold. For fuck's sake, cunt must
have a fuckin' butler. Aye, it's me. We're sendin' ye the contract so
the devious cunt cannae back out now, right? Well, just keep an
eye oan him, right? Dinnae want him headin' oot tae the green-
house like Kurt Cobain, eh? Deid singers sell records, but it's a bit
fuckin' awkward sellin' a live gig if the frontman's fuckin' topped
himself, ken? Right. Aye. The money's no' a problem. Ma secretary's drawin' up the papers. Right. See ye at the rehearsals.'

Phone call #4:

'Hullo, aye, it's Max Mojo. Ah wis tae phone this mornin' tae see
if ma test results were in. Aw, aw'right. Naw, ah dinnae have the
time. Ah'm fuckin' double busy, hen. Ah'll phone back.'

Phone call #5:

'Haw, Hairy Yin … just a reminder. Dinnae fuck this up, or ah'm
puttin' ye in an old folks home full ae Daniel O'Donnell fans, so
think on, eh?'

Phone call #6:

'Ma, it's me … dinnae forget tae feed the goldfish and the carp.
Call ye later.'

Phone call #7:

'Hullo. Ma name's Max Mojo. Ah'm phonin' tae set up a meetin'
wi' Councillor Crockett. Aye, Cramond Crockett. Just tell him
tae call ma secretary, Hamish May, oan 01563 73859. He kens me,
an' he kens whit it's about tae. Aye, thanks.'

Phone call #8:

'Hi, how's it goin'? Ma name's Max Mojo an' ah'm the promoter ae The Big Bang Festival. Ye've probably heard ae it. Aye, that's right. Well, ah'm lookin' tae negotiate a price tae hire yer boat. Aye, the *Waverley*. That's the very fella. Day trip … aye. Probably about five hundred. 29th ae August. Right. Ye can get me on this number. Cheers pal.'

Phone call #9:

'Hullo Norman? Izzat Norman Blake? Joe McAlinden gie'd me yer number. Aye, it's Max Mojo. Hopefully ye'll remember me. Aye, the same yin. Ye aw'right? Ah'm good man. Listen, ah wis hopin' tae book the band tae support The Miraculous Vespas on this big comeback gig. Aye. Aye. Aye. Joe told me ye'se were back th'gither, rehearsin' an' that. New record comin' oot? Aye, well here's a big opportunity for ye … Teenage Fanclub an' The Miraculous Vespas oan the same bill. Ah ken when we tried tae sign ye for Biscuit Tin, ye said that. Aye. Naw, that'll be cool, man. *Star Sign*'s one ae Grant's favourite records. Okay, you speak tae the guys an' ye can let us ken, eh? Right, cheers Norman.'

Max Mojo is thumbing through a black book with alphabetised names, many of whom Bobby knows from their elevated public profiles. The list of contacts is incredible. How many of them are legitimate contacts, and morever, how many of them would welcome the name 'Max Mojo' flashing across their smartphone screens is another matter, but it gives Bobby some comfort that, as unlikely as it all seems, Max might just pull this crazy stunt off.

Phone call #10:

'Hullo. It's Max Mojo, the manager of The Miraculous Vespas. Is that Chris? Chris Blackwell? Aye, cheers man. Wondered if ye had the chance tae consider the offer yet? Aye? Aye, that sounds good, man. We've had loads ae interest in their new record. It's fuckin' amazing, man. They might've been oot the game for twenty years, but fuck me, it's gonnae be like that Bowie record, 'Where Are We Now'. When it draps, it's gonnae shock every cunt tae their core. There's so much fuckin' emotion in it, ken? Aye, well ah'd be lyin' if ah told ye otherwise. Branson's been chasin' us, but frankly, ah just don't like the cunt. Aye, ah always wanted us tae be on Island Records, an' Grant fuckin' loves Bob Marley, ken? Aye. There's a cover ae 'Redemption Song' gettin' planned for the gig. Aye. Magic. Thanks, man. Look forward tae it. Bye.'

The car has reached Glasgow airport.

Chapter Thirty-One

March 2015. Manchester, England

'You're here with us on BBC Breakfast. Coming up we have Max Mojo and Bobby Cassidy, who'll be talking about a bizarre music festival they are staging on Ailsa Craig, a tiny uninhabited island in the Irish Sea…'

'…But first, here's Carole with the weather.'

Bobby Cassidy is shaking. He's watched the BBC Breakfast News programmes regularly on the World Service, and perhaps, like many viewers, he felt that he knew these idiomatic and composed pre-senters personally. They were like neighbours that you saw every morning as you went out to start your car and head for work. Or at least if he had neighbours or daily employment that required him to get up before lunchtime, he imagined a relationship similar to the one he thought he had with the handsome man in the suit, the beautiful woman with the perfect teeth, and Carole, whose smile was as radiant as the sunshine she seemed to promote daily. Since returning to Scotland, Bobby has never seen Carole downcast, a murderous look in her eyes on account of the rain coming down in javelin-tipped stairrods. They all look unfeasibly healthy. His teeth, by comparison, look like the results of a police baton-charge in a ceramic-tile factory. He is determined not to smile.

He is surprised to feel so ill at ease, sitting on their curved red sofa. It is undoubtedly due to the extensive paraphernalia of their TV studio in Manchester. Robotic cameras and miles of taped-down cables, which are always just out of shot. He knows these things are a necessary part of the process, but being ushered in, over and past them has unnerved him. He feels like he has been up all night and the perspiration on his brow is driving the make-up down into his eyes. They shouldn't have gone to that late party last night with members of The Charlatans, three Premier League footballers and a busty teenager who claimed to be from a place called *Geordie Shore*. Bobby is hungover. Max Mojo, on the other hand, is in his element. There is a glint in his eye; the type of sparkle that betrays his mordant thoughts. He is preparing to say something outrageous and Bobby knows it.

The male presenter reprises the morning's headlines. Despite a life lived largely overseas, Bobby knows him like he knows his own reflection, but he suddenly can't remember his, or his co-presenter's names. Neither can Max – but only because he wasn't paying attention when he was being briefed.

It's a slow-news day. Preparations for an upcoming general election are still forming with the main parties, so the news features some minor stories about red meat and how it could now apparently prolong life, and a devastating monsoon named Fred in a far-flung part of the world that Bobby hasn't even heard of.

'Max Mojo and Bobby Cassidy, good morning,' says the female presenter.

Bobby thinks she's lovely.

Max isn't so sure. The malign voice in his head is now under medicinal control, by and large. But, given an audience and the correct circumstances for carnage, it still takes some suppressing. Right at this moment, it is forming lewd racist and sexist phrases for Max to spew at this brown-skinned woman with the boy's haircut. These would result in the wrong type of news headlines. Max tries to concentrate. He focuses instead solely on the BBC's male anchor.

'Hiya,' says Max, calmly.

'Y'awright?' whispers Bobby through thin lips.

'Now tell us, you're putting on a one-night music festival on a remote uninhabited island off the west of Scotland. Why?' she asks with a rehearsed incredulity.

''Cos we can!' replies Max, folding his arms, still looking at the man in the expensive suit.

246 DAVID F. ROSS

'Aye,' says Bobby.

'Like Everest, an' that,' adds Max, patting Anchorman's knee. 'But no' the double glazing, hen … 'cos it's there!'

Bobby is staring at this elegant female, transfixed. It helps settle his nerves.

She is beginning to suspect this might be her Russell Harty / Grace Jones moment.

'But why Ailsa Craig?' asks the suit, trying to help out his colleague.

Max breathes deeply and then says, 'The gig's just a smokescreen, ken? See Scots folk? They're aw mouth an' attitude but bugger all else.'

Bobby is forced to wipe the moisture from his brow. He has no idea where Max is headed with this.

'See aw that independence bollocks last ye—'

The man – Bobby suddenly remembers he's called Charlie Something – intervenes sharply and apologises for the use of the word. He tries to laugh it off and politely warns Max Mojo. Max stares down the camera with the red light on and he too apologises to the nation before continuing.

'Never mind the bollocks, we had a referendum last year … ye'se might ae heard about it, doon here in Enger-land.'

Charlie Something nods whilst trying to remain composed. This isn't the interview he thought they would be having.

'But we blew it. So *we* thought that if wee Alex and Nicola could declare independence, then so could we!' Max quickly takes off his shirt, dislodging the microphone in the process. He is wearing a t-shirt bearing the slogan

INDEPENDENCE FOR AILSA CRAIG – HANDS OFF OOR FISH!

Charlie Something grapples for his notes. It's clear he is receiving instructions to cut this piece sharply. So heavily is Bobby now perspiring and shaking, he is worried viewers might think he is having a stroke.

Before they can cut to an item about breast-feeding, Max Mojo shouts, 'The Miraculous Vespas are the greatest fuckin' band in history. FREEDOM!' His microphone is trailing by his side, but he still makes himself heard.

The two professionals glance at one another and then try to laugh the incident off, but it's clear they are rattled. No news presenter wants to be the subject of the news itself, and by that evening hundreds of thousands of people around the world will have watched this short clip after it has gone viral. Who needs a publicist when Max Mojo is on the case?

Unsurprisingly, the car that picked them up from the Lowry Hotel two hours earlier to take Max and Bobby to the BBC Media Centre in Salford Quays isn't driving them back. They have been dumped out of the soulless steel-and-glass building with such force that Bobby expects security to follow them outside and give both of them a severe kicking. Max wears a smugly satisfied look on his face.

'Right, now we can get tae work. We've finally got a fuckin' audience!'

Back in Crosshouse, Joseph stares at the estimate. Five hundred thousand pounds to construct the small, eyelid stage out of a durable hardwood. Ten percent more to construct the 'hull' with a more contemporary production using glass-reinforced plastic. This alternative, but recommended, process proposes constructing a large mould and essentially forming the outer structure from a layer of fibreglass laid to the mould, then applying a core of balsa wood or foam before the inner skin is laid. This option for the parts that will be underwater takes special materials and specialist knowledge. They are basically building a boat, although the timescale is almost as pressurised as for the much bigger one once constructed by Noah. They have to cut the build time down by three months. Needless to say, faster construction times mean even more money. Max Mojo better be right about the sponsorship deals or they will all be going to prison over substantial unpaid debts.

Joseph lifts the phone and punches the numbers. It's a short call; essentially confirming his wish for the specialist joiners to proceed. They will build it all from cedar. It needs to be ready in four months. He will pay twenty-five percent up front. The working capital is long gone, and although Bobby has reserves from the sale of the villa and Max clearly has money, even if he is loathe to part with any of it, this uniquely designed floating stage is being funded from Joseph's sale of his shares in M(cubed) and from his redundancy. If it weren't in some parts exciting, it would represent financial madness on a scale that only disgraced RBS boss, Sir Fred Goodwin, would sanction.

At Heatwave's Ayrshire HQ, Hammy is dealing with an increasing amount of calls and correspondence. The rate of these has ramped up dramatically in the three hours since the Breakfast TV incident. Everyone wants to speak with Max, including someone senior from the Scottish National Party. Hammy has been told to simply log names and numbers, or *favourite* and *like* the social media posts to the venture's new accounts. That way they can filter out the time wasters and focus on the ones who will pay well for apparent exclusives. Max Mojo is from the Malcolm McLaren School of Music Business Hustling. He is looking for advances that most likely won't – or can't – be paid back, for exclusive access rights that will be 'sold' to multiple competing organisations. If it all works out as he sees it in his head, the subsequent legal actions brought by any of them will be immaterial. Max has one ace card up his sleeve. But it gives him a negotiating position. The Miraculous Vespas have never been signed to a major label. A recent reissue of the original mix of 'It's A Miracle (Thank You)' was released by Max himself to coincide with the film premiere. He narcissistically recorded a live interview with the journalist Norma Niven and put an edited version of this on the single's B-side. In fact all of the recorded material of The Miraculous Vespas now is now owned exclusively by Max. The protracted and bitter legal dispute that followed this settlement were the principal reason that Grant Delgado vowed never to record music again. Why would *he* now wish to put any more money in the pockets of someone whom he considered to be on a par with Rupert Murdoch in terms of devious duplicity?

This is exactly the conundrum being extensively considered over the dinner table in a small but handsome house in Portland, Oregon. The opportunity to turn his debut novel into celluloid is now everything to Grant. Maggie knows it and her regular chipping away at his intransigence is slowly but surely working. She has noticed that the one remaining guitar he has kept – the classic Rickenbacker bought in a small Kilmarnock music store on the same day he first met both Maggie *and* Max – has been retrieved from the loft and has been placed under his bed. It is as if he is nervously working up to a first date with an old girlfriend. Steve Buscemi has sweetened the deal with Grant by suggesting that he also score the movie. It is an interesting if unusual proposition that Grant hasn't previously considered. Although anxious about committing to composing new music for the first time in almost twenty years, his novel *The First Picture* originated from an idea contained within the lyrics of the song of the same name. He recalls how impressed he was by Jonny Greenwood's soundtrack for the film *There Will Be Blood*, particularly as Greenwood's day job – guitarist in Radiohead – offered so few clues about the austere and minimalist tone of the film's music. Grant is enticed, undoubtedly, but agreeing to the Miraculous Vespas gig is a high price to be paid. It has taken him two months, and an intensive course of counselling, to cope with the unpredictable panics the situation has induced, but he has decided to say yes to Max Mojo, via Maggie, of course.

Simon Sylvester is still in prison. Not as an inmate, though; he is now a senior figure in an organisation called Jail Guitar Doors – named after The Clash song and founded by Billy Bragg and Mick Jones. The organisation has grown and Simon is now the head of its activities in Scotland. His job is important. It requires him to travel around the country's various penal institutes, encouraging younger offenders to find rehabilitation through music, as he once did. Simon still occasionally teaches music but only to those whom his colleagues consider to have a real aptitude, talent or ability to concentrate. Simon Sylvester's attitude to the prospect of playing with The Miraculous Vespas is surprising. He welcomes it, but purely because of the positive example this increased profile will potentially give to the various lost boys he now feels compelled to help. Simon Sylvester has changed in many ways.

Simon's younger brother Eddie – The Miraculous Vespas' mercurial but troubled guitarist – is less convinced about the merits of restringing his guitar for this particular gig. Eddie Sylvester was known as The Motorcycle Boy in the band's initial, short-lived burst of fame. Eddie suffered from a multitude of mental-health issues, which were traced back to seeing his mum die in the family's front garden. Eddie had been watching from his bedroom window as she cut the sodden grass following a heated argument with her husband, who should have done it earlier before the rain had started. She cut through the lawnmower cable. Eddie Sylvester played on stage wearing a full-face motorcycle helmet. It allowed him to block out the demons – the insistent voices in his head – and lose himself in the only thing that offered him sanctuary: playing guitar, like an effortless combination of Jimi Hendrix and Johnny Marr.

The reasons for Eddie Sylvester's nonchalance about the impending gig are unsurprisingly complex. He has conquered many of his previous disorders and has normalised his relationships with others within his circle; which is now a religious one: Eddie Sylvester is a preacher. In 1995, he was informed by a psychic that he had been placed on Earth for a purpose, and that he would begin to receive messages from the spirit world. Subsequently, and using the money he was paid for appearing with the rest of The Miraculous Vespas on the now legendary '95 *Top of The Pops* Christmas Special, Eddie Sylvester invested in a Doctorate of Divinity from an obscure community university in Utah. He is now the Reverend Doctor Edward Sylvester, leader of the Church of the Infinite Mind, based in Prestwick in a rented dilapidated shed on the local airport's estate. The Reverend only wears emerald green clothes, believing the distinctive colour to be a conduit for positivity. Gone is the nervousness; it has been replaced by a stupidly deluded self-confidence. Edward Sylvester is considered a figure of fun by his local community. He refers to himself in the third person. In a local radio interview fifteen years ago, he proclaimed that the world as some knew it would end before he, the Reverend Doctor Edward Sylvester, was fifty. He knew this as the spirit world regularly contacted him and calmly informed him that he had been chosen as its saviour. The end, when it came, would be by earthquakes and tidal waves. Their initial epicentre was to be the Isle of Arran. In the aftermath of Edward's subsequent public shaming, Simon had stopped trying to reach his brother. The negative associations were affecting his work with aggressive, hard-bitten youngsters, who were still capable of being saved, but in a different, more tangible way. Now, Edward Sylvester's only contact is with his flock. They normally number ten, but only six if it's methadone day at the clinics. The good Reverend Doctor spends every day communicating with the spirits and preparing for when the time comes for him to save the world. He prays that it's soon. Some angry, vindictive people just don't deserve to be saved.

Chapter Thirty-Two

June 2015. Crosshouse, Ayrshire

After a tempestuous and unpredictable May, June is shaping up to be more measured. A number of interviews have been carried out and all have swollen the Heatwave coffers, to some degree covering the escalating infrastructure costs. The social media campaigns are skyrocketing, and although it has taken him a while, Hammy is becoming a master of retweeting and instagram posting. The event's Twitter account has almost half a million followers. BBC Scotland has filmed a feature comparing the growing clamour for the gig tickets as similar to that of the new Apple iPhone release. Max still hasn't revealed that the tickets will be distributed freely via *The Big Issue*: he'll leave that to the last few weeks in order to avoid some overeager young journalist blowing the promotional impact.

Hairy Doug has sourced the requisite sound and light equipment and has roped in a crew. They are nearly all as old as him but their experience will count for a lot, given the unusual nature of the rigging.

Joseph has approached Hettie to create a series of abstract posters advertising The Big Bang. They are beautiful and mysterious, and, as a series, they are increasingly colourful. They are being treated like collectable works of art in their own right and several are now being replicated in spray-paint on concrete as far afield as Barcelona and Buenos Aires. Hettie is glad to be able to help, and the poster campaign has also boosted interest in her own upcoming Gallery show.

Bobby has also been spending more time with Lizzie King. They have been out to dinner several times and, despite Hammy's continued warnings that she'll just break his heart again, Bobby considers it a risk worth taking.

Joseph Miller has been interviewed extensively by a series of design magazines keen to understand the conceptual philosophy behind the emerging stage design. He has been encouraged to enter the design for a number of European Design Awards, all coming with an entrance price tag, but again Max Mojo has encouraged this, 'all publicity being good publicity etc'.

The Miraculous Vespas have arrived in Scotland and, despite the periodic activity of newpaper men, media men and fans of the band from various locations hoping for tickets or information about how they can be acquired, the band – minus the Reverend Doctor – have been smuggled into the Manse without anyone knowing they are there. After the scrutiny around Operation Double Nougat, Washer Wishart erected a large boundary wall around the church grounds. All involved in the Big Bang are very grateful that he did.

Simon did visit his brother in Prestwick but left quickly. Edward had talked in riddles. He wanted to pray with, and for, his brother. He hoped to offer him salvation, although he found it hard to explain exactly what Simon needed saving from. Simon pities his brother. He has always seemed lost, but this wilderness is something different altogether. The only saving grace appears to be that he is content in this advanced state of madness. Simon asked him to do The Big Bang in the hope that the comparative normality of a one-off gig on a floating stage, playing to a small audience of sea-faring travellers, all compressed on the tiny shingle beach of an uninhabited island might shake the shite out of him; but as he explained the premise in detail, Simon Sylvester began to feel that his words seemed more mental than his brother's. He left with the get-out clause: *'Well, if ye'll no' dae it for anythin' else, just dae it for the money. Every other cunt's only dain' it for that. Ye'll can get the roof on this fuckin' place fixed at least!'*

Back at HQ, Max reasoned that of all of them, the artist formerly known as The Motorcycle Boy was the most dispensable. Just stick a helmet on any cunt that can pass the first round of a *Britain's Got Talent* audition and nobody would be any the wiser. But much of the Vespas distinctive sound came from Eddie's guitar, so Grant Delgado wants him in; Eddie's inclusion has therefore become just another potential obstacle Max has to fix.

For now Bobby and Joseph are sitting on a small speedboat, chartered privately. They are heading across calm water towards Bobby's island. With only two months to go, they have concluded that a detailed recce of the place is essential. The final documents of sale have been concluded and Bobby feels they should now spend a night on the island, protected only from the arbitrary elements by the tent they have brought with them, at the very least because they're expecting five hundred other people to do the same.

The shape of the rocks changes gradually as they approach the shallower water. They have sailed from Ayr. From a number of places on the coast – Ayr, Girvan, Troon, Irvine – the island looks the closest. But it's merely an optical illusion exaggerated by the curvature of the Ayrshire coastline that seems to surround it – the same type of illusion that doubtless persuaded prisoners on Alcatraz that they could swim to the mainland. The boat slows as it closes in. The swell of the sea seems to grow out of the flat calm they have traversed. Razorbills swoop and guillemots bob. The boat sails closer, slower again. The bird population becomes apparent. There are thousands of the fuckers.

'Never mind them bein' aggravated by the music, they'll have a fuckin' field day wi' aw the chips and cheese!' Bobby remarks.

The speedboat pulls close to the narrow wooden jetty. The island's unique shape looks totally different now they're standing on it. It actually does feel like a desert island, especially today, with the unseasonal heat of the Ayrshire coast at its warmest. Joseph has studied plans of this part of the island's shore. It is where the available ground widens most and in truth is the only useable terrain on which to locate a crowd of people in comparative safety. The jetty will need reinforcing: this is Joseph's first observation; plus there is clearly no way that the bulk of the world's oldest operating paddle steamer, which has been taking Glaswegian punters 'doon the watter' for over fifty years will get anywhere near the island's only dropping off point. As the stage construction has developed, Joseph has become more interested in the techniques of ship and yacht design and construction. He researched the *Waverley* when it became a possible, if unlikely, transportation option for band and audience, and knows that, despite its relatively low draught, there is no way the waters around the perimeter of such a tiny island are deep enough to take the vessel. This is noted in the Joseph Miller ledger as Problem No.1.

In a series of post-sale conversations with the Conservation Trust, which initially tried to block his purchase, Bobby has agreed a tentative compromise. The existence of another private landowner isn't an issue for the Trust *per se*; and their reservations about the damage that could be done to the breeding colonies have been assuaged by Bobby's offer to gift the parts of the island that he won't be using back to the Trust, post the event. Everyone has their price, it seems and everyone's principles are ultimately up for sale. He's learned this from Max, who so far, has proved to be pinpoint accurate. But, as they walk the flat base-land that should become the area for tents, allowing everyone to remain here overnight, Problem No. 2 emerges. Beyond the ruined Ailsa Craig Castle, there is only one reasonably substantial structure on the island: the old white lighthouse. The only other structures are four separate cottages for the lighthouse men. As should have been anticipated, they all need refurbishment to a greater or lesser degree. It remains the plan that the band, crew and Heatwave Promotions' directors, staff, media pack and sponsor VIPs will stay in the buildings overnight. It is a romantic notion, but this isn't Ibiza; the Scottish climate is unpredictable and the beaches of the Balearics have a regular supply of public utilities that seem to be missing from Ailsa Craig. The lighthouse has been converted to run on solar power – a persuasive notion on such a mesmeringly beautiful day: the type of day that can persuade a pale-blue skinned Scotsman like Joseph Miller that sleeping out here, under a blanket of glistening stars, is exactly what Gary Cassidy longed for. The peace and tranquility and the raw, natural, rugged beauty of the bizarre topography makes the two even more determined that the lack of services can be overcome. They press on.

'It's the only island ever tae have won a gold medal at the Olympics,' says Bobby, rhyming off some of the impressive facts that he has become aware of.

'Whit d'ye mean?' asks Joseph, unsure if Bobby is talking about a participant having represented the island independently.

Bobby acknowledges his confused look.

'Naw, ah mean the curlin' stones. That women's team fae Britain that won the Olympics in 2002 … their stones were aw fae here.'

'Ah, right,' says Joseph.

'An' ah'm only the third owner in six hunner fuckin' years!'

'Aye?' This does surprise Joseph.

'Aye. A bunch ae monks fae Ayrshire got their hands on it in the fifteenth century.'

'Whit for?'

'Fuck knows. Pagan sacrifice probably. We'll probably find the charred bones ae drunken bastards an' auld hoors just up behind the lighthouse wall,' says Bobby. 'See twenty years ago, a bunch ae daft fuckin' students took a snooker table up tae the top ae it, an' played some frames…'

'Fuck off!'

'They did, an' more than that, they did it in their fuckin' y-fronts.'

'Gie's peace,' says Joseph, laughing.

'Fuckin' tellin' ye! It's aw there in the sales documents,' says Bobby proudly.

They both look up towards the summit. The sides are so steep that they can't see it. Even Bobby starts to think that last 'salient fact' was simply a prank played on him by the selling agents. 'Bloody impressive though, eh?'

'Aye,' Joseph agrees. 'It is.'

'Gary would've loved aw this.'

'Ah know, Bob. This is a great thing yer dain' for him.'

Bobby turns away when Joseph says this, and walks off slowly, hands in pockets. Joseph knows to give him some space.

Joseph wanders through the lighthouse building alone. It was built

in 1886 by the father of the writer Robert Louis Stevenson. This revelation more than any other had Bobby in raptures, convinced that
the island might have been the inspiration for the son's most famous
book – the one that meant so much to Gary and helped sustain him
while he was in prison. 'Aye, we might need tae find some fuckin'
buried treasure once aw the bloody bills start comin' in,' Joseph said
when Bobby revealed this particular fact. The lighthouse building
is in reasonably good condition, Joseph notes. He is pleasantly surprised to find a small helipad on the open ground just beyond it.
He makes an asterisked note of this. One of his own fears about the
event is someone falling seriously ill or an emergency occurring that
requires urgent hospital attention. A working helipad indicates that
the lighthouse occupants of the past had the same concern.

The built structures adjacent haven't fared as well as the lighthouse. They wear the faded grandeur of an old Hollywood actress:
dusty and dishevelled but still trying to appear serene. Wild Atlantic
gales have blasted their walls, and their roofs look as if demolition is
their only safe option. Joseph wanders further. The four cottages at
the foot of the cliff are all uninhabitable. He makes a capitalised note
that the joiners who are working on the stage construction will need
to have their remit extended to cover a 'sixty-minute makeover'-type
regeneration of these buildings. In one of the cottages, Joseph finds
some papers. He quickly leafs through the sheaf, pausing at unusual
statements or grainy photographs that jump out. One hundred years
ago, nearly thirty people occupied these cottages: granite miners and
lighthouse keepers, but also farmers and occasional birdwatchers.
He is surprised to learn that, until 1970, there was even a tearoom
on the island for day trippers. Granite blasting is now prohibited.
The previous owners acceded to environmentalist pressure that it
disturbed the seabird population. But enough of the smooth, blue
hone granite boulders remain loose to justify the £25,000 lease paid
by Kays Curling, the local curling-stone industry specialists. Beyond
this, there isn't much sign that man has ever been here. An old light
railway line that led from the quarry to the pier has distintegrated.

Large fog signals to protect approaching craft are long since inoperative. And as he strolls on, it becomes apparent why. Hettie once told him that Gary Cassidy imagined there was a different type of life on the west-facing side of this strange, granite knuckle, and he was right. Joseph peers through dense undergrowth and sees evidence of the third-biggest gannet colony in Britain. If they decide to come to the party, the carnage portrayed in Alfred Hitchcock's film will seem as tame as a couple of swooping budgies by comparison. Problem No. 4 is noted: *About forty fucking thousand hungry nicotine-headed gannets the size of flying rabbits dive-bombing the audience for food scraps.*

That'll certainly make the news, Joseph muses.

When he returns to the beach, Bobby has pitched their tent and started a fire. Joseph half expects him to have waded out into the Irish Sea and caught fish with a wooden branch whittled into the shape of a spear. In fact, Bobby has simply brought along a portable barbecue, a box of Swan Vestas and a few burgers from McGarritys the butcher. It is almost 8 pm and it is beginning to cool rapidly on the shaded side of the island, where they are. They watch the streetlights slowly emerge along the edge of Ayrshire, ten miles away. It still feels that you could almost reach out and touch the mainland.

Joseph takes out his iPod and plugs it into a small, circular, metallic speaker. He has made a playlist.

Bobby calls him a geek. 'Fifty-odd an' still a fuckin' music anorak,' he says.

They both laugh, and then sit in contemplative silence, eating charred burgers and drinking from bottles of Budweiser as the Super Furry Animals yearn for life in the Presidential Suite.

Chapter Thirty-Three

July 2015

'There's a problem,' admits the fat councillor.

Judging by how much this heavy man is sweating, Max Mojo isn't sure if that problem is personal hygiene-related, or Big Bang-related. He regards the obesity statistic seated next to him on a bench on an elevated banking of land that faces west, allowing a panorama in which the Ailsa Craig is the centrefold. Max tries hard to conceal his utter disdain and contempt for people like Cramond Crockett. Max has concluded – without evidence to support his theory – that Cramond Crockett is a product of a previous era's Scottish Labour-driven, union-orientated political class, which permitted widescale abuse of everything from personal expenses to commercial junkets to chauffeur-driven taxis ferrying officials home pished from every conceivable event where they'd be (mis)representing their constituents. Such men – and they are almost exclusively men, in Max's experience – are easy prey for the bribe. The Big Bang needs such a man on the inside of the local Ayrshire Council chambers. The event has stoked a mass of opprobrium and the Council are being placed in a difficult position. Since Ailsa Craig is a privately owned entity, it is difficult to invoke legislation that would prevent an essentially private event taking place there. Max has appeared on television in the last few weeks arguing successfully that The Big Bang differs little from the many times the previous owner held private barbecues on Ailsa Craig's beaches for his friends. It should matter not, Max has argued, that Bobby just happens to have many more friends, and a more powerful sound system. A Green Party spokesperson, who was invited to appear on the same programme, was shouted down by the youthful audience for suggesting that Max's associates would be guilty of a form of gannet genocide, and that all involved should be arrested if the gig goes ahead.

With the gig's momentum building up, rehearsals going as well as can be expected from such a bunch of temperamental fuck-ups, and the dramatic eyelid stage almost complete, Max has elected to remove the one remaining blockage that he feels might threaten proceedings. Max has paid Cramond Crockett to ensure the gig's smooth passage through the local Council's Licensing Board hearing. For Heatwave Promotions to sell food, alcohol and any gig-themed merchandising requires a licence granted by the nearest authority. Cramond Crockett serves on the committee and has apparently secured this licence by spreading about some of the £15,000 Max has given him. Unfortunately, in a drunken night out with colleagues, the Councillor has let it slip that the gig is only proceeding because he intervened.

'Ya stupid fat cunt, ye!' Max screams.

'Keep yer voice, doon, for fuck's sake,' says Cramond Crockett. 'This'll no' come tae anythin'.'

'So whit are ye fuckin' botherin' me aboot it for, then, ya dick?'

'Ah just felt ye needed to know, ken?' says Cramond patting Max's arm in a condescending manner. In fact, Cramond Crockett has concealed the worst of this story. He is actively under investigation and has just been suspended. Not for Max Mojo's Big Bang licensing bribe – that is as yet undetected – but for a series of similar cases over the course of the last five years. It is only a matter of time, however, before this latest transgression is discovered.

'So whit happens next then? An' where's ma fuckin' money?'

'It's fine,' Cramond assures Max, in a way that only serves to worry the band's manager more. 'None ae this'll track back tae you, even if somebody makes an issue ae it.'

'Whit d'ye mean "if"? Look Cramond, ye better be tellin' me the whole fuckin' story here, right?' Max is blazing. ''Cos if ah find out yer linin' us up here tae save yersel'—'

'Calm doon,' says Cramond, even though it looks to Max like a heart attack is on his immediate horizon, 'Ah've got it covered. Like ah says, ah just thought ye should be aware … in case some daft *Daily Record* reporter starts sniffin' aboot.'

Max Mojo leaves the sweating Councillor sitting on the bench. But only after he has unleashed such a voluble tirade of profanity that it prompts a woman in a house more then fifty yards away to emerge into her garden from her kitchen and yell an ignored protest.

Max catches a taxi back to the Manse in Crosshouse. The twenty minutes it takes to get there dissipates his anger sufficiently for him to be able to conceal it. But when he opens the door to the church hall where The Miraculous Vespas are practising, he receives another surprise. Eddie Sylvester is there, dressed in an emerald-green track suit and strumming a guitar as if he has never put it down.

'Holy fuck,' laughs Max. 'Whit've you come as … the Jolly Green Giant? It's no' a fancy dress gig, ya diddy!'

'Leave it, Max,' says Simon. 'He's here, aw'right, can we just leave it at that?'

'Aye, aw'right, keep yer fuckin' wig oan … Christ sake, ah huvnae even seen the cunt in nearly ten … naw, fuck … twenty years. Ye can imagine the shock, eh?'

Eddie Sylvester moves to his brother's side and whispers in his ear.

'He says he disnae want anybody swearin' around him, or else he's no' doin' the gig.'

Eddie leans in and whispers again.

'An' he also says that we've aw tae pray on stage before the gig.'

Max sniggers. 'Anythin' else for Pastor Jack Glass, eh?' says Max. 'Some Holy Ribena oan the rider? They wee communion wafer biscuits that the Catholics eat? A few fuckin' loafs an' fishes?'

Eddie leans in for a third time.

'As well as the fee, he wants his church roof in Prestwick fixed for free,' says Simon.

'Aye? Whit a fuckin' surprise, eh? In it for the money … just like every other cunt then!'

'Fuckin' shut it, Max,' Grant Delgado stands up to face off with

Max. 'Just fuckin' leave him, right. Who cares why he's dain' it …
why any of us are dain' it!'

'Aw, the big man finally speaks,' says Max.

Maggie instinctively moves closer to Grant, in order to try and
hold him back if necessary. But Max backs away. He turns and
heads for the house, to find his fellow Heatwave directors and to go
through outstanding actions.

As he leaves, he shouts, 'An' get fuckin' practisin' … ye'se sound
like fuckin' Coldplay!'

But they don't. Amazingly, given the time they have all, apart from
Simon Sylvester, spent away from their instruments, they sound
great. Grant's awkwardness instantly diminished as Simon Sylvester
hugged him warmly on meeting. And although Eddie occupies a
different state of mind, he too seemed happy to see the others when
he joined them, viewing them as potential converts rather than old
colleagues, no doubt, but still, he appears content to be once again
in their company. The rehearsals were going on for a fortnight before
the guitarist appeared. But he is a natural musician and picked up
the old songs instinctively, despite the lengthy passage of time since
he or anyone played them. Max's old faithful portable record player
is again back in the church hall, as it was during their first incarnation, and the band's initial nerves have given way to a renewed confidence as they reacquaint themselves with the vibes and the rhythms
of their troubled debut album.

Grant Delgado has been momentarily rocked, though, by Max's
confirmation that Joe McAlinden and Teenage Fanclub will be their
support acts. Teenage Fanclub are a Scottish institution, a band with
an incredible back catalogue of songs. It will be difficult to find
someone that doesn't like them. And Joe McAlinden has just released
a wondrous new record under the band name Linden. Both are very
accomplished acts with their own substantial, core support, so Grant

was initially surprised that they have agreed to appear on the under-
card, so to speak, particularly as Max Mojo tried to sign both of them
in the early 90s, in a vain attempt to refloat Biscuit Tin Records. The
Bellshill band were, however, impressed both by Max's bravado and
his personality, and why they went with Alan McGee at Creation,
neither manager nor the individual musicians can now recall.

The Big Bang setlist is emerging: the full content of their debut
LP, naturally, sustained by some of the band's favourite cover versions, and then three original songs written by Grant that didn't
make the initial album cut. The set runs to just over an hour, and
fifty minutes has been allocated to both support bands. Heatwave
Disco will provide the music before, between and after the bands,
and with no curfew, beyond that which the gannets and the gulls
might dictate, plans are being made to ensure enough records are
present, unlike on the Disco's first ever outing for Lizzie King's eighteenth birthday party.

Chapter Thirty-Four

August 2015

Max Mojo has secured countless promotional initiatives. On behalf of a formerly dormant company, he has banked lucrative advances from Apple, Sony, McDonalds, and Canal+ from France for the rights to capture the gig for a future feature film.

Heatwave Promotions Ltd, on the other hand, is accumulating increasing monthly losses. The company has taken on personal loans from Bobby Cassidy, one of its three directors, to cover the accelerating expenditure that the venture is now racking up. Joseph has mulled this over recently with Bobby, but they both accept that, although unconventional, Max appears to know what he is doing, and since they didn't actually set out to *make* money from the gig, achieving the most unlikely event anyone has ever contemplated has a heroic, even intoxicating, sense of folly about it .

Nevertheless, the fame that is now knocking daily on the big, wooden Manse doors is blinding them to a number of obvious concerns, ones which should seriously worry them, were they able to examine them more closely. First among these is the fact, unknown to his collaborators, that Max Mojo has set up the new promotions company with three designated directors, of which Max himself isn't one. Equally unknown is that Hamish May *is*. Max's long-term accountant has been controlling this process: establishing and registering the limited liability company and setting up the shareholders' rules of agreement to permit Max – a named non-executive director, and one-time bankrupt – access to the expenditure via the signature of one of the named shareholders: most conveniently, the oblivious Hammy.

Just like his hero, Malcolm McLaren, Max has accepted a verbal financial offer from Richard Branson at Virgin Records just as he is putting pen to paper on a better one that assigns future The Miraculous Vespas releases to the more appropriate Island Records. But this contract, like the other ones that deal with the incoming funds, is filtered through Biscuit Tin Ltd, a company with paper ownership largely assigned to Molly Wishart, Max's old and infirm mother. By the time the legal consequences of all of these complex deals and agreements are sorted out, Max plans to be long gone.

Bobby, Joseph, and the rest, know nothing of these important details, but Max has impressed everyone involved with The Big Bang. Even Grant Delgado now holds a grudging admiration for his ability to keep this runaway rollercoaster on track.

Max appears on Scotland Tonight; a late-night, current-affairs television programme. Questions are asked but it's a light grilling, nothing heavy. Like Jim White interviewing Brian Laudrup, as opposed to Jeremy Paxman torturing Michael Howard, the young presenter brown-noses Max, and it seems clear that she is hoping for an invite to The Big Bang, so regularly does she drop into the conversation that she's free that particular Saturday. Max laughs it off and focuses on the main intent.

'See, when we talked aboot independence for Ailsa Craig? We were bein' serious,' he says.

Abigail, the young presenter laughs.

'Whit are ye laughin' about?' he asks.

'Well, it's just a small island, it isn't actually a country,' she says. She is trying to play along with what she assumes is simply a jokey statement.

'So's Malta,' says Max. He isn't smiling.

'True,' she says.

'Wee Alex Salmond went tae the polls wi' less chance ae winnin' than us,' Max says, 'And now, Nicola's gonnae keep tryin' it until she gets what she wants.'

'How did you vote in the 2014 campaign?' asks Abigail.

'Never mind that,' says Max. 'Our campaign will have nothin' tae dae wi' that sham. We've got a justified case, and ownership, *and* self-sufficiency.'

Abigail has been warned about this interview. Colleagues have put Max Mojo up there with The Fall's Mark E. Smith and Shane McGowan of The Pogues as the interviewer's universally acknowledged 'short straw'. But she is ambitious and jumped at the opportunity. She is now unclear, though, whether Max is taking the piss on live television or whether he actually believes what he is saying.

'But what would you want to achieve from Independence for Ailsa Craig?' Abigail asks.

'Freedom,' says Max calmly. 'The freedom to do what we wanna do ... the freedom...' Once again he stares straight down a live camera and reaches right into the living rooms of thousands. '...to get loaded!'

Abigail wraps the interview up sharply. Max promised he wouldn't swear and he hasn't, but his final line – stolen from Primal Scream – has lit up social media once again.

As he speaks, The Big Bang tickets are being secreted into copies of *The Big Issue* the length and breadth of the UK. The deal done with the magazine is a genuine one this time. In the fraught months following the explosive trial in 1985 that sent numerous members of a Glasgow crime cartel to prison, Max Mojo disappeared. He and The Miraculous Vespas were unknowing pawns in a complex police sting that deliberately filtered substantial amounts of gangland money through the band via Washer Wishart, Max's moneylaundering father. Rather than accept any formal witness protection, Max elected to vanish and look after himself. As a consequence, he too was homeless for a time, before surfacing on Bobby Cassidy's bleached Ibizan doorstep with an old, suntanned producer, the 'lost' master tapes of the band's only recorded LP, and a new plan for world domination in tow.

Abigail Smart wants to ask him about these times past, and about the bizarre kidnapping of a Boy George lookalike. But Max has assured STV that such questions, if asked, would simply be ignored. He is a difficult but engaging person, Abigail surmises, and when the 'live recording' red lights go off, she finds him funny and grateful for the extensive plugs she has given the event and *The Big Issue* as they prepare to distribute their most unique printrun ever, the following morning.

Joseph Miller is back on the Ailsa Craig. He is watching something he never thought he would see: five helicopters chartered from the nearby Prestwick Airport and containing scribes and lenses representing some of the world's media are swarming around a small, half-domed timber structure that is being pulled into position by two small barges. Two wooden pillars, which were already there, have been supplemented by two others. These will be the four points the stage will be tied to using heavy nautical ropes. Joseph's concerns about the impact of Scotland's unpredictable and often volatile weather are shared by almost everyone involved – apart from Eddie Sylvester, that is, who seems perversely certain that a storm to make Hurricane Bawbag look like some light drizzle is coming. The construction of the stage has pragmatically incorporated Hairy Doug's sound and light rigs, the generators that will power them and portable dressing rooms and toilets. These have all been fitted back on the mainland, to allow them to be tested in advance and to save the additional carriage and complexity of fitting them *in situ*. Had the stage been planned for terra firma, everything would be fine. As it is, the sailing across was without major incident and the sea played along. Now though, fixing the structure to the posts using only ropes seems ill considered. But it's only two weeks until the gig, so there's no going back.

The project's costs are now running at £3.5 million, including the fees to the headline performers, which will be paid on invoice, but only post-gig. It's evident that no one on the band's side of the deal trusts anyone else. Three days after *The Big Issue*: Big Bang Special, and three-quarters of the golden tickets have been claimed. *The Big Issue* has a normal circulation of around a hundred thousand copies every week. With the organisation buying into the initiative described by Max Mojo, a printrun of five times that much was agreed. Almost ten thousand individuals, many of them vulnerable through drug dependency, abuse or homelessness, have been involved in the selling of them. A special price of three pounds per issue was accepted by the organisation and a reduction in the cost to the vendors of a pound has been negotiated. In addition, the Homeless World Cup has now also been added to the growing list of sponsors keen to be associated with this unusual and exciting act of twenty-first-century altruism.

Every night, the national news is carrying interviews with punters who have successfully acquired a ticket for one of the most eagerly awaited events in modern music. Inevitably, some tickets are finding their way onto eBay, and the buy-it-now figures are truly eye-watering, but Max has limited these apparent abuses by the late announcement and the mechanism of the release of the tickets. Perhaps inevitably, there have been some negative consequences. Three separate *Big Issue* sellers have been assaulted for their stock, but by and large, the success of the venture has been claimed by almost all.

It's the evening before the gig: 28th of August 2015. A large table has been set up in the church hall of the Manse. Max has organised external caterers and in the kitchen of the old house adjacent, a modern-day Ayrshire banquet is being prepared.

'Did ye'se get the Killie pies?' Max shouts from the hall doorway.

A muffled reply confirms.

'It's no' a fuckin' scranfest without the Killie pies, man,' he says to his fellow dinner guests. They number thirteen including Max. He is sat at the centre, naturally. To his left sit Bobby Cassidy and then The Miraculous Vespas: Maggie, Grant, Simon and Eddie. At the end of the table is Andy Fordyce, a young follower of the Reverend Doctor who has been brought in to bless not only the dinner, but The Big Bang event and the apocalyptic scenario that Eddie is certain will follow it. For Eddie and Andy this is a 'last supper' in every conceivable interpretation. To Max's immediate right are Joseph Miller, Hammy May and Hairy Doug. Next to Hammy is Donald McDonald, the local joiner who has embraced the challenges of building the stage and making the cottages on Ailsa Craig temporarily habitable. Donald was an old friend of Washer Wishart, Max's equally larger-than-life father. He wouldn't have accepted this thankless task otherwise. He has now submitted his invoices, but sees his work also as a way to repay an emotional debt to the old man, an opportunity denied him when Washer died in 2007.

Next to Donald sits Jimmy Stevenson. Jimmy was the original van driver for both Heatwave Disco and The Miraculous Vespas. Like Hammy, Jimmy Stevenson is confined to a wheelchair, albeit Jimmy's looks like a serious bit of standard NHS kit. By comparison, Hammy's looks like a toy. Jimmy Stevenson is, to some extent, the guest of honour, but he is now well into his eighties and no longer has any idea where he is, or even who his dinner companions are. He has been retrieved from the old folks' home where he now resides. The final guest is Bernadette, a nurse accompanying Jimmy in the event that he struggles to make it to the dessert.

Max turns the volume of his old faithful record player down. It has been playing *Electric Warrior* by Marc Bolan & T. Rex. Appropriately, Max waits until the end of 'Life's A Gas.'

'Friends, compadres, musicians, fellow travellers … Jimmy's nurse,' he says. 'Welcome all. This is a momentuous night for aw ae us. We aw stand on the brink ae immortality.' He glances at Jimmy, and the oxygen mask that covers the old man's mouth and nose. 'Well, nearly aw ae us.'

Two young chefs walk through from the Manse kitchen, carrying four plates each. As Max continues his opening address, they work their way around the rear of the table, setting the starter plates down from left to right along the wooden table. Wine is freely flowing; grapes are theatrically placed around long-stem candles. It feels like the opening scenes of a low-budget Peter Greenaway film.

'So, before we get stuck in, ah'm gonnae pass tae Joey, who's remindin' us why we're aw here,' Max concludes.

'Fur the dosh?' suggests Simon Sylvester.

Everyone laughs as if he is being deliberately ridiculous, whilst secretly acknowledging the truth in his statement. It still isn't clear how or when that money will work its way to each of those to whom it is due.

'Fuck off!' says Max. 'Joey?'

Joseph stands. He reaches into his pocket and takes out a piece of paper that has seen better days. Sellotape is keeping it together. He unfolds it, and then passes it to a surprised Bobby. 'Here, mate. This is your night,' says Joseph.

Bobby takes the paper, and with it, several deep breaths. He stands and reaches for his glasses. His arthritic hands hold the paper awkwardly. They, like the rest of him, are trembling. He says nothing in introduction, pressing straight into a recitation of *The Man Who Loved Islands* by his brother, Gary Cassidy. Bobby reads the last line slowly and sits down again.

Joseph has been watching the reactions of the others. He notices Maggie has taken Grant's hand. Eddie Sylvester and Andy, his disciple, appear to be praying. Jimmy Stevenson is rocking slowly back and forth. Hammy is still eating and eyeing up Jimmy's untouched plate. Hairy Doug's eyes are closed. He may be asleep.

As Bobby finishes the reading, tears roll. He wipes them, embarrassed at how regularly they flow nowadays. He makes a joke about how their fathers – his, Joseph's and Max's – would've booted their collective balls for not acting like real men. He reinforces this point by highlighting the love of golf from their father's generation: 'Ye can communicate wi' yer mates as ye walk away in a different fuckin' direction fae each other. Standin' oan the tee whisperin' that ye've got a lump oan yer baws, then ye head intae the rough for ten fuckin' minutes tae recover fae sayin' it out loud. There wis nae call for face-tae-face revelations.'

The younger diners nod in acknowledgement of the Scottish temperament. They toast absent friends. Joseph thinks of two young women: first his daughter Jennifer, to whom he has recently posted an extensive and very personal written apology. A strange birthday present, admittedly but one that might make future birthdays with her a possibility. It is a long shot, but if this unusual experience has demonstrated anything, it is that long shots are sometimes worth taking, despite their risks. The other woman about which he has thought is Megan Carter, in many ways the catalyst for the whole situation. If she hadn't prompted him to confront the obvious fact that he missed his oldest friend, he wouldn't have responded to Hammy's SOS call in the way he did. Joseph hopes Megan is safe and content, wherever she now finds herself. The others listen. No questions are asked. It's beginning to feel like one of Grant Delgado's group-counselling sessions. Bobby wishes Hettie was here, but she is preparing for the opening of her newest exhibition the following weekend. Bobby suspects she wouldn't have come, anyway. It is enough that they are speaking again, but too much to hope for more, perhaps. However, her absence is notable, for Joseph as well as Bobby. More than this though, Bobby naturally wishes Gary was here, although if he was, none of this would be happening. Bobby, and Joseph for that matter, have found a form of redemption in this crazy stunt. They have recaptured something that had been lost: a joy for life and for all of the possibilities it still presents. They have appreciated that ambition isn't only for the young. It is their chimera; both of them clinging to this fantasy for different reasons and outcomes. Bobby Cassidy has been slowly but gradually drowning in the strangeness of life; of no longer being the carefree youngster he once was – the physicality of his impermanence writ large across his aching, misshapen hands and his inability to walk long distances without feeling like a stroke was imminent. But the vision that he now shares with his childhood friend has taken these debilitating thoughts and placed them in a locked box under the stairs. They will return no doubt, but he is focused on the here and now, and, despite his reservations, he owes Joseph, Hammy, Laurie Revlon and, improbably, Max Mojo for restoring the balance.

Joseph, on the other hand, knows the source of his depression has been an overactive and sensitive brain. His anxiety only manifests itself in dark, disturbing thoughts that force him to retreat. He has found himself at odds in a world in which cheerfully faked apathy is the default setting. He has struggled to cope with the knowledge of having one day to die, and with every exhausting morning following another night of patchy pockets of sleep, he began to assume that that day had come. An irrational response, admittedly, but the brain is defiantly strong and his worked out how to overpower the various medications ascribed to keep it dormant. But now, that same, uncertain brevity of life has provided a stimulus of positivity that Joseph Miller didn't previously realise he possessed. The Big Bang has become everything, almost to the point that, if death suddenly came after its conclusion, he begins to feel it would all have been worth it.

So they all drink and fondly recall those who can't be there. They indulge the emerald-green Reverend Doctor and let him say a prayer to an invisible entity above their heads, despite his inference that this god will smite them all the following day. They laugh as Max Mojo lifts a slightly downbeat mood and regales them with self-depracatory – and undoubtedly libellous – tales of nights out with such luminaries as Jimmy Somerville, Pete Burns and the girls from Bananarama. Bobby notices Max's phone on the table vibrating on silent. It's an incoming call from a 'CC'. Max ignores it. He tells of a bacchanalian orgy involving surviving members of The Sex Pistols and also of Camden lock-ins with The Pogues and Nick Cave's Bad Seeds. Finally, Max talks of the time he headbutted Bob Geldof at the recording of the Band Aid single. Where Max's other stories have the definite aura of elaboration and exaggeration, Bobby knows this one to be true, as Geldof also appeared in The Miraculous Vespas documentary to confirm it. Grant Delgado isn't aware of this, despite having been present at the Live Aid recording. The story from Max's perspective is revealing and so full of apparent regret and yearning, that Grant appears to soften his attitude slightly to Max. Although never as close as Bobby and Joseph, Grant and Max once shared something unique. They were friends briefly, and over these last two weeks a tiny part of why that was once important to both of them has returned. Only Bobby seems to have noticed that 'CC' has tried to call Max five times. A message alert has also flashed up briefly. It read 'Max. Call me. It's URGENT...!!!' It, too, goes unanswered.

Bizarrely, given the multitude of things that could yet go wrong, almost everyone is looking forward to the gig now; everyone except Jimmy Stevenson. His nurse goes to the loo, leaving Hammy watching over Jimmy. She returns to find that the old man has fallen forward and his face is now fully submerged in pie and mash. Hammy had just turned away for the briefest of seconds, he proclaims, defensively. An ambulance is called. It arrives sharply. Jimmy is lifted into it like an old Marshall amp being carefully loaded into his own old 1972 Campervan. He won't have long, his nurse says. But she assures them that he really wanted to come tonight, to see old faces.

Bobby and Joseph are standing outside, watching the ambulance pull away. Both doubt that Jimmy even knew where he was, and perhaps not even who he was. There's a sudden prevailing sadness as they regard the indignity of an almost lifeless Jimmy Stevenson being pushed around, fed, cleaned up, unable to do anything for himself. He's close to death and they know they won't ever see him again. Jimmy was once a close friend of Bobby's dad, Harry. Another link with the past now all but severed.

Inside the hall, old classic records are getting an airing and Grant and Maggie are dancing. The relaxed air is thick with marijuana smoke.

Still outside, Bobby and Joseph are reflecting on how far they've come in just a few short months. Thanks to The Big Bang, people across the world now know the story of Gary Cassidy, the Scots Guardsman who saved his friend and comrade's life during the Falklands conflict and returned to the UK to find a malignant newspaper media accusing him of desertion. The tragedy of the Cassidy family, and of Gary's very specific battles with Post Traumatic Stress Disorder, are now the subject of a bidding war between several film companies. Max Mojo's assertion that this outrageously expensive venture will eventually more than wash its face financially appears, amazingly, to be coming to fruition.

'Ye aw'right, boys?' A voice in the darkness, beyond the wall.

'Aye,' says Bobby.

'Ah'm Stevie Dent. Ah'm wi' the *Daily Mail*. Ah'm a pal ae Max's. Is he in?'

'Wait there,' says Bobby.

But Joseph innocently opens the gate and ushers the man in. He stands next to the journalist and asks him if he is on the press list for tomorrow.

'Eh … aye. Like ah said, me an' Max go way back. Ah'm from Crosshouse tae. Him an' I used tae be in a band th'gither.'

There is a flicker of recognition as Joseph remembers the Henderson church hall riot. Heatwave Disco, in the form of Joseph Miller and his minder for the night, Malky McKay, were supporting the original Vespas, who were playing a farewell gig. Back then, Max was known by his real name, Dale Wishart, and he was the amateur band's singer and frontman. The balding, fat man in front of Joseph was also on the stage that night. He played bass. What a strange coincidence.

Suddenly there's a crack, and then another two in rapid succession. The *Daily Mail* journalist hits the gravel as if he's been shot. It's dark and the lack of illumination is concealing the colour of his face. *Fuck sake*, thinks Joseph, *two ambulances called in the space ae twenty fuckin' minutes!*

'Whit a fuckin' shot, eh?' Joseph turns around to see Max strolling towards him. He is holding a rifle.

'What the fuck, Max? Have you just shot this guy?' Joseph is stunned.

Bobby is behind Max but seems surprisingly relaxed. *What is going on here?* thinks Joseph.

'Calm doon, Joe-boxer. It's just an air rifle pellet,' says Max. 'Get up ya fat cunt,' he adds, rolling a kick at the stricken journalist's stomach.

Steven Dent moans. Another dull Doc Marten is delivered to his face.

'Fuck sake, Max … calm down, man!' Joseph yells.

'This devious cunt killed The Miraculous Vespas first time around. He's no' dain' it again this time.' Max cocks his air rifle. 'Ah used tae shoot big coos on the arse wi' this wee beauty. So fuckin' glad ah kept it for one last spree on this fuckin' shitebag.'

Steven Dent is dazed and confused. A pellet is embedded in his cheek. It's unclear yet if the other two hit their target. Helped by Simon Sylvester and Hairy Doug, the three drag Steven Dent into the church hall and proceed to gaffa tape him to a chair.

Grant, Maggie, the Reverend and his flock have gone to bed in the Manse. Donald the boatmaker left just after Jimmy swan-dived his dinner. The surrealism of the evening was becoming too much for him, plus, he had agreed to head over at dawn on the first of the small flotilla of private-hire boats that have been corralled into service following the recent FaceBook appeals.

As they huckle the hack into the hall, Hammy watches on, bemused.

'You're fuckin' finished this time, ya mad bastard!' croaks Steven Dent before the tape seals his mouth.

'Remember that scene in Reservoir Dogs?' says Max calmly. 'Get me the shears!'

Steven Dent's eyes display panic over the top of the battleship-grey tape.

'Ach, fuckin' behave yerself, ya prick! Think ah'm dain' a stretch for a waster like you?' Max turns to Bobby. 'This dick once called me the most hateful man in Britain. He'll need tae think ae a better headline this time.'

Max aims a kick at the chair and in trying to avoid it, Steven Dent overtopples the chair. Man and chair now lie on their side, where they will remain for the whole night.

Chapter Thirty-Five

29th August 2015. The Big Bang, Ailsa Craig

When the guests at the Crosshouse Church Manse awake in the morning, they find that one of their number is missing. Max Mojo is nowhere to be seen.

'Where the fuck's Max?' This is becoming the morning's clarion call. No one knows where he is.

Bobby assumes he's headed over to Ailsa Craig at the crack of dawn. Steven Dent is also gone, freed from his chair of taped captivity.

The official order of travel was to be first Max, along with The Miraculous Vespas and Hammy. With Hairy Doug's prefabricated setting up work completed, he was scheduled to head over on a later boat, along with the sound technicians and the support bands. But with Max gone, Hammy and Hairy Doug leave to take the next official boat.

Hammy's deeply-rooted thalassophobia resurfaces. 'Ma stomach's in knots,' he admits to Hairy Doug, before adding, 'but ma arse is definitely workin' in miles per hour!'

A separate boat has been hired for the sponsors. Bobby and Joey remain to do local press and media interviews at Troon Harbour before going across on the last of the official boats. The *Waverley* idea has been aborted. It was a romantic and very photogenic notion, but practicality and cost prohibit it. The paddle steamer *Waverley* is a Class V craft. The scale of the vessel and the lack of any substantial jetty mean that the closest it could get to the tiny island is almost half a mile offshore. This hadn't fazed Max Mojo initially. He had assured the bands that launching the *Waverley*'s two remaining lifeboats to carry the five-hundred-strong audience onto the island would look fantastic and would be captured by the worldwide coverage being planned for the event. The owners of the vessel, Waverley Excursions, disagreed, however, and a plan B was needed. Social media answered the call and now nearly seventy boats of varying sizes and safety classifications are lining up for the trip across the Irish Sea. Max argued that the evacuation of Dunkirk had involved rowing boats and no one now viewed that as anything other than an unqualified maritime success. Why would anyone object to a similar, smaller sailing over a shorter distance? he reasoned. But complain they did. Numerous environmentalists, a small group from Amnesty International, and a splinter protest group claiming Independence for Arran are all attempting to blockade the vessels docked in Troon Harbour; the designated pick-up point for those with golden tickets. Troon Harbour has been selected because the local speedboat club responded to the May-Day Hammy had issued. A sizable donation has been promised. The Coastguard is circling them all, trying to keep the narrow entry to the harbour clear. Speedboats are the order of the day due to the time factor, their general manoeuvrability, and the worry over yacht fins grounding on the rocks. On the mainland shore, the police are in heavy attendance, although they are maintaining something of a watching brief. Helicopters circle out to sea, and a biplane on a repetitive fly-past trails a large 'John 3:16' banner from its tail. Bobby figures Eddie Sylvester has been behind this one.

It's just after lunch when Bobby Cassidy and Joseph Miller appear at Scott's restaurant overlooking Troon Harbour. The car park is mobbed and individuals from various security firms are patrolling the gate, checking that people either have guest passes for the gig or for the press conferences, or, more specifically, that they possess a golden ticket. Joseph's betablockers are working overtime, and although he remains excited, he is nervously anticipating some disasterous, unforeseen drowning event just beyond the next wave. *Anxiety is a complete cunt!* he thinks.

Bobby and Joseph are ushered into the restaurant's glazed conservatory. The weather has been kind to them so far, but it is not expected to hold. Sunlight glistens on the water as the collected boats stock up for their anticipated passengers. Bobby has been here on many occasions recently, almost all with Lizzie, who lives only a few hundred yards away. She has turned down the opportunity to come over for the gig. She feels it is still too soon and that his thoughts should be with Gary and Hettie on this particular day.

They sit with their backs to the glass. A red cord line is in front of them, separating them from a multitude of flashing cameras and people holding small, shiny tape recorders or smartphones. The questions are conducted by a young girl Bobby recognises. He thinks she works for STV. She introduces herself as Abigail Smart.

First question:

'Bobby, why is this event so important to you?'

Bobby pauses, takes a deep breath. 'It's tae honour my brother, Gary. He died a few years back but he loved islands, that wee yin over there particularly. He had a hard time after the Falklands, ken? We just wanted tae dae something unique tae remember him.'

'Bobby, how much money did you make as MC Bobcat?'

'Eh,' Bobby looks at Abigail for help. She steps in.

'That isn't relevant, I'm sorry.' She points. 'Yes … Jenny.'

'Who's idea was it to reform The Miraculous Vespas?'

'Em, ah knew Max from way back … ah worked on The Miraculous Vespas remixes in the 90s. Once we had agreed tae try this, he suggested the band. So, ah suppose it was him.'

'…And where is he now?' journo Jenny continues.

'We're no' really sure,' Bobby says, laughing nervously and looking at Joseph, who instinctively shrugs. 'No, seriously, ah think he's over on the island. He's a perfectionist. Nothin' left tae chance.'

'It's the *NME* here. Have you heard the band, Bobby? Rumours are that they still aren't speaking to each other.'

'Well, ah can confirm that that isnae true. The rehearsals have sounded brilliant,' Bobby confirms.

'Any possibility of new material?'

'Aye. Every chance. Deal's already been signed wi' Island Records for a new LP.' Bobby says this and then wishes he hadn't. He isn't sure if Max has made this known to anyone, least of all the band themselves. The audible gasps as he reveals this suggest the exclusive nature of his news; he feels worse.

'How difficult has this event been to put on? It's the *Daily Record*, and can I direct this one to Joseph Miller?'

This startles Joseph. He hasn't wanted to be in the forefront of any of the publicity. His role, as it was for Heatwave Disco back in their day, was by preference a supporting one. But now, with numerous cameras trained on him, he has no option.

'Eh … it's been pretty tough.'

Joseph appreciates that elaboration is needed, but he isn't sure where to start. Should he talk about the multi-million-pound costs being incurred? Should he focus on the complex interpersonal relationships between all of the participants and how their fragile egos have threatened the whole thing right up until last night? Should he highlight his worries about the impending weather change and the safety implications of that? For the last three nights in succession, Joseph has dreamed of a returning Hurricane Bawbag suddenly sweeping in across the Irish Sea and submerging the island and all of its temporary population. The storm-force winds that battered Scotland in late 2011 and were colloquially named after the Scottish slang for an annoying or irritating person, reached more than 100 mph on the west coast. Anything similar and his timber-lined eyelid stage and all aboard it will be heading to Oz faster than Judy fucking Garland. Max Mojo and The Miraculous Vespas are one thing, but imagine being implicated in the whole of Teenage Fanclub being lost at sea? It doesn't bear thinking about. So, given all of this, and that it is the *Daily Record* asking, he keeps his words short and his tone upbeat.

'…but we have a great team. No challenge is too much for them.'

The lights are strong and Bobby is finding it difficult to focus closely.

'Yes,' says Abigail, acknowledging a tall man in a dark suit whose hand has been raised.

'Are you Bobby Cassidy and Joseph Miller, directors of Heatwave Promotions Ltd?' The question seems unusually formal and the other members of the media pack turn to look to the rear, where the voice has come from.

'Eh, aye. Ye know that … it's on the board outside,' says Bobby.

The suited man and three colleagues step forward.

'I'm arresting you in connection with an ongoing enquiry into fraud and the bribery of a Council official. You do not have to say anything but it may harm your defence if you do not mention when questioned something which you later rely on in court. Anything you do say may be given in evidence.'

There are stunned faces everywhere. Someone shouts, 'Fuck me, are you getting this? Hector … tell me you're getting this?'

'Do you understand,' says the suit.

'Whit the fuck's goin' on?' Bobby pleads. 'We huvnae done anythin'!'

'Ye've nothin' tae worry about, then, sir,' says the suit.

Handcuffs seem unnecessary but they are deployed anyway. Bobby yelps as his fragile hands suffer from their steely grip. Joseph Miller's mind is swimming with the likelihood that Lucinda must be behind this. An unacceptable irritation at him having had the gall to contact their daughter to explain his absence from much of her life.

As they progress down the wooden stairs of Scott's Restaurant, they are mobbed. No one is quite sure what is happening. Over to the left, at the gated entrance to the marina, gig-goers are beginning to assemble. It's an ordely queue, Joseph notes; not what he has anticpated. He foresaw five hundred drunken, hallucinating, rabble-rousing youngsters fresh from their first T in the Park, abusing the boat owners and falling into the water. But they all look like male or female versions of him. Middle-aged, respectable, respectful. Out for a good time, but not at any cost. As he is led to the waiting unmarked police cars, he reflects on how the gig-going audience has changed over the years. Fifty-year-olds go to see bands on stage. Teenagers go to see DJs in an aircraft hanger or a field; DJs who play other people's records and get paid about fifty grand a night for it. On their first night out, Heatwave Disco was paid thirty pounds, which, due to a variety of unforeseen circumstances, turned into a loss of about a hundred pounds.

'Mind your head, sir.' Joseph can't help but feel the irony that these thoughts invade as he is being arrested for alleged fraud and bribery. It is only a cry from behind the car which snaps him out of it.

'Dad!'

He turns sharply.

A young, blonde girl is trying to push her way through the throng. She waves. He shouts her name from inside the car as it edges away.

'They should fuckin' be here by now!' says Hammy to Hairy Doug.

The weather has shifted ominously from bright sunshine to threateningly overcast. Behind his helmet, Eddie Sylvester is grinning. Hammy is watching anxiously from the stage deck where he has been deposited earlier. The beach is no place for a wheelchair, and Hairy Doug has suggested he's better out on the floating stage.

All three bands are now backstage in the tiny, makeshift compartment that is doubling as a green room. Beer is being consumed, and perhaps because no one has a viable phone signal, they all seem to be getting along famously. Grant Delgado has relaxed as Raymond McGinley declares his love not only for The Miraculous Vespas LP and its influence on the Fanclub *Grand Prix* album, but for Grant's novel, too. Joe McAlinden is deep in conversation with Eddie Sylvester, who has lifted the visor and is trying to convert him. Maggie is showing Norman Blake a camera that she has brought along with her. She has secured her own personal assignment with *Rolling Stone* magazine to record the event from her perspective.

Hammy watches the boats hustle and harry around the buoys at the end of the tiny jetty like they are frantic America's Cup competitors elbowing for room. He finds it absolutely astonishing that there have been no collisions so far. The helicopters continue to circle the island and, although it's still early evening, arc lights are now detectable.

'Maybe you should start the DJ-ing?' says Hairy Doug. It's only an hour until Joe McAlinden's band is due to open the show. Hammy can't believe that Bobby and Joey – and also Max *fucking* Mojo – aren't here. But the majority of those who have secured golden tickets are. They have pitched tents to the rear of the beach. No one is entirely sure about the tidelines, so the stewards hired by Max have been urging caution. The catering stalls are no more than covered, branded trellises, but their sponsors' logos are illuminating the shaded beach with their vibrant dayglo livery. It isn't as Hammy pictured it: it's way better and much more impressive, in his opinion. Max might be a mental cunt – and an AWOL one at that – but he has put on a show that few in the inner circle thought possible. He seems to have considered everything, from the food to the transportation to the acquisition of the necessary permits.

'Do you know a man called Cramond Crockett?'

'No, I've never heard of him. Who is he?' asks Joseph naively. The left side of his neck is throbbing. He feels the tension rising. He has been on double-doses these last few weeks. His answers are being recorded.

In an adjacent, windowless room, a question in a similar vein is asked: 'Did Councillor Cramond Crockett solicit payments from your company in return for licences being granted?'

'Eh?' says Bobby 'Ah really don't know what you're talkin' about, mate.'

The questioning of the two men continues in a small police station in Ayr while reporters and televison cameramen amass in the car park outside. None of the waiting hacks are quite sure why they are there, but something unusual seems to be occurring.

Joseph assumes last night's air-rifle incident is somehow connected, but that hasn't been raised and he isn't intending to assist. Bobby's mind flashes back to Max's phone and the ignored calls from a 'CC'. Likewise, he keeps that concealed until clarity on the wider issue dawns. Following another series of questions about the mysterious Councillor, Bobby stares up at what he assumes is a CCTV camera.

'Ah'd like tae speak tae a lawyer please.'

The detective laughs at this.

'Appealing to a smoke detector won't do ye much good, pal.'

Bobby feels foolish.

'Look, yer under caution but this isn't CSI Ayrshire! Just help us with the enquiries and then ye can be on yer way.'

'Ah don't know whit we're supposed tae have done, so how the fuck can ah help ye?' Bobby tries not to sound aggressive but he is rattled. God knows how the gig is going, if it hasn't actually been abandoned already amid the chaos of its organisers detainment.

The detective sighs. 'Okay,' he says. He sits down, legs over the chair and leaning on the front as if auditioning for the CIA. 'Councillor Cramond Crockett has been arrested. He is accused of accepting bribes to facilitate clean licences for pubs, nightclubs and numerous events over the course of five years. In tandem with others on the Licensing Board, they have accepted in excess of two hundred thousand pounds in illegal payments.' The detective pauses. He scans Bobby's face for cognitive signs but all he sees is the confused face of a toddler trying to work out how to solve a Rubik's Cube by eating it. 'Heatwave Promotions Ltd – the company that you are a director of – paid Cramond Crockett fifteen grand to secure a licence for this occurence on the Ailsa Craig.'

'Did we fuck!' says a genuinely startled Bobby Cassidy.

'Yes, ye did. The Councillor has admitted it. Too late to prevent the licence getting withdrawn, mind you,' says the detective. 'Are you still pleading innocence?'

'Too fuckin' right,' says Bobby. 'Where's the evidence beyond some dodgy official sayin' it happened?'

'Well…' The detective smiles and look at his colleague, who also smiles knowingly. 'Ye wrote him a cheque!'

'Whit? Don't talk pish. We don't even have a chequeboo– … Haud on, whose name's on the cheque?' Bobby asks, a realisation of sorts beginning to dawn.

'The cheque was signed by a Hamish May, one of the three designated directors of your company.'

'Holy fuck!' says Bobby. 'That fuckin' devious, connivin' cunt!'

Hamish May is behind the Heatwave Disco decks. He will not be touching any microphones. Painful memories are the ones that take longest to fade. But, despite the unforeseen circumstances, he seems relaxed playing the records. He has watched Bobby Cassidy doing it enough times to appreciate the relative simplicity of it all. It's all about knowing your audience. He starts with a Clash song, which brings cheers from the beach. He follows it with well-known songs by The Happy Mondays, The Charlatans and Oasis: safe choices for a nostalgic demographic. The sound quality is fantastic. He might be a rustic old fucker, thinks Hammy, but fair play to Hairy Doug … the crusty old bastard knows his stuff. Hammy experiments. He takes a calculated risk. He picks out a record solely on the basis of its title: 'North American Scum' by a band called LCD Soundsystem. The crowd on the shingle goes collectively mad. People are dancing. It has started to rain lightly but no one seems to be caring. A string of well-received records is played before the allocated stage time for Linden. Their guitars have been checked one last time, the lights are illuminating the stage. The film crew from Canal+ have given their own thumbs-up … and Joe McAlinden follows his young band onto the stage. Joe is dressed in a heavy green parka with a furry hood. He lives up the coast in Argyll and knows how quickly the weather on this exposed coastline can change.

'Hi, we're Linden,' says Joe to hooting and hollering from the five hundred. 'This is a bit mental, eh?' he admits. 'We're gonna do a few songs for ye, but first, can ah point out the fire exits? One to the left of the beach – into the sea – and the other, up there tae the right an' into the scary woods.' Joe strums. 'This is a new song, called "Rest and Be Thankful".'

Linden's set is polished and well received. The blond-haired frontman looks genuinely pleased to be on this unusual floating stage, although by the time he leaves the front of it, the waves around it are swelling. Hammy wonders how much attention Joey paid to the rising tide, never mind the impact of any developing waves. He looks across at the Teenage Fanclub consortium and imagines that few of them will have Patrick Swayze or Keanu Reeves-level surfing skills. They are wearing rollneck sweaters, for fuck's sake; they just don't look the type.

It's 9 pm, on the mainland *and* on the island. Despite an outrageous claim in Max Mojo's impromptu independence manifesto, Ailsa Craig hasn't reverted to the non-GMT time zone that Max had suggested it once occupied; not yet anyway. Bobby Cassidy and Joseph Miller are being released from Ayr Police Station. A car has been called for them but they aren't entirely sure where it should take them. They can't get to the gig now. Even if they find a boat owner willing to take them in the darkness, the weather is worsening, and the gig will be over before they get there. After some anticipated paparazzi pursuits, with flashbulbs blinding the occupants, Bobby explains the complex position to his close friend and business colleague, Joseph Miller.

'Max has fuckin' fucked us, the fuckin' cunt! He's always been a shifty bastard. He probably sneaked out the womb usin' the umbilical cord as a rope tae climb down.' He spits the words like a venomous cobra.

'Eh? How?' It's clear that Joseph's interview has been far less illuminating than Bobby's.

'He set up the promotions business wi' his accountant, an' we sat back an' let the cunt get on wi' it. There wis three designated directors…'

'Aye, ah know aw that…'

'…but he wisnae one ae them!'

'Eh?'

'It's you, me and Hammy. Max wis designated as non-exec director but wi' powers over the expenditure.'

'How the fuck did he get away wi' that?'

'Remember that night where he brought out aw they papers for us aw tae sign?'

'No' really,' says Joseph.

'It wis a night we were aw pished. We signed the documents agreein' the shareholders' terms. The cunt even got Hammy tae sign as a fuckin' witness. Turns out that wis his shareholding agreement he wis signin'. Hammy's a fuckin' director an' he disnae even fuckin' know it!'

'Jesus Christ … whit a bastard!'

'Aye. He's fuckin' landed us right in it, mate.' Bobby draws in sharp, deep breaths sharply through gritted teeth. 'But the worst bit is … he's pushed aw the sponsorship payments for the gig intae a separate company.'

'Fuck sake,' says Joseph. 'How we gonnae settle aw these fuckin' bills?'

'Well, he better have an answer for that yin! We're gonnae have enough tae deal wi' with this fuckin' Councillor shite!'

'What'll we dae if he's buggered off?'

The rain is falling steadily and the wind has risen. Small waves are splashing up against the edge of the stage. Teenage Fanclub have been immense, finishing an incredible set of cast-iron guitar classics with Grant's favourite song of theirs, 'Star Sign'.

Hammy is back behind the decks, although he nervously notes that he has to apply the wheelchair's brakes as the structure gently sways in the emerging swell.

He has half an hour to fill before the headliners come on. Grant Delgado is drunk, but to be fair to him, he has told everyone in advance that he would need to be. Eddie Sylvester has been praying backstage. Maggie is in one of the two portaloos. Simon seems the calmest of all. 'An hour an' it'll be aw by,' he keeps reminding everyone.

The two support bands are waiting by the side of the stage. They have no real option, given the stage's waterborne location, but they are happy, too, as Grant Delgado has suggested an encore of 'Maggie May' featuring all of them. Hammy plays 'She Cracked' by Jonathan Richman & The Modern Lovers, 'No Fun' by The Stooges and Joy Division's 'Love Will Tear Us Apart', all at eardrum-bursting volume. The beach bums are in raptures. The lightshow is having a real effect now, strobes rippling and dancing on the water's crests and troughs. It is supplemented by the helicopters' searchlights. They have been a constant throughout this weird day. Media 'copters, police surveillance ones and chartered observers, all coming and going, swarming over and around the activities below like insistent massive midgies.

As Grant Delgado ambles onto an increasingly unstable stage, Bobby Cassidy and Joseph Miller are standing on wet, slippy rocks at Troon Beach. They are truly scunnered. The lights at the base of Ailsa Craig are visible and it still seems like a few swift strokes from Michael Phelps would be all it would take to reach them. So tantalisingly close, but yet still so physically far. They say nothing to each other, both speechless at the turn of events. Joseph imagines Max, over on the island, holding court, and forms the angry words that he'll say to him. Bobby also imagines Max on an island, but not the one they are looking at. Bobby thinks of Gary, the whole point of this ridiculous idea. He envisages Gary laughing at this monumental fuck-up. It momentarily makes him feel a bit better. A few pieces of bright-yellow paper are washing up on the rocks not far from where they are standing. They are posters designed by Hettie Cassidy, advertising The Big Bang event and containing some words from Gary Cassidy, the man who loved islands.

'Hi … ah'm Grant. This song's called 'The Wind.' Grant Delgado stands on stage on his own. He opens the headline set with a fragile, beautiful solo version of the Cat Stevens song, his mellifluous voice immediately captivating the beach-bound. Hammy is unsure whether this is totally spontaneous given the worsening weather or a planned part of the set that the band haven't had the chance to rehearse. He certainly hasn't heard them play it, but Grant's version is incredible. The rest of the band wander on stage while the five hundred cheer wildly and loudly from the windy, wet beach. The Reverend Doctor Edward Sylvester has agreed to wear the full face helmet, provided it is painted emerald green. He immediately drops to his knees in prayer. The rest of the band wait for him and then tear into 'It's a Miracle'. The crowd goes bananas. It's like they've never been away. Very few people have witnessed a live gig by this band, yet their debut LP was rated the eighty-seventh best in history by the same magazine Maggie is photographing the whole happening for. Flashbulbs and flashlights are everywhere; on the beach, in the air and even backstage, as everyone seeks to capture an experience that logic suggests will never ever happen again.

Bobby takes Joseph's arm and drags him off in the direction of Lizzie King's flat. He has texted her and asked if they can come round. It is now raining heavily and at least the island can be seen from her window. There is some form of visual connection in that, although for both of them, the spirit of the moment has gone.

The Miraculous Vespas have played their entire LP to a rapturous ovation. Only Hammy seems concerned about the emerging gale that has developed to such an extent that the lighting rig above Grant's head is now visibly swinging backwards and forwards. Grant decides that going off backstage to prompt the crowd to call for an encore in this context is pointless and he summons the other musicians on. Grant dedicates 'Maggie May' to the girl who loved him, and the woman who saved his life. Hammy pictures Bert Bole's bony blue-cheese-veined arse going slowly up and down as the opening chords come through the amps. He can't shake the image.

Halfway through their collective cover of the popular Rod Stewart classic, a sudden unexpected gust hits the stage structure. There is an audible roar from the beach as the lights go out. Although nowhere close to the apocalyptic tsunami Eddie Sylvester has been predicting for the last month, larger waves are now hitting the curved shell and the floating structure is straining against its tethers. Unlike the one on the Titanic, this particular band don't play on. Hairy Doug is already in the water. He has his emergency life jacket on, though. Eddie Sylvester yells, 'It's time … Hallelujah Lord!' Grant grabs Maggie and the life jackets and they inflate. Simon Sylvester follows, attempting but failing to drag his rampant, ecstatic brother behind him. Teenage Fanclub dive impressively into the water headfirst, like a synchronised five-man Olympic swimming team. Joe McAlinden dithers, but his delay is purely about saving his fur-lined parka. Eventually he rips it off and leaves it on the sodden stage, bombing into the cold, dark sea just after his band. Hammy realises that he is alone, behind the decks, and out of the sight of the others, who have forgotten him. He hears loudspeakers informing the crowd to stay on the beach but some have heroically headed in to assist the flailing performers. Canal+ are filming it all as live action.

'Fuck sake,' cries Joseph Miller. 'C'mere an' see this!' Bobby and Lizzie run through to the front room. The Big Bang is being shown live on the evening televison news as a current breaking story. The three watch open-mouthed as the stage Joseph designed breaks free of its mooring and begins lolloping out to sea. A spotlight scans the stage. Thankfully, it appears to be empty.

'Aw fuck … naw!' shouts Bobby. 'That's Hammy. He's still on the bloody thing!' The spotlight has caught a panicking Hamish May. He has wheeled his chair to the edge of the stage and is waving furiously. A camera closes in. Hammy looks petrified. Bobby has his hands over his mouth as if knowing exactly what is coming next.

'Naw, Hammy don't dae it. Jesus, stay there … YA DAFT BASTARD!'

But it's too late. Hammy obviously can't hear him, nor anyone else in much closer vicinity, yelling similar instructions through loudspeakers. Despite the level of the rescue helicopter that has been circling intermittingly during the course of the day being almost close enough for the man on the end of the winch cable to reach the stage, Hammy rolls his wheels off the edge. He flops out of the chair with arms forward, like he is stage-diving at the Barrowland Ballroom. He disappears.

'Fuck me, he's just committed fuckin' suicide live on telly!'

'He'll be aw'right, Bobby,' says Lizzie, trying to calm her former boyfriend. 'Look at aw the folk there!'

But the rescue copter has to pull up suddenly. The stage has reared up and its edge catches the suspended rescue man. It's not clear if it has knocked him out, but he isn't moving. He is dangling lifelessly.

'We're staying with these dramatic breaking pictures from Scotland,' says ITN's Tom Bradby, with a little too much glee for Joseph's liking. It looks like Hammy is doomed. He was once hospitalised with hypothermia after being bundled into a rowing boat and cast into these very same waters. He has regularly told of how he had actually briefly died that night in 1982. Now it seems that the Irish Sea is back for him. It hasn't forgotten or forgiven his escaping its depths all those years ago. Bobby Cassidy is heartbroken, and in that moment, Joseph Miller fully understands that the bond between him and Hammy is even stronger than theirs once was.

The flashlight catches something in the dark, murky water. It is shiny and colourful. It looks like an emerald-green mermaid. Joseph thinks he is seeing things: the legend of the Ailsa Craig selkie perhaps … Daryll Hannah in *Splash*, all flowing hair and bare flesh. Bobby shakes him from the dwam.

'Look … it's Eddie! That daft, dopey cunt Eddie Sylvester is savin' him.'

The Revered Doctor Edward Sylvester has Hammy and is pulling him slowly backwards towards the shore, swimming strongly, one-armed like Hasselhof on *Baywatch* through the rough waves as the eyelid stage drifts out and into the distance. The winchman is over them; he has recovered his bearings. He manages to hook the rope around Hammy's torso and up they go, his spindly legs rotating uselessly, like a damp puppet on a single string. Eddie Sylvester is still in the water, fifty yards from shore. Two flashlights follow the ascending winch, before one dips back down to hold vision on Eddie. But he has gone. He is nowhere to be seen. The acquatic brilliance of his colourful shell-suit has vanished under the waves.

Chapter Thirty-Six

September 2015

'Keep away from people who try to belittle your ambitions. Small people always do that, but the really great make you feel that you, too, can become great.'

(Mark Twain)

It has been a beautiful service, all present are agreed. They have learned funny and unusual things about his life, his background and the closeness of his relationship with his family, especially his mother. As a celebration of a life lived fulsomely if unconventionally, it is warm and comforting. Following an extended period of early autumn rainfall – virtually every day, in fact, since the calamitous night of the Big Bang – the sun has shone and it somehow eases the pain of the funeral for everyone. The words of Mark Twain on the order of service resonate with everyone. They are appropriate for the life being celebrated, but they ring true for many others in the congregation, too. The chapel doors open and the melancholic words of his favourite song ring out:

'Sad, deserted shore, your fickle friends are leaving,
Ah, but then you know it's time for them to go.'

Two remarkable arcs of rainbow colours signal the way for the slow procession, away and up the steep hill and into their centres of gravity, led by a formal black vanguard. The rolling hills of the picturesque little cemetery are within walking distance, but Bobby and Joseph take the car for Hammy's benefit. They park and get out slowly, soberly; Bobby helps Hammy into his chair. The chair is awkward, its newness and stiffness of operation not quite having been bedded in yet. The awkward topography requires Bobby to push Hammy. Hammy, for once, is happy to be dependant.

'Aye, who knows where the time goes, right enough, eh?' says Joseph softly.

'Hmm.' The burial plot is at the crest of the hill.

'A fine spot,' Hammy suggests, although he doesn't elaborate and clarify for whom the spot is 'fine'.

They all secretly acknowledge that respectful formality and soft cliché are the order of the day for funerals. They are amongst the first to arrive, but they hold back. Bobby doesn't want to be at the front, near the grave. It is nothing to do with the shameful memories of the last time he was in such a position, and more with avoiding any additional stress that his prominence might put Hettie under.

Pete died the night after Hettie's showcase gallery exhibition of their work was finished. It was like he sensed his extended time was finally up; like the work and the emotional support Hettie needed was the only thing sustaining him. His condition had actually seemed to improve slightly near the end, but they both knew he had already survived much longer than all available medical expertise had predicted. His borrowed time was deep into *extra* time and everyone on the sidelines was checking their watches in disbelief. It was perhaps a relief, perhaps even to Pete himself, Hettie was being assured, when the final whistle was finally blown.

Hettie asked Bobby if he might want to help carry the coffin, but her request seemed half-hearted, and Bobby felt – wrongly in Joseph's opinion – that it would be the height of hypocrisy to step forward for a man he barely knew, and a sister with whom his reacquaintance remained fragile. Joseph argued that he'd be doing it solely for Hettie, not Pete, but it seemed to make little difference. So Joseph Miller takes his place as cord number five. Joseph has his own historically strained relationship with Pete D'Oliveira, but carrying him for this last mile seems like the best way to lay this to rest, along with the body of the man he unfairly and unreasonably envied.

It is fine, eventually. Hettie understands her brother well. There is no malice; he just has no stomach or sensitivity for these things. It would have been infuriating, had they not accommodated their relationship to acknowledge their respective faults.

The small group of mourners head back to a quaint country pub on the edge of Loch Lomond. It was one of Pete's most favourite places to think, to work and to relax. It is cold but beautifully serene and crisp. Bobby, Joseph and Hammy sit outside. Hammy lights a cigarette. His habit has grown substantially from the odd social puff, back up to the level it once was when they were all at school. He puts this down to the stress of a second near-drowning, but Bobby knows Esta Soler brought him six cartons when she surprised him with a visit in hospital during that first week when the story of his rescue became worldwide news. Esta only stayed for a day. The Blood Oranges had planned a short break away to London in order to reassess their charter; opportune given that it coincided with The Big Bang weekend.

'They things'll kill ye,' says Joseph.

'Well, somethin's got tae. Might as well be the Marlboro Man.'

'Ye should try the vapin'. Wean yerself off the nicotine,' offers Bobby.

'Away an' shite,' says Hammy. 'Vapin'? Fuck that! It looks like yer playin' a tiny wee flute. That kinda thing can still get ye a swift kickin' in the west ae Scotland, ken? No' good for an aul' geezer like me wi' ginger hair an' nae legs, is it?'

'Naw … ah suppose not,' says Joseph.

Hammy was naturally thrilled to see Esta Soler but he is now over her. There will be no extensive pining. Life was too short for that. As Heatwave Promotions' main social media co-ordinator, Hammy has now discovered Tinder. He's swiped right and now has irons in the fire, especially since his profile includes being involved with The Big Bang experience.

'Would you three like a drink?' It is Hettie. They hadn't even noticed her approaching.

'Ach, you sit down. Ah'll get them,' says Joseph.

She begins to insist and then gives up. The exhaustion is writ large in the furrowed ridges around eyes that look like they are carrying sacks of coal.

'Four gin and tonics, right?'

They nod.

'Ye alright now, Hammy?' she asks, reaching for one of his cigarettes.

'Aye, hen,' he replies. 'A bit scunnered wi' aw the interviews but ah suppose it wis necessary, ken?'

'How's Eddie?' she asks.

'Jesus, man, that daft bastard's in his glory. He's got about three hundred followers now, every one ae them as mad as him. Simon's sayin' that he's been offered this telly show on the God Channel.'

They all laugh at the lunacy of this.

'He's got a new slogan,' says Bobby. '"The world's about tae end ... but fear not, ah'm here tae save it!"'

'Sylvester saves ... but Dalglish scores fae the rebound!'

They laugh loudly.

'When's the trial?' asks Hettie.

'Ah'm no' sure,' says Bobby. 'Don't really care much either, now that we're out the firin' line.'

'Thought ye'd both be called as witnesses?' she asks.

'Aye, probably. But the phone recording Max made cleared us, and him. He definitely edited it, though. Christ knows how he did it, mind. Made it sound like Crockett was blackmailin' us. The Councillor admits that the words are his ... but his defence was that he didnae say them in that order. When ye add in aw the other cases, though, he looks fucked aw ways up.'

'Where is Max?' Hettie asks.

'Who kens?' says Hammy. 'He's like fuckin' Batman, that yin.'

The subject of Max Mojo's apparent disappearance has vexed

commentators everywhere since the night of The Big Bang, the journalist Steven Dent most especially. Dent claims he was shot by Max, assaulted, drugged with Rohypnol and then photographed indulging in lewd, graphic sexual practices at an underground sex club involving three magistrates and a member of the Scottish Parliament.

Washer Wishart's reputation has endured long after his death, it seems, and Max tapped into it for some very specific favours. Mobile-phone footage of the last of these incidents has surfaced at the *Daily Mail*. It suggests his involvement was anything but coerced. Steven Dent narrowly escaped jail following the enquiry into phone hacking. The court of public opinion was never going to be on his side in respect of his new claims.

Grant Delgado and Maggie Abernethy have returned to the States, as unwitting co-directors of the newly formed Biscuit Tin Music Ltd, owners of the entire Miraculous Vespas back catalogue and administrators of the lucrative new sponsorship deals and contracts that Max Mojo put in place. A separate subsidiary company – Big Bang Leisure Ltd – has also been established, with Bobby and Joseph as co-directors. Bobby Cassidy and Joseph Miller are also non-executive directors of the parent company, and between them they are in the process of settling the invoiced accounts of all who participated in The Big Bang. Grant has made it clear that his only interest is in recovering the one-off gig fee agreed with Max for the band members to reform but, according to Bobby, he is currently in discussions with Island about a new record, as well as the raft of remastered, repackaged reissues that Chris Blackwell has planned. Grant likes Chris a lot and feels that he is someone that the whole band can trust completely. Max Mojo is a maverick, and it certainly seems that he has been operating to a grand but unlikely plan all along, but Grant knows deep down that, if it all turned to shit – if Cramond Crockett didn't play ball and that if the expenditure accounts for Heatwave Promotions didn't imply that blackmail was contributing to the substantial losses – then Max would've fucked them all over without a second thought. Nevertheless, he's repaired the damage done all those years ago. Fuck knows where Max or his devoted old mum are now, but Maggie, Simon, Bobby, Joseph, Hammy and even Grant all hope he is happy. He at least seems to have earned it.

'An' how's things wi' Jennifer now, then?' asks Hettie. She's aware that all she has seemed to do this morning is ask questions of people, but so much seems to have happened to them all over the last month, and, typically of middle-aged west of Scotland males, she is having to drag it out of them.

'Aye. It's fine, ah suppose,' says Joseph, half-heartedly. 'Ach, it's gonnae take time. She's bitter about loads of things. To be fair, it's no' just wi' me, it's wi' her mum tae.'

Hettie nods as if she understands.

'To be fair tae Lucy, she disnae seem tae be blockin' me fae seein' her.'

'Christ, Jennifer's an adult,' says Hammy. 'She cannae fuckin' stop the lassie!'

'Aye, ah know. But still, her no' bein' a cow about it all makes it a wee bit easier,' admits Joseph. 'She's comin' down tae the Manse tae stay for a few days, so we'll see what happens after that.'

'Bloody hell, are you three still livin' in that auld church?' Hettie laughs. 'The Hardy boys an' Nancy there, on the Broo!'

'Hey, ah might be on benefits, but still … fuck sake,' moans Hammy.

'…or Last ae the Summer Whinin'!' adds Hettie.

'We're just lookin' after it for Max. He left a few notes about doin' it up, some ideas an' that. We're thinkin' ae turnin' it intae a museum an' a recording studio an' a bar an' that,' says Bobby with a fair degree of excitement.

Bobby and Joseph sailed over to the Ailsa Craig late on the Sunday afternoon, the day after The Big Bang. The clear-up operation was in full swing, but the two Scottish impresarios were still in shock at the anticipated costs. However, the stage had been lassoed and towed back to shore. The crowd had left the beach area in surprisingly good condition and the large containers intended for separating rubbish for recycling had been reasonably faithfully utilised. The returning power boats picking up the punters waited for their numbers to be called, then edged in slowly, two at a time. It was as organised a maritime withdrawal as the still-temperamental weather would allow, and astonishly, no craft was damaged in the whole exercise.

They were both devastated that they had missed the gig and part of the justification for going over to the island was to hunt Max Mojo down and confront him. But Max had never been on the island. No one had seen him since the eve-of-concert dinner at the church hall. In the weeks that followed, and with the dawning understanding of Max's complex initiative, Bobby and Joseph considered future plans for the island. They had done the hard bit, after all … the Ailsa Craig was now on the world map. They just had to work out how to take advantage of it.

Chapter Thirty-Seven

June 2016. The Ailsa Craig

Joseph Miller stands back and shields his eyes. The sign looks very cool. Flat, cut letters, just like the New York Guggenheim, spread across the white-painted frontage of the new, two-storey structure:

THE GARY CASSIDY HOTEL

The design fits perfectly with the adjacent lighthouse tower. The hotel is nearly ready for its opening day in two weeks' time. Channel 4's *Grand Designs* programme will be featuring the build in the next series. Filming has wrapped, and although numerous construction issues emerged – the ongoing problem of maintaining services through the winter being the main one – the project has finally completed and guests are clamouring for bookings for the four months the hotel will be open. The culmination of the season will see another celebratory free concert, given on the eyelid stage, which has now been permanently fixed to properly driven timber piles. There is an outdoor table-tennis table: an in-joke in honour of Joseph's dad, who told him that there used to be one on Rothesay – perhaps the windiest place in the entire country – when he was a kid. A comparative fortune has been spent, but the revenue from The Big Bang initiative has continued to roll in. Bobby Cassidy and Joseph Miller feel they are putting it to good use, and hope that Max Mojo will agree, if he ever returns.

Grant Delgado is part-funding a film of his novel, with Steve

Buscemi directing and James Franco in the starring role. From the rushes and the Production Company's PR machine, the film is being hotly tipped to win the Grand Jury Prize at the 2017 Sundance Film Festival in Utah next January.

Maggie now teaches photography. They still live in Portland, Oregon and Johnny and Angie Marr are their neighbours.

Simon Sylvester continues to work with disadvantaged incarcerated youngsters across Scotland, using music as a way to reach them. He is now regularly booked for conference speaking slots across the world.

The Reverend Doctor Edward Sylvester has built a new church in Prestwick. Its capacity is five hundred and it is regularly packed to its rafters. As well as his daytime slot on God FM, he writes a weekly newspaper column for the local *Ayrshire Press*. Eddie Sylvester – once a local figure of ridicule – is now a national, emerald-green-clad hero.

Hairy Doug is happily retired. There will be no comeback.

Bobby Cassidy and Lizzie King are now, once again, a couple. Bobby still lives in the Manse with Hammy, running the Biscuit Tin club, studios and museum, but Lizzie has chosen to keep her own flat in Troon, from which she runs a corporate cleaning business. The arrangement suits all three just fine.

Joseph Miller has moved out to Ailsa Craig to run the hotel. There is a skeleton staff here at present, although he is preparing to interview potential hotel personnel for the four months of the summer it will be open. There are ten rooms – all designed for quiet contemplation – a spa and a small fitness club. Big Bang Leisure Ltd has gifted the vast majority of the island to the National Trust and has put a number of environmental protections in place to secure the seabird colony and allow it to prosper harmoniously with the human population in return for the annual one-off gig at the end of the season. Despite a question being raised about its future in the Scottish Parliament at Holyrood, Ailsa Craig remains a part of Scotland … for the time being.

Joseph watches the small power launch get closer. It takes fifteen minutes from when he first sees it. There are two people on board. Normally it is only old Harvey, the boatman, bringing supplies and mail, and taking back any necessities or messages for Bobby. The lack of phone or network signals was a major issue to begin with, but Joseph Miller is slowly coming to terms with it. The other person is a woman. A young woman. She has blonde hair, which billows in the wind. He sighs and wipes away a tear. He walks along the jetty. It's hard for him to take in that she has actually come. She said she would, but he didn't fully believe her.

'Hello,' he says.

'Hi,' she replies.

He helps her out of the boat as if she was a Ming vase, and she hugs him.

She stands back and looks at him. 'So, any vacancies for a Manager of Guest Relations?'

'Aye, possibly.'

He takes her bags and she hands him various items of mail that Harvey has given her. Among them, he spots a postcard. It has a picture of a sun-drenched desert island. He turns it over. It has come from the Bahamas. The text reads:

'To Bobby & Joey…
I lost track of my friends, I lost my kin. I cut them off as limbs.
I drove out over the flatland, hunting down you and him.
It's a wide open road, my friends.'
M.M.

(Is This) The *(Happy)* End?

The Incidental Music: *(or music that underscores these incidents)*

'Thick As Thieves'
The Jam
(written by Paul Weller)
Available on Polydor Records, 1979

'Otis'
Durutti Column
(written by Vini Reilly)
Available on Factory Records, 1989

'We're All Going To Die'
Malcolm Middleton
(Written by Malcolm Middleton)
Available on Full Time Hobby Records, 2007

'Love Letter'
Nick Cave and the Bad Seeds
(written by Nick Cave)
Available on Mute Records, 2002

'The Adventures of Robinson Crusoe'
The City of Prague Philharmonic Orchestra
(Theme music composed by Robert Mellin and Gian-Piero Reverberi)
1964

'Summer'
Calvin Harris
(written by Calvin Harris)
Available on Deconstruction Records, 2014

'Last Night a DJ Saved My Life'
Indeep
(written by Michael Cleveland)
Available on Sound of New York/Beckett Records, 1982

'(Are You Ready) Do The Bus Stop'
Fatback Band
(written by Bill Curtis and Johnny Flippin)
Available on Perception Records, 1975

'Me, Myself & I'
De La Soul
(written by Clinton, Huston, Jolicouer, Mason, Mercer, Wynne)
Available on Tommy Boy Records, 1989

'Dropping Bombs on the Whitehouse'
The Style Council
(written by Paul Weller, Mick Talbot)
Available on Polydor Records, 1984

'Bigmouth Strikes Again'
The Smiths
(written by Morrissey and Marr)
Available on Rough Trade Records, 1985

'Fine Time'
New Order
(written by Gilbert, Hook, Morris, Sumner)
Available on Factory Records, 1988

'Loaded'
Primal Scream
(written by Gillespie, Innes, Young)
Available on Creation Records, 1990

'Fools Gold'
The Stone Roses
(written by Ian Brown and John Squire)
Available on Silvertone Records, 1989

'La Ritournelle'
Sebastien Tellier
(written by Sebastien Tellier)
Available on Record Makers/Astralwerks, 2004

'(Love Is Like A) Heat Wave'
Martha and The Vandellas
(written by Holland, Dozier, Holland)
Available on Gordy Records, 1963

'Don't Look Back'
Bettye Swann
(written by Robinson, White)
Available on Money Records, 1968

'Ivo'
The Cocteau Twins
(written by Fraser, Guthrie, Raymonde)
Available on 4AD Records, 1984

'Star Sign'
Teenage Fanclub
(written by Gerard Love)
Available on Creation Records, 1991

'Presidential Suite'
Super Furry Animals
(written by Rhys, Bunford, Ciaran, Pryce, Ieuan)

'Too Much Too Young'
The Specials
(written by Jerry Dammers)
Available on 2 Tone Records, 1980

'She Cracked'
Jonathan Richman & The Modern Lovers
(written by Jonathan Richman)
Available on Beserkeley Records, 1976

'No Fun'
The Stooges
(written by Pop, Asheton, Asheton, Alexander)
Available Elektra Records, 1969

'North American Scum'
LCD Soundsystem
(written by James Murphy)
Available on DFA Records, 2007

'The Wind'
Cat Stevens
(written by Cat Stevens)
Available on Island Records, 1971

'Maggie May'
Rod Stewart
(written by Rod Stewart and Martin Quittenton)
Available on Mercury Records, 1971

'Who Knows Where The Time Goes?'
Matthew Sweet & Susanna Hoffs
(written by Sandy Denny)
Available on Shout! Factory Records, 2006

'Wide Open Road'
The Triffids
(written by David McComb)
Available on Mushroom/Domino Records, 1986

'The First Picture' and 'It's A Miracle (Thank You)'
The Miraculous Vespas
(written and performed by Robert Hodgens, and engineered by
Chris Gordon at Three Hands Studio, Glasgow)
Listen to these songs at http://orendabooks.co.uk/book/the-rise-&-
    fall-of-the-miraculous-vespas/

Dialogue from the MGM movie, *The Laurel-Hardy Murder Case*
Written by H.M. Walker
Starring Stan Laurel and Oliver Hardy
Directed by Hal Roach
1930

Acknowledgements

The writing of this trilogy of books, which began with *The Last Days of Disco*, detoured slightly with *The Rise & Fall of the Miraculous Vespas*, and has now finally docked here with *The Man Who Loved Islands*, would not have been possible without the helpful advice and direct assistance of a number of wonderful people. I remain indebted to those acknowledged in the previous two novels but to those lists, I'd like to add the following people:

Markus Naegele, Thorsten Nagelschmidt, Irvine Welsh, Alan McCredie, West Camel, Johnny McKnight, Alastair Braidwood, Liam Rudden, Mark Callan, Joe McAlinden, Norman Blake, Teenage Fanclub, Nicola Meighan and Janice Forsyth … and of course, Elaine, Nathan, Nadia, my mum, my sisters and Karen Sullivan.

The music is such an intrinsic part of these stories and I hope the songs noted in the appendices prompt you to seek out some sounds you haven't heard before, or simply to rediscover great records that remind you what it was once like to have the world at your feet.

Until next time …
David. X